THE STOBRIMORE CHRONICLES

The Beginning

by

Matthew Eric Johnson

The Stobrimore Chronicles, Book One

Published by Worldgate Press

ISBN-13: 978-1-971576-01-5 (Paperback)

Cover design by: Matthew Johnson
Printed in the United States of America

The Adventures continue in:
"The Stobrimore Chronicles - New Lands"

For more, check out MatthewEricJohnson.com

CHAPTER 1

The ringing of the phone echoed through the house. Seven-year-old Jack put his toy dragon down on the floor, stood up, and left his bedroom to find his grandfather. Walking down the stairs and into the living room, Jack found his grandfather, Artemis, asleep in the recliner.

"Grampa Art! Grampa Art!" Jack said as he shook his grandfather's shoulder. "Grampa Art! Wake up!"

Artemis slowly opened his eyes, blinking a few times before looking over at Jack. He cleared his throat.

"What is it, Jack?" he asked.

"Grampa Art! The phone!" said Jack.

Artemis finally noticed the sound of the phone ringing in the other room. He stood up from the chair and let out a slight moan as he stretched. He gave Jack's head a quick pat before walking to the kitchen to answer the phone. Artemis cleared his throat just before picking up the receiver.

"Hello?" he said, in a gravelly voice. "Yes, this is he."

A moment passed before his expression changed. He slowly walked over to the kitchen table and sat down. His voice quivered with his next words.

"Are you sure?" asked Artemis.

A few more moments went by. A tear rolled down his cheek. He cleared his throat again as he wiped the tear away.

"I'll make the arrangements. Thank you," he said.

Artemis hung up the phone and then returned to the seat at the kitchen table. The tears began to flow as he placed his head in his hands. Jack peeked his head into the kitchen and saw Artemis silently weeping at the kitchen table. He slowly approached his grandfather and placed his hand on Artemis's forearm.

"Grampa Art, what's wrong?" said Jack. "Why are you crying?"

Artemis turned to Jack, pulled his chair out, picked him up and placed him on his lap. He then wrapped his arms around Jack, holding him tightly. He cleared his throat once again as he softly spoke to Jack.

"Jack, there's something I need to tell you. Mommy and Daddy were in an accident. It was a very bad accident." he said.

Jack started to tremble.

"Are they okay?" Jack asked.

Artemis shook his head.

"No, Jack... no. I'm so sorry, Jack. They were hurt really bad, and..."

Artemis's voice started to shake.

"...they're gone, Jack. They died."

Jack sat there in a daze. His ears had shut out all sound other than the beating of his own heart. Thoughts of his mother and father filled his mind, and the realization that he would never see them again suddenly hit him. Tears began pouring from his eyes. But though he was crying, he didn't make a sound. He just sat there in Artemis's lap as the tears silently rolled down his cheeks.

#####

The days leading up to the funeral passed by in a fog. Artemis found himself preoccupied with the funeral and burial arrangements, leaving Jack alone in his thoughts. As the day of the funeral grew closer, Jack found himself crying less and less, and by the time the funeral day came, Jack was left with a general feeling of numbness. He had cried all of the tears he was going to cry and had come to accept the loss of his parents. It wouldn't be until much later that Jack would realize that even while Artemis was preoccupied with all of the funeral arrangements and his own grief, he was always watching over Jack.

The day after the funeral, Artemis called Jack into the kitchen.

"Jack, come here. There's something I want to show you." he said.

Jack walked into the kitchen and sat down at the kitchen table. Artemis then took out a small leather pouch from his pocket and placed it on the table. He removed the string keeping the pouch closed to reveal a number of colored stones. Each stone was about the size of a quarter and together they looked like opaque gemstones. There were six different colors of stone. There were two red ones, a blue one, a green one, a yellow one, a white one, and a black one. He arranged them on the table in front of Jack.

"Jack. Do you remember those stories I told you about the other world? The one with elves and beastfolk and dragons and magic?" he asked.

Jack nodded while continuing to stare at the stones on the table.

"Do you like those stories?" asked Artemis.

Again, Jack nodded, but this time with a slight smile.

Artemis picked up one of the stones.

"Then let's call these story stones. Let me show you how they work."

Artemis placed one of the red stones in the center of his palm and closed his hand. He then closed his eyes and took a deep breath. When he opened his hand, the stone was gone. Jack was surprised to see that the stone had disappeared.

"Wow! Is that magic?" Jack said.

"Something like that," said Artemis, with a slight grin. "Now it's your turn. Place each stone in the palm of your hand, hold them tight, and close your eyes. For each stone you can make disappear, I will tell you a new story."

Jack got excited and picked up one of the stones. He placed it in the center of his palm, closed his hand, and then closed his eyes tightly. After a moment, he opened his eyes and then opened his hand. The stone was gone.

"I did it!" said Jack.

A smile beamed across Jack's face. It was the first time that Artemis had seen Jack smile since the death of his parents.

"Very good, Jack! Now try another one," he said.

Jack picked up the next stone, placed it in his hand, closed it and then closed his eyes. Once again, when he opened them, he saw that the stone had vanished. Jack's smile grew bigger. Artemis smiled as well.

"Keep going, Jack," said Artemis.

Jack repeated the routine with the next stone, and then the next and the next one, until all six stones had disappeared. Artemis was visibly surprised.

"Remarkable, Jack! That's absolutely remarkable! Not many can make all six stones vanish. You're very special," he said.

At that point, Jack was smiling from ear to ear.

"That's six stories, Grampa Art!" said Jack.

"Yes, it is. And I'll be happy to tell them to you. But first, you need to go wash up for dinner. Then we can start on the first story." he replied.

Jack hopped off of his chair and ran to the bathroom to go wash up for dinner. Artemis stood up and walked to the refrigerator to get everything he needed to start cooking. As he pulled the ingredients out of the fridge, he began talking to himself as he smiled.

"Six attributes. Incredible. Who would have thought that he would have an affinity for all six magical attributes? Simply incredible," he said.

#####

Once dinner was ready, Jack practically inhaled his food, filled with anticipation at the new stories about the world filled with elves and fairies and beastfolk and dragons and magic. Each night, the routine continued. Jack would make all six stones vanish, and Artemis would tell him six stories. This nightly routine continued all the way up until Jack graduated from high school. As he got older, Jack even tried to see how many of each stone he could make disappear at a time. By the time he graduated high school, Jack was able to make six of each stone disappear at once. And he so enjoyed the stories that Artemis told him that he began recording and transcribing them so he could revisit them whenever he wanted. After he graduated high school, his fascination with magic led to a bachelor's degree in chemistry. Upon graduating college, the sense of honor and service that were common in the stories told by his grandfather led to Jack enlisting in the US Army as an officer, thanks to his college education, where he eventually earned a Ranger tab and quickly rose to the rank of Major. He would often tell the many stories he had recorded to the men and women under his command, earning him the nickname of "The Bard". Throughout his time in military service, he never failed to stay in touch with Artemis in between missions.

CHAPTER 2

It was just after returning from a month-and-a-half-long extended mission, a mission that Jack had decided would be his last one before retiring from military service, that Jack received a small package in the mail from his grandfather. He opened the package, and inside he found a smaller package and an envelope. He opened the envelope first and pulled out the letter. He read it out loud to himself.

"*My dearest grandson:*

I hope this letter finds you in good health. I can never fully express the pride I have for you for the man you have become. I write this letter while you are still off on your mission, and by the

time you read it, you will have already reached your 35th birthday. That will make you one year older than your mother and father when they passed. There were many things that I had hoped to pass on to them when they reached this age, but it was not to be. But now I am proud to be able to pass these things on to you. Contained in the small package, you will find two sets of keys. The first set you will likely recognize. They are the keys to our house in the hills where you grew up. The second set of keys is to a small cupboard in the basement. Inside that cupboard, you will find a small chest containing some things I'm sure you will find of interest. I would tell you what they are, but why spoil the surprise? Let's just say that the contents may send you on a small quest. Nothing so extravagant as the ones I used to speak of in the stories I've shared with you over the years, but still, a quest nonetheless. And speaking of quests, I have decided to go on my own quest. Not to battle dragons or anything of that sort, so you need not fear for me. I just felt that it was about time for me to see everything this world has to offer, and even at the ripe old age of nearly 200 years old, I figure there's no better time than the present to do so..."

Jack chuckled at the joke of his grandfather's age. As far back as he can remember, it was a recurring joke that Artemis had told him as he was growing up. The letter continued.

"I wish you all the best and look forward to seeing you when I return from my epic quest, which hopefully includes a lot of first-class travel and high-end hotels whenever possible. I'll be sure to buy you a souvenir or two along the way.

All my love,

Artemis."

Jack let out another chuckle, imagining his grandfather, dressed in full garb of the characters in his many stories over the years, sitting in a first-class seat on an airplane, getting stares from everyone around him. He then thought about the house where he had grown up, remembering that he had often asked Artemis about what was in that little cupboard in the basement, only to be told that he'd find out when he was older. He couldn't deny that he was a little bit excited to finally find out what was in there. He opened the small package and removed the sets of keys. He looked at them briefly before placing them in his pocket.

Just as he folded the letter and placed it back in the envelope, he heard a knock at the door. He opened the door to find the battalion commander of his unit standing there.

"Colonel Brandt! What can I do for you, sir?" said Jack, as he stood at attention in the doorway.

"At ease, Major. I just came by to congratulate you on another successful operation and say that we're all going to miss you around here when you leave. Especially those stories you always tell. I also wanted to hand you these. Your exit papers have all been filed. Here are your copies," said Colonel Brandt.

Colonel Brandt handed him the envelope with his exit papers.

"Thank you, sir," said Jack.

Colonel Brandt peeked into Jack's quarters, looking at the single duffel bag packed in the corner. He grinned as he looked back at Jack.

"All packed, I see," said the colonel.

"Yes, sir," said Jack.

"From what I hear, your unit is throwing you a bit of a retirement party of sorts," said Colonel Brandt, still grinning.

"Yes, sir. But how did you hear about that?" asked Jack.

Colonel Brandt patted his jacket over his shirt pocket.

"They were kind enough to include me in the invitation list. I'm actually looking forward to it," he said.

Jack tilted his head upon hearing that.

"Really? I mean no offense, sir, but in all the time I've served under you, you've never really struck me as the party type," said Jack.

"I could say the same thing about you, Major," said the colonel.

Jack shrugged.

"Then I guess it looks like we can both be a little bit uncomfortable for a while. You know... for the sake of the troops," said Jack.

"Exactly, Major. For the sake of the troops," replied the colonel.

They both nodded as they smiled. Colonel Brandt then gestured down the hallway.

"Shall we head over there now?" he asked.

Jack stepped out of his quarters and closed the door behind him.

"Lead the way, sir," said Jack.

The two of them walked down the hallway towards the entertainment room where the party was going to take place. Colonel Brandt turned to Jack as they walked.

"Oh. And by the way. I saw on your discharge paperwork that it was your birthday last week. Happy belated birthday, Jack," he said.

"Thank you, Colonel," said Jack.

#####

The party went on for several hours. Fun was had by everyone there, even Jack and the Colonel. A few gifts were given, and Jack told one last story to the men and women in his unit. When the party ended, Jack returned to his quarters, placed the gifts into his duffel bag, placed it by the door and then got ready for bed.

#####

The next morning, Jack grabbed his bag, said his final goodbyes to his subordinates and colleagues and caught a taxi to the airfield. From there, he caught a military transport back to the United States, and then a commercial flight, and a long drive later, he finally arrived at the house where he grew up. By then, it was fairly late, so he grabbed a quick bite to eat, took a shower, and then went to bed.

#####

The next morning, Jack woke up, unpacked his things, did a quick workout, and then had some breakfast. As he did the dishes, he looked over at the door to the basement. Today was the day he was going to finally see what was in that little cupboard. He couldn't help but feel a bit excited. He placed the last dish on the dish rack, dried off his hands, and then went to the bedroom to grab the keys his grandfather had sent him. As he made his way down the basement stairs, he felt a sense of giddiness, like a young child heading down the stairs to look at the gifts under the tree on Christmas morning. He made his way over to the cupboard. He fiddled with the keys until he fit one into the lock and unlocked the cupboard door. He opened the door, and just as the letter his grandfather sent him said, there was a small chest, about the size of a shoebox, sitting on the bottom shelf. The chest looked like the typical treasure chest one might see in a movie or a fantasy game, with iron trim and hinges on a dark wooden box, leather straps on each side of the front latch, and a small locked padlock securing the latch in place. Jack picked up the small chest and carried it back upstairs to the kitchen. It was a bit lighter than he had expected it to be. He placed it down on the kitchen table and sat down to get a closer look at it. He looked at the padlock for a moment and then back at the key set he had just used to unlock the cupboard. Inside a small rubber sleeve attached to the key ring, Jack found the tiny key that looked like it would fit into the padlock on the chest. He pulled the key from the sleeve and inserted it into the opening on the padlock. He took a slow, deep breath in before turning the key. When he did, he heard that satisfying click of the padlock unlocking. He carefully took it off the latch, undid the leather straps, and opened the chest. Inside the chest, he found an old map, a compass, a peculiar-looking key and an envelope. He opened the envelope and found another letter written to him by Artemis. He read it.

"Jack,

By the time you read this letter, I will be gone. And when I say gone, hopefully I mean gone on my round trip around the world and not a one-way trip to the Great Beyond. Because that would be rather unfortunate. For you, too, but mostly for me. The map you see included in this chest is the way to a secret that has been kept by this family all the way back to the days when I was a child. I know you are aware of the rather vast amount of land on which this house sits, and you would spend many hours playing in the forest as a child, but the land belonging to our family goes even further than you may think. The location marked on that map should be about a day's hike from the house, so I have prepared a pack with all of the things you may need for your hike there. You can find it in the hall closet. It's a bit heavy for me, but nothing you shouldn't already be used to from your time in the Army. When you reach the spot on the map, use the enclosed key. There is so much more I want to tell you, but that will have to wait until I get back. In the meantime, enjoy your new quest, young warrior, and good luck.

Artemis"

Jack placed the letter back in the envelope and took out the map. He unfolded it and studied it carefully. He was surprised to see just how much property his grandfather owned. What he thought would have been measured in acres turned out to be measured in square miles. He couldn't imagine how much it cost to purchase that amount of property, but he figured that he would just ask Artemis about it once he returned from his trip. He examined the terrain leading toward the marked location and realized that he was in for far more than a leisurely stroll through the woods to get there. He placed everything from the chest onto the kitchen table and then walked to the hall closet to retrieve the backpack. When he opened the closet door, he saw the rather large backpack leaning against the back wall of the closet, partially concealed by the various coats hung on the rail. He moved the coats out of the way and pulled the backpack out. As he did so, he noted the weight of the pack.

"Holy crap! What's in this thing? Dumbbells and bricks?" he said.

He brought the backpack into the living room, opened it, and removed all of the contents to inventory all of the gear. It was something he had done many times before a mission while he was in the Army, so it had become almost a habit. The backpack included everything he might need for a difficult hike. It was almost obsessively thorough. There was rope and climbing gear, fishing gear, cooking gear, a rather comprehensive first aid kit, the usual camping gear, flashlights, rechargeable batteries, a solar-powered charger, a few MRE military food rations, some handheld radios, a takedown rifle and ammunition, a few knives, rain gear, a water filter, and various odds and ends. Jack was impressed at just how thorough his grandfather had been in packing the backpack.

"Wow," he said, "Grampa Art could give the supply guys

in the Rangers a run for their money. You'd think I was getting deployed again with all of this."

Jack slowly and carefully placed everything back into the backpack. Looking at the clock on the wall, Jack noticed that a few hours had passed since breakfast and it was already after noon, so he set the backpack by the door and decided to start his hike the next morning. He spent the rest of the day studying the map before eating dinner and hitting the sack soon after, in preparation for an early morning start.

#####

When the next morning came, Jack dressed for the hike. He wore black cargo pants, hiking boots, a light gray t-shirt, and a dark gray button-up shirt with extra pockets on the upper sleeves. Given that the temperature in the area had started to get cooler, he figured the darker colors would help him to absorb any heat from the sunlight, helping him keep warm. He rolled up a lightweight trench coat and secured it to the backpack. He walked over to the gun safe, opened it up and took out an old Colt 1911 .45 caliber handgun, a holster, a few extra magazines, and an extra box of ammunition. He wanted to be prepared in the event he ran into any wolves, bears, or mountain lions on the hike. A rule he had always lived by was that it is better to have something and not need it than to need something and not have it. He put the holster on his belt and placed the extra magazines and the ammo boxes in the backpack. He made himself a quick breakfast, filled a canteen with water, placed the map, compass, and key in his pocket, picked up the backpack, and left the house, locking the door behind him.

#####

The hike was surprisingly difficult, but save the occasional distant sighting of a number of wild animals on the property, it was otherwise uneventful. Jack was still glad that his time in the military kept him in decent shape, because without that steady training and exercise, he likely would have found himself exhausted long before reaching the point marked on the map. The spot indicated on the map brought Jack to the base of a twenty-foot-tall cliff face. Not knowing exactly what he was looking for, Jack began to explore the area. After about ten minutes of exploring, he came across a spot in the cliff that was concealed by a rusted wire mesh covered in rocks and plants. When he moved it aside, he found an opening in the cliff face and a stairwell leading down. He pulled a flashlight from his backpack and headed into the opening.

#####

The stairwell was carved out of the rock, and as Jack made his way further down, he noticed several old torches mounted to the walls. They looked centuries old. Jack found himself getting more and more excited to see what was at the bottom of the stairway. When he finally reached the bottom, he was met by a large wooden door held together with iron bars and rivets. Jack noticed the keyhole by the handle and recalled the odd key that had been included in the chest from the cupboard. He reached into his pocket and took out the key. He carefully inserted it into the lock and turned it. He heard the heavy clanking sound of the locking mechanism disengaging. He removed the key, grabbed the handle, and pushed at the door. It didn't move, and he ended up walking face first into it. He then looked over toward the edge of the door and saw the hinges. Feeling slightly embarrassed, he gently pulled the handle. The door opened.

"Smooth move there, Ranger. Glad no one saw that," he said to himself before walking through the doorway.

Just to his left as he entered the room, he saw a small wooden lever. Next to it, was a wood plaque that said "off" and "on" on it. It was written in his grandfather's handwriting. He moved the lever to "on". Suddenly, stones embedded in the walls of the room began to glow, filling the room with a soft amber light. Jack grinned.

"Heh. Cool," he said.

As the light grew brighter, Jack shut off the flashlight and put it in his pocket. He began looking around the room. To his left, there was a workbench with various pieces of odd-looking equipment. To his right was a series of baskets, each containing a number of the colored stones Artemis had given to Jack before telling him stories. Jack smiled as he approached the baskets. He picked up a number of the stones, placed them in the palm of his hand, closed his hand, closed his eyes, and then opened them. The stones had vanished from his hand.

"Ha! Still got it," he said.

On the far end of the room was an archway leading further in. He took a brief peek through the archway, seeing nothing but darkness, before exploring the room he was in a bit more. He approached the bench with the equipment on it and started to examine it. Along with the equipment, he saw an old leather-bound book. He opened the cover of the book and found a photograph tucked inside. When he looked at the photo, he saw his grandfather as a young man, standing with an older man that appeared to be Artemis's father. They were standing at the top of the stairway by the cliff face. Jack flipped the photograph over and noticed writing in the corner. It said,

"*Father and I. Guardians of the gate. April 12, 1907*"

"No way," said Jack. "That can't be the right date. That would make him..."

Jack tried to do the math in his head.

"...really old. Like really really old. Like not joking about his age old."

Jack made a mental note to ask his grandfather about that photo when he returned from his trip. He then began to flip through the pages of the book. He saw various sketches and a language he was unfamiliar with. A few things were written in English in the margins on a number of pages. Most of the things written in English were in Artemis's handwriting.

From what Jack was able to decipher, the book appeared to be an instruction manual on how to create the various colored stones, which, according to the book, were called affinity stones.

As Jack continued to flip through the book, trying to figure out the true purpose of the stones, he heard the sound of rocks shifting and collapsing from the tunnel beyond the archway on the far end of the room. As he approached the archway, he heard what sounded like distant muffled explosions, almost like the sounds of a faraway battle being fought.

With his curiosity piqued, Jack took out his flashlight, turned it on, and slowly made his way down the tunnel. The further down the tunnel he got, the louder the sounds of battle became. Halfway down the tunnel, Jack was met with some resistance, as if he was suddenly walking through chest-deep water. He pushed forward, feeling momentarily dizzy before the resistance faded. Soon he saw a light at the end of the tunnel. The sounds of battle grew even louder. When he exited the tunnel, he found himself in the remains of what looked like some sort of ancient temple. Just as he began to look around, the floor beneath him collapsed, and he found himself tumbling downward.

CHAPTER 3

Archers on the western ridge of the canyon drew their strings back, generating glowing energy arrows from their bows, preparing to fire another volley at the approaching pack of draphnir, grotesque-looking creatures with spines down their backs, sharp black claws, speckled gray skin, deep blood-red eyes, and patches of thick, wiry fur. Blue blood flew as the glowing yellow arrows pierced their flesh. Lia, commander of the Vedyrian Army, shouted out orders to the troops from the front line.

"Archers! Prepare for another volley! Mages! Keep those shields strong! Give the healers time to recover the wounded! Don't let the Dark Army gain any ground!" she said as she deflected an incoming dark arrow with her sword.

At the other end of the canyon, the Dark Army prepared to fire another volley of dark energy at the Vedyrian Army. Several squads of the Demonborne moved massive red crystals mounted on carts to the center of their ranks. They directed the points of the crystals toward the Vedyrian Army, and a team of necromancers gathered behind each crystal and placed their staffs on them, charging them with dark magic. An archer from the Vedyrian side spots the crystals being charged and calls to the commander.

"Commander! Triple C's!" he yelled.

"How many?" asked Lia.

"Three!" he yelled back.

"Dear gods! Fall back! Fall back!" Lia said as the Vedyrian forces began to retreat.

The archer fired an arrow into one of the Demonborne, causing them to fall, shifting one of the crystals off course and causing it to discharge before it is fully charged. The massive sphere of energy impacted the side of the canyon in between the two armies, striking near the ruins of an old temple carved into the wall, causing stones to shift violently. The Vedyrian Army continued to fall back as the archers attempted to provide cover fire. Lia yelled to the mages.

"Prepare to bring up the shields. Give them everything you've got! If we get hit with just one of those cannon bursts, we're done!" she yelled.

As they continued to fall back and the mages began work to raise the magic barriers, Lia looked over to the temple ruins that had just been struck. There she saw someone tumbling down the hill from the temple. The bag he had on his back went flying and landed against the opposite wall of the canyon. Just as he reached the canyon floor, the Dark Army fired two of the three crystal cannons. Lia watched as the person slowly stood up, dazed from the fall. She looked up to see the massive spheres of energy from the cannons beginning to arch toward the stranger.

"They're headed straight for him." she said.

She tried to get his attention.

"You there! Run! Run!" she yelled.

Jack slowly stood up, shook his head and looks around. He looked behind him to see a woman in the distance yelling at him and pointing. He turned to see what she was pointing at, and he saw the massive energy spheres heading right for him.

"Holy hell!" Jack said as he raised his hands reflexively.

Suddenly, Jack's hands began to glow. The spheres seemed to become attracted to him, speeding up as they approached. In a moment that surprised all on the battlefield, Jack started to absorb the energy of the massive spheres. His whole body began to glow, and bolts of energy started cascading from his hands and arms. As he absorbed the energy, glowing purple cracks appeared to form along his arms, leading all the way up to his chest. As the cracks worked their way along his arms, the sleeves of his long-sleeved shirt began to char and burn away, flaking off like the burning pages of a newspaper in a bonfire. The battlefield fell silent as both sides stood there in shock at this stranger who just took two direct hits from the crimson crystal cannons and was still breathing. At that point, Jack's entire body was glowing a deep purple hue. He turned his head and faced Lia for a moment. She saw a look of fear and confusion on his face. His eyes glowed brightly as he turned back toward the Dark Army. He dropped to his knees in a significant amount of pain. A sphere of energy began to appear in front of his chest. The sphere was black in the center, with purple and deep red vapors emitting from it. It began to grow in front of him. He let out a yell as the sphere discharged, growing outward in a cone of energy that engulfed the entirety of the canyon where the Dark Army stood. The glow was blinding. Lia and the soldiers of the Vedyrian Army shielded their eyes. As the blinding light faded, Lia looked up to see Jack slumped over, still on his knees, before fully collapsing to the ground.

"That's not possible," she said.

As she and the rest of her army stood and looked down the canyon, they saw that the place where the Dark Army once stood was now a mile-long trail of ash, glowing stone, and sand turned to blackened glass, all coming to a point right in front of Jack. She stood up, wiped the dust off of her armor and began to cautiously approach Jack. Captain Alivair, Lia's second in command, saw her approaching Jack and ran to her.

"Be careful, Commander! We don't know what it is, yet!" said Alivair.

"It's OK, Captain. I'll be careful," she said as she got closer. She could see smoke still rising from his shirt where the sleeves had burned away.

When she reached Jack, she walked carefully around him in order to get a look at his face. She knelt down and rolled him onto his back. Jack briefly looked at her before losing consciousness.

Captain Alivair looked shocked after getting a look at

Jack's face.

"He's... he's human!" he said.

Lia looked up at Alivair.

"And he's still alive. Bring the healers." she replied.

Alivair seemed confused.

"But, Commander, we don't know anything about this... human," he said.

Lia gestured toward the now smoldering path where the Dark Army once stood.

"We know that he did that to the Dark Army, Captain. And, as impossible as this whole thing looks, he saved us. Now get the healers over here," said Lia.

"Yes, Commander," said Alivair.

Alivair raised his hand to call the healers forward.

"Bring a stretcher!" he said, before looking down at Jack, "And bring the suppression collar!"

Lia gave Alivair a stern look. Alivair gave her a slight shrug in response.

"Better to be safe than sorry, Commander," he said.

The healers arrived, along with a number of soldiers carrying a stretcher. They loaded Jack onto the stretcher.

Alivair turned to Lia.

"Where do you think he came from?" he asked.

Lia looked up at the temple ruins.

"If I didn't know better, I'd guess he came from the temple," she said.

Alivair looked up at the temple ruins.

"You mean the old Worldgate temple? You think he's an Otherworlder? But that temple has been inactive and abandoned for almost two hundred years," he said.

He then looked back at Lia.

"So... what now?" he asked.

Lia watched as they loaded Jack onto the stretcher before looking at the path burned into the canyon.

"For now, we return to camp and tend to our wounded. And when he wakes up... if he wakes up, hopefully we can get some answers. Just to be safe, though, let's send some scouts to check out the area," said Lia.

"Yes, ma'am," said Alivair.

Jack and the wounded soldiers were loaded up onto stretchers and brought to what could best be described as ambulance carriages to be transported back to camp. The biggest difference between Jack and the wounded was that Jack was the only one wearing that suppression collar. The journey back to the base camp took two days. Jack remained unconscious for the journey. Once they arrived at camp, Jack was taken to a tent where he was placed under guard.

CHAPTER 4

Jack's eyelids felt like they were made of lead when he tried to open them. As the light began to reach his eyes, he noticed a familiar sound of purring. Almost reflexively, he reached his right hand out. He felt fur and began to gently stroke it. The purring grew a bit louder. Once he fully opened his eyes, he lifted his head, which, much like his eyelids, felt like it was made of lead. When he looked to where his hand was petting, he saw a humanoid feline figure with its head resting on the edge of the bed, sleeping. The feline figure slowly opened its eyes and looked over to Jack.

"Hi there," said Jack.

"Hi," said the feline figure in a sleepy voice.

"You remind me of a cat I used to have when I was younger," said Jack.

"Nice," said the feline figure, right before its eyes opened wide and its pupils dilated fully.

"You're awake! You're awake! He's awake!" it said, and then jumped to its feet and ran out of the tent.

Jack could hear it yelling "He's awake!" over and over again as the voice faded into the distance. He took a look around, first looking at his arms, which were bandaged from the tips of his fingers up to his upper chest. He was lying on an actual mattress as opposed to a cot. There was a blanket covering him and a pillow beneath his head. He looked to his right and saw the chair where the feline figure had been sitting. Further on was a small desk with a second chair. Leaning against the desk was his backpack. As he looked around, he noticed how roomy the tent really was. It was slightly larger than the living room of his childhood home.

There were small glowing crystals in light fixtures all around the tent, similar to the crystals Jack had seen in the cavern.

As the mental fog fully lifted, Jack saw the front flap of the tent open up. The daylight from outside the tent was momentarily blinding. Two silhouettes appeared in the bright light and then entered the tent. As his eyes readjusted to the light inside the tent, the silhouettes gained form. The first figure he noticed was the humanoid feline. It stood about four feet ten inches tall. Getting a better look at it, he noticed that it was wearing a burgundy-colored vest and a long, denim-blue-colored skirt. A tail was visible at the base of the skirt. This, along with the feminine figure, led Jack to conclude that it was a female feline. Around her waist, she had a wide brown leather belt with a dagger in a sheath on each hip. The second figure caused him to momentarily flash back to the canyon where, after he had absorbed that massive amount of magical energy, he had turned to see the woman now standing before him. She was about five foot nine, had bright blonde hair, almost the color of polished gold, and her eyes were a soft shade of lavender. She was clad in impressively intricate and ornate armor, with an equally ornate sword hanging from the black leather belt around her slender waist. As she brushed her hair behind her ear, Jack noticed that the tip of her ear came to a point. Needless to say, he was slightly confused.

The woman spoke.

"I heard that you were awake," she said.

Jack nodded and then looked over at the feline.

"With the way she was yelling, I think pretty much everyone heard that I was awake," he said with a grin.

The feline turned her head away in embarrassment.

The woman smiled.

"Yes. You may be right. How do you feel?" she asked.

Jack took a moment to evaluate himself. He looked at his bandaged hands and arms.

"I'm not entirely sure. I can't really feel my hands or arms. They're completely numb. Everything else... kinda hurts," he said.

"That doesn't seem that surprising, given what you've been through. Though, what is surprising is that you weren't immediately vaporized when those two triple-C shots came down right on top of you," said Lia.

"Triple-C's?" asked Jack.

"Crimson crystal cannons," said Lia, "They're..."

Jack interrupted.

"Let me guess. They're cannons controlled by a crimson-colored crystal. Am I correct? Wow. That was a lot of C-words. I can see why you call them triple-C's."

Lia smiled.

"Yes, indeed. Now, I'm sure you have many questions, but first, introductions. I am Lia, commander of the Vedyrian Army, and this is Crescia, my attendant," she said.

"Uh... hi. I'm Jack," he said.

"Hello, Jack. It is nice to meet you. So, do you have any questions?" asked Lia.

Jack took a deep breath.

"Yeah. What happened? Where am I? How did I get here? Why am I covered in bandages? What's the deal with this collar? Are you an elf? And, um, since when do military commanders have attendants?" Jack paused for a moment. "Yeah. That's a good start."

Lia's eyes widened at the sudden machine gun-like barrage of questions. Crescia chuckled, leaned toward Lia, and whispered.

"You did ask, your Highness," she said.

Lia leaned back to Crescia.

"I certainly did," she said.

Lia walked over to the chair next to Jack's bed and sat down.

"As far as what happened, that's a bit of a complicated question, so we'll put that one aside for the moment. As for where you are, you're currently in the main camp for the Vedyrian Army, which, for the time being, is set up on the outer edges of the Kupari province, one of the most eastern territories in the Vedyrian Kingdom. You got here because we picked you up from the battlefield and brought you here while you were unconscious. You're covered in bandages because of the damage you sustained on the battlefield that our healers appear to be unable to fully heal. The collar is intended to stabilize and suppress your magic because it was highly unstable when we found you. Yes, I am, in fact, an elf. And..."

Crescia interrupted.

"I'll take that last one. I'm an attendant serving the Crown Princess of the Vedyrian Kingdom," she said, as she gestured toward Lia.

Jack's eyebrows raised in surprise at that last part.

"So... you're the commander of the army and a princess, huh?" he asked.

Lia nodded.

"Cool," he said.

Jack's eyebrows lowered as he started to process what she had said.

"*Vedyrian Kingdom. Why does that sound familiar? Of course. The stories that Grampa Art used to tell me. She's gorgeous. Cat's kind of weird. This must be a dream. I probably fell at the bottom of that tunnel, hit my head, and now I'm having this dream as I lay unconscious at the bottom. But I don't recall ever having a dream that hurt this much. This collar's uncomfortable. I hope I can get it off once my magic stabilizes... Wait. My magic?*" he thought.

Jack turns to Lia.

"I'm sorry, but did you say magic?" he said.

Lia nodded.

"Yes. Magic of the likes I've never seen before, in fact. Let alone magic from a human Otherworlder," she responded.

Crescia chimed in.

"From what I heard, you kind of redesigned the landscape. That canyon used to have twists and turns. Now it's a straight shot all the way to the end," she said, gesturing with her hand to imitate the twists and turns and then the straight line.

Jack furrowed his brow again in confusion.

"Otherworlder? What's an Otherworlder?" he asked.

"Someone from the other world, silly. You'd think that the name was pretty obvious," Crescia said with a hint of sarcasm in her voice.

"Now, Crescia, I'm sure that he's just as confused as we are. There's no need for that."

Lia turned to Jack.

"Otherworlder is a term that we use for people who have passed through a Worldgate, like the one in the temple ruins you came from. There are a number of gates around this world. Few are active, but most are not. The one you traveled through had been inactive for almost two hundred years. Only those with some affinity for magic are able to pass through the gates. Do you know what types of magic you have an affinity for, Jack?" she asked.

"To be totally honest, um, Princess? Your Majesty? Sorry. What do I call you?" asked Jack.

"Please call me Lia," she said.

Crescia seemed a bit surprised that she would suggest that he address her with such familiarity, setting all titles aside.

"Oh. Thank you. So, uh, what I was trying to say, um, Lia, is that before you just told me a few moments ago, I had no clue that magic was a real thing, let alone what sort of affinity I might have for it," said Jack.

"I see. Well, perhaps when you're feeling better, we can get an affinity crystal in here to test your magic," said Lia.

"Sure," said Jack.

Lia smiled gently.

"Oh, by the way, how long have I been unconscious?" asked Jack.

Lia thought for a moment, briefly looking at Crescia.

"I'd say it's been a little under three-and-a-half weeks,"

she said.

Crescia nodded in agreement.

"Three-and-a-half weeks?!" said Jack, sitting up quickly, causing a significant amount of pain.

"Oww!" he said.

"Be careful," said Lia.

Jack thought for a moment.

"Wait. If I've been unconscious for almost three and a half weeks, how am I not dead from starvation and dehydration?" he asked.

"You have Crescia to thank for that," said Lia.

Crescia nodded with a smile beaming across her face, making her look like a child who had just been praised for getting an A+ on their report card.

"Yep! I cut your food up really small, chewed it up nice and soft, mixed it with water, and used my water magic to feed you." she said.

"Oh. Wow. Ok. That's... uh... that's kinda gross, but thank you. I appreciate the effort," said Jack.

Crescia nodded again, continuing to smile like a child, completely ignoring the part about Jack saying that it was gross.

"So, you can use magic, Crescia?" asked Jack.

"Mmm hmm. I'm not super strong, but I have an affinity for water magic." she said.

Jack chuckled.

"What?" asked Crescia.

"It's just that, where I come from, cats and water generally don't mix too well," said Jack.

"Well, I think I mix pretty well," said Crescia.

Jack smiled. He then went to adjust his position in bed and noticed something.

"Um... why am I naked? Where are my clothes?" he asked.

Lia cleared her throat, momentarily flustered at the thought that she had been conversing with a naked man.

"Uh, yes. Your clothes. They were badly damaged when you appeared. We'll have someone prepare some new clothes for you," she said, nodding to Crescia to get that started.

Crescia nodded and then left, waving to Jack as she exited the tent. Lia then stood up.

"Well, I have some things I must attend to. I will have some clothes and food brought to you. Once you've eaten, I'll return later to give you a better description of what happened when you first appeared. If there's nothing else?" she said.

Jack shook his head.

"No. Thank you. It was nice meeting you, Lia," said Jack.

"You as well. We'll speak again later." Lia said.

Lia gave Jack a nod and left the tent.

Jack leaned back into the bed.

"So. This is actually happening. Grampa Art will definitely have some explaining to do when I get back... if I even can get back," he said to himself.

He shifted in bed.

"Why did they even take my underwear? On second thought, I'm not sure I even want to know," he said.

He reached his bandaged right arm over to the backpack and unzipped a side pocket. He then pulled out a spare pair of boxers from the pocket and put them on.

"Much better," he said, after getting back under the sheets of the bed.

CHAPTER 5

About an hour had passed before Crescia returned with some clothes to replace the ones damaged during the battle. She placed them on the chair next to the bed and left to get Jack some food. By the time she returned, Jack had gotten dressed in the newly supplied clothing. The pants were black with two pockets in the front and two in the back. The knees were reinforced with black leather patches. The supplied undershirt felt a little abrasive, so Jack dug into the backpack once again and was able to find the spare dark gray t-shirt he had packed. The long-sleeved shirt that was supplied was black in the torso, with dark blue sleeves. The shirt had a banded collar with two buttons, which he left unbuttoned. A leather vest and cloak were also included, but Jack decided to set those aside. He also chose to stick with his hiking boots over the supplied boots for the time being. He wasn't in the mood to try to break in a new pair of boots after spending so long in bed. As he looked at himself in the mirror, he said a silent prayer for all the pockets of his original shirt and pants that would never serve their purpose.

Crescia returned with some food. She saw Jack in his new clothes.

"Well? How do I look?" asked Jack.

Crescia looked him up and down.

"You look... better?" she said.

"I'll try to ignore that pause and the way that sounded more like a question than a statement and just say thanks." Jack said with a smile.

Crescia placed the tray of food down on the small desk.

"Lady Lia will be with you shortly. Please eat," she said.

"Thank you," said Jack.

Crescia smiled and bowed before leaving the tent. Jack sat down at the desk to eat. On the plate were two small but thick slices of meat, some potatoes and what looked like white and purple carrot-like vegetables. As Jack ate, he thought to himself that, although this wasn't his first meal since arriving, it did happen to be the first meal that he chewed and swallowed himself. He paused for a moment, realizing just how messed up of a thought that was, and then continued eating.

#####

It wasn't long after Jack finished his meal that he heard Lia's voice outside the tent.

"May I come in?" she asked.

"By all means," said Jack.

Lia walked in with an older man behind her. The man was mostly concealed in a cloak, but Jack could see that he had long silver hair and a short beard. He was carrying an object the size of a serving tray wrapped in a blue cloth with gold trim. Jack arranged the two chairs and sat down on the bed.

"How are you feeling, Jack?" she asked.

Lia sat down, but the cloaked man remained standing by the opening of the tent.

"A lot less naked than before, thanks," said Jack.

Lia was slightly flustered by his reply.

"Is Galdalf over there going to sit down, too?" asked Jack.

The man spoke.

"I know not of this Gandalf you speak of. My name is Bilen," he said.

"Ok, then. Pop a squat, Bil. Take a load off," said Jack.

"Pop a what?" Asked Bilen.

"It means have a seat," said Jack, as he gestured to the empty chair.

Bilen looked over at Lia. She nodded. Bilen then walked over to the empty seat and sat down. He removed his hood, revealing that he, too, was an elf. He placed the item he was carrying in his lap.

Lia took a deep breath.

"You wanted to know what happened, so we're here to tell you. For the last two hundred and fifty years, the Vedyrian Kingdom has been at war with the Dark Army. The ruler of the Dark Army is known only as the Great Demon Emperor. His true name has been lost to history. All that is known is that he was a Grand Mage who became so consumed by dark magic that he turned into a being so evil that words still don't exist to properly describe him. His constant quest for more power led him to spread across the land like a plague, conquering kingdom after kingdom. Elf kingdoms, Beastfolk kingdoms, and the kingdoms of men all fell in the wake of his evil. Those who fell in battle or were captured were turned into Demonborne and made soldiers of the Dark Army. The dark elves joined with the Great Demon Emperor of their own free will, hoping to capitalize on the ever-expanding territory. Mages were turned into necromancers, like the ones who fired the triple-C's when you first arrived. And then there's the Draphnir. They are horrible beasts with razor-sharp claws that travel in packs and follow the commands of the necromancers on the battlefield. As long as they remain under the control of a necromancer, they will tear through anything in their way, with no sense of self-preservation." she said.

"Sounds like a real friendly bunch." Jack said sarcastically.

Lia continued.

"The remaining kingdoms and survivors all joined together under the flag of the Vedyrian Kingdom. We were engaged in what was a losing battle in the Arnin Canyon when you appeared. Somehow, when you appeared on the battlefield, you were able to absorb the massive amounts of magic from the triple-C's, and then you directed an even more massive display of magic back at the Dark Army that left nothing of the enemy on the battlefield. You fell unconscious soon after, and we brought you here," she said.

"I see," said Jack. "Could you do me a favor?"

Lia nodded.

"I still don't have that much feeling in my arms yet, so could you just pinch my leg as hard as you can?"

Lia looked a bit confused, but after Jack lifted his left leg in her direction, she gave it a hard pinch.

"Oww!" said Jack.

"For what reason did you wish for me to do that?" Lia asked.

"Just checking something," said Jack, confirming in his mind that this wasn't a dream.

He then lowered his leg before continuing.

"So, to sum up, I somehow traveled through something called the Worldgate, fell down a canyon, and found myself in the middle of a battle in a long-running war between good and evil, with you guys being the good guys, and I have some sort of super scary magical powers I didn't know that I had. Does that pretty much sum it up?" he said.

"I guess if you want to put it in simplest terms, yes," said Lia.

"Ok. Cool. That tracks. So what's the deal with Bil, here?" asks Jack as he gestures toward Bilen.

"Bil is... excuse me, Bilen is here to determine what magical affinities you possess," Lia said as she pointed toward the item wrapped on Bilen's lap.

Bilen then removed the fabric covering the item to reveal a large hexagonal crystal mounted to a wooden backing, with a metal frame around the crystal. The center of the crystal was slightly raised with six triangular facets leading down to the metal frame. Bilen stood up and then placed the object on the seat. Lia turned back to Jack.

"This is a magical affinity scale. It measures the strength of your magic and the affinities that you possess," she

said.

Jack takes a closer look at the scale.

"What do you mean by affinities?" he asked.

Bilen spoke.

"Magic is divided into six affinities. There is fire magic, water magic, wind magic, earth magic, light magic, and dark magic. Each facet of this crystal indicates a different affinity, and the glow indicates the strength. When it comes to magic users, many have only one affinity. Some have two or three. There are very few, such as Her Highness, who have an affinity for four types of magic," he said.

"Fire, water, earth, and light magic, to be specific," said Lia.

Jack tilts his head back in thought.

"Ok, fire, water, wind and earth magic all sound somewhat self-explanatory. I assume that it involves manipulating those elements in some way. But what's the deal with light magic? Do you use that to make it bright and dark magic to make it dark?" he asked.

Lia smiled.

"Light magic is used for things such as healing, restoration, purification, and protection spells. Dark magic is destructive magic. It's powerful, but it starts to damage the user the more it is used. Used extensively, it can even corrupt a soul," she said.

"Well, that doesn't sound very good," said Jack. "So, how does this gauge work?"

"With your permission, your Highness?" said Bilen as he gestured to the scale. Lia nodded, approving his request to demonstrate.

"First, you must close your eyes and imagine energy flowing through your body. Then imagine it flowing to your hand. Then imagine it flowing to your index finger. Once you have done that, place the index finger on the apex of the crystal, and it will show you what affinities you possess."

As Bilen gave the explanation, he demonstrated each

step. When he placed his index finger on the apex of the crystal, three facets began to glow. The fire facet glowed a bright red. The water facet glowed a bright blue, and the light facet glowed a bright white. Bilen spoke again.

"As you can see, I have an affinity for three types of magic, and the intensity of the glow shows that my magic is quite strong in these affinities. Now, your Highness?" said Bilen, as he gestured for Lia to demonstrate her affinities on the gauge as well.

Lia placed her index finger on the apex of the crystal, and four facets began to glow. The first was the red facet. Then the blue facet, then the green facet, and then the white facet. The glow of each facet slowly grew in intensity, indicating that Lia was quite powerful with the four attributes of magic that she possessed.

"Nice," said Jack.

"And now, it is your turn," said Bilen.

"Uh... shouldn't we take this collar off first?" said Jack. "If I remember correctly, you said that this thing suppresses magic."

"That is true," said Lia.

She gave a nod to Bilen, who walked over to Jack, placed two fingers of his right hand against the clasp of the collar, spoke a silent incantation, and then the collar was released. Jack rubbed his neck where the collar once rested.

"Thanks," he said.

Jack then took a deep breath and tried to imagine the energy inside him was flowing like a river, but when he didn't feel anything, his mind began to wander a bit. Various phrases entered his thoughts. Phrases like "Use the force!" and "There is no spoon," and "You're a wizard, Harry," entered his thoughts and made him smile. Not sure if he was actually getting anywhere, he decided to try touching the apex of the crystal anyway. The moment he touched it, it began to react. Each facet began to glow, one after the other, until the light was blinding. Jack took his finger off the crystal the moment it shattered into several pieces, making a loud popping sound like a flashbulb on an old camera. Jack was taken by surprise and leaped back, placing himself completely on the mattress.

"Crap! I'm so sorry! Was that expensive? That looked expensive. Did I break it?" he said.

Bilen took another look at the now broken gauge.

"Impossible! And all six attributes! Your Highness, a word, please!" he said as he moved toward the opening of the tent, waving to Lia to follow.

"Excuse us for a moment," Lia said to Jack as she stood up and followed him outside of the tent.

As they left, Jack poked at the gauge, causing a shard of the crystal to fall to the floor. He quickly picked up the shard and tried to place it back where it was, with limited success. He then backed up onto the bed again, worried that he might be in trouble.

Outside the tent, Bilen leaned in close to Lia.

"Your Highness, we must be cautious with that human! To possess all six attributes and with such power, he could be a bigger threat to us than the Great Demon Emperor himself! His magic is chaotic! He has the potential to level a country or even split the world!" he said.

"From what I have seen of him, he seems to be a kind man. I sense no hostile or evil intentions from him. And if he is truly as strong as you say, imagine the help he could provide us in defeating the Dark Army. You saw what he did at the canyon," said Lia.

"He must be controlled, Your Highness! He has no idea of his power and no knowledge of how to control it! Regardless of intent, he could level this entire camp even by mistake! We should return the collar to his neck at once!" said Bilen.

"He is our guest, Bilen. Not our prisoner. We simply need to teach him how to control his powers, and if you will not do so, I will teach him myself," Lia said in a stern tone.

Bilen collected himself for a moment, took a deep breath, and stood up straight.

"As you wish, Your Highness. But let it be known that I advised against it," he said.

"Noted," said Lia. "You may go."

Bilen bowed to her before turning around and walking away.

Lia returned to the tent to find Jack still sitting on the bed, looking like a child who had just broken an expensive vase. He had put the collar back on his own neck and was repeatedly trying to latch it.

"I'm so sorry about breaking your gauge. I didn't mean to do it. You're not going to have me executed or anything now, are you?" he asked.

Lia smiled.

"No, Jack. It's ok. You just caught us both by surprise. That's all. There's no need for that collar anymore. You can stop trying to put it back on." she said.

"Oh," said Jack, as he set the collar down on the bed. "So... what now?" he asked.

"For now, I think you should get some rest. Tomorrow, I think we should work on teaching you how to control your magic," she said.

"Yeah. Sure. That sounds like a good plan. Let's do that," said Jack, as he nodded rapidly.

"Very well. Then I bid you good night, Jack," said Lia, as she gave a slight bow of her head.

"Yeah, uh... good night, Lia. Sweet dreams," he said, still flustered by what had just transpired.

Having never heard that before, Lia found the saying quite interesting.

"Hmm. Yes. I like that. I wish you sweet dreams as well,

Jack." she said with a gentle smile.

Lia then left the tent. The evening light was much dimmer than the light that had first shone in when they had entered, leading Jack to finally realize just how long they had been talking. He flopped back down on the bed and let out a big sigh before grabbing the blanket and pulling it over his head.

"Smooth, Jack. Real smooth," he said.

CHAPTER 6

The next morning, Jack woke up early. He noticed a bowl of fruit on the desk that wasn't there the night before. He grabbed a few of the apples and put them in his pockets. He walked to the opening of the tent and peeked his head out. To the left and right of the tent's opening were two guards.

"Morning, boys," he said to the guards.

The guards both looked at him.

"Here. Have an apple," he said as he took two of the apples out of his pockets and tossed one to each guard.

He took the third apple out and started eating it.

"A couple of questions for you boys. First, are you here to keep people from coming in or to keep me from coming out?" Jack asked.

One of the guards spoke.

"We are here for your protection, sir," he said.

"Sweet," said Jack. "Second question. I know that this is a question that is almost never asked in movies and fantasy books, but is there any chance one of you two strapping young gents could direct me to the latrine?"

The guards looked confused. Jack tried to clarify.

"The latrine. The bathroom. The place where you relieve yourself. Where you go number one or number two. The toilet, boys. The porcelain throne. Is any of this ringing any bells, guys?"

The guards still looked a bit confused. Jack changed his tactic.

"I'm gonna be blunt. I. Have. To. Pee. Where do I do that?" he said.

The guards finally understood, and one of them spoke.

"This way, sir." he said as he directed Jack to the tent where "business" is done.

Once he was finished with his business, Jack stepped out of the tent.

"Hmm. A magic outhouse. Neat. Mystery solved, I guess," he said to himself before speaking to the guard who was waiting outside. "Thanks. Now, onward to my tent, my armor-clad friend!"

The guard escorted Jack back to his tent.

#####

Not long after Jack returned to his tent, Lia arrived.

"Good morning, Jack. Did you sleep well?" she asked.

"Yeah. You?" asked Jack.

"I slept quite well, thank you. Before we talk about your magic, I thought it might be a good idea to show you around the camp," she said.

"Sure. Sounds like fun," said Jack.

With that, Lia and Jack left the tent. They talked as they walked.

"You seem surprisingly comfortable in this setting, Jack," she said.

"Well, where I come from, I was a soldier for quite a while, so I'm used to spending a lot of time in the field," he said.

"You were a soldier?" she said.

"Yeah. I was a Major. I was in charge of a unit of specialized soldiers known as Rangers," he said.

"I see. And did these Rangers of yours also possess magic?" she asked.

"No. As far as I know, magic doesn't really exist where I come from. But we were well trained and well armed, so we were more than capable of completing even the most difficult of operations," said Jack, with a hint of pride as he thought back on the soldiers he had under his command.

As they continued to walk, Lia showed him the various

specialty tents and structures, including the one where meals were prepared, the briefing and command tents, the soldier barracks, and the supply tents. They then came upon the medical tent.

"This is our medical tent," Lia said, as she opened the flap, revealing rows of beds where soldiers with varying degrees of injuries were being attended to by healers.

Jack's expression turned serious as he looked into the tent. He had seen more than his fair share of similar scenes during his time in the military. A glow came from the hands of the healers as they tended to the wounded. He turned to Lia.

"Didn't you say that it's been more than three weeks since the battle in the canyon? How are there still so many wounded?" he asked.

"That battle ended over three weeks ago, but some of the soldiers were severely injured before you showed up, and we are still fighting skirmishes every day. The healing is slow because some of our strongest healers are among the wounded from the battle at Arnin Canyon, and we can't get any more healers in to replace them for at least a month, even by dragon," she said.

"I'm sorry to hear that. Wait... Did you say dragon?" Jack said.

"Yes. Follow me," said Lia.

They walked toward the outer edge of the camp and came up to a covered area where peculiar noises could be heard. As they got closer, Jack could see what looked like small dragons, only slightly larger than Clydesdale horses. There were saddle-like mounts attached to some of their backs.

"These are our dragons. Lesser dragons, to be more precise. With a rider and equipment, they can travel distances much faster than it would take on foot, but we only have so many," she said.

Jack cautiously approached the dragons. One in particular seemed to be rather aggressive, opening its mouth and hissing at anyone who passed by.

"What's the deal with this one?" asked Jack.

"That one is a recent addition. She was fine bringing her here, but soon afterward, she wouldn't allow any rider and grew aggressive to anyone who approached her. We fear that we may have to put her down," said Lia.

"What's her name?" asked Jack.

"Nava," Lia said.

Jack approached Nava slowly and carefully. She started to hiss. Just as he got within reach, Jack noticed something in her mouth. Along the gumline on the left side of her back teeth, Jack noticed what looked like a bone wedged deep into the gums. It was then that he noticed that she was rubbing at the area with her tongue.

"Can I try something?" asked Jack.

"Be careful," said Lia.

Jack took a few more steps forward, and Nava hissed again, but she didn't lunge toward Jack. She only opened her mouth to hiss. Jack slowly raised his right hand and placed his left hand on his own jaw, tapping as if to tell Nava that he wanted to help. As she held her mouth open, Jack reached his hand in. One of the handlers noticed what Jack was doing from a distance and began to approach from behind Lia.

"Is he insane? Is he trying to lose a hand?" said the handler, but Lia raised her hand to stop his approach.

"Wait. Let him try," she said.

Jack slowly reached his hand toward the fragment in the back of the dragon's mouth. The moment he touched it, Nava winced and pulled back slightly but didn't close her jaws. Jack carefully grabbed an edge of the fragment and gently pulled it out. It was a two-inch-long shard of bone, likely from a meal that the dragon had eaten soon after arriving. The moment he pulled it out, Nava's demeanor changed. Jack turned to Lia.

"I don't know about you, but I'd be pretty cranky with a shard like this sticking in my gums and no way to reach it," he said as he tossed it on the ground. When he turned back to Nava, he noticed that her head was down and she was stretching her neck toward him. Lia seemed surprised at this action.

"What's happening?" asked Jack.

"She's thanking you. Touch your forehead to hers," she said.

Jack leaned in and gently placed his forehead against Nava's head and closed his eyes.

"You're most welcome," he said to Nava as he pet her on the side of her neck.

As he pulled his head back, Nava made eye contact with him. He smiled at her before turning back to Lia, who still had a somewhat surprised look.

"What?" said Jack.

"Dragons are sensitive and selective creatures. They generally don't take too kindly to strangers. Let alone allow one to put their hand in its mouth. That she took a liking to you so quickly is exceedingly rare. I'm thoroughly impressed," she said with a smile.

"Always happy to be of service, Your Highness," Jack said while bowing in an exaggerated manner.

Right after Jack stood back up, Nava placed her chin on top of Jack's head. He reached up and scratched behind her jaw.

From a distance, Captain Alivair sees this happening and approaches Lia.

"Your Highness. May I speak to you?" he said.

Lia turned to him.

"Of course." She turned to Jack, who was still playing with Nava. "Excuse me for a moment, Jack."

Jack waved in acknowledgment before going back to playing with Nava.

Alivair had a look of concern on his face.

"Your Highness. Should we really be letting this stranger walk around freely in this camp? He's dangerous, and for all we know, he could be a spy for the Emperor. I don't trust him. He should be detained and interrogated immediately," he

said.

"Captain Alivair, look over there," Lia pointed at Jack. "Does that really look like a spy to you?"

Jack was playing with a dragon like it was a completely normal thing to do.

"And are you forgetting about the nearly twenty-three thousand Dark Army troops that he reduced to nothing at Arnin Canyon?" She asked.

"Of course not, Your Highness, but that may very well have been a sacrifice in order to get us to take him in." Alivair said.

"Captain, consider this. If the Dark Army had someone capable of wiping out an entire legion of soldiers in a single shot, would it not make more sense for them to simply use it on us directly instead of sacrificing their own soldiers for the sake of some sort of subterfuge?" she asked.

"Perhaps. But I still don't trust him," he said before walking up to Jack.

He pointed a finger at Jack as he spoke.

"If you do anything to threaten Her Highness, I will not hesitate to put you down, Otherworlder. That's a promise," Alivair said in a threatening tone.

Alivair stood slightly shorter than Jack, with long hair the color of blue calcite. His bright silver armor was accented with strips of gold and was intricately engraved, showing his high status. The woven black leather long sleeves extended beneath black leather gauntlets covered in fine metal scales, leading to studded knuckles and larger scales running down each finger.

"Gotcha. You're kind of a dick, huh?" Jack said as he continued to pet Nava, showing that he wasn't the least bit intimidated by Alivair's threat.

"I don't speak Otherworlder, human. What is the meaning of this 'dick' you speak of?" Alivair asked.

"Oh, it's an Otherworlder term that means that you're kind of a big deal." As Jack was saying this, he briefly looked at

Lia and subtly shook his head before turning back to Alivair.

"I am second in command of the Vedyrian Army, Otherworlder, so if what you say is true, then I am very much a 'dick', and you best not forget it," said Alivair.

"Oh, don't worry. I won't forget it." Jack said, trying his best to hold back a laugh.

As Alivair walked away, he spoke to Jack one last time.

"I will be keeping an eye on you, Otherworlder," he said.

"Looking forward to it!" said Jack in reply, as he waved to Alivair.

Jack pets Nava one more time before walking back over to Lia. He is no longer making any effort to hide his smile.

"From your reaction, am I to assume that this word you used does not mean what you told him it means?" Lia asked.

"It does not. But it will be really funny if he starts telling people what I told him," said Jack.

Lia shakes her head.

"I do hope that you both eventually get along. For now, there are a few more places I'd like to show you," she said as she gestured the direction that she wanted Jack to walk.

Jack nodded and followed.

#####

As they continued to walk through the camp, Jack was amazed at the diversity of the occupants of the camp. The camp was populated by not just elves, but a wide variety of beastfolk and other races. Among the beastfolk, there were wolves, bears, lizards, felines, and rabbits. Towering above all the other occupants were the orcs. Their skin was a light-bluish gray, and their eyes were the color of antique gold. The shortest among the ones he saw was at least eight feet tall, with muscles that would put even the biggest of bodybuilders to shame. Their facial features included pronounced brows and thick, squared jaws. There were complex raised ritualistic scars along their faces, necks, arms, and chests. One thing in particular began to stand out to Jack. He didn't see any other humans.

"Quick question, Lia. Where are all of the humans?" he asked.

"Unfortunately, there aren't that many left anymore. The human kingdoms were among the first to fall to the Dark Army. Many became Demonborne. The survivors are scattered throughout the land." She said.

"Oh. So I'm kind of an endangered species here, huh?" he said.

"It would seem so," she said, in a slightly somber tone.

Eventually, they came to a tent surrounded by large wolf beastfolk guards.

"This is the armory," she said as she nodded to the guards to let her and Jack pass.

As they walked into the tent, Jack saw rows and rows of weapons, including swords, bows, daggers, and staffs. As he looked around, he noticed something missing.

"Where are the arrows?" he asked.

Lia picked up one of the bows and pointed to a gem mounted into the grip.

"Since there are many who don't possess a magical affinity, we have many tools that have been infused with magic through these gems."

"How do you infuse magic into gems?" Jack asked.

"It's a technique and skill known exclusively to the fairiefolk. Their skills in magic and alchemy have been quite useful for generations." she said.

"Wait. There are fairies here, too?" asked Jack.

"Indeed. And not only are they skilled in magic and alchemy, they have also been very helpful to us as messengers and spies," Lia said.

She handed the bow to Jack. He examined it thoroughly and was surprised at how light it was. He drew the string back, but nothing appeared.

"How does it work?" he asked.

He handed the bow back to Lia, and she angled it in a way that Jack could see the gem mounted into the grip.

"You begin by placing two fingers of your firing hand on the gem and then draw back the string."

She touched her index and middle fingers against the gem and brought them directly back to the string. As she did so, a glowing yellow line of energy formed between the gem and the string. When she raised the bow and drew the string backward, the line grew to a full-sized glowing energy arrow. The string itself glowed as she drew it back. She slowly brought the string back to the bow, resulting in the energy arrow shrinking back down to a line between the string and the grip, and when she released the string, the glowing line vanished.

"Cool!" Jack said, as he tried to process what he had just witnessed. "So what other kinds of objects can you infuse magic into?"

"There are many tools used for everything from cooking to the transporting of heavy supplies that have been infused with fairy magic." she said.

"Oh! Like the toilet, right?" Jack said with a surprising degree of enthusiasm.

Lia laughed at his excitement.

"Yes. Like the toilet," she said, still laughing.

"Yeah. That was cool. I liked that," said Jack.

"You are a very peculiar man, Jack," said Lia, as she began to catch her breath.

Jack nodded.

"You know, you're not the first person to tell me that," he said.

"I should think not," said Lia, as she returned the bow to the racks. She then gestured toward the opening of the tent.

"There is one more place I'd like to show you," she said as they walked out of the tent.

#####

They walked for some time through the camp, engaging in some idle small talk as they walked. Eventually they reached a row of tents on the outskirts of the camp, opposite to where the dragon stables were located. As they approached the tents, a familiar person came out of one of the tents.

"Oh! Hey, Gandalf! Wait... sorry. Bil, right?" said Jack.

Bilen shook his head, knowing that he was likely about to be in for a rough time, as he approached Lia and Jack. He greeted them both.

"Greetings, Your Highness," He turned to Jack. "And... you, as well."

Lia slightly bowed her head in greeting. Jack raised a hand and waved. Lia turned to Jack.

"Bilen here is the leader of the Mage Corps. They are the ones responsible for the majority of large-scale offensive and defensive magic on the battlefield," she said.

"Nice! So you're kind of a badass, huh? Good for you, Bil. Oh, and I'm still really sorry about breaking your crystal gauge. I feel really bad about that," Jack said.

"No need to worry yourself any further, young man. It can be repaired." Bilen said.

Jack let out a sigh of relief.

"Oh good. That's good to hear," he said.

Lia places a hand on Jack's shoulder.

"The reason I brought you here, Jack, is because Bilen will be assisting me in trying to teach you to control your magic," she said.

"Try being the operative word here, I'm guessing," said Jack as he held up his bandaged arms.

"I have faith in you, Jack," she said in a reassuring tone.

Just as she finished saying that to Jack, a fairy flew up from behind them. Jack flinched, thinking that a large insect had flown up to them before turning and seeing what appeared to be a humanoid with light mint-green-colored skin, short and spiky dark green hair, and four rapidly beating dragonfly-like wings flying up to Lia's shoulder. The tiny figure whispered something into her ear. Lia nodded and thanked the fairy before it jumped off of her shoulder and took flight, returning in the same direction from which it came. Jack didn't blink a single time watching what had just transpired between Lia and the fairy.

"Wow. That just happened," he said out loud to himself.

"I have some issues I must attend to, gentlemen. If you'll excuse me. Jack, will you be able to find your own way back to your tent?" she said.

Jack nodded. She then turned to Bilen.

"Bilen, I'd like you to join me this evening in Jack's tent in order to begin his instruction."

Bilen bowed his head.

"As you wish, Your Highness," he said.

Lia then turned around and walked away in the same direction the fairy took a few moments earlier. Jack stood there, looking around awkwardly for a moment before looking at Bilen.

"So... I guess I'll see you later, Bil," Jack said.

Bilen gave a nod to Jack.

"Until this evening, then. Try your best not to blow anything up in the meantime," he said in a mildly condescending tone.

"Gotcha," said Jack as he turned and headed back to his tent.

CHAPTER 7

As evening came, Jack sat impatiently on his bed, awaiting the arrival of Lia and Bilen. The thought of actually learning how to use magic made him feel a bit like a kid again, listening to all of the stories that Artemis told him. The evening meal was delivered by a beastfolk rabbit, standing all of four feet tall, not counting the ears. Jack thanked him and asked him a question before he left.

"Where's Crescia?" He asked.

The rabbit paused at the opening of the tent and turned to Jack.

"She is attending to Her Highness at the moment," he said.

"Oh, ok. Thanks," said Jack.

The rabbit nodded and left.

Jack practically inhaled his meal, still excited about learning magic. No sooner had he finished his last bite when he heard Lia's voice outside the tent.

"Jack, may we enter?" she said.

Jack shot up from the chair, threw the utensils onto the plate, and slid it over to the end of the desk.

"Yes! Of course!" he said.

Lia and Bilen walked in.

"Please, sit!" Jack said excitedly while gesturing to the chairs.

Lia and Bilen both calmly walked over to the chairs and sat down. Jack then sat down on the bed.

"So, where do we start?" said Jack.

"I get that you're excited, Jack. But we need to do this properly and safely," Lia said.

Bilen clears his throat.

"Since we both have an affinity for it, and it's the one type of magic that has the least possibility of you completely destroying the camp should you use it, the first type of magic we shall teach you to use is light magic," he said, not even attempting to hide his feelings of objection to teaching Jack magic at all.

"Makes perfect sense," said Jack.

Bilen pulled a small dagger from a sheath on his hip.

"Give me your hand, Jack," he said.

Jack was a bit hesitant.

"Why do I get the feeling that you just want an excuse to cut me?" he said, half jokingly.

Lia chuckled.

"If you wish to learn to control your magic, give me your hand." Bilen said, clearly in no mood to laugh.

Reluctantly, Jack held his hand out. Bilen lowered the bandages wrapped around his palm and placed the blade of the dagger against the edge of his palm, about two inches below his pinky finger. He quickly pulled the dagger, creating a deep cut in Jack's hand.

"Oww!" said Jack as he pulled his hand back.

Bilen held his hand out, waiting for Jack to place his now injured hand back down.

"Magic is something that you feel. It is something you control with your thoughts," Bilen said.

Jack was still cradling his injured hand.

"Right now, all I feel is that you cut me like you're holding a grudge. I think you hit bone, Bil. Seriously. Not cool," he said.

Bilen again held his hand out, more forcefully this time, trying to get Jack to give him his hand again.

"Give me your hand. I'll heal it," he said in a frustrated tone.

"No!" said Jack before looking to Lia. "You can use light magic, too. Can't you?"

Lia nods while smiling at the scene unfolding before her.

Jack offers his injured hand to her.

"Then can you heal it? I'm worried that he might just stab me again," he said.

Lia gently took his hand.

"Sure." she said.

Lia held her other hand over his injury, closed her eyes and her hand began to softly glow.

"Magic is all about visualization. When you're healing someone, you must imagine their wound healing, and if you concentrate enough, the magic will start to heal the wound."

As she spoke, Jack watched as the fresh wound in his hand began to close. By the time she was done speaking, the wound had completely closed, leaving not so much as a scar. When she was done, the glow began to fade. She then placed the hand she used to heal Jack's wound onto his palm. She opened her eyes and smiled. Jack just sat there, amazed at what he had just witnessed. The pain that was so sharp only moments ago was gone. All that was left was the warmth of Lia's hands holding his.

"Wow," he said. "And you're telling me I can do that?"

Lia smiled and nodded.

Bilen cleared his throat again, noticing that Lia had yet to release Jack's hand. Lia released Jack's hand and he brought it up to his face, examining it closely.

"Would you like to try?" Lia asked Jack.

Jack immediately looked over to Bilen.

"Can I cut him?" he said.

Bilen leaned back, slightly threatened by Jack's excitement. Lia took the small dagger from Bilen and placed it against her own hand. She drew the blade slowly across her own palm and offered her hand to Jack. Jack cradled her hand with one hand and held his other hand a few inches above her palm.

"Now close your eyes and imagine the wound healing,"

she said.

Jack took a deep breath and closed his eyes. As he began to concentrate, his hand began to glow. The glow rapidly became very bright, and the wound on Lia's hand quickly closed. She reached up and grabbed his hand, breaking his concentration.

"Excellent! You did it! Well done, Jack!" she said.

Jack opened his eyes and brought her previously wounded hand close to his face, running his fingers over the area where the wound had vanished.

"I can heal people?" Jack said.

"Yes. It seems you can," Lia said. "And quite quickly, it would appear."

Jack suddenly stood up.

"I'll be right back," he said.

As he ran out of the tent, Bilen shouted to him.

"There is much more to learn! You are far from finished here!" he yelled.

#####

By that time, Jack was well on his way to the medical tent. Having seen as many wounded soldiers over the years as he had, the idea of being able to heal even one was something he couldn't wait to do. When Lia and Bilen exited Jack's tent, he was already out of sight.

#####

Jack burst into the medical tent and was greeted by one of the healers.

"May I be of assistance?" the healer said.

Jack was almost manic in response.

"I can heal. Can I help?" he said.

The healer looked somewhat confused but allowed Jack to pass. Jack walked up to one of the soldiers lying in a cot. The soldier had a number of deep wounds across his face and chest.

Jack placed his hand over the wounds, closed his eyes, and concentrated. Soon his hand began to glow. The glow became brighter and brighter. After a moment, Jack opened his eyes. The wounds on the soldier had healed completely. The healer approached the soldier and examined him, confirming that the wounds had fully healed.

"Thank you, stranger," he said.

But by that time, Jack had moved on to the next soldier. Again, he closed his eyes, concentrated, and began to heal the soldier's wounds. Eventually, Jack thought he would try to heal many soldiers at once. He stood in the middle of the tent, closed his eyes, and concentrated as hard as he could. The glow from his hands became so bright that it engulfed the entire tent. Those who were able to do so shielded their eyes from the glow.

#####

In the distance, Lia and Bilen saw the immense glow coming from the medical tent and began to run toward it.

"Young fool," said Bilen as they ran.

#####

When the light faded, Jack was breathing heavily. He looked around at the soldiers. Many of them were now looking at him with shocked expressions, including the healers. Not only were they shocked by the glow from this stranger who had just burst into the tent. Many of them were also shocked to find that recently severed limbs and recently lost eyes had returned. Jack slowly stumbled out of the tent as the healers began to examine the soldiers. Just as he closed the flap of the tent after stepping outside, Jack began to wobble before collapsing face down in the dirt.

"That was awesome," he said into the dirt.

Just then, Lia and Bilen arrived to see Jack on the ground. A healer came out of the tent and saw Jack. Bilen raised his hand.

"Don't worry about him," he said.

Jack, still face down in the dirt, raised his hand and gave a thumbs-up. The healer then energetically waved for Lia to come into the tent.

"Your Highness! Your Highness! You must see this!" the healer said.

Lia walked into the tent, following the healer. She looked around in the tent to see previously seriously wounded soldiers now sitting up in their cots. The healer rushed her from cot to cot.

"Your Highness! Look! Even lost limbs have returned!" he said.

"Remarkable." She said as she greeted each of the soldiers with a smile.

Meanwhile, Bilen was crouched in front of Jack, who was still face down in the dirt.

"What you failed to hear when you ran from the tent, young man, is that use of magic comes at a price. The more you use, the weaker you become. It takes a toll on your body that you must recover from," he said.

"Yeah. I'm starting to understand that now." Jack said to the dirt, slightly slurring his speech. "Still, totally worth it. That was awesome."

Bilen shook his head and stood up. Lia came out of the tent.

"Bilen, you should go in there and take a look," she said before looking down at Jack, who was continuing to lay face down in the dirt.

Bilen went into the tent. Lia crouched down and rolled Jack onto his back.

"Woah. That's much better. Oh, hey! You're pretty. I healed some people. That was fun. I can't move. Am I gonna die? Still, totally worth it," he said, sounding like he was highly intoxicated at that point.

Lia began to laugh.

"No, Jack. You're not going to die. You just used too much magic too fast. You'll be just fine after you rest for a while. You did very well. Thank you, Jack," she said as she gently patted Jack on the head while calling some guards over to help pick him up.

As the soldiers lifted him up, each one holding him by an arm, Lia noticed that the bandages that had been wrapped around his arms were almost completely burned away, revealing dark, almost tattoo-like scars where the glowing cracks had initially formed when she first saw him absorb the massive amounts of magic energy in the canyon. His head was slumped forward, as he was so weak that he was unable to hold it up. Lia's expression changed.

"But why did you feel the need to rush over here so quickly, Jack?" she asked.

With his head still slumped forward, he spoke in fragments.

"Had to... lost so many... couldn't help... now I can... had to," he said as he drifted off into unconsciousness.

Lia then noticed a few tears falling down his cheeks. She gently placed her hand on his head for a moment before speaking to the soldiers holding him up.

"Bring him back to his tent... carefully." she said.

The soldiers nodded and carried him away.

#####

Bilen walked out of the tent with a look of surprise and confusion on his face. Lia spoke.

"Still think he's a threat, Bilen? Would a threat do something like this?" she asked.

"I don't doubt his intentions, Your Highness. What he did here was... miraculous, to say the least. But imagine if he had done something with one of the other magical attributes. It's his lack of control that is dangerous," he said.

"All the more reason for you to help teach him to

control it, then," she said before turning around and walking away, heading in the direction of Jack's tent.

Bilen looked back at the medical tent briefly before walking toward the direction of the Mage Corps tents.

#####

As Lia approached Jack's tent, she saw the two soldiers leaving. She thanked them as they passed by her, giving her a slight bow. She opened the flap of the tent and entered. Inside, Jack was lying face up on the bed. His head was shifting around on the pillow, and he was quietly muttering something. Lia got close to try to hear what he was saying. As she tilted her head and got about a foot away from him, she was able to make out what he was saying.

"Had to. Too many. Had to. No more. Too many. Had to," he muttered.

Lia began to realize that there was a much deeper meaning to his actions as she saw another tear fall from one of his eyes. Remembering that he had mentioned being a soldier to her earlier, she imagined that he must have had regrets about his own soldiers being wounded in battle. She softly stroked his head as he continued to shift.

"You did well, Jack. You did very well. Now rest. Just rest," she said as she continued to stroke his head.

When Jack finally drifted off to sleep, Lia placed a blanket over him and then stepped out of his tent.

#####

As she returned to her own tent, Alivair approached.

"I hear your little pet performed quite the trick earlier, Your Highness," he said.

"He is not my pet, Captain, and I advise you to remember to whom you are speaking," she said in a firm tone.

Captain Alivair's posture and expression changed. He straightened his armor, recognizing that his condescending comment had clearly crossed a line, though he was surprised at just how firm her tone actually was. It was a tone she had not often used when speaking to him.

"Forgive me, Your Highness. I meant no offense," he said.

"Yes, you did. But that aside, is there something I can do for you, Captain," she said in the same firm tone.

Alivair cleared his throat.

"I was simply saying that word has begun to spread about what the human did in the medical tent," he said.

"The human's name is Jack," she said, continuing the firm tone.

"Yes, Your Highness. Jack," he said, realizing that he was continuing to dig himself into a hole.

"Is there anything else?" she asked.

"No, Your Highness," he said.

"Then good night, Captain," she said.

Alivair stood at attention.

"Yes, Your Highness. Good night," he said.

He remained there for a few moments as she entered her tent. After a quick look around, he walked off to go to his own tent for the night.

CHAPTER 8

The next morning, Jack woke up feeling like he had just spent the previous night drinking half the contents of a liquor store. He poked his head out of the tent just as Crescia was arriving with his breakfast. He held the tent flap open for her and followed her into the tent. She placed the tray down on the desk and turned to Jack.

"How are you feeling today?" she asked.

"Worse than good. Better than dead, I guess," said Jack.

Crescia looked thoroughly confused at his statement.

"I'm pretty achy, but otherwise not too bad," Jack said to clarify.

Crescia nodded, getting a better idea of how he was feeling.

"Oh. I think I get it now. Well, I hope you feel better soon," she said.

"Thanks," said Jack.

Crescia then walked up to Jack. Standing only a few feet from him, the difference in height between the two of them became much more apparent. They almost looked like a parent and child. Crescia smiled.

"Word has spread throughout the camp about what you did yesterday." she said.

"Is that a good thing?" asked Jack.

"Of course! Very good! That you were able to heal everyone, be they elf or beastfolk, is all that everyone has been talking about," she said enthusiastically.

"Cool," said Jack.

"Well, I have to get back to my duties. See you later, Jack!" Crescia said.

She hummed to herself as she left the tent.

After she left, Jack sat down at the desk and ate the breakfast. When he was done, he decided to go for a walk around the camp.

The one thing that stuck out to him was how friendly everyone was to him. It wasn't that anyone was particularly unfriendly to him before, Bilen's constant condescension and Captain Alivair's blatantly overt hostility notwithstanding. But he found that people were smiling at him as he passed, with some even greeting him with the occasional "Good morning." His walk eventually brought him to the stables. As he approached, Nava's head perked up. Jack walked up to her and put his hand out. She leaned her head down. He leaned his head forward and touched his forehead to hers while petting her neck.

"Good morning, Nava. Did you sleep well?" he said.

Jack was still somewhat giddy at the idea that he was standing there and petting a dragon. It was something that he had imagined doing all the way back to when he was a young child, playing with his toy dragons in his bedroom. Soon, the handler that had approached the day before walked up to Jack.

"She sure has taken a liking to you," the handler said.

"Yeah. She's a real sweetheart," said Jack as he continued to pet Nava. "I'm Jack, by the way."

"Good to meet you, Jack. The name's Barvan."

"Nice to meet you, Barvan. How's she doing this morning?" he asked.

"Much better. She's getting her appetite back. Perhaps in a few days, if Her Highness is ok with it, I'll let you take her out for a quick flight." Barvan said.

"Really? That would be incredible!" said Jack. "Wouldn't that be nice, Nava?"

Nava nudged Jack.

Jack gave Nava a few more pets before turning to Barvan.

"Well, I should probably be heading back. It was nice to meet you, Barvan," he said.

Jack reached his hand out to shake Barvan's hand. Barvan grasped Jack's wrist, and Jack did the same to Barvan.

"You as well, Jack," said Barvan.

Jack gave Nava a few more pats on the neck before heading back to his tent. On his way back, he saw Captain Alivair doing his morning rounds. Jack had hoped to avoid making contact, but sadly the stars were not with him at that moment. Alivair approached him.

"Good morning, human," said Alivair.

"Good morning, dick," said Jack.

Alivair took a deep breath before speaking again. Making it very clear that what he was about to say was being said begrudgingly.

"I suppose I should thank you for your efforts yesterday evening," he said.

"No thanks necessary. I did it because I could." Jack said.

Wanting to engage in further conversation about as much as he wanted to take a face-first dive into a raging bonfire, Alivair chose to end it as quickly as possible.

"Very well, then. Good day," he said.

"Back at you," said Jack.

Alivair walked away to continue his morning rounds. Jack took a slight amount of joy in knowing just how much it irritated Alivair to say anything even remotely positive to him. As his tent came into sight, Jack noticed Lia approaching. When she saw him, she briefly recalled the complex emotional state he was in the night before after healing the soldiers in the medical tent. Jack greeted her first.

"Good morning, Lia," he said.

"Good morning, Jack. Are you well?" she asked.

Jack gave a slight shrug.

"All things considered, I'm not too bad," he said. "How

about you?"

"I'm well," she said.

"That's good. So what's on the agenda for today?" Jack asked.

"Today I think we should try working on some water magic. Nothing too flashy. Just some basic magic," she said.

Jack was a bit doubtful about his ability, given how much he had overdone it the evening before.

"This should be interesting," he said in a half enthusiastic and half worried tone.

Lia opened the flap of the tent and gestured for Jack to enter.

"Shall we get started?" she said.

"Where's Bil?" Jack asked.

"He's working with the Mage Corps today. But I think we can handle this one without him," she said.

"Ok, then," Jack said as he entered the tent.

After they both entered the tent, Lia opened the pouch she had brought with her and took out two small glass bowls and placed them down on a chair before sitting down on the other chair. Jack once again sat on the bed. Lia began the instruction.

"As I said yesterday, magic is all about visualization and concentration. In order to create or manipulate water, you first need to see it in your mind. Let me demonstrate," she said.

She held her hand over one of the bowls, momentarily closed her eyes, and then opened them. When she opened her eyes, Jack noticed a slight blue glow coming from her pupils. As she focused on the bowl, a small sphere of water began to form between the bowl and her hand. She slowly moved her fingers and the sphere of water came to rest in the bowl. She then waved her hand over to the other bowl, and the water slowly raised up from the first bowl and then gently cascaded into the other bowl. Finally, she turned her palm upward, causing the sphere of water to rise up to face height. She brought her other hand up and brought both hands together for a moment before quickly pulling them apart, causing the sphere of water to suddenly burst into a cloud of vapor.

Jack was awestruck by what he had just witnessed. He had a big smile across his face. Not knowing what else to do, he began to clap.

"That was amazing," he said.

Lia smiled.

"Thank you," she said, somewhat taken aback by his enthusiastic response. "Do you think you can do that?"

"Not even a little bit," Jack said, while continuing to smile.

Lia was unable to suppress a laugh at his bluntly energetic denial.

"Give it a try," she said.

Jack stretched his arms out and shook them, as if he were preparing to throw out a first pitch at a baseball game. He did a few stretches and then took a couple of deep breaths. He then began to talk to himself.

"Visualize and concentrate. Visualize and concentrate. C'mon, Jack. You can do this. Just visualize and concentrate."

He held his right hand over one of the bowls and closed his eyes. Below his outstretched hand, a small orb of water began to form. He opened his eyes. Unlike Lia, Jack's eyes began to glow a bright and vivid blue, encompassing his entire eyes. At the same moment that his eyes began to glow, the small orb of water grew into a raging torrent, spraying an absurd amount of water into the bowl at speeds comparable to a fire hose. The sudden onslaught of freezing cold water hit both Jack and Lia. It caused Lia to momentarily let out a scream before she stood up and quickly exited the tent. Having heard the scream, a number of soldiers had come running to see what had happened. When they arrived at the tent, they saw Lia standing there, dripping wet and breathing heavily. Shortly after that, Jack came walking out of the tent, also dripping wet from head to toe.

"Boy, that was cold! But surprisingly refreshing! And

hey! I didn't pass out, so... progress!" said Jack, trying to make the best of the situation. He looked over to Lia and noticed that she was still shaking off the water.

"Sorry," he said.

"I think that perhaps we should do any further magic lessons outside from now on," Lia said after catching her breath.

"I wholeheartedly concur," said Jack.

"I'm... going to go change into something dry," she said before walking away in the direction of her tent.

Jack turned around and faced his tent.

"Everything of mine is wet now," he said sadly.

As Jack walked into his tent and sat down on his bed, the full force of the regret hit him alongside the disturbingly loud, soggy, squishing sound of his now entirely waterlogged mattress. After a few moments of soaking, Jack considered seeking assistance from one of the mages in the Mage Corps. Even though Bilen had told Jack that he had an affinity for all six forms of magic, he felt like any further attempts would likely only make things worse, so he decided it was best to rely on a professional, so he left his tent and made his way toward the Mage Corps tents.

#####

When he arrived at the section of the camp where the Mage Corps were stationed, he decided to just call out to see if anyone would help.

"Excuse me! Does anyone here know wind magic?" he yelled.

As he stood there, waiting for anyone to reply, he felt a rather large hand on his right shoulder. He turned to see who owned the rather large hand and found it connected to a rather large slate gray wolf beastfolk soldier. Standing at least six-and-a-half feet tall, this soldier had the crest indicating that he was a member of the Mage Corps.

"Are you in need of someone skilled in wind magic, my friend?" he said in a deep, booming voice.

Jack suddenly realized that he had seen this soldier before. The last time he saw this soldier, he was lying on a cot in the medical tent, minus the hand that was now gently resting on Jack's shoulder.

"Hi," said Jack. "Yes. I think so, at least."

The wolf soldier patted Jack's shoulder a few times.

"You seem a bit damp, my friend," he said.

"Yeah. I had a bit of a water magic mishap in my tent. I kind of flooded it," Jack said.

"Impressive," said the soldier.

"Lia didn't think so," said Jack.

"Oh. I see. My sympathies, friend," he said. "Close your eyes and hold your breath for a moment."

Jack saw no reason to object, so he closed his eyes and held his breath.

"Raise your arms as well," said the soldier.

Jack complied.

As Jack stood there, eyes closed, breath held, and arms raised, he began to feel a strong wind building around him. It was quite warm and spun around him like a Jack-sized tornado. It increased in speed for almost fifteen seconds and then died away completely. Jack then opened his eyes and exhaled. He looked down to find that his newfound friend had used his wind magic to completely dry Jack's clothing.

"If you can do that same thing to all of the stuff in my tent, I will make you my best man at my wedding if I ever get married." Jack said.

"Lead the way, my friend," he said.

"I'm Jack, by the way."

"Greetings, Jack. I am Rhandor."

"I have a feeling that this may be the start of a beautiful friendship, Rhandor," said Jack as they walked to his tent.

#####

After they arrived at the tent, Rhandor did his magic, systematically drying each item in Jack's tent by first raising the item up into the air and then surrounding it in a sphere of wind to dry it before bringing it back down into Jack's hands.

#####

As Lia stepped out of her tent, she noticed that nearly everyone was facing in the same direction and their heads would rise and lower in sync. She looked toward the same direction as everyone else only to see all of Jack's possessions, one by one, floating up to the sky, momentarily hovering in place, and then slowly returning back down. She looked around a second time at all the people who seemed almost hypnotized by the sight before making her way to Jack's tent. By the time she arrived, she was able to witness Jack's entire mattress slowly levitating upward into the sky like it was being abducted by aliens in need of a good nap.

"Rhandor?" She said.

"Yes, Your Highness?" said Rhandor.

"What are you doing?" she asked.

Jack interjected as he popped his head out of the tent.

"He's quickly becoming my best friend," he said.

"That's good, I suppose," Lia said.

"Yeah. Thanks to Rhandor, pretty much everything in my tent is dry again," said Jack.

"I see," she said. "That gives me an idea."

As Rhandor lowered the mattress into Jack's waiting hands, Lia approached Rhandor.

"What would you say to assisting Jack in learning how to use wind magic?" she asked.

Rhandor turned to Lia and bowed.

"It would be my honor, Your Highness," he said.

"Excellent," she said. "But for the safety of all involved, it would be best if we do this outside the camp. Perhaps at the practice range?"

"Of course. I shall make preparations," said Rhandor, bowing a second time before heading in the direction of the Mage Corps tents.

Jack came out of his tent, having returned the mattress to the bed.

"Where's Rhandor?" he asked.

"He is off to make preparations for you to try some wind magic," she said.

"Are you sure that's such a good idea? Given... you know." Jack said as he pointed to his tent.

"No need to worry, Jack. I've asked Rhandor to set up a practice range outside of the camp in order to minimize any potential collateral damage." she said.

"Oh. Good," said Jack. "I don't think my tent could take much more."

"Come, let us grab something to eat before we head to the range. You will need your strength," Lia said.

#####

Jack and Lia proceeded to the tent where the food was prepared, and they each had a small meal. When they were done, Jack made sure to grab a piece of cake and carefully wrapped it in a cloth.

CHAPTER 9

When they arrived at the practice range outside of the camp, Rhandor had already set up a number of targets.

"Greetings," he said as Jack and Lia approached.

Jack held up the wrapped piece of cake, offering it to Rhandor.

"I got you a piece of cake as a treat for helping me out," said Jack.

For a moment, Jack became preoccupied by his use of the word "treat." He hadn't intended to imply that Rhandor was a dog deserving a treat and a "good boy." He looked at Rhandor's face as he handed him the piece of cake, checking for any hint of a change in his expression that might indicate offense. When the only expression he saw was one that appeared to be an expression of gratitude, Jack realized that he was probably overthinking it and that the whole concept of doggy treats could very well be a completely foreign concept in this world. His realization was confirmed by the friendly response from Rhandor upon receiving the piece of cake.

"Thank you, Jack. Your thoughtfulness is most appreciated," he said, before taking a big bite of the cake.

Jack let out a subtle sigh of relief before looking around the range. There were a number of straw man-shaped targets connected to wooden poles embedded in the ground. There was also a large basket containing a number of softball-sized leather balls.

Rhandor finished his piece of cake and walked over to a pile of straw with a number of small bundles of something mixed in. He turned to Jack.

"The thing about wind magic that distinguishes it

from many of the other forms of magic is the fact that you can't see the magic itself. Unlike fire or water, air has no form, so to help you understand..."

He then turned to Lia.

"Your Highness. If you would be so kind?" he said as he gestured to the pile.

Lia nodded and crouched down, and with a quick flick of two of her fingers, a flame formed on the pile and rapidly spread. The bundles mixed in with the straw produced a massive amount of smoke. Rhandor then turned back to Jack.

"...this smoke will serve as a medium to allow you to see some of the manipulations involved in wind magic."

Rhandor took a few steps away from the fire and then flicked his fingers like he was waving for the fire itself to follow him. His action caused one of the bundles in the fire to jump out of the fire. He then waved his hand like he was directing where he wanted the bundle to go, and the bundle followed his gesture, landing about halfway between Rhandor and the targets he had set up. The smoke gently rose from the bundle. He then turned to Jack again.

"Wind magic has multiple uses, on top of the rather entertainingly novel use you saw earlier. Wind magic can be used both offensively and defensively. When concentrated, wind can be thrown like a blade at a target. Allow me to demonstrate," he said.

Rhandor turned to face the target that he had placed the smoke bundle in front of and took what looked like a fighting stance, with his body facing forty-five degrees from his target. His hands were at his sides. Jack took a close look at Rhandor's eyes and noticed a subtle yellow glow from his pupils. Suddenly, Rhandor's right hand shot up diagonally across his body like an upward chop at the air. A fraction of a second later, Jack saw the smoke in front of Rhandor split momentarily like it was sliced in half by a sword. A fraction of a second after that, the target that stood beyond the smoke bundle exploded, and when the debris had settled,

Jack saw that the target had been sliced along the same angle that Rhandor's chop had traveled. When Rhandor looked back at Jack, he was surprised to see Jack's head repeatedly darting back and forth between the now destroyed target and Rhandor, still somewhat confused about what had just transpired.

"That strike involves imagining a blade that reaches out from your hand and strikes your target. It has a limited range, but it is quite effective at stopping anyone or anything that gets within reach," he said.

Jack then turned to Lia.

"And you think I should start with that? Not trying to blow the flame out of a candle or make a leaf float or anything like that?" he asked.

"Given the strength of your previous attempts with magic, you might as well make the destruction intentional," Lia said with a smirk.

"Fair point," Jack said, smirking back.

Jack then walked up to Rhandor. Rhandor pointed to one of the other targets.

"Just remember. Visualize a blade of air. See it in your mind. Focus on your target and then throw the blade," said Rhandor.

Jack nodded, took a deep breath, and then got into the fighting stance that Rhandor had when he did his strike. He then closed his eyes and visualized the blade. Rhandor walked over to Lia and stood next to her to watch Jack. When Jack opened his eyes, they were glowing bright yellow. He moved his hand in the same way that Rhandor had done, throwing the "blade" at the target. A massive cloud of dust traveled along the path that Jack was facing, leading all the way to the target. Along with the dust cloud came a deafening, thunderous boom. As the ringing in his ears began to subside, Rhandor lifted his hands to clear the dust from the air to get a better idea of what had just transpired. When the dust cleared, Rhandor and Lia first noticed that Jack was down on his knees, breathing heavily. Starting where Jack had stood and leading several yards beyond what little remained of the target was a sharp furrow carved into the ground. It was shallow on the end close to Jack and nearly two feet deep at the opposite end. Rhandor walked up to Jack, crouched down, and placed his hand on Jack's shoulder.

"Are you well, Jack?" he asked.

Continuing to breathe heavily, Jack responded.

"Yeah. I'm fine. That was just a bit intense. And loud. I just need to catch my breath."

"It was a quite impressive attack, my friend. And you hit your target. Well done," said Rhandor.

Jack looked up at where the target once stood.

"Oh wow. I didn't even realize it. Yay for me. Woo!" he said before sitting down on the dirt. He looked over to Lia.

"I didn't pass out, fall flat on my face, or unintentionally drown anybody. I think I'm starting to get the hang of this stuff," he said.

"Indeed," said Lia.

"I think I'm going to need five minutes or so, though," he said.

Rhandor stood up and walked back to Lia.

"Most impressive. His power is unlike any I have ever seen, but I fear his true problem lies in his inability to properly control that power. We may not have anyone here who can help him. We might have to eventually send him to see her," he said.

"Perhaps," said Lia. "But I still believe it may be a bit too early to consider such a drastic move. He is still new to this world and still new to magic. He may yet learn to control it himself. I have faith in him."

"As do I, Your Highness." Rhandor said, raising the hand that Jack's healing powers had regenerated. "But faith can only carry one so far."

Rhandor then turned and approached Jack, who was still sitting on the ground catching his breath. He offered his hand to help Jack up. Jack grabbed his hand and stood up.

"A most impressive effort, Jack. But perhaps you should refrain from any more magic for the day. It appears to be taking its toll," Rhandor said.

"Yeah. You're probably right," said Jack.

"But worry not, my friend. The demonstration is not yet over. Follow me."

Rhandor led Jack over to the basket filled with the leather balls.

"I shall walk over there. When I say so, I want you to throw these balls at me as fast and as hard as you can. I will show you how wind magic can also be used defensively," he said.

"Ok. Cool," said Jack.

Rhandor gave Jack a nod and then walked about twenty feet downrange before turning around.

"When you are ready, my friend," said Rhandor.

Jack thought back to his days in school when they would play dodgeball. Though he never imagined that he would one day be using those skills on a six-and-a-half-foot tall humanoid wolf with magical powers. He picked up the first ball, wound up, and threw it as hard as he could at Rhandor. Holding up his index and middle finger, Rhandor made a small swiping movement like he was turning the page of a book in front of him. The ball was sent off-course long before it reached him. Jack then repositioned himself behind the basket and proceeded to throw ball after ball as fast as he could at Rhandor. Each ball was easily deflected to the left or right with the subtle swiping motion of Rhandor's hand. Jack threw the final ball directly at Rhandor's head as hard as he could. This time, Rhandor flicked his wrist upward, sending the ball toward the sky. Without even looking, Rhandor held his right hand out, and the ball landed squarely in his palm.

"That is so cool," said Jack.

"It is not just solid objects that can be deflected with wind magic," said Rhandor before turning to Lia. "Your

Highness, if you'd be so kind?"

Lia nodded and then placed her palms together. Jack saw a reddish glow start to form in her pupils. As she parted her hands, a fiery sphere began to form between them. By the time she stopped parting her hands, the fireball had grown to nearly the size of a basketball. Lia then took a fighting stance, and with an open palm, thrust her left hand forward, aiming at Rhandor. The fireball launched at impressive speed toward Rhandor. Once again, he waved his hand. When he did so, the fireball immediately deflected and burst like an overinflated balloon. Jack began to applaud.

"That was incredible!" he said.

Jack then turned to Lia.

"That was fire magic?" he asked.

Lia smiled and nodded.

"Wow," he said.

Jack imagined himself trying to do fire magic. Then, taking into account his track record with overpowered magic up to that point, he then imagined the fireball growing out of control. The thought caused him to shudder for a moment.

"Are you all right, Jack?" asked Lia.

"Yeah. I just had a scary thought, but it's gone now."

Lia turned to Rhandor.

"Your assistance today has been most appreciated, Rhandor," she said.

Rhandor bowed.

"It was my pleasure to be of service, Your Highness," he said.

Lia then turned to Jack.

"Perhaps that should be all for today, Jack," she said.

Jack nodded and then thought for a moment before metaphorically rolling the dice.

"Would you be able to join me for dinner tonight?" he asked.

Lia was slightly surprised by the question but considered that there was still a lot about Jack that she didn't know.

"Yes. I'd like that," she said. "Now, if you'll both excuse me, there are things I must attend to."

Rhandor bowed. Jack saw that and awkwardly followed suit. Lia saw the awkwardness of Jack's bow and smiled as she walked away.

After she walked out of view, Jack walked up to Rhandor. Rhandor placed his hand on Jack's shoulder.

"You possess an uncommon level of bravery, my friend," said Rhandor.

Jack paused for a moment and thought about what he had just done.

"Rhandor?" he said.

"Yes, Jack?"

"Did I just ask the future ruler of a kingdom and the current commander of its army on a date?" he asked.

"I believe you did, Jack," Rhandor said.

"And she said yes?" Jack asked.

"She did indeed," said Rhandor.

"Rhandor?" said Jack.

"Yes, my friend?" he said.

"I do hope to see you in the front row of my likely public execution," Jack said.

"Front and center, my friend," said Rhandor as he patted Jack on the shoulder.

"Thank you, Rhandor," said Jack.

"You're welcome, Jack," said Rhandor.

CHAPTER 10

When evening came, Jack found himself pacing in his tent. Questions filled his mind as he paced. Is this a date, or is it just dinner? Does Lia know it's a date? Is she already involved with anyone? Can someone even date royalty? The questions continued to occupy his thoughts, making him more and more anxious. The moment he was on the verge of hyperventilating, he heard Crescia at the entrance of his tent.

"Jack? Are you there?" she asked from outside the tent.

"Yeah!" Jack said, at a volume much louder than he had intended.

Crescia poked her head into the tent.

"Her Highness has requested your presence in her tent," she said.

"Ok!" Jack yelled, before clearing his throat. "Ok. I'll be out in a moment," he said at a much more reasonable and calm volume.

Crescia smiled at his obvious nervousness.

Jack walked up to the mirror and made one final check. He straightened his clothing and ran his fingers through his hair a few times. He took a deep breath and turned toward the opening of the tent to find Crescia trying her best to suppress her giggling.

"What?" asked Jack.

"Nothing. Nothing at all," she said. "This way, please."

As Jack and Crescia made their way to Lia's tent, Jack's anxiety only grew. To those around him, he looked more like a condemned man walking his final steps toward a firing squad than a guy walking to have dinner with someone. Crescia couldn't help but find it amusing. When they reached

Lia's tent, Crescia turned to Jack and placed her hands on his shoulders.

"I have never seen someone so nervous to eat a meal. Will you be all right?" she said in a mildly mocking tone.

Jack nodded and then did a quick shake of his head and arms to try and shake out the tension. He took a deep breath.

"Ok. I'm ready," he said.

Crescia entered the tent, and Jack could hear his introduction.

"Your Highness. Your guest has arrived. Shall I show him in?" she asked.

Jack could tell from her voice that Crescia was trying not to laugh.

"Please," said Lia.

Crescia held open the tent flap and gestured for Jack to step inside. As he passed her, she whispered to him.

"Good luck," she said with a wink.

When Jack walked in, Lia was standing there, smiling. He could tell that, thanks to Crescia, she was fully aware of Jack's awkwardness. Her tent clearly reflected her status. Her armor was mounted on a wooden stand near a small desk with a mirror. There was a full-sized bed along the back wall of the tent. The tent was illuminated by a number of lanterns with softly glowing amber crystals. In the center of the tent was a small table with two chairs. When Jack's eyes met Lia's once again, he momentarily panicked and started to clumsily attempt to bow. As thoroughly entertained as she was by his awkwardness, Lia finally spoke.

"Breathe, Jack," she said with a smile.

It was only after she said that to him that Jack realized that he had stopped breathing upon stepping into the tent. After he started to breathe again, he awkwardly raised his right hand and waved.

"Hi," he said.

"Hi," said Lia. "Come sit down."

Jack walked over to the table and began to sit, but

immediately shot up again and walked over to Lia's chair and pulled it out for her. She sat down.

"Thank you, Jack," she said.

Jack then walked back around the table and plopped down into his seat, adjusting his position several times before placing his hands on his lap.

"You seem nervous," Lia said with a smile.

"Does it show?" said Jack.

"A little." she said. "This is hardly the first time we've been alone, Jack."

"Yes, Your Highness, That's true. It's just..."

Lia interrupted Jack.

"Jack. I told you that you can call me Lia. No need for formalities here."

"Oh, yeah. Right. Lia. Yes. You did. Yeah. Lia. Yes," he rambled.

"Would you like some wine?" she asked, gesturing to the bottle on the table.

"Absolutely," said Jack as he took the bottle, filled the glass, and chugged it down like he had just found water for the first time in days after a brutal trek through the desert. Upon realizing what he had just done, he placed his glass down and cleared his throat.

"Sorry. Would you like some wine?" he asked.

"Yes, please," she said as she chuckled.

Jack picked up her glass and carefully poured a much more reasonable amount than what he had poured into his own glass and handed it back to her.

"Thank you," she said.

Jack poured a second glass for himself, took a sip, and set the glass on the table.

Crescia popped her head into the tent.

"Dinner will be ready shortly. You ok in there, Jack?"

Lia could no longer hold it back and began to laugh. Jack's head drooped as he realized how awkward he had been up to that point.

"Yes, Crescia. I'm fine, thank you," he said, as he felt the tension begin to release from his shoulders.

Jack raised his head and smiled as he saw how entertaining Lia had found the whole situation so far. Lia took a sip of wine.

"I've been meaning to say this for some time, but for an Otherworlder, you certainly seem to be taking all of this surprisingly well," she said.

Jack thought for a moment.

"Yeah. That's weird, huh?" Jack said. "Part of it might have to do with the stories that my grandfather told me."

"What kind of stories?" she asked.

"Stories that, now that I think about it, seem surprisingly similar to this place. Almost to the point where I wonder if this is where he got the stories," he said.

"What do you mean?" she asked.

"Well, the gate that I passed through to get here is actually in an underground tunnel on my grandfather's property," he said.

"But that gate hasn't been active for nearly two centuries," Lia said.

"Why not?" asked Jack.

"It's said that it was intentionally destroyed by King Deromar to prevent the Dark Army from pursuing him and his family after his kingdom fell," she said.

"Deromar? Why does that name sound familiar?" Jack asked.

"He was the king of one of the last human kingdoms to fall to the Dark Army. The Kingdom of Stobrimore was..."

Jack suddenly interrupted.

"The kingdom of what?" he asked.

"Stobrimore," said Lia.

"Stobrimore?" asked Jack.

"Yes. Why? Is that important?" asked Lia.

Jack cleared his throat.

"It's my last name," he said.

Lia looked a bit confused. It occurred to Jack that the concept of a last name isn't always a given, so he attempted to clarify.

"It's my family name. My name is Jack Stobrimore."

Lia placed her wine glass down on the table and thought for a moment.

"What is the name of your grandfather?" she asked.

"Artemis. Why?" said Jack.

"That was the name of the young prince that King Deromar brought with him through the gate." she said.

Jack was beginning to have difficulty processing what he was hearing.

"Wait. I need a second here," he said.

He leaned back in his chair and looked up at the ceiling of the tent, trying to comprehend the direction the conversation had taken. As he was still processing, Lia spoke up.

"If what you say is true, Jack, that would make you the direct descendant of the last human kingdom."

"Which would make Grampa Art... a king?" Jack asked, partly to Lia and partly to himself.

"And your mother and father, a prince and princess." she said.

"Unfortunately, my parents died in an accident when I was very young. It's not something I really like to talk about, though," said Jack.

"If that is true, Jack, that would make you the crown prince of the fallen Kingdom of Stobrimore."

Jack placed his elbows on the table and put his head in his hands. It was certainly not what he had expected to discover when he initially asked to have dinner with Lia. As he was still trying to process the new information, Crescia entered the tent carrying a tray with their food. Jack and Lia both looked over to Crescia as she walked in.

"Is your conversation going well?" she asked them both.

Jack's face still broadcast his confusion.

"Well, apparently I'm a prince now," he said.

Crescia's eyes grew wide.

"Before dinner was even served? Wow! Um... I congratulate you both on your betrothal!" she said, totally misunderstanding the situation.

Lia laughed.

"Apparently young Jack here just found out that he is the crown prince of the fallen human kingdom of Stobrimore," Lia said, attempting to clarify.

"Oh," said Crescia as she placed the plates of food in front of each of them. "So you're not betrothed?" she asked.

"No," said Lia. "Not today."

"I see," said Crescia, before turning to face Jack. "Congratulations, Your Highness," she said to him in a slightly sarcastic yet playful tone.

Crescia's tone broke Jack out of his loop of shock and confusion. He smiled before looking at Crescia.

"Hey, now don't you start with that," he said.

Crescia gave an exaggerated curtsy in response.

"Yes, Your Highness. A thousand apologies, Your Highness," she said before sticking her tongue out at him.

Once again, Crescia had broken some of the tension that Jack had been struggling with. While he certainly hadn't come to terms with the new discovery, he was no longer spiraling trying to understand it.

"This is certainly not how I expected this date to go," said Jack.

"Date, you say?" said Lia.

Jack suddenly began to panic again.

"Wait. Is it not... ? I thought... It's just... You know..." he rambled.

"Calm down, Jack. A date is fine. I, too, see this as a date," she said with a smile.

"It is? You do? Oh, thank god," said Jack as he breathed a sigh of relief.

"Shall we eat?" she asked.

"Yes. Eat. Food. Yes. Good idea," said Jack.

As they ate, they continued to talk.

"Jack, I've been meaning to ask you something. When you learned that you could use light magic and you went to the medical tent to heal the soldiers, you seemed rather..." she paused to try to find the right word. "...passionate about feeling the need to do so. May I ask why that is?" she said.

Jack placed his utensils down and took a sip of wine before answering her.

"In my time as a soldier, I fought many battles with the soldiers under my command. Not all of them came home. There was one mission in particular that stands out. A local had given us intelligence on the location of a high-value target, a well-known human trafficker..." he clarified after seeing a slight look of confusion on Lia's face. "That's a criminal who sells people, often women and children, into slavery, often sex slavery."

She was slightly shocked by that, but nodded. He continued.

"We checked the intelligence, and it appeared to be valid. We organized an operation to take him out and free the victims. Everything was going smoothly... until it wasn't. As it turned out, the local who had informed us had also informed the trafficker, and we ended up walking into an ambush. My team and I found ourselves caught in a kill box. We were surrounded. We were eventually able to get to cover, but by that time, two-thirds of my team was either dead or dying. A secondary team was able to move in, and we ultimately completed the mission, but at one hell of a cost. I lost a lot of good people that day. I never want to see that again. I just wish I had the power then that I have now. Maybe things would have turned out differently."

Lia reached over and placed her hand on his.

"That is a pain I know all too well," she said.

Jack let out a deep breath through his nose.

"So, changing the subject entirely, is it common here for royalty to be leading the charge in battle? When I first appeared here, I recall seeing you front and center on the battlefield," he said.

"I can't say that my father was particularly pleased with the idea at first, but my mother can be surprisingly effective when it comes to changing his mind," Lia said.

"He may be the king, but she rules the kingdom, huh?" Jack asked with a bit of a grin.

Lia laughed.

"I suppose, in some ways, that may very well be true. My mother is a very strong woman."

"Like mother, like daughter, I see," he said as he raised his glass.

"Indeed," she said with a smile.

Their conversation continued as they finished their meals. They were both sipping wine when Crescia entered, again carrying a tray. This time, on the tray were two plates with slices of cake. After placing the plates on the table and collecting the dinner plates, Crescia turned around and faced Lia and bowed.

"Your Highness," she said.

Lia nodded.

Crescia then walked out of the tent but quickly poked her head back into the tent, looking at Jack.

"And Your Highness," she said quickly before once again sticking out her tongue at him.

Jack raised his napkin, pretending he was going to throw it. Crescia quickly ducked out of the tent. He turned back to Lia.

"She's having way too much fun with this," he said.

They were close to finishing their slices of cake when Alivair suddenly came bursting into the tent.

"Your Highness! Pardon the interruption, but we've received reports of a Dark Army scouting party approaching from the north."

Lia wiped her mouth with her napkin before responding.

"Prepare a team to intercept them." she said.

Jack jumped at the opportunity.

"Permission to join the intercept team," he said. "No magic. I promise."

Lia thought for a moment.

"Very well. Captain?" she said, turning to Alivair.

"With all due respect, Your Highness. I don't see what the human can do to assist us," he said, not even trying to conceal his displeasure.

"The human has a name, Captain. And Jack is also a highly skilled soldier, and on top of that, he also happens to be nobility, so you would do well to treat him as such," she said.

"Him? A noble? Of what?" Alivair asked.

Jack waved.

"Hi. Jack Stobrimore."

"Stobrimore? And what title do you supposedly hold?" Alivair asked.

"Crown prince, apparently," said Jack with a slightly smug expression.

Alivair's expression darkened.

"Very well... Your Highness. We shall assemble at the stables in five minutes. Don't be late, or you will be left behind."

"No problem, Captain. I'll just grab my bag and meet you there." Jack said.

Jack stood up and turned to Lia.

"I very much enjoyed this. I hope we can do it again soon," he said.

"As do I," said Lia.

"Did he say the stables?" Jack asked.

"Yes. He did."

Does that mean that I get to ride a dragon?" he asked.

"I believe it does," she said with a smile.

"Wow. A date with a gorgeous princess, discovering that I'm royalty and I get to ride a dragon. Best day ever!" he

said.

Lia couldn't help but smile as Jack ran out of the tent like a kid.

CHAPTER 11

Jack rushed into his tent and quickly placed his backpack on the bed. He opened the flap to check and make sure that all the necessary equipment was there. He patted down the side pockets to check the contents and then secured all of the various zippers and flaps. He threw the backpack around to his back and ran out of the tent to head toward the stables.

#####

When Jack arrived at the stables, he was surprised to see all of the lesser dragons being fitted with harnesses. What surprised him the most was that Barvan was there, fitting a harness onto Nava. He ran up to Barvan.

"Barvan, is someone taking Nava out?" he asked.

"Well, you are, I'm assuming." Barvan said.

Jack walked up to Nava, and she bowed her head. Jack rested his forehead against hers.

"Did you hear that, Nava? We're going to fly. Isn't that cool?" he said to her.

Jack walked back to Barvan.

"So, how does this harness work?" he asked.

The harness ran the length of Nava's back. By the tail, there were two calf-length cuffs ending in stirrups. Up by the wings, there were two raised handles that looked like joysticks. Barvan gave Jack a quick tutorial.

"First, you grab the handles. Then you lay down on her back, and lastly you put each leg into the cuffs and put your feet into the stirrups. Dragons are smart creatures. All you have to do is lean the handles in the direction you want them to turn. If they trust you, they will quickly become an extension of you. She'll know what to do. Just enjoy the ride," he said.

Jack once again approached Nava.

"Ok, Nava. My life is in your hands... or wings. Let's do this," he said.

Nava nudged Jack. In his mind, that was her way of saying, "Don't worry. We got this."

As Jack was petting Nava, he heard a familiar voice from behind him.

"I hear you will be accompanying us, my friend," the voice said.

Jack turned around to find Rhandor standing behind him.

"Rhandor! You're on the intercept team, too?" said Jack.

"Indeed. As are you, I see. Good to have you," Rhandor said.

"Yeah. It will be my first time flying a dragon, which is not a sentence I ever expected to say," said Jack.

"How was dinner?" asked Rhandor.

"Oh, it was awesome. Next time I hope to learn more about her, though. And yeah, can you believe that there will be a next time? It went that well. And guess what? Apparently I'm a descendant of the king of the last human kingdom, which I guess makes me a prince, which is weird. But the best part about that is how much it irritates Alivair to acknowledge it. Watch what happens when he gets here. You can practically see the veins bulging in his temples when he says it," said Jack.

"Marvelous. I look forward to hearing more about it once this task is over, and I congratulate you on your good fortune, Your Highness," said Rhandor.

"Jack. Please, Rhandor. Call me Jack."

"Of course, my friend," said Rhandor.

It wasn't long before Alivair arrived at the stables with one of the fairies sitting on his shoulder. He reluctantly approached Jack.

"Watch this." Jack whispered to Rhandor.

"I see that you have arrived at the stables... Your Highness. Are you prepared?" Alivair asked.

"Ready, willing, and able, Captain. I'm sure I will be of some use. Right, Rhandor?" Jack said.

"Yes. Indeed. Of that, I have no doubt," said Rhandor, trying his best to not snicker.

"Very well. We shall be moving out quite shortly... Your Highness. Be sure not to get separated," said Alivair.

"Who's this?" Jack asked, pointing to the fairy on Alivair's shoulder, asking both out of curiosity and knowing that Alivair had no more desire to speak to him.

"This is Fyn, one of our best and most skilled members of the reconnaissance unit. Fyn will be directing us to the location of the Dark Army scouts.

Jack waved to Fyn. Fyn waved back.

"Nice to meet you, Fyn," said Jack. Fyn bowed from Alivair's shoulder.

"If you will both excuse me, I do have my own final tasks to attend to. Rhandor... Your Highness," said Alivair before turning away from the two of them and heading over to his own dragon to make the final preparations.

Jack turned to Rhandor.

"Did you see the veins? Every time he said 'Your Highness', you could see the veins in his temples bulge, right?" he said.

Rhandor couldn't help but laugh at that point.

"Indeed I could. They were quite prominent," said Rhandor, trying his best not to laugh too loudly.

Not too far off, Alivair made a hand gesture in the air that suggested that they were prepared to head out.

"Oops. Game time. You stay safe out there." Jack said.

"You as well," said Rhandor.

Rhandor walked over to his dragon and effortlessly secured himself in the harness. Jack walked up to Nava's head.

She bowed her head down. Jack gave the top of her head a quick kiss.

"Remember. It's my first time doing this, so be gentle," he said.

Jack then followed the instructions that Barvan had given him and properly secured himself in Nava's harness.

Alivair gave a signal with his hand, and soon all of the dragons took flight. As the dragons leveled out and began to fly in formation, Jack was unable to hide his smile. He raised himself up to look around as they flew through the evening sky. He couldn't help but think back to his early childhood, when he would place his action figures on the back of the toy dragon he would always play with, imagining what it would be like to fly through the air. It was a wish that he never expected to be fulfilled, but there he was, flying through the sky on the back of a dragon. For a moment, he completely forgot the reason for the flight and just closed his eyes and held out his arms to feel the wind. The sharp turn that the dragons made once they approached the landing site brought him back to his senses. He quickly grabbed the handles to avoid falling off and switched his mind back to mission mode.

#####

The dragons landed in an open field surrounded by trees and rocky outcroppings. Jack and the other members of the team dismounted the dragons and assembled in a small group for the next briefing from Alivair.

"When we get to the top of the ridge, we should soon be able to see the scouting party approaching down below from the west. When they come into sight, we will then determine if we can hit them from the ridge or if we shall need to reposition. Should we need to reposition, it will put us at greater risk of a skirmish, so stay sharp, and we shall all make it back alive. Let us move out," Alivair said.

Everyone in the team nodded, and they began to make

their way up the hill to the ridge. When they reached the top, all of the members of the team got into the prone position and carefully crawled to the edge of the ridge to get a look at the terrain down below. Jack reached into his bag and pulled out a pair of binoculars. He put the binoculars to his eyes and scanned the terrain, looking for any sight of the scout team. Alivair noticed this and tapped Jack on the shoulder.

"Your Highness, what is that device?" he asked.

"You don't need to call me that, Captain. Please just call me Jack. I'd prefer that to any title, and I'd like it a whole lot better than being called human or Otherworlder. Just Jack."

"Very well, Jack. What is the purpose of that device in your hands?" Alivair asked.

"They're called binoculars. They can be used to magnify one's vision in order to see objects or people at long distances." Jack said as he handed them to Alivair.

Alivair placed the binoculars to his eyes.

"Fascinating. It is as if we were much closer to the ground below. These are a most useful tool," said Alivair.

"Yeah. They do come in handy," said Jack.

As Alivair was scanning the landscape with the binoculars, one of the other team members caught sight of the approaching scout team.

"There!" the team member said.

Everyone looked toward the direction the team member was pointing. Alivair aimed the binoculars in that direction to see the scout team. The team was comprised of four Demonborne soldiers with a necromancer in the middle.

"I see them. Damn. They have a necromancer," he said.

Alivair lifted the binoculars.

"They are too far away to reach with magic, and that necromancer may be a problem. We will have to reposition," he said.

"Captain, with your permission, I might be able to take them out from here," said Jack.

"Not even your magic could reach them without

alerting them to our presence, and frankly, I would prefer it if you didn't destroy half of the land in your attempt," Alivair said.

"No magic needed. I have something that can reach them without it," said Jack as he began to open his backpack.

Jack began to pull out the individual sections of the takedown bolt-action rifle. He first pulled out the barrel section, then the stock section, followed by a magnifying scope, a 10-round box magazine, and lastly, a suppressor. He started to assemble the rifle.

"What sort of device is this?" Alivair asked.

"It's called a rifle. It's a device that fires a projectile at a high velocity over a long distance, allowing you to kill an enemy who is far away. It uses these." Jack said as he held up one of the cartridges.

It was a .308 caliber round. Jack assembled the rifle and attached the scope to the mounting rail and the suppressor to the end of the barrel. He then placed the magazine into the magazine well. He pulled the bolt back and pushed it forward to chamber a round.

"This rifle has a suppressor, so it won't be as loud, but I would still recommend everyone here cover their ears," said Jack.

Alivair nodded and then turned to the other team members and made a gesture telling them all to cover their ears.

"When you are ready, Jack. I hope your device works as you say it does," said Alivair.

Jack was momentarily surprised that Alivair had finally referred to him by name but he put that surprise aside to do what needed to be done. He unfolded the bipod attached to the barrel segment of the rifle and positioned his eye behind the scope. He aimed the rifle at the scout team. He made note of the wind speeds based on the amount of movement in the robes of the necromancer and used the gauge on the reticle in order to estimate the distance. After making the calculations in his head, Jack made the necessary adjustments to the scope. He then took aim at the head of the necromancer.

"Target in sight. Be ready. Preparing to fire," he said.

Alivair once again made the gesture to cover ears to all of the team. Alivair covered the ear closest to Jack and raised the binoculars to his eyes with the other hand.

Jack disengaged the safety, took a deep breath in, and exhaled slowly. Near the end of the exhale, Jack squeezed the trigger. The loud crack of the gunshot startled the members of the intercept team. Through the binoculars, Alivair watched as the necromancer collapsed to the ground. The other members of the Dark Army recon team looked around, confused about what had just happened. Jack chambered a second round, took aim at another member of the recon team, and pulled the trigger. Another one down. He chambered a third round, took aim, and fired. Three down. Then four. Then the fifth and final Dark Army scout team member collapsed to the ground, dead. Jack then did a quick scan of the area through the scope before re-engaging the safety.

"All targets neutralized, Captain," he said to Alivair.

Alivair took another look at the bodies through the binoculars.

"Remarkable! Absolutely remarkable!" he said.

Alivair sat up and turned to the other members.

"All clear! The enemies are dead! We're all clear!" he said.

The rest of the team members sat up in surprise. All of them were looking at Jack. Jack ejected the magazine, pulled the bolt back to eject the spent casing, checked the chamber, and then placed the stock end of the rifle on the ground before sitting up. He looked around to find everyone looking at him.

"That's how it's done where I come from," he said.

Alivair placed his hand on Jack's shoulder.

"Absolutely fascinating. That is a truly remarkable tool you have, Jack. You must tell me more about it some time," he said.

Jack was a bit surprised at the sudden turnaround in Alivair's behavior toward him.

"Sure. I'd be happy to," said Jack.

Everyone began to stand up. Alivair offered his hand to Jack to help him up. Jack took his hand and stood.

"Thank you," said Jack. "We should probably get down there and check the bodies for intel."

"Yes. Indeed," said Alivair, before turning to the other members of the team. "Prepare to move out," he said.

Jack picked up the rifle, disassembled it and placed the sections back into his bag. As the team made their way down the ridge to check the bodies of the Dark Army soldiers, Rhandor approached Jack.

"A most interesting tool you have there, Jack. Most interesting indeed," said Rhandor.

"Well, where I come from, magic isn't really an option, so we use tools like that in order to fight," said Jack.

"It is a very formidable weapon," said Rhandor.

"It certainly gets the job done," said Jack.

When they reached the bottom of the ridge and began to approach the fallen Dark Army soldiers, Alivair ordered several of the team members to establish a perimeter while he, Jack, and Rhandor approached to examine the bodies. As they got close, a gem in the staff that had been carried by the necromancer began to faintly glow. Jack started to feel lightheaded. He stumbled, and was caught by Rhandor.

"Are you all right, Jack?" he asked.

"I think so," said Jack. "I just got a little dizzy."

The closer they got to the staff, the more the gem began to glow, and the more lightheaded Jack became. Rhandor noticed the glow coming from the staff and called to Alivair.

"Captain! The staff!" he said.

Alivair looked at Jack and noticed he was being affected

by the staff, so he picked up the staff, threw it a good distance away, and then, using fire magic, sent a small fireball at the staff, causing it to burst into flames. As the staff was reduced to ash, Jack's dizziness faded.

"Are you all right now, Jack?" Alivair asked.

"Yeah. I'm feeling a bit better now. That was weird," said Jack.

"It would appear that dark magic has some sort of adverse effect on you," Rhandor said.

"Given that I was hit with such a massive dose of it when I first got here, and I ended up unconscious for three weeks afterward, you may be right," said Jack.

As Alivair began to check the bodies, he noted how the uniforms of the dead soldiers were entirely undamaged, which was seldom the case when it came to the use of magic. Given that Jack had taken each of them out with a headshot, there was no concern about any intelligence items being damaged by the battle. Alivair collected a number of items from the bodies and placed them into his satchel. He stood up and walked over to Jack and Rhandor.

"Jack. I feel I must apologize for the way that I have treated you. You are clearly a skilled warrior. I apologize for my previous behavior," Alivair said.

"Apology accepted, Captain," said Jack. "I hope we can be friends."

"I would like that," Alivair said.

Alivair then reached into the satchel and pulled out the binoculars to hand them back to Jack.

"Keep them. They're a gift. Every captain needs a good pair of binoculars," said Jack.

Alivair was surprised at Jack's offer.

"Thank you, Jack. That is most gracious of you. I shall make good use of them," said Alivair.

Alivair placed the binoculars back into his satchel before signaling to all of the intercept team.

"Return to the dragons! Our job here is done!" he said.

Alivair then turned to the bodies and fired a number of fireballs at them, quickly reducing the bodies to ash.

As they climbed back up the hill to get to the dragons, Rhandor gave Jack a tap on the shoulder.

"A most interesting turn of events, my friend. Turning the captain from an adversary to an ally is quite the surprise," Rhandor said.

"I'm as surprised as you are," said Jack. "It's a pleasant surprise, though."

"Indeed," said Rhandor.

When they returned to the dragons, the events of the day had begun to catch up to Jack. Not long after they took flight, Jack decided to take a brief nap.

#####

A quick nudge by Nava before they came in to land woke him up. After walking Nava back to the stables, Jack gave Nava a few quick pets and a kiss on the forehead before turning her over to Barvan. Alivair gathered everyone for a final debrief.

"You've all done well today. Go get some rest. I shall report our success to the commander," he said.

Rhandor accompanied Jack until they reached Jack's tent.

"Well done today, my friend. Sleep well," said Rhandor.

"You too, Rhandor," said Jack before walking into his tent, dropping his bag and collapsing onto the bed for some well-deserved rest.

#####

Alivair stood outside of Lia's tent.

"Your Highness. I've come with a report of our mission," he said.

"Come in, Captain," said Lia.

Alivair entered the tent and bowed to Lia.

"Your Highness. I've come to report a successful operation," he said.

"Very well. Any casualties?" Lia asked.

"None, Your Highness. Not so much as a scratch," he said.

"That's very good to hear. And what of Jack?" she asked.

"He was most impressive, Your Highness. He brought a remarkable tool that allowed us to eliminate the enemy with no risk to ourselves. It was loud like thunder, and the members of the Dark Army fell with each shot. It was quite remarkable. Jack is a very skilled warrior and was certainly an asset to this mission," he said.

"I'm pleased to see that your opinion of him has changed for the better, Captain," said Lia.

"Indeed, Your Highness. He was even so gracious as to give me this gift," said Alivair as he reached into his satchel and pulled out the binoculars. "He said that they are called binoculars. They are a fascinating device that, when placed against one's eyes, allow one to see far away objects as if they were up close."

Alivair handed the binoculars to Lia. She looked them over and then placed them to her eyes.

"Fascinating, indeed," she said before handing them back to Alivair. "I hope you are able to make good use of them."

"I shall, Your Highness," said Alivair.

"Anything else?" she asked.

"I was able to recover a number of items from the enemy. I shall review them more thoroughly and report on them later," Alivair said.

"Excellent. Is that everything?" she asked.

Alivair thought for a moment.

"There was one thing of note that occurred when we approached the bodies. It appeared that the necromancer's staff began to glow as Jack approached, and the glow appeared to have some sort of adverse effect on Jack. The moment I destroyed the staff, his discomfort seemed to disappear, but I wonder if there is something more to his reaction to the dark magic item," he said.

"I see. Perhaps I will speak with him about it tomorrow. Is that all?" she said.

"Yes, Your Highness," said Alivair.

"Very well. Congratulations on your success, Captain. Go get some rest," she said.

Alivair bowed again.

"Yes, Your Highness," he said. "Good night."

Lia thought back to what Jack had once said to her.

"Good night, Captain. May you have pleasant dreams," she said.

"Thank you, Your Highness. You, as well," he said before leaving the tent.

Lia smiled as she returned to the documents she had been reviewing before Alivair had entered.

CHAPTER 12

The next morning, Jack woke up early. The events of the prior day gave him a lot to think about. The one event that was front and center in his mind was the date, even though his previous day's activities had also included flying through the sky on the back of a dragon. After doing a few morning stretches, he decided to go for a run to get the blood flowing. It was somewhat of a routine that Jack had picked up during his time in the military. The day after completing a mission and returning to base, he would go for a run and listen to some music. He opened up one of the pockets of his backpack and pulled out his music player with an arm strap and a pair of earbud headphones. After strapping the music player to his left arm and selecting a song from his 80's music running playlist, he hit the play button and began his run.

The run started by heading toward the stables and then running around the perimeter of the camp. Occasionally, a soldier would wave to Jack as he ran by, and he would return the wave. Even though he was now in a world with fairies, beastfolk, elves, dragons, and numerous other beings that, prior to passing through the gate that brought him there, were little more than fictional characters in the stories his grandfather used to tell him, Jack found himself feeling surprisingly comfortable in the setting. To him, a military camp was a military camp, regardless of the occupants. As he rounded the corner toward the area of the camp where the Mage Corps were staying, one of the members waved him down. Jack paused his music and removed the headphones.

"Good morning," said Jack.

"Good morning," said the Mage Corps member.

"What's going on?" Jack asked.

"We were just about to head over to the target range and work on some fire magic. We've heard quite a bit about you and wondered if you'd like to join us," he said.

Jack thought about it for a moment. He had seen a little bit of fire magic demonstrated the day before when Lia lit the straw at the wind magic tests and when Alivair used it to destroy the staff and burn the bodies of the Dark Army members. He figured that it couldn't hurt to see it in action one more time.

"Sure. I'm Jack, by the way."

"I'm Veris."

"Nice to meet you, Veris," said Jack.

"You, as well, Jack. Just follow me," said Veris.

As they walked in the direction of the fire magic range, Jack was able to hear what sounded like distant explosions.

"Will Bilen or Rhandor be there?" Jack asked.

"They are currently having some discussions with Her Highness. They may be along later," said Veris.

When they arrived at the practice range, Jack could see a number of Mage Corps members launching volleys of fireballs far downrange. When they hit, they would create large, fiery explosions in the distance. Veris turned to Jack.

"What we're trying to do today is to make the fireball as compact as possible, while trying to get the largest explosive yield out of it when it hits downrange," said Veris.

"Interesting. Mind if I watch for a while?" Jack asked.

"Sure," said Veris.

Jack stayed back about fifteen feet from the firing line. He watched as the Mage Corps members, one after another, held out their hands and created melon-sized fireballs between their palms and then launched them downrange, resulting in large explosions.

After a while, Veris approached Jack, along with a few other Mage Corps members.

"We heard from Rhandor that you're surprisingly powerful when it comes to magic. Have you done any fire magic yet?" asked Veris.

"Not yet," said Jack. "I don't quite have the control part down yet."

"Well why don't you give it a try now?" Veris said. "This is the fire magic practice range, so you don't have to worry about damaging anything out here."

"I don't know if that's a good idea," said Jack.

"It's ok. We'll show you how to do it. Right?" said Veris as he turned to some of his colleagues. A number of them nodded.

Veris began his instruction.

"I'm sure you're already aware of how magic is all about visualization. When it comes to fire magic, you must first visualize magic flowing through your hands and into a sphere between your palms. Your magic becomes the fuel for that fire, so the more fuel you pour into it, the stronger the explosion will be when it hits its target. Once you feel like the sphere is concentrated enough, you simply push it forward. That will send the fireball toward your target. Let me demonstrate." Veris said.

Veris took a few steps toward the firing line and closed his eyes. When he opened them, a red glow appeared in his pupils. He placed his hands together and then slowly parted them. As his hands parted, a flaming sphere grew between them. When the sphere was roughly the size of a cantaloupe, Veris took a fighting stance, and with a quick pushing motion, he sent the fireball downrange. Two hundred yards away, the fireball landed and immediately exploded. Jack applauded.

"That was awesome," said Jack.

"Now it's your turn," said Veris.

"I'm not sure. I might just end up overdoing it again," said Jack.

"Just try it once. If you only fire one, you shouldn't have to worry about overdoing it," said Veris.

"Ok," said Jack. "But you might want to all stand back a bit, just to be safe."

The members of the Mage Corps all filed into lines to the left and right of Jack, about ten feet away from him on each side. Jack closed his eyes for a moment and placed his palms together. When he opened his eyes, they were fully enveloped in a bright red glow. As he separated his palms, a fireball began to form. As the fireball grew, the tattoo-like scars on his arms began to glow. Since he was wearing a T-shirt for his run, the glow from the scars was visible to those around him, and some of them began to step back. Once the fireball was about the size of a basketball, Jack stood in the fighting stance and prepared to fire. He took a deep breath and then thrust his arm forward, projecting the fireball downrange. All of the members of the Mage Corps ran to the edge of the firing line as they watched the fireball travel on its heavy arc, sailing well beyond the two hundred-yard mark where Veris's strike had impacted. The fireball finally began to descend nearly eight hundred yards out. When it hit the ground, there was a massive explosion that caused the ground around them to shake. The fiery explosion continued to climb into the sky, resembling a smaller version of a nuclear mushroom cloud. Everyone was so fixated on the explosion that no one had noticed that Jack had collapsed to the ground. As the shockwave finally reached the members of the Mage Corps, a cloud of dust surrounded them. Jack was lying face down in the dirt.

"Yep. I think I overdid it again." he said to the dirt.

#####

Lia was in the middle of a morning briefing with Rhandor and Bilen in the command tent, with Crescia attending to their needs. The sudden shaking followed by the near deafening sound of an explosion caught their attention, and the four of them all raced out of the tent. They looked in the direction of the Mage Corps practice area to see the mushroom cloud rising in the distance.

"What the hell is that?" said Bilen.

Lia and Rhandor looked at each other for a moment before they both realized that there could only be one person who could do that.

"Jack!" they both said.

The four of them started running as fast as they could toward the practice range.

When they arrived, the whole area was still shrouded in a dust cloud. The air was so thick with dust that they could hardly see anything. Rhandor waved his hands as he used wind magic to clear the air. When the air had finally cleared, they saw the Mage Corps members, still standing at the firing line, watching the mushroom cloud continue to rise into the atmosphere. Several yards behind them was Jack, still lying face down in the dirt. Lia and Crescia ran to Jack while Rhandor and Bilen ran over to the other Mage Corps members.

Lia dropped down to her knees next to Jack and rolled him over so his head and upper back were resting on her lap.

"Jack! Jack! Can you hear me? Jack!" she yelled as she shook him.

Jack's eyes began to open, and he tried his best to look at Lia.

"Sorry," he said in a near whisper.

Lia then turned to Bilen.

"Bilen! Assemble everyone here, right now!" she said.

Bilen turned to the Mage Corps members.

"You heard Her Highness! Assemble, right now!"

The Mage Corps members all fell into formation, facing Lia.

"Whose idea was this?" she asked.

Veris stepped forward.

"It was mine, Your Highness. I didn't think that one attempt could cause that much damage. Especially from someone who had never done it before. I take full responsibility," he said.

"You're damn right you take full responsibility! What would have happened if Jack had lost control and sent that fireball anywhere else?! Look at that!" she said, pointing at the crater formed by Jack's fireball as the mushroom cloud finally dissipated. "Do you have any idea what sort of destruction that could have caused if it had hit the camp?!"

"No, Your Highness. I didn't realize how powerful he was," said Veris.

What Lia didn't realize at the time was that the more she yelled and chastised the members of the Mage Corps, and Veris, in particular, the tighter and tighter she began to hold Jack.

"Of course you didn't! There is a reason why we have been limiting Jack's use of magic! And did anyone even realize that he was lying face down on the ground, or were you all too busy looking at the explosion?!" she yelled.

All of the Mage Corps members shook their heads, realizing that they had all been too caught up in the explosion to even think about Jack. At that point, Lia was holding Jack's head firmly against her chest. The angrier she got, the tighter she held him there. By that time, Jack was beginning to struggle to breathe. As weak as he was from the magic, he wasn't able to put up much of a struggle. His right hand began to weakly flop on his leg, like he was trying his best to tap out. Crescia noticed this.

"Um... Your Highness?" said Crescia, trying to get Lia's attention.

Lia continued to chew out the Mage Corps. Eventually, Jack's hand stopped tapping. It was then that Crescia decided it was time to speak up.

"Your Highness!" yelled Crescia.

"Yes! What is it, Crescia?!" said Lia.

Crescia pointed to Jack.

"I think you broke him, Your Highness."

Lia looked down and realized that she had been inadvertently smothering Jack for quite some time. She immediately loosened her grip, and Jack rolled back onto her lap. After a moment, he suddenly gasped for air. His eyes popped wide open, and he looked around. Lia's face was turning red, partly from all of the yelling and partly from the embarrassment of nearly suffocating Jack.

"Jack! Are you all right? Forgive me. I did not intend to harm you," she said.

"Hey. There are worse ways to go," said Jack as he began to catch his breath.

Realizing what he had meant after giving it a moment of thought, Lia became even more embarrassed and let Jack go completely. He slid off of her lap and landed face up on the ground. Lia stood up and dusted herself off, clearly flustered by Jack's tongue-in-cheek comment.

"Rhandor. Would you please see to it that Jack makes it safely back to his tent?" she said as she tried to regain her composure.

"Of course, Your Highness," said Rhandor as he bent over and picked Jack up in a fireman's carry.

From over Rhandor's shoulder, Jack spoke.

"Hey, buddy," said Jack.

"Hello, friend," said Rhandor.

"Sorry 'bout this," said Jack.

"Worry not about this, Jack. Let's just get you back to your tent so you can rest," said Rhandor.

"Rhandor?" said Jack.

"Yes, Jack?" said Rhandor.

"You're a good friend," said Jack.

"Thank you, Jack. So are you," said Rhandor as he carried Jack away.

#####

Lia turned to Bilen.

"I expect a full report on this later. I will leave the disciplinary actions to you to decide," she said.

"Understood, Your Highness," said Bilen. "It will be done."

After giving the members of the Mage Corps a final look of disapproval, Lia turned and walked back toward the camp.

#####

As Rhandor arrived at the tent, Jack was even more dazed from his overuse of fire magic. Once inside, Rhandor carefully laid Jack down on the bed.

"Rhandor?" said Jack.

"Yes, Jack?"

"I messed up, huh?" said Jack.

"Let's not worry about that right now, Jack. Just get some rest," said Rhandor.

"She's mad at me, isn't she?" asked Jack.

"Perhaps. But I think she's more worried than angry," said Rhandor.

As Jack began to drift off into unconsciousness, he tried his best to get one last sentence out.

"Tell her... I'm sorry... letting her down," he said before unconsciousness claimed him.

Rhandor gave Jack a few pats on his shoulder.

"Just rest, my friend." he said as he stood up.

When Rhandor exited the tent, Lia was just arriving.

"How is he?" she asked.

"Unconscious now, but feeling quite guilty beforehand," said Rhandor.

"I think you're right. We may have to send him to Zavyra. She may be the only one who can help him stabilize his magic. Otherwise, he has a good chance of eventually destroying himself or others," she said.

"Should you decide to send him to her, I would like to volunteer to accompany him," said Rhandor.

"I shall give it some serious thought. For now, let's let him rest. I will speak with him tomorrow," she said.

"Yes, Your Highness," said Rhandor as he bowed.

#####

The next morning, Jack woke up once again feeling like he had been on an all-night bender. As he rolled out of bed, the vision of that massive mushroom cloud that he had made the day before occupied his thoughts. He remembered how he was able to feel the shockwave of the blast passing over him while he was face down in the dirt. Thoughts of the nuclear explosions over Hiroshima and Nagasaki, the nuclear tests of the past, and even the few uses of the MOAB bomb and how they compared to what he had done the day before left him with a sense of fear. Jack recognized that power without control is dangerous, and it made him more of a liability than an asset. He began to realize that something would have to change if he wanted to prove useful in the fight against the Dark Army. He made the decision to go talk to Lia.

#####

When he arrived at Lia's tent, a feeling of anxiety began to build in his gut. A part of him was worried that the only reason that she was keeping him around at all was because of the powers he had, and if he couldn't use them properly, his days would be numbered. Those thoughts were being contradicted by the thoughts of how their relationship had developed during his time there. While he was standing there fighting with himself in his head, Lia exited her tent.

"Oh! Hello, Jack," she said.

"Um... Hi," said Jack.

"I was just about to come see you, actually," said Lia.

"Is that a good thing or a bad thing?" asked Jack.

"What do you mean?" she asked.

"Well, I kind of messed up big time yesterday. I figured that some disciplinary measures may be heading my way. Whatever you choose to do, I will accept it. Even if you ask me to leave. I take full responsibility for my actions," he said.

Lia was surprised and somewhat confused by Jack's behavior.

"I... um... Why don't you just join me in my tent. There's something I'd like to talk to you about," she said.

"I see. Of course," said Jack, imagining the worst.

Jack and Lia went inside her tent. Lia sat down in a chair and gestured for Jack to do the same. Jack straightened his outfit and then sat down in a stiff position, as if he were sitting in front of a disciplinary review board in the military. Lia found his behavior somewhat amusing.

"Calm down, Jack. I'm not going to ask you to leave," she said.

Jack released a bit of the tension in his shoulders.

"Then what did you want to talk about?" he asked.

"I did want to talk to you about your use of magic. Between what I've witnessed and what I've heard from reports when you've used magic or been around dark magic like you were when you approached that necromancer's staff, I can't say that I'm not concerned," she said.

"I know. I'm a liability as I am now," said Jack.

"That's not what I mean. What I'm saying is that I'm worried about you, Jack. I'm worried that if you stay the way you are now, your inability to control your magic may eventually get you seriously hurt or killed. That's the last thing I want to happen to you, Jack," she said.

"I see. So what can I do about it?" Jack asked.

"I'd like for you to see Zavyra. She is what you'd call a specialist in all things involving magic. There is no one else in this world who knows more about magic than her," Lia said.

"So where is this Zavyra?" asked Jack.

"She lives in the mountains to the far north of here. It would be a long journey for you to reach her, but I believe that she can help you," Lia said.

"So... wait a sec. You do want me to leave, then," he said in a slightly joking tone.

"Of course not!... Well... technically, yes. But it's just temporarily. I want you to come back! When you've learned how to control your magic, you'll come right back to me, right?" she said.

Jack noticed that she started to get flustered there for a moment, and the words "come right back to me" echoed in Jack's mind. He fixated on the part where she said "me" instead of "us," and in doing so, it alleviated many of his concerns about her possibly wanting to get rid of him. It also gave him a small degree of hope that she may have been starting to feel for him the same way he found himself increasingly feeling for her.

Lia clears her throat.

"You're teasing me, aren't you?" she said.

Jack smiled.

"A little bit. I'll come back. I promise. So how do I find this Zavyra?" he asked.

"While I wish I could accompany you on your journey, unfortunately, reports are coming in that the Dark Army is gaining ground, so I must remain here. But you won't be going alone. Rhandor will be accompanying you. I have also asked Fyn to fly ahead and make contact with the fairy network so you both know what you're heading into," said Lia.

"Cool. I like Rhandor. So, when will this journey start?" he asked.

"A few more preparations must be made, so you should be prepared to leave by tomorrow morning."

Jack thought for a moment.

"Tomorrow morning? Then would there be any chance we could have dinner together tonight?" he asked.

Lia smiled.

"Yes. I would like that," she said.

"So, do you really think that this Zavyra can help me?" he asked.

"I do," said Lia.

"Well then, I look forward to meeting her," said Jack.

"As I said, it will be quite a long journey, so you should start preparing now," said Lia.

Jack stood up.

"Will do. So, I'll see you for dinner tonight?" he said.

"Yes. Indeed," said Lia.

Jack left Lia's tent feeling energized. The journey he was about to go on would not only help him to learn how to control his magic, it would also give him a chance to see much more of this new world that he found himself in. On top of that, a second date was planned for the evening.

#####

He rushed to his tent to do a quick inventory of what he might need on the journey and then made his way to the Mage Corps tents. When he arrived, a number of the mages seemed a bit hesitant to approach him, given how their last interaction ended the day before, but they still greeted him with a nod or a wave. When Rhandor stepped out of his tent, Jack jogged over to him.

"Rhandor! Good morning!" Jack said as he ran.

Rhandor looked over to see Jack.

"Good morning to you as well, my friend. How do you feel today?" Rhandor asked.

"A bit hungover, but other than that, pretty damn good," said Jack.

"I take it that you've spoken with Her Highness, then," said Rhandor.

"Yeah. She told me that the two of us will be going on a bit of a trip," Jack said.

"Indeed. I look forward to joining you on this journey,"

said Rhandor.

"So, what do you know about this Zavyra?" Jack asked.

"There are legends about her that say that she is well over a thousand years old. Personally, I have never seen her, but I heard that she isn't particularly fond of beastfolk, so I don't know how much I can tell you. I do know that she knows far more about magic than any other. Some say that she was among the first in this world to truly master magic," said Rhandor.

"Oh. Well, here's hoping she can help me. Lia said that she lives pretty far away from here. Any idea of how long it will take us to reach her?" asked Jack.

"It may take some time. We will likely have to stop several times to rest. We may have to stop at a number of towns on the way," Rhandor said.

"So this will be kind of like a real quest of sorts, I guess," said Jack.

"I suppose so," said Rhandor.

"Oh, and guess what? I have another date with Lia tonight." Jack said excitedly.

"I see. I wish you luck, my friend. Just remember that we shall be leaving tomorrow morning, so try not to drink too much. It is never good to drink and fly," said Rhandor.

"Good advice. I'll keep that in mind. Wait... Are we taking the dragons?" he asked.

"Of course, my friend. To take this journey on foot would take far longer," said Rhandor.

"Oh, yeah. I guess that makes sense. That means I get to fly again. This is going to be awesome," said Jack.

Rhandor was amused by Jack's growing enthusiasm.

"I'm going to go to the stables and talk to Barvan, then. I don't even know what to feed a dragon. If we're going to be gone for a while, I wouldn't want Nava mistaking me for a snack because I didn't bring the right food," said Jack.

"A wise idea, my friend," said Rhandor.

Jack gave Rhandor a quick wave and then headed

toward the stables.

#####

When he arrived, he saw Barvan tending to the dragons.

"Barvan! Good morning!" said Jack as he jogged up to the stable where Barvan was working.

"Ah! Good morning, Jack. How are you this day?" asked Barvan.

"Quite well, Barvan. Quite well," said Jack.

"Glad to hear it, Jack. Is there something I can help you with on this fine morning?" Barvan asked.

"It looks like Rhandor and I will be going on a journey. I had some questions about caring for Nava here." Jack said as he moved to Nava's stall.

"Ah. I see. It would be my pleasure to instruct you on this, Jack," said Barvan.

"Great! First question. What do I feed her, and how often?" Jack asked.

"That's a good question, Jack. The good thing about these lesser dragons is that they have a wide variety in their diet. They can eat both plants and meat. Nava here is particularly fond of a variety of fruits and mushrooms. She does eat meat, of course, but apples are a nice treat for her," said Barvan.

"Ok. Good to know. Will I have to bring food, or is it something we can pick up on the way?" Jack asked.

"When will you be leaving?" asked Barvan.

"Tomorrow morning," said Jack.

"I will make sure she gets a full meal tonight and a good breakfast tomorrow. Beyond that, you should probably feed her whenever you land for the night. If you are near a town, it shouldn't be too difficult to find a stable that will feed her. If you plan to camp in the wilderness, I would recommend doing a bit of hunting or gathering when possible. A single spiny boar would be enough to feed you, Rhandor, and both dragons with little difficulty, and they're very common in these lands," said Barvan.

"Good to know. I'll remember to bring my rifle," said Jack.

"Where is this journey taking you?" asked Barvan.

"To see someone named Zavyra," said Jack.

Barvan paused what he was doing.

"You're going to see Zavyra?" he said.

"Yeah. Why?" asked Jack.

"I've only heard rumors, but from what I hear, not all who go to see her return, and those who do return seldom speak of it," said Barvan.

"Oh," said Jack, suddenly finding himself questioning his excitement.

Barvan notices the look of apprehension on Jack's face.

"With your power, Jack, I wouldn't worry too much," he said, trying to be of some comfort.

"I guess we'll see," said Jack. "On that disturbing note, I think I'll return to my tent for now."

Jack walked over to Nava and gave her a few pets before leaving. Barvan felt a little regretful for how he had phrased things, but all he could do at that point was watch Jack walk back to his tent.

#####

When Jack returned to his tent, he decided to do another inventory of his backpack. When he checked the small pocket in the front of the backpack, he felt something he hadn't noticed before. He unzipped the pocket and took out what was inside. When he opened his hand, he saw that the object was an old ring connected to a gold chain. He took a closer look at the ring and noticed that it was the ring his grandfather had given to him when he was still a child. The ring was gold and had an enameled symbol on the front. The symbol looked like a stylized dragon behind a shield with two swords crossed in front of the shield. Artemis had told him that it was a ring that he had received from his father when he was young and that it had brought him good luck. It had been some time since Jack had seen the ring. He spent a few minutes studying it before putting it in his pocket.

#####

When evening came, Jack found himself feeling nervous. While the journey he was mere hours from taking was occupying his mind to a degree, it wasn't the journey that was making him nervous. It was the second date. Once again, he found himself pacing and repeatedly checking his appearance in the mirror. A part of him realized that he was a 35-year-old man acting like a 15-year-old kid getting ready for his first high school dance, but another part of him was able to recognize that, of all of the issues he had to be nervous about, going on a date was the most normal thing. He was in a parallel world where there was a war with an evil army controlled by a leader known only as the Great Demon Emperor; magic was a thing, and he apparently had the ability to use it but lacked the ability to control it, and that there were dragons and beastfolk all around him. Being nervous to go on a date was the one normal thing. Jack was able to find a small amount of comfort in that normality, right up until the moment that the four-foot-ten-inch walking, talking cat popped her head into his tent.

"Hi, Jack. Her Highness would like your presence in her tent," said Crescia.

"Thank you, Crescia," said Jack.

After doing a last quick mirror check, Jack followed Crescia to Lia's tent.

#####

When they arrived, Crescia once again announced his

arrival the same way she had done the previous time. As Jack walked into the tent, Crescia gave him a quick wink and a smile as he passed by her. Jack responded by sticking out his tongue at her. Jack then turned his attention to Lia.

"Hi," said Jack.

"Hello," said Lia.

Lia gestured toward the table.

"Would you like some wine?" she asked.

"Yes, please. And I promise not to chug it down like I did last time," said Jack.

Lia smiled.

"That's good," she said.

Jack first held out Lia's chair, and she thanked him as she sat down. Jack then poured her a glass of wine before pouring himself one and sitting down.

"Are you nervous about tomorrow?" she asked.

"A little," said Jack. "But I think I'm as prepared as I can be."

"I wouldn't worry, Jack. I have faith in you," said Lia.

"Thank you. That really means a lot to me," he said.

"I'm happy to hear that, Jack," Lia said.

Jack found himself captivated by Lia's beauty in the soft amber glow of the tent.

"You know, you have really incredible eyes. I've never seen eyes of that color before. They remind me of the lavender flowers that grow near my house. They're quite lovely," Jack said.

Lia was slightly embarrassed by the compliment.

"Oh my. Thank you, Jack. That's very kind of you to say," she said.

"It's true," said Jack.

Trying to change the subject in order to hide her embarrassment, Lia took a sip of wine and asked Jack a question.

"What is your home like, Jack?" she asked.

"Well, I live in a state called Michigan. On my

grandfather's property, there are trees as far as the eye can see. Beyond those trees is a lake called Lake Superior. It's a lake so massive that you can't see the other side. It's a beautiful area," said Jack.

"It sounds wonderful. I wish I could see it someday," said Lia.

"If we win this war and get back to the gate I came through to get here, who knows? Perhaps that's a wish that could be granted," said Jack.

"I would like that very much," said Lia.

"What about your home? What's it like?" Jack asked.

Lia thought for a moment.

"Well, I spent much of my youth in the castle in the capital city of Vedyria. My father was often busy with his royal duties, and my mother spent much of her time handling diplomatic matters for the kingdom. With no siblings, I spent a lot of time on my own. Because of that, I spent a lot of time sneaking off to the royal guard training grounds. At first, I would just watch them train, but then one day, Morgryn, the Captain of the Guard, saw me mimicking the moves and decided to let me train. My father wasn't particularly pleased to see his little girl picking up a sword, but he allowed Morgryn to keep training me. I think my mother had a little something to do with that decision, too. Over time, I became quite skilled, and I would even join the occasional guard patrol of the city, in disguise, of course, because I didn't want to risk the public discovering that the crown princess was beating up thieves and other criminals on the streets and alleys of Vedyria."

"Yeah. I can imagine that would complicate things," said Jack.

"Indeed," said Lia.

"So what was the city like?" asked Jack.

"It's a wonderful city. It's filled with people of all races. There are elves, beastfolk of every sort, orcs, and dwarves, all living in harmony together. There are even a few humans there. There are thriving businesses of all sorts and markets where you can find anything to suit your taste. I'm quite fond of the berry cream puffs at a bakery near the city square. I would often sneak out of the castle as a child to buy one. My mother loves them, too, so whenever I was on patrol, I would stop by and pick up a few, and we would share them in secret while my father was busy with his duties." she said.

"It sounds amazing," said Jack.

"Oh, it is. I would very much like to show it to you someday. Perhaps when this war dies down," said Lia.

"I very much look forward to that," said Jack.

As they both took a sip of wine, Crescia appeared with their meals. As she set the plates down on the table, Jack took the opportunity to ask about them both.

"So how did you two get to know each other?" he asked.

Crescia chimed in first.

"My mother works for the queen, and when the time came for Her Highness to need an attendant, I begged for the opportunity, and the queen was gracious enough to approve my request," said Crescia.

"We have been together for quite a few years now. Crescia has become like family to me. I often find myself thinking of her as my little sister," said Lia, as she gently held Crescia's hand.

"That's really nice. I'm glad that you two have each other," said Jack.

"You don't have any siblings?" asked Crescia.

"Nope. I'm an only child," he said.

"That's too bad," said Crescia. "But hey. You have me, now," she said with a wink.

Jack smiled.

"Thanks," he said.

"Now, you two enjoy your dinner," said Crescia as she walked out of the tent.

Jack turned to Lia.

"She's the type to say whatever comes to her mind, huh?" he said.

Lia chuckled.

"Yes, but that's one of the things I love about her," she said.

"I wonder what she'd be like on catnip." Jack said quietly to himself.

"What did you say?" Lia asked.

"Oh, nothing important. There's just this herb that affects cats where I come from. It makes them all goofy. But the cats where I come from walk on four legs, and most of them are a lot smaller," said Jack.

"I see. There are similar herbs here. Crescia gets quite chatty when she partakes in them. It can be very entertaining," said Lia.

"More chatty than she is now? I didn't think that was possible. I'd kind of like to see that at some point," said Jack.

"Who knows what may happen in the future?" Lia said with a slight grin.

"At least wait until I get back." Jack said with a smile.

"Of course," said Lia.

They continued to talk as they ate. As the evening went on, Jack didn't want it to end. After they finished dessert, Jack came to his senses enough to remember the journey he was only a relative few hours from taking. He set his napkin down on the table.

"Well, I should probably get back to my tent. I have a long journey ahead of me tomorrow." He said reluctantly.

"Yes. Indeed you do," said Lia, equally as reluctantly.

They both stood, and Jack slowly made his way to the opening of the tent. Lia followed closely behind him. Jack opened the tent flap and turned around to find Lia right behind him.

"I really enjoyed this," he said.

"As did I," said Lia as she moved a little closer.

As Jack's sense of reason began to slip, he moved closer to Lia.

"I can't think of anything else to say," he said.

"Then don't say anything," Lia said as she moved in for the kiss. It was a soft and gentle, but passionate kiss. No sooner had their lips parted that Crescia appeared at the opening of the tent.

"Your Highness, I'm here to collect the dishes before... oh," Crescia's train of thought completely derailed the moment she saw them.

Lia and Jack both looked at Crescia, surprised by her sudden appearance. Crescia looked back and forth between them before holding two thumbs up.

"Nice," said Crescia.

Lia looked slightly embarrassed. Jack cleared his throat.

"Well, um, I, uh, I should probably be getting back to my tent. Early morning and all," he said.

"Yes," said Lia, trying her best to regain her composure.

"So, um, good night. Sweet dreams," said Jack.

"Yes. Good night, Jack. Sweet dreams to you, as well," said Lia.

"Oh, that's definitely going to happen," said Jack with a smirk.

Jack said good night to Crescia as he exited the tent and made his way back to his tent. Lia was left standing there, awkwardly waiting for what would likely be a barrage of questions from Crescia before going to bed.

CHAPTER 13

When morning came, Jack was filled with energy. The events of the night before were still fresh in his mind. He made one final check of his gear and then headed to the stables. On his way there, he ran into Alivair, making his morning rounds.

"I heard that you're going to see Zavyra, Jack," said Alivair.

"That's the plan," said Jack.

"I wish you luck on your journey," Alivair said.

"Thank you, Alivair. I really appreciate that," said Jack.

"I must attend to my rounds, but I will try to be there to see you off," said Alivair.

"I look forward to it. If I don't see you there, stay safe. Make good use of those binoculars. They'll help you see danger long before you're in its reach." Jack said.

Alivair offered his hand. Jack gladly took it, and they shook hands. There was a part of Jack that was going to miss teasing Alivair, but on another level, he was also glad to no longer be at odds with him. After the handshake, Jack continued on toward the stables. When he arrived, he saw Barvan just finishing up with the morning feeding of the lesser dragons.

"Good morning, Barvan," said Jack.

"Ah, Jack. I see you're up early on this fine day. A good day to fly," said Barvan.

"Yeah. I'm looking forward to it," said Jack.

"I've secured a pouch to the harness with some apples and some dried fish. Should be enough of a treat to keep Nava happy on the way," said Barvan.

Jack looked over at Nava and saw that she had the

harness already secured and the pouch that Barvan had mentioned was secured to the chest part of the harness. As Jack began to give Nava her morning pets and scratches, he heard a familiar voice coming from behind him.

"Good morning, my friend!" said the voice.

Jack turned to see Rhandor approaching, carrying a large pack.

"Good morning, Rhandor. All set for this quest?" Jack asked.

"Indeed," said Rhandor, as he held up the pack.

"Good, because we're going to have a lot to talk about on the way," said Jack.

Rhandor tilted his head, curious as to what Jack meant by that, but then he shrugged and smiled.

"Looking forward to it," he said.

As the minutes passed, a small group began to form. In the group were Bilen, Veris, and a number of the other Mage Corps members, a few of the soldiers who had been healed by Jack in the medical tent, and eventually even Alivair appeared. They were all there to see Jack and Rhandor off. As well-wishes were traded back and forth, Lia approached the stables, with Crescia not far behind her. Lia was carrying something wrapped in a black cloth in her left hand. As she approached, she acknowledged and responded to everyone wishing her a good morning. When she reached Jack, there was a noticeable change in her tone of voice. It went from the normal commanding voice that she was expected to use when greeting her troops to a softer and gentler voice as she greeted him.

"Good morning, Jack," she said softly.

"Good morning, Lia," Jack responded.

Momentarily looking over to Crescia, Jack noticed that she was giving the same double thumbs up that she had given the night before.

"Did you sleep well?" asked Lia.

"Oh yes. Quite well. And my dreams were very sweet,"

said Jack with a grin.

Lia smiled for a moment before regaining her composure, remembering that she was currently surrounded by her own soldiers.

"I have something for you," she said.

She held up the object that was wrapped in the black cloth and carefully began to unwrap it. Beneath the cloth was a quite ornate sword. It had a gold pommel and cross guard, with a black leather grip with twisted gold wire wrapped in alternating spiral patterns along the length of the leather grip. The sword was in a black leather sheath accented with gold and silver on the top and bottom. The sheath was already pre-attached to a black leather belt. The blade was slightly wider than a rapier and roughly three feet in length. Affixed to the cross guard was a bright red jewel. She handed the sword to Jack.

"The gem on this sword is infused with fire magic. My fire magic. Should you encounter anything on your journey, as long as you keep this sword by your side, you will have no need to risk using your magic. Allow mine to keep you safe," she said.

Jack carefully studied the sword.

"Wow. This is amazing. Thank you, Lia," he said.

"The blade is made with elven steel. It is razor sharp and virtually unbreakable," she said.

"I will treasure it," said Jack.

Just as Jack was about to speak again, he heard Rhandor's voice.

"Jack! If we wish to make our first destination before nightfall, we must leave very soon!"

"Ok, Rhandor! I'll be right there!" replied Jack.

Jack turned to Lia.

"I have something for you, too. Close your eyes," he said.

Lia was a bit reluctant but chose to close her eyes. Jack reached into his pocket and pulled out an object. When he partly released the object, the ring connected to the gold chain that he had taken out of his bag the night before appeared. He undid the clasp on the gold chain and carefully put the necklace onto Lia's neck, taking extra care so as not to get it caught in her golden blonde hair. Lia's eyes remained closed. Jack whispered something to her as he was placing the necklace around her neck.

"This belonged to my great-grandfather. I've been told that it brings good luck to any who wear it, so I want you to have it," he said.

"Jack! We must go now!" said Rhandor, who was already sitting atop his dragon, preparing for takeoff.

"Ok! I'll be there in a second!" said Jack to Rhandor. He then turned to Lia.

"I'll be back as fast as I can. Stay safe," he said just as he was turning to head to Nava.

#####

Lia's eyes opened, and she looked down at the ring attached to the chain. On the ring, she recognized the royal crest of the kingdom of Stobrimore. She quickly looked at Jack just as he was securing his legs into the harness and preparing to take off.

#####

Rhandor looked briefly at Lia and then at Jack. Once Jack was fully secured, both he and Rhandor turned to wave at the small crowd right before the dragons took flight. As they gained altitude, Rhandor steered his dragon, Aris, toward Jack in order to be close enough to speak.

"You are far more bold than I gave you credit for, my friend! I'm impressed!" said Rhandor.

"What do you mean?" asked Jack.

"I saw the gift that you gave Her Highness!" said Rhandor.

"What about it?" asked Jack.

"Was that not a signet ring you gave to her?" asked Rhandor.

"Yeah! It belonged to my great-grandfather! It's apparently the family crest!" said Jack.

"Since you were not born in this world, I can see why you would be unfamiliar with customs here!" said Rhandor.

"What the hell are you talking about?" asked Jack, as he grew more and more confused by the moment.

"The ring you presented to her! That was your family ring! By presenting your family ring to a woman, you are asking for them to become part of your family!" said Rhandor.

"I did what, now?!" asked Jack, finding himself completely shocked by the words he had just heard.

"Congratulations, my extra bold friend! You just asked the crown princess of the Vedyrian Kingdom to marry you!" said Rhandor.

Jack's eyes grew wide as he turned around and looked toward the camp, which was already fading away into the horizon. The gradually increasing lightheadedness eventually became substantial enough to remind him to start breathing again. As he gasped for air, his mind became flooded with panicky thoughts, like hoping that Lia would, on some level, realize just how unfamiliar Jack is regarding local customs and not take his action as anything more than an offering of a token of good luck. Though he had clearly developed feelings for Lia, thoughts of marriage were hardly at the forefront of his mind. He hoped he would be able to eventually clear up the misunderstanding upon his return. Rhandor just laughed at the sight of Jack in full-blown panic mode, and the teasing continued for some time as they flew.

Back at the camp, Lia watched as Jack and Rhandor vanished from sight. She then took a closer look at the ring before quickly tucking in inside her armor and looking around to make sure no one had noticed. Alivair approached her.

"Your Highness. Did he... ?" asked Alivair.

"Not a word, Captain. Not one word," said Lia as she straightened her armor and turned to return to her tent, trying her best not to look flustered.

"Yes, Your Highness," said Alivair, as he watched her walk away.

#####

When the evening sun began to make its way below the horizon, Rhandor signaled to Jack that it was time to land. He pointed to an open area next to a river not far ahead, and they began their descent. The dragons hovered for a moment before touching down. Rhandor hopped off of Aris's back and gave him a few pats before walking over to the riverbank. When Jack hopped off of Nava's back, he immediately plopped onto his butt. Rhandor looked over at Jack and laughed.

"Your legs fall asleep, my friend?" he asked.

"Well, I'm not exactly used to long-distance dragon travel. Or short-distance dragon travel. Or dragon travel at all, for that matter," said Jack from the ground.

Rhandor walked up to Jack and helped him up.

"You'll get used to it, my friend," he said.

Jack got back to his feet and stumbled around a bit. As he walked, he bobbed up and down slightly, like someone who had just spent days on a ship at sea in rough waters and was just setting foot on dry land again.

"Are we setting up camp for the night?" asked Jack.

"Indeed," said Rhandor. "The dragons can still fly at night, but it gets quite cold up there, so it's best we keep our travel to days."

Rhandor rummaged through one of the bags he had packed.

"Speaking of cold, take this." He said as he handed Jack

a bundled piece of black fabric.

When Jack removed the string securing it and unfolded the fabric, he realized that it was a hooded cloak. He immediately put it on.

"This is cool. Now I can look like a Jedi," said Jack.

"What's a Jedi?" asked Rhandor.

"Oh. Um... Nothing," Jack waved his hand slowly in front of Rhandor's face. "You do not need to know of the Jedi."

"What are you doing with your hand?" asked Rhandor.

Jack dropped his hand, finally realizing that continuing the gag would only be entertaining to him and no one else.

"Any fish in that river?" Jack asked, trying to change the subject.

"I would assume so," said Rhandor.

"Let's do some fishing, then," said Jack as he set down his backpack.

After digging through the backpack for a few moments, Jack removed a small plastic case. He opened the case and pulled out a small collapsible fishing rod. He connected the reel, strung the line through the eyelets, and connected a hook and bobber.

"What is that device?" asked Rhandor.

"It's a fishing rod," said Jack as he flicked his wrist to the side, causing the rod to fully extend.

"You use that device to catch fish?" asked Rhandor as he walked over to the riverbank.

"Yeah," said Jack. "How do you catch fish?"

Rhandor crouched down by the edge of the water. He stared into the water for a moment, and then, in a move so quick Jack could hardly see it, Rhandor reached into the water and pulled out a fish. He turned and showed it to Jack.

"Well... Sure. If you want to take all the fun out of it," said Jack.

#####

After about an hour of fishing, Jack had reeled in four fish. Rhandor had scooped up seven. By that point, the sun had completely set. Jack gathered some sticks and kindling for a fire. After he arranged them in a pile, he had an idea. He walked over to Nava and unstrapped the sword that Lia had given him before he left. He walked up to the pile of sticks and drew the sword from the scabbard.

"What are you doing?" asked Rhandor.

"Watch this," said Jack.

Jack placed his thumb on the red crystal on the hilt, and the blade suddenly became engulfed in flame. He placed the blade against the sticks and set them on fire. He removed his thumb from the crystal, and the fire on the blade extinguished. Rhandor just shook his head.

"I'm sure Her Highness will be overjoyed to know that you're using the flaming sword she gave you, powered by her very own magic, to light a campfire," he said.

"Well, I guess that's just going to be a conversation between me and my fiancé, apparently," said Jack, jokingly.

Jack cleaned and gutted the fish. He was thankful that Artemis had included some basic camping gear in his backpack, because it included some cooking tools and some basic seasonings. When they were finished cooking, Jack and Rhandor ate their fill and gave the remaining fish to the dragons, who happily finished them off in no time. Afterward, they took some time to relax by the fire.

"That was a quite tasty meal, Jack," said Rhandor.

"Thank you. So what's the plan for tomorrow?" Jack asked.

"A little more than half a day from here is the town of Estin. That's our next stop. The further north we go, the greater the risk that we may run into Dark Army scouting parties, so we need to gather intelligence whenever we can," said Rhandor.

"That makes sense. We should probably turn in if we're

going to be heading out early," said Jack.

"Indeed," said Rhandor.

Jack stood up and kicked some dirt onto the fire to extinguish it. Rhandor adjusted his pack to use as a pillow and used his cloak as a blanket. Jack walked over to the dragons and placed his bag down next to Nava. He laid down next to her and draped his cloak over himself. Just as he closed his eyes, he heard something. When he opened them he saw that Nava was extending one of her wings to cover him. He gave her a few pats and closed his eyes, falling asleep soon after.

#####

The next morning, Jack was woken up by Nava poking at his head with hers. When he opened his eyes, she was standing right above him, with her face mere inches from his.

"Morning," he said.

It occurred to him that he had never expected to be woken up by a dragon poking at his head, and what was even more unexpected was that he wasn't the least bit afraid in that situation. He reached into his bag and pulled something out.

"Here. Apple," he said as he held the apple between his face and Nava's face. Nava carefully took the apple from his hand.

"Dragon snooze button," Jack said to himself before closing his eyes again.

#####

About ten minutes later, Jack woke up to the sound of Rhandor packing up his gear. He stood up and dusted himself off and shook the dust off the cloak before putting it on.

"Good morning, Jack," said Rhandor.

"Morning," said Jack as he stretched.

Rhandor reached into his pack and pulled out a few strips of dried meat.

"Here. Have some breakfast," he said.

"Thanks," said Jack as he walked toward the riverbank to splash some water on his face.

"We have been blessed with another day of good weather," said Rhandor.

Jack wiped the excess water off his face before taking a big bite of one of the strips of dried meat.

"Hey! These are pretty good!" said Jack.

"Yes. And if you drink some water, they will stave off any feelings of hunger for many hours," said Rhandor.

"That's convenient," said Jack as he walked over to Nava and gave her a piece of the meat.

Jack grabbed his canteen from his backpack, opened it, and drank it before walking back to the riverbank to refill it. After filling the canteen, he returned to Nava and began securing all of his gear. When both Jack and Rhandor were ready to go, Jack tossed Nava another apple, and then both dragons took to the sky.

With the shock of the ring revelation from the previous day now behind him, Jack was able to take the opportunity to actually look around and enjoy the scenery as they flew. He took everything in. The air was clean, cool and refreshing. There were forests and fields, rivers and streams, and occasionally he would see a small farm with some beastfolk tending to the crops or a distant village filled with people going about their daily lives. They were sights that he wouldn't soon forget.

CHAPTER 14

The sound of raindrops hitting the canopy of the trees was all that Fyn and the two other fairies with him could hear, other than the buzz from the beating of their wings. They were conducting routine long-range patrols in order to check for any approaching Dark Army soldiers. They flew in a wide V-formation, zipping back and forth between the trees. As the rain began to pour, Fyn started to consider halting the patrol and ordering the other two fairies to seek shelter until the rain let up.

Just as he was about to give the order, the fairy to his right gave a signal that he had spotted something. Fyn and the fairy to his left flew over to where the other fairy had landed. When they looked in the direction the fairy was pointing, they saw some movement up ahead in a clearing. The three of them carefully approached the edge of the clearing, making sure to minimize the noise of their wings. When they reached the edge of the clearing, they flew up to a high branch of one of the trees in order to remain concealed. What they saw in that clearing was a massive assembly of Dark Army soldiers. They saw at least a hundred Demonborne soldiers, with each formation being commanded by a dark elf. The dark elves had blood-red hair, black eyes with white irises, reddish-gray skin and ears that were slightly longer and more tapered than the Vedyrian elves. Behind each formation of Demonborne stood four necromancers, each carrying a wooden staff with glowing crimson crystals embedded in the top. To the west of the formations, child-sized goblins were corralling at least seventy draphnir using long, serrated spears. The draphnir were clawing and nipping at each other like a pack of wild dogs. One of the goblins went to jab at a draphnir and missed, causing the goblin to fall forward. When it placed its hand on the railing of the makeshift corral to catch its balance, it only took an instant for one of the draphnir to strike. It was pulled into the pack of draphnir and immediately torn to shreds. The other goblins did nothing but stand there and listen to the screams of their colleague, knowing that it was too late to rescue it, and even if it wasn't, it was guaranteed suicide to try.

Flying between the formations were a number of imps, which were the Dark Army counterparts to fairies. Unlike fairies, who have four wings, imps have only two, and imp wings are dark, with a thorny appearance. Imps also have dark red, almost black skin and razor-sharp teeth.

Having seen all that they needed to see, Fyn signaled the other two fairies to return to the camp, but just as they were about to take off, they were spotted by one of the imps who was patrolling the perimeter. The imp let out a shrill cry that immediately caught the attention of a number of Demonborne and Necromancers near the perimeter. Fyn and the other two fairies took off as fast as they could. Bolts of dark magic flew past them, fired from the bows of some of the Demonborne soldiers. Beams of dark magic let loose from the staffs of the necromancers sliced through the trees as if they were made of sand. Fyn and the other two fairies did their best to dodge the onslaught of dark magic attacks as they fled. As they weaved back and forth between the trees, constantly adjusting their elevation to make themselves harder to hit, a beam from one of the necromancer's staffs caught the wing of the fairy to the right of Fyn. He hit a number of branches on his way down and rolled several feet upon impact. Fyn and the other fairy dove down to retrieve their injured colleague. They flew down, and each one grabbed an arm of the injured fairy before taking flight once again.

#####

Eventually, when they got far enough away from the clearing that the Dark Army no longer had a clear line of sight, they climbed up above the tree canopy and flew high into the sky, because getting battered by the ever-increasing rain was still far more preferable than the alternative.

#####

A half-hour after their encounter with the Dark Army, Fyn and the other two fairies arrived back at the Vedyrian camp. Exhausted from their flight, they crashed through the opening of Alivair's tent. Alivair immediately rushed over to pick up the fairies. When he saw that one of them was injured, he called for one of the soldiers outside of the tent to rush the injured fairy to the medical tent. Alivair brought the other two fairies over to his desk and poured a small amount of water into a bowl. Fyn and the other fairy crawled over to the bowl and began to drink as much water as they could. After drinking his fill of water, Fyn waved for Alivair. Alivair picked Fyn up and placed him on his shoulder. As Fyn gave his report, Alivair nodded. Afterward, Alivair placed Fyn back on the desk.

"Excellent work. You two should go get some rest. I shall report this information to Her Highness immediately," he said.

Alivair then raced out of the tent and headed in the direction of Lia's tent.

#####

Lia was sitting at her desk in her tent. She would occasionally lift the ring attached to the necklace and look at it. Just as she tucked the ring back into her shirt, she heard Alivair's voice from outside her tent.

"Your Highness! I have urgent news to report from the fairies!" he said.

"Enter," she said.

Alivair hurriedly entered the tent, still dripping water

from the pouring rain.

"Excuse my present state, Your Highness, but I have something most urgent to report," he said.

"What is it, Captain?" she asked.

"The fairies have returned from their patrol with news of a large assembly of Dark Army soldiers assembled nearly a half a day's march from the camp. Fyn reported at least a hundred Demonborne, each formation commanded by dark elves, with at least sixteen necromancers and almost eighty draphnir. They appear to be readying for an attack," Alivair said.

"Assemble the soldiers and be ready to head out in an hour's time," said Lia.

"Yes, Your Highness," said Alivair.

He bowed to Lia and immediately left the tent. Lia stood up and loudly called to Crescia in the next tent over. A short time later, Crescia appeared at the entrance of her tent.

"Yes, Your Highness?" said Crescia.

"Assist me with my armor," said Lia. "We are preparing for battle."

"Right away, Your Highness," said Crescia.

A few minutes later, Alivair returned to Lia's tent.

"The troops are assembled, Your Highness," he said.

Lia unrolled a map on her desk.

"Show me where the Dark Army is located," she said.

Alivair pointed to a spot on the map.

"Fyn reported that they were assembling here," he said.

Lia studied the map for a moment.

When we arrive, we will place squads here, here, and here." she said, pointing to several locations on the map.

"Hand out as many shield braces as we have available. And from here on out, remember to refer to me by my rank," she said.

"Yes, Commander," said Alivair.

"Prepare to move out. I will be there shortly," said Lia.

Alivair bowed and exited the tent. Lia once again pulled

out the necklace and held the ring.

"Here's hoping that this truly brings us good luck," she said to herself before picking up her sword and securing it to her belt. Lia then left the tent and headed toward the formation of soldiers.

#####

When she arrived at the area just outside of the camp where the soldiers were assembled, she walked to the front of the formation and turned to face them.

"We are heading into a battle where the enemy is more than a hundred strong. There will be many draphnir there as well, so make sure to watch yourselves and those around you. The terrain where we will be fighting is heavily wooded, so watch your step. We shall not let the Dark Army take one more step into Vedyrian territory. Be smart. Be sharp. Be brave. Leave no one behind. Is that clear?" said Lia.

"Yes, Commander!" said the entire formation in unison.

"Very good. Now move out!" said Lia.

The soldiers stood at attention and then began the march to the clearing.

#####

The sky grew darker and the rain grew heavier as they continued to march through the increasingly muddy terrain. Water poured off the armor of the soldiers as they marched. A number of fairies flew beside the soldiers, on constant lookout for any enemies. In the distance, flashes of lightning and rumbles of thunder echoed through the skies. When they reached a half-mile from their target, Alivair held his fist up in the air, signaling the soldiers to stop. Holding his index and middle finger up together, he signaled for the units to split off and head to their designated positions. Once the other units were ready, they began their march again.

#####

The heavily wooded area surrounding the clearing, along with the near-deafening sound of the heavy rain, proved beneficial for the Vedyrian forces because it made it much easier to mask their approach. Lia and Alivair remained with the middle formation. As they approached within a few hundred yards of the clearing, one of the fairies noticed an imp on patrol. The fairy waved her hands, and small vines shot out from the surrounding trees, capturing the imp. Thicker vines wrapped around the imp's mouth, preventing it from calling out. Lia's pupils glowed red as she snapped her fingers, sending a spark that lit the imp on fire, quickly burning it to ash.

By that point, the Dark Army soldiers had set up a number of tents and small structures. To signal the attack, Alivair fired an energy arrow high into the sky. The arrow arced back down and landed in the center of the Dark Army camp, exploding. With that explosion, a number of Vedyrian soldiers from each unit began to pour into the clearing, firing arrows and launching fireballs at the enemy. One of the goblins took his axe and cut the rope securing the corral that contained the draphnir. As a group of seven draphnir approached Lia's position, her pupils began to glow with a blue light as she held her hand up, freezing a large number of raindrops in place. The drops formed into the shape of spikes and rotated to aim at the oncoming draphnir. Lia lowered her hand, pointing her palm at the draphnir, sending the water spikes at them at high velocity, piercing the draphnirs' skin like dozens of arrows. They collapsed to the ground, dead. By that point, the Dark Army soldiers were scattering to fend off the surprise attack. Energy arrows were flying in all directions. Necromancers began firing their staffs at the Vedyrian soldiers. Many of them were able to activate the shields using the crystals on the shield braces on their arms, but some were too slow and were cut down by the beams of dark magic energy.

Alivair charged toward one of the dark elves and drew his sword. The dark elf raised his hand, preparing to launch a sphere of dark magic at him, but Alivair was quicker and fired a fireball right at the dark elf's hand, burning it. The dark elf drew his sword just as Alivair got within reach and deflected Alivair's first strike. Sparks began to fly as their blades clashed. The dark elf thrust his sword forward to Alivair's chest. Alivair deflected the blade, but not fast enough to avoid the edge of the dark elf's blade from slicing into his upper shoulder. Alivair winced in pain but brought his foot up and kicked the dark elf in the chest, sending him flying backwards a few feet, landing on his back in the mud. The dark elf raised his sword as Alivair approached, but Alivair swung his sword faster and chopped off the hand of the dark elf. He then followed that move with a forceful thrust, plunging the blade of his sword into the dark elf's throat. Alivair then leaned his sword to the left and right, severing the head of the dark elf from his body. Alivair pulled his sword from the ground and swung it out to his side, casting off the blood on the blade.

Elsewhere on the battlefield, a group of eight Demonborne soldiers charged towards Lia. Her pupils began to glow green as she pressed her hand against the ground, causing the earth below the feet of the charging soldiers to liquefy. The soldiers sank into the mud above their heads, struggling to free themselves. Lia removed her hand from the ground, and it returned to its more solid state, trapping the Demonborne in place.

Bilen and Veris, along with a number of other members of the Mage Corps, bombarded the necromancers with wind blades and fireballs. A number of the mages fell to the necromancer counterattacks, but the remaining mages were ultimately successful in wiping out the necromancers.

By that point, the draphnir were scattered around the battlefield. The Vedyrian soldiers were cutting them down as they approached, but a few of the soldiers were unable to stop them, and they were brutally attacked.

#####

The battle raged for what seemed like forever, but when it was over, the Vedyrian Army stood triumphant, surrounded by the fallen Dark Army soldiers. Celebratory cries could be heard from a number of the soldiers as they realized that the battle had been won. Lia stood in the middle of the battlefield and held up her sword in victory.

"Collect the wounded and bring them to the healers! Scan the area for any who may have escaped, then prepare to return to camp!" she said.

The soldiers cheered.

Alivair came out of one of the tents.

"Commander! You need to see this!" he said as he waved for Lia to come over to him.

Lia rushed over to him.

"What is it, Captain?" she asked.

Alivair brought her over to a table with a number of documents lying on it. He picked up one of the documents and handed it to her.

The document outlined the objective of the Dark Army soldiers. They were ordered to locate a human with dark hair and crack-like scars along his arms. The orders were to bring him back alive. There were a number of sketches accompanying the text on the document.

"Commander. Who does this description sound like to you?" asked Alivair.

Lia looked closely at the document.

"They were here looking for Jack," she said.

"How do they even know about him?" asked Alivair.

"There must have been some survivors of the battle at Arnin Canyon." she said.

"They don't know that he's no longer at the camp," said Alivair.

"It appears not," said Lia. "And we should keep it that way. Gather up all of these documents."

"Yes, Commander," said Alivair.

"I just hope that Jack and Rhandor haven't run into any trouble with the Dark Army on their journey," said Lia.

CHAPTER 15

It was mid-afternoon when the town of Estin came into sight. Rhandor pointed to a clearing near the main road leading into Estin as a good place to land. When they landed, Jack and Rhandor hopped off the dragons and walked toward the main entrance to the town with the dragons walking closely behind them. Rhandor stopped for a moment and reached into his pocket. He took out two small items that resembled brass knuckles. He handed one to Jack.

"Before we left, Her Highness gave me these. These are royal treasury seals. Should you need to purchase anything, simply show this to the merchant. They'll present you with a small notebook. When they do, just press the seal against the page of the notebook and think of the price of the items you are purchasing. The seal will do the rest," said Rhandor.

"So I press this against the page, and the seal leaves a mark based on the price? Then what happens?" asked Jack.

"The merchant will present the notebook to the local royal treasury officer in the town, and they'll be reimbursed by the officer," said Rhandor.

"Oh. So it's kind of like a voucher of sorts," said Jack.

"Indeed," said Rhandor.

"That's handy," said Jack.

"Put it on and place your thumb here," Rhandor said as he pointed to an indentation above the index finger hole.

Jack did so, and the seal glowed for a moment.

"There. Now the seal is bonded to you. That way, should you lose it or should it be stolen, it won't work for anyone else," he said.

"Nice. It even has security," said Jack as he looked at the

seal before placing it in his pocket.

"One more thing," said Rhandor. "It's best you keep your hood up for now. The people in this town rarely see humans, so it would be better if we didn't draw too much attention."

Jack put the hood of his cloak up.

"Now, let's head to the stables first," said Rhandor.

#####

They walked into the town. As they walked, Jack looked around. The town was mostly populated by beastfolk. There were numerous shops selling everything from weapons and armor to clothing and knick-knacks. On the streets were various stands selling food, with some selling prepared meals and others selling fruits or vegetables. A number of restaurants were visible on the main street as well. Jack was surprised at how modern the city looked. If not for all of the beastfolk walking around, the town could have easily been mistaken for any one of the many small towns of Europe. As he was occupied looking at the shops, a small ball rolled up and tapped his left foot. Jack bent down and picked it up just as a young rabbit beastfolk child ran up to him. He handed the ball to the child.

"Here you go," said Jack.

"Thank you, mister," said the child.

"You're quite welcome," said Jack.

"Hey, mister. Is that your dragon?" asked the child.

"It sure is," said Jack.

The child got excited.

"Can I pet her?" the child asked.

"I don't see why not," said Jack before turning to Nava. "You don't mind, do you, Nava?"

Nava slowly lowered her head to the child's level. The child carefully raised his hand and placed it gently on Nava's nose. He rubbed it a few times, and then Nava let out a little snort. The child giggled.

"Thanks, mister," said the kid before turning and waving as he ran back to his parents to continue playing with his ball.

Jack turned to Rhandor.

"Seems like a pretty friendly town," he said.

Rhandor nodded.

#####

The stables soon came into sight. They led the dragons into the stables as Rhandor spoke with the owner. He presented the seal to the owner, and just as he had described to Jack, the owner brought out a notebook, and Rhandor stamped it. One of the handlers came over to Nava. Jack pulled out an apple and gave it to her.

"Ok, Nava. You be good, ok?" said Jack as the handler led her to a stall.

After both dragons were secured in their stalls, Rhandor approached Jack.

"Next, we should find some lodging for the night. When that's done, I'll go and speak to the local guards and see what information I can get about Dark Army movements in the area," he said.

"Sounds like a plan," said Jack.

#####

They walked for a few more minutes before they came up to an inn. They walked in and Rhandor spoke briefly with the clerk. When he was done, he walked back to Jack and handed him a key.

"We're in the last room at the end of the hall upstairs," he said.

"Roger that," said Jack as he took Rhandor's bag. "I'll go put our things up in the room so you can go check in with the guards."

"Thank you, my friend," said Rhandor.

Rhandor walked out of the inn.

#####

Jack headed up the stairs to their room. He put the key into the lock and opened the door. The room was surprisingly large. It had two beds, two large wardrobes, and a small bathroom. Jack lowered his hood.

"Nice. All that's missing is a mint on the pillow," said Jack.

He placed the bags at the foot of each bed and then sat down on one of the beds. He looked at the pillows and saw a small object resting there. He picked it up and examined it. Sure enough, it was a small mint candy.

"I'll be damned," said Jack with a smile.

Jack opened his backpack and took out the Colt 1911, still in its holster, and clipped the holster behind his right hip.

"Can't be too careful," he said.

Jack then placed the bags in wardrobes, put his hood up, and left the room, locking the door behind him.

#####

His stomach growled a bit, so he decided to check out some of the food vendors they had passed by on their way to the inn. One of the vendors was selling a variety of baked goods. Jack scanned over the selection. One thing in particular jumped out at him. It was a jam-filled pastry with frosting drizzled on top.

"I'd like one of these, please," said Jack to the vendor.

"That'll be three coppers, please," said the vendor.

Jack reached into his pocket and pulled out the seal. He showed it to the vendor and the vendor pulled out the notebook. Jack placed the seal against the notebook and thought about the three copper pieces. The seal glowed momentarily and left a mark on the paper. The vendor looked at the notebook briefly and then put it away. He grabbed a small piece of paper, picked up the pastry with it, and handed it to Jack.

"Thank you," said Jack.

He ate the pastry as he walked. It was well made. The pastry was flaky, the frosting was sweet, and the jam had a flavor quite similar to strawberries. As he strolled along, Jack would occasionally look into the windows of the various shops he passed. One window in particular contained an item that caught Jack's eye. Displayed in the window was a small brooch. It was a small sword wrapped in a vine. The blade of the sword was a white gem. The grip was a ruby red gem, and the pommel was an emerald gem. Each gem was finely bordered in gold. From the pommel to the tip of the sword was a thin gold vine that loosely wrapped its way around. Each curve of the vine was accented with marquise-cut dark green gems for leaves, bordered in gold. Below the brooch was a small price tag. The price was eight gold coins.

Jack thought that it would make for a nice gift for Lia, but he felt weird about using the seal to purchase it. It would essentially be like buying her a gift with her own money. Jack didn't have any coins on him, so he made a mental note of the store's location and continued walking.

#####

As he walked, he thought about ways he could get the money to buy the brooch. When he reached the town square, he heard a voice that piqued his interest.

"Step right up! Ladies and gentlemen, step right up and test your magic! Free the ball from the tube and win ten gold coins! Many will try; few will win! Give it your best shot! Step right up!" said the voice.

Jack walked up to see what he was talking about. The man was standing next to a large, free-standing wall. Weaving from the bottom of the wall to the top was a tube. The tube was wider in some spots and smaller in others. There was a small amount of water at the bottom of the tube, and a cork ball was floating on top of it. Attached to the wall was a small pedestal with a blue crystal similar to the affinity gauge that Jack had used at the camp. Jack watched as one of the town residents gave it a try. The resident placed his palm down on the blue crystal and closed his eyes. When he opened his eyes, there was a pale blue glow in his pupils. Water slowly began to build in the tube, moving the ball through. The flow of water began to slow when it reached the wider section of the tube. The player began to strain as the ball reached the midway point of the tube. Eventually, he gave up, and the ball slowly settled back at its starting point. Jack watched as a second man attempted. That time, the ball only reached about a quarter of the way through the winding tube. Jack walked up to the man.

"Mind if I give it a try?" asked Jack.

"Give it a shot, friend. First try is free. Next one will cost you one silver," said the man.

Jack stepped up to the crystal. He placed his hand on it, and began to coach himself.

"Ok, Jack. Remember the camp. Not too much. Not too fast. Just for a second. Try not to break the wall." he said to himself.

Jack closed his eyes for a moment. When he opened them, his eyes glowed a bright blue. In that moment, water began gushing into the tube, propelling the ball through the twists and turns in an instant. The ball then popped out of the top of the wall like a champagne cork. Jack pulled his hand off the crystal and looked up just in time to catch the ball in his right hand. There was a moment of stunned silence among the crowd that had gathered, followed by applause. Jack walked over to the man running the game and handed him the ball.

"Quite impressive, friend. Quite impressive, indeed. Well done. As promised, here you are. Ten gold coins. A fine display of magic," said the man.

"Thank you very much, sir," said Jack as he received the

ten gold coins.

#####

After receiving the coins, Jack made his way back to the shop where he saw the brooch. He walked into the shop and purchased it immediately. The shopkeeper gave it to him in a small box wrapped in purple fabric and tied with a golden string. Jack placed the box in his pocket and left the store to make his way back to the inn.

#####

When Jack returned to the room, Rhandor was there.

"Hello, Jack. Did you enjoy exploring the town?" asked Rhandor.

"I certainly did," said Jack. "There's a bakery that makes some damn good pastries not too far from here. We should get some before we leave town."

"Certainly," said Rhandor.

"What did you find out from the guards?" asked Jack.

"There have been a few sightings of Dark Army soldiers in the area over recent weeks. We best not spend too much time in any one place and keep our eyes and ears open as we continue northward," said Rhandor.

"Understood," said Jack.

"And we should try to keep any use of magic to a minimum. Wouldn't want to draw any unnecessary attention to ourselves," said Rhandor.

"Oh, uh, yeah," said Jack.

Rhandor could tell from Jack's response that something had happened.

"Jack?" he said.

"I only used a little bit of it. Not too much. Nothing too flashy. I just played a game of sorts to win a bit of prize money. I didn't break anything or blow anything up. I promise," said Jack.

"I see," said Rhandor. "How much did you win?"

"Ten gold coins," said Jack. "I used them to buy something for Lia."

"Well, from now on, best not to use any magic unless it's absolutely necessary," said Rhandor.

"Heard and understood," said Jack.

"Very well. Let's head downstairs to the dining hall and get something to eat. After that, we should return here and get some rest. We will be leaving tomorrow morning."

"Good idea. I was getting a bit hungry," said Jack as they left the room, locking the door behind them.

#####

When they got down to the dining hall, they chose a table off in the back corner. Jack pulled his hood back a little, but not so much that his ears were exposed. They ordered their food and drinks and talked as they ate.

"So, this gift you spoke of...," said Rhandor.

"Oh, yeah. Here. Let me show you," said Jack as he pulled it out of his pocket.

Jack carefully undid the string and unfolded the fabric before opening the box. He handed the box to Rhandor.

"My. Would you look at that? That's quite nice," said Rhandor. "I'm sure Her Highness will be most grateful to receive it."

"Here's hoping," said Jack as he re-wrapped it and placed it back in his pocket. "So, where to after this?"

"From here, we travel to a town called Ackhard. It's about a day's journey from here. From Ackhard, we travel about a half-day's journey to the base of the Firespring mountain. That's where you'll find the path to Zavyra's abode," said Rhandor.

"Ooh. Firespring. Sounds hot," said Jack.

"There are a number of hot springs near the base of the mountain that are said to be good for healing," said Rhandor.

"Wait. Where I'll find the path? You won't be joining me?" said Jack.

"No. The journey up the mountain path is one that you will take alone. You are there to seek her help. She's not a fan of visitors," said Rhandor.

"Oh. Well, let's hope we find her in a good mood on a spa day at the base of the mountain, then," said Jack.

Rhandor chuckled.

"Not likely, my friend. She is only seen by those who seek her," he said.

"Well, a guy can hope," said Jack.

"Indeed," said Rhandor as he held up his glass before taking a drink.

When they finished their meals, they returned to their room.

#####

Jack took the Colt 1911 from the holster and placed it under his pillow. They each got into their bed and were both fast asleep soon afterward.

CHAPTER 16

The foul stench of rotting meat caused the dark elf to wince as he walked past the draphnir pens near the castle. At each side of the entrance to the castle stood greater goblins. Unlike the child-sized goblins that tend to much of the grunt work, greater goblins are much taller and much stronger, making them useful for serving as castle guards. Standing upwards of seven feet tall, each greater goblin carried a massive serrated sword with a blade that was five inches wide and nearly five feet in length. The dark elf nodded to the greater goblins, and they immediately opened the door for him. As he approached the throne room, he could hear the screams of prisoners being brought before the Emperor. He entered the throne room just in time to witness the prisoners, all beastfolk, down on their knees with the Emperor standing in front of them. The Emperor stood nearly seven and a half feet tall. He was cloaked in long black robes. A hood covered his head. His face was completely hidden by a cloud of dark magic energy, with only the red glow of his eyes visible.

The dark elf watched as the Emperor raised his right hand. When the Emperor extended his arm forward, what looked like a jet-black flame began to shoot out of the Emperor's hand, splitting seven ways with each string of black flame reaching out to one of the prisoners. The prisoners each became engulfed in the black flame, screaming in agony. When the black fire extinguished, the screams were no more. The beastfolk's fur had turned to a dark gray. Their claws and fangs had grown. A black ooze dripped from their mouths. Then the Emperor spoke. His voice was deep and echoed throughout the throne room.

"Rise, Demonborne, and serve me," the Emperor said.

The newly changed Demonborne stood and bowed to the Emperor. They then turned and exited the throne room through a doorway on the right. The dark elf approached the Emperor and knelt down, placed his right hand over his heart and bowed his head. The Emperor once again spoke.

"Greetings, General Karvan. What news do you bring?" said the Emperor.

Karvan raised his head.

"Great Emperor, I bring news. The squadron we deployed has been defeated by the Vedyrian Army," said Karvan.

"What of the human?" asked the Emperor.

"He was not among the Vedyrian soldiers, Your Excellency," said Karvan.

"Have you come before me only to report your failures, General Karvan?"

"No, Your Excellency. One of our imp spies has reported a sighting of an unusual magic user in the town of Estin. He wore a cloak, and his face was concealed, but his magic was quite strong. It could be the human we seek," said Karvan.

"Did he bear the scars?" asked the Emperor.

"Unknown," said Karvan.

"Very well. You will send dark elves to every town along the border. Find the human and bring him before me," said the Emperor.

"As you command, Your Excellency," said Karvan.

Karvan stood, bowed to the Emperor and then left the throne room.

#####

He walked down one of the halls of the castle until he came upon the infirmary. He entered the infirmary and approached a dark elf lying in one of the beds. The dark elf in the bed was his brother, Corvan.

"Greetings, little brother. How are your wounds?" asked Karvan.

The entire left side of Corvan's body was severely burned. His left ear was gone, and the left side of his face was badly burned. Corvan sat up in his bed.

"The pain is tolerable now, Brother. I wish to return to service," said Corvan.

"You're in luck, Corvan. The Emperor wishes for me to deploy dark elves to the border towns in order to search for the human who did this to you. I would like you to join them," said Karvan.

"Excellent, Brother. I shall get my revenge for what he did to me at Arnin Canyon," said Corvan.

"His Excellency wishes the human to be captured and brought before him," said Karvan.

"Alive?! Brother! I have witnessed firsthand the destruction that this human can bring! You weren't there! That human reduced nearly twenty-four thousand of my men to ash at Arnin Canyon! Not even the canyon itself could withstand his attack! I fear his power may even rival that of the Emperor! He must be eliminated!" said Corvan.

"It is the wish of the Emperor, Brother. He must be captured and brought before the Emperor alive. Is that understood?" said Karvan.

Corvan let out an exasperated sigh.

"Yes, Brother. I will do as His Excellency commands," said Corvan.

"See that you do, Brother. I will send men to Estin to investigate. I want you to make your way to Ackhard." Karvan said.

"Yes, Brother. As you wish," said Corvan.

CHAPTER 17

The rain was finally letting up when Lia and the soldiers returned to the camp. Lia turned to Alivair.

"Get me a full casualty report as soon as possible, Captain. And let me know if you find anything else in the documents," said Lia.

"Right away, Commander," said Alivair.

Lia returned to her tent. Crescia was waiting there.

"Your Highness! I'm so happy that you've returned safely!" said Crescia.

"Thank you, Crescia. It was a tough battle, but we came out on top," said Lia.

Lia pulled the necklace with the ring that Jack had given her out from under her armor and began to fidget with it. Crescia noticed Lia's anxiety.

"Is there something bothering you, Your Highness?" asked Crescia.

"It's Jack," said Lia.

"Oh no! Did something happen to him? Is he ok?" asked Crescia anxiously.

"No. Nothing like that. He's fine, as far as I know," said Lia.

"Oh, thank goodness," said Crescia. "Then what is bothering you about Jack?"

"It seems the Dark Army is looking for him. For what reason, I'm not sure," said Lia.

"Do they know that he's not here right now?" asked Crescia.

"As far as I can tell, they remain unaware of Jack's absence, but I can't be sure. All I know is that they're looking for him," said Lia.

Crescia placed her hand on Lia's shoulder.

"Well, if they're still looking, at least that means that they haven't found him yet. So he should still be safe, and Rhandor is with him, and no one would mess with Rhandor," said Crescia, trying to be optimistic.

"That's true," said Lia.

"Where are they now?" asked Crescia.

"If they stick with the plan that Rhandor gave me before they left, they should be in the town of Estin or en route to Ackhard by now," said Lia.

"I wonder if he knows that they're looking for him," said Crescia.

"The least we can do is try to send word. Summon a fairy. We will try to send them a message through the fairy network," said Lia.

"Right away, Your Highness," said Crescia before bowing and leaving the tent.

#####

A few minutes later, Alivair appeared in front of Lia's tent.

"Your Highness, I have the casualty report you requested," he said.

"Come in," said Crescia.

Alivair entered the tent.

"Your Highness," said Alivair after bowing.

"Proceed with the report, Captain," said Lia.

"Total casualties of sixteen, Your Highness. Twelve wounded and four dead," he said.

"Understood, Captain. See to the arrangements for the fallen," she said.

"Yes, Your Highness," said Alivair.

"Have all the wounded made it to the medical tent?" she asked.

"Yes, Your Highness. The healers are currently administering treatment," he said.

"Very good. Have you had a chance to review any more of the documents?" she asked.

"Not yet, Your Highness. I intend to do so as soon as I return to my tent," he said.

Very well, Captain. I won't keep you," said Lia.

Alivair bowed to Lia before leaving the tent.

Lia once again began to fidget with the ring. Soon afterward, Crescia returned with a fairy. Lia wrote down a message on a small note, rolled it up, and handed it to the fairy.

"I want you to pass this message on through your network to every town on the way to Firespring Mountain. Tell them to be on the lookout for their dragons at the stables. This is a most urgent matter, so pass it along as fast as you can," she said to the fairy.

The fairy took the message, nodded, and flew out of the tent.

#####

Nearly an hour later, Alivair returned to Lia's tent.

"Your Highness. I have reviewed the documents we recovered from the Dark Army encampment," said Alivair.

"Very well, Captain. Proceed," she said.

"It appears that there were a few survivors of the battle at Arnin Canyon. Most notably a high-ranking commander by the name of Corvan. It was his report that appears to have informed the Great Demon Emperor of Jack's existence. While it is still unknown what they intend to do with him once they have him, it appears that the emperor wants Jack alive. I can only assume that he seeks Jack in order to make use of his power," said Alivair.

"A safe assumption," said Lia.

Alivair continued.

"Aside from Jack, it appears that they intend to expand

their territories to both the north and south. I'd advise sending word to the southern camps to be on the lookout for enemy advancements," he said.

"Very well. See to it, Captain," said Lia.

"Yes, Your Highness," said Alivair.

"Anything else?" asked Lia.

"No, Your Highness. That's all I have to report at this time," said Alivair.

"Ok, Captain. Have you eaten yet?" she asked.

"Not yet, Your Highness," said Alivair.

"Then please, go get something to eat and get some rest. It has been a rough couple of days. We should get some rest wherever we can." she said.

"Yes, Your Highness. What about you?" Alivair asked.

"I'll have Crescia bring me something," said Lia.

Alivair noticed that Lia was fidgeting with the ring.

"He's going to be fine, Your Highness," he said.

"Hmm?" said Lia, looking up from her documents.

"Jack, Your Highness. Even before he learns to control his magic, we've both seen what he can do, so I pity the poor soul who finds themselves standing against him... or any of the ones standing in the general vicinity of him, for that matter," Alivair said, trying to make a joke.

"Yes. Let's hope you're right, Captain," said Lia, not really in the mood for jokes.

Sensing that it was time to leave, Alivair stood at attention and bowed.

"Your Highness," he said.

Lia nodded in response, and he left the tent.

#####

After a while, Lia grew tired of going through all of the documents and decided to take a walk. She walked through much of the camp and eventually found herself standing in front of Jack's tent. She entered the tent, looked around for a moment, and then sat on the bed. Something caught her eye sticking out from under the pillow. She lifted the pillow to reveal a small note with her name written on it. She unfolded the note and read it.

"Are you snooping? Look under the chair."

Lia smiled and looked under the chair. There was a second note. She unfolded it and read it.

"Ha! I knew you were snooping. Look in the desk drawer."

Lia stood and walked over to the desk. She opened the drawer and saw another note. The note was wrapped around an object. She read what was written on the top of the note.

"Lia. Do not open until you have returned to your tent."

Lia carefully placed it in her pocket and returned to her tent. When she got there, she placed it down on her desk and began to unwrap it. Inside the note was Jack's digital music player with headphones. Written on the inside of the note were instructions.

"Place this one in your left ear and the other one in your right ear. Press the triangle button to play, the square to stop, and the two vertical lines to pause. Press this button to make it louder and this button to make it quieter. Hope this helps you to relax."

Lia followed the instructions and put the earbuds in her ears. She pressed the triangle button and was surprised to hear music playing. She quickly took one of the earbuds out to see if the music was playing elsewhere, but she couldn't hear it from anywhere but the earbuds. She carefully placed the earbud back into her ear and listened to the music. She was fascinated by the little piece of Otherworld technology that Jack had left for her and amused by the little game he had used to lead her to discover it. She tried all of the buttons on the device in order to begin to understand how it functioned and then began to listen to the music again. Eventually, she started to feel the stress begin to melt away, bit by bit. She walked over to her bed, laid down and soon fell asleep as the music continued to play.

CHAPTER 18

Jack and Rhandor woke up at mid-morning. They were both grateful for sleeping on a mattress instead of the ground, as they had done the night before arriving in Estin. They packed their gear and left the inn. On their way to the stables, they stopped by the bakery that Jack had mentioned and bought a number of pastries. When they reached the stables, Jack walked up to Nava and offered her a piece of his pastry. To his surprise, she ate it happily.

"I'll be damned. Who would have thought that a dragon would like pastries?" Jack said to himself.

He gave Nava a few pats on the neck. She then started to pick at the bag of remaining pastries he was carrying.

"No, no. These are mine," he said before leaning in close. "I'll share with you later. Don't tell Rhandor."

Once the dragons were released from the stables, Jack and Rhandor led them out of town. When they got far enough outside of town, they mounted the harnesses. Jack turned to Rhandor.

"How long of a flight do we have today?" he asked.

"We should reach Ackhard by dusk if we don't run into any complications," said Rhandor.

As they prepared for takeoff, Jack made a joke.

"Welcome, and thank you for flying Dragon Airways. Please make sure all luggage is firmly secured to the dragon before takeoff. In the event of a water landing, your dragon can swim. Emergency exits are... well... everywhere. Thank you, and enjoy your flight," he said.

Rhandor gave him a confused look and shook his head.

"It's an Otherworld thing," said Jack as he shrugged.

"I see," said Rhandor.

#####

The dragons both took flight and quickly climbed into the sky. As they soared through the sky, Jack once again took the opportunity to take in the sights. To the southwest he saw sheets of rain falling from a distant storm cloud. Straight ahead, the weather was clear. There was hardly a cloud in the sky. Occasionally, Jack would take a bite of a pastry, then tap Nava on the neck. When she would turn her head for a moment, he'd stretch out to give her a piece of the pastry, which she would happily eat. Beyond the sightseeing, the flight was otherwise uneventful.

#####

As evening came, the town of Ackhard came into view. From the air, Jack could see that Ackhard was a much larger town than Estin. Unlike Estin, Ackhard was surrounded by a large stone wall. There was a line of people near the front gate, waiting to get in. Rhandor gave the signal to land, and they both touched down a few hundred yards from the front gate. As they began walking with the dragons closely behind them, Jack turned to Rhandor.

"What's the deal with the wall?" he asked.

"Ackhard is a town of strategic importance, and it has been for quite some time. Back before the unification under the flag of the Vedyrian Kingdom, many tried to take this town due to its proximity to a number of important resources. Now, Ackhard isn't just a town; it's the northernmost outpost of the Vedyrian Army," said Rhandor.

"Impressive," said Jack. "So we won't have any problem getting in, I'm guessing."

"I should think not," said Rhandor.

When the guards at the gate saw Jack and Rhandor, they waved them forward, recognizing that Rhandor was a member of the Vedyrian Army.

"Sir. Welcome to Ackhard. Right this way," said the guard to Rhandor.

The guard signaled for a smaller gate to be opened. When the gate was completely open, Rhandor and Jack entered, followed by the dragons. As they walked through the other side of the wall, two soldiers came up to the dragons and began to lead them. That caught Jack by surprise.

"Hey! Wait! Who are you? Where are you taking her?" he said.

Rhandor turned and placed his hand on Jack's shoulder.

"Don't worry, my friend. They are Vedyrian soldiers. They are simply taking the dragons to the outpost stables. They will be well cared for," he said.

"Oh," said Jack before turning to the soldier directing Nava. "Just be careful with her."

The soldier nodded in response as Jack removed his gear.

Another soldier came running up to Rhandor.

"Sir! We've been waiting for your arrival. An urgent message arrived for you earlier this morning," said the soldier.

"Very well," said Rhandor before turning to Jack. "We'll be staying in the officer's quarters tonight. This soldier will escort you."

"Ok," said Jack.

Rhandor left with the soldier, leaving Jack standing there with his escort.

"Hi," said Jack to the soldier.

"Hello, sir," said the soldier.

"Lead the way," said Jack.

#####

Instead of walking through the town, the soldier escorted Jack through the various passageways that ran along the inside of the wall. Jack was a little disappointed that he wasn't able to get a good look at the town. When he lowered the hood on his cloak, the soldier seemed momentarily surprised.

"Oh. You're a human," said the soldier.

It was then that Jack got a better look at the soldier and noticed the pointed ears partially concealed by his helmet.

"Is that a problem?" asked Jack, testing the waters of this soldier's potential biases.

"No, sir," said the soldier. "Just don't see too many humans around here anymore."

"Anymore?" asked Jack.

"This place used to be a major trading hub with a number of the human villages on the outer edges of the kingdom of Stobrimore, before it fell," said the guard.

"Ah," said Jack.

"Pardon my rudeness, sir. My name is Marath. I'm working to become a junior mage in the Mage Corps here in Ackhard," he said.

"Nice to meet you, Marath. The name's Jack."

Jack chose to withhold his last name so as not to draw too much attention or make things any more awkward than they already were.

"So what brings you this far north, Jack?" asked Marath.

"Looking to see a lady about some help with my magic," said Jack.

"Oh! You're a magic user?" said Marath with a hint of excitement. "What affinities do you possess?"

"Um, all of them," said Jack.

Marath stopped in his tracks. He turned and faced Jack.

"All of them? Surely you're joking," he said.

"Nope. At least not according to Bilen and his affinity gauge, which I kind of broke," said Jack.

"You've met Master Bilen?" said Marath with a look of surprise on his face.

"Yeah. Not sure he particularly likes me very much, but I can definitely say that we've met," said Jack.

"I would love to see a demonstration of your magic," said Marath.

"Yeah, I don't think you would. When I use it, I have a tendency to break things," said Jack. "That's why I'm going to see this Zavyra person. I'm told that she can help me learn how to control it."

Marath's expression changed.

"You're going to see Zavyra?" he asked.

"Why does everyone's face do that when I mention that name?" Jack asked.

"It's just the rumors, sir," said Marath.

"Yeah. I've heard them. The ones about how not everyone who sees her returns, and those who do tend not to talk about it. Right?" said Jack.

"Yes, sir. It is said that she is quite fearsome," said Marath.

"I wish, just once, that someone would tell me something good about her. Like she makes great pies or she loves fluffy bunnies or something. But no. It's always everyone looking at me like I'm walking to my own execution when I bring up her name. It doesn't exactly fill me with loads of confidence," said Jack.

"My apologies, sir. I shall speak no more of it," said Marath.

"Don't worry about it, Marath," said Jack.

They eventually came to a large hallway with doors on each side. Marath stopped in front of one of the doors.

"This shall be your room, Jack. Sir Rhandor will be staying in the room across the hall," said Marath.

"Sir Rhandor?" asked Jack.

"Yes. Sir Rhandor is a high-ranking knight among the Mage Corps," said Marath.

"Hmm. You learn something new every day, I guess," said Jack.

Jack opened the door and looked around. The room was quite spacious, and it had a comfortable-looking bed, a desk, a wardrobe, and a small nightstand.

"If there's nothing else...," said Marath.

"Nope. Everything's good here. Thanks, Marath," said Jack.

Marath stood at attention for a moment, bowed, and then returned to his duties.

#####

A few minutes later, after Jack had settled in his room, he heard Rhandor approaching. Jack walked to the doorway and looked down the hall as Rhandor approached.

"So, Sir Rhandor, huh?" he said.

Rhandor shrugged.

"I felt that the use of titles was unnecessary at this point, Your Royal Highness, Crown Prince Jack of the Kingdom of Stobrimore," said Rhandor.

"Ok, yeah. Sure. I guess that's fair. Wow. Couldn't even fit that one on a business card," said Jack. "So what was that urgent message all about?"

"We received word from Her Highness that it appears that the Dark Army is looking for you," said Rhandor.

"Well, that sucks. Any idea why?" asked Jack.

"Unknown, but it appears that they want to take you alive," said Rhandor.

"Oh boy. That can't be good. Let's make sure that doesn't happen," said Jack.

"Indeed," said Rhandor.

"So, do they know where we are?" asked Jack.

"I don't know. But it would be best if we don't do anything to draw too much attention to ourselves. The Dark Army has spies everywhere. They may very well even have them here," said Rhandor.

"With all the soldiers here? Do you really think they would have the balls to try something here?" asked Jack.

"One cannot be too careful. The Dark Army has ways

of infiltrating places even as strongly fortified as this. Were this only a base for the Vedyrian Army, I would say that it would be very unlikely for them to try something here, but with Ackhard also being a vibrant and heavily populated town, there is still a chance that agents of the Dark Army could make their way in, undetected," said Rhandor.

"So... keep my hood up again when I'm outside?" asked Jack.

"Indeed. At the very least. And no use of magic unless it is absolutely necessary. We cannot afford to have you taken when we are so close to reaching our destination," said Rhandor.

"Gotcha," said Jack.

Jack walked over to his bag, opened it, and took out the Colt 1911 and the holster and clipped it to his waistband behind his right hip. Realizing the seriousness of the situation, Jack walked up to Rhandor.

"I'm going to teach you something that we used when I was in the military. It's called clock positioning. It's a way to indicate the location of an enemy quickly without having to physically point them out," said Jack.

"Sounds interesting. How does it work?" asked Rhandor.

"Ok. Picture a circle around you on the floor. Directly in front of you is twelve o'clock. Directly to your right is three o'clock. Directly behind you is six o'clock. Directly to your left is nine o'clock. Are you with me so far?" said Jack.

Rhandor nodded.

Jack then used his hand to indicate each position on the clock.

"This is twelve o'clock, this is one o'clock, this is two o'clock, three, four, five, and so on," said Jack.

"I see," said Rhandor.

"Now, if there is an enemy above or below us, you add the word 'high' or 'low' to the clock position. For example, if we're walking down the street and there is an enemy up on the roof of a building directly in front of us, you would say 'enemy, twelve o'clock high' in order to indicate where the bad guy is. Make sense?" said Jack.

"Indeed. A quite useful shorthand for communication," said Rhandor.

"And if we're not facing the same direction, you can make it clear by saying 'my' or 'your' before the number to tell where the bad guy is. So if I'm facing toward you and you're facing to my left, and I see an enemy behind you, I would say, 'enemy, your six o'clock', and that would let you know where the bad guy was in relation to the direction you're facing," said Jack.

"I think I understand. Yes. Most interesting," said Rhandor.

"One more thing," said Jack.

Jack then walked over to his backpack, dug around for a moment, and pulled out two handheld radios. He turned them both on before handing one of them to Rhandor.

"These are radios. They will allow us to communicate with each other from far distances. You just press this button before you talk, speak into the radio, and release the button when you're done talking. Let's test them out. Go into your room across the hall, go to the far wall, and leave the door open so we can see each other."

Rhandor walked across the hall and into his room, leaving the door open as Jack had instructed.

Jack pressed the button on his radio.

"Can you hear me, Rhandor?" he said into the radio.

Rhandor was surprised to hear Jack's voice through the radio. He looked at Jack and nodded energetically. Jack once again spoke into the radio.

"Now you try it. Press the button and speak into the radio," he said.

Rhandor examined the radio again and then pressed the button and spoke.

"Is my voice reaching you, Jack?" he asked before

releasing the button.

"Loud and clear," responded Jack through the radio.

Rhandor then ran back to Jack.

"A most remarkable device, my friend! Truly remarkable! What magic does it use?" asked Rhandor.

"Um, it doesn't really use magic. It uses something called radio waves, which, now that I say it, probably doesn't mean much to you."

Jack thought for a moment and realized that now probably wasn't the time to try and explain the ins and outs of electromagnetic radiation and its applications in communication.

"Let's just say it works because of Otherworld technology," said Jack, hoping that explanation was good enough.

"Fascinating," said Rhandor.

Jack was secretly relieved that Rhandor wasn't insistent on getting details. He then showed Rhandor the clips on the back of the radio.

"With this clip, you can attach the radio to your waistband or pocket," said Jack.

"Ah. Yes! I see!" said Rhandor as he clipped the radio to his waistband.

Jack put the hood on his cloak up.

"Now, let's go explore. I want to check out this town," he said.

"Indeed," said Rhandor.

When they left the barracks and got out into the town, Jack noticed how crowded it was.

"Is something going on, or is it always this crowded?" he asked.

Rhandor looked around.

"There appears to be a festival of some sort," said

Rhandor.

Rhandor then walked up to one of the soldiers walking in the crowd. After talking to the soldier for a moment, he returned to Jack.

"It seems that this is an annual harvest festival," said Rhandor.

"So... tasty baked goods?" said Jack.

"Yes, my friend. Tasty baked goods," said Rhandor.

"Yay!" said Jack.

As they walked along the streets filled with stalls for the festival, both Jack and Rhandor took in the sights, sounds and smells. At one stall, Jack noticed a small elf child trying her best to use the little crossbow to hit the target so she could win the doll. He saw the look of disappointment on her face when she failed. Jack walked up to the stall and showed the treasury stamp. He was given three blunted arrows. Jack turned to the little elf girl.

"Watch this," he said.

Jack cocked the crossbow and inserted the first arrow. He took careful aim at the target below the doll. His first shot hit the bullseye, but the target didn't move far enough back to trigger the flag indicating a win. He turned to the little elf girl and gave her a wink before cocking the crossbow and loading the second arrow. Once again, he took careful aim at the target. Again, he hit the bullseye. That time, the flag was triggered. The man behind the stall saw the flag.

"We have a winner!" he said as he reached up and took the doll down.

He handed the doll to Jack. Jack turned and handed the doll to the little elf girl. She smiled a big smile and hugged the doll tightly.

"Thank you, mister!" said the little elf girl.

"Sure thing, kiddo," said Jack.

Jack then turned and looked at some of the other prizes along the wall. One thing caught his eye. It was a tiny sword about the size of a pocketknife. Jack took aim and hit the target, triggering the flag. The man behind the stall picked up the tiny sword and handed it to Jack. Jack nodded to the man and placed the crossbow down on the counter. He then walked back up to Rhandor and handed him the tiny sword.

"Here. For those little battles you might run into. Or maybe a toothpick," he said.

"Thank you, Jack," said Rhandor.

"No problem," said Jack with a smile.

By that time, the sun was fully set, and the only light was from the lights of the town. Rhandor turned to Jack as they walked.

"Shall we get something to eat? There's a pub coming up to the right, here," he said.

"Yeah, sure. I'm starving," said Jack.

#####

They walked into the pub and grabbed a table in the back corner. The server came over, and they ordered their food. The pub soon became very crowded. As they ate, Jack occasionally looked around the pub. There were elves and beastfolk, adults and children, all having a good time. Jack noticed one person sitting near the entrance who wasn't looking particularly festive. The man was wearing a cloak, much like Jack, and, like Jack, had his hood up, covering his face. Other than the fact that the man wasn't looking very happy, Jack didn't see anything out of place. He figured that it was probably just someone who was having a bad day or had tired themselves out at the festival and continued eating. When they were done, Rhandor signaled for the server, showed the stamp to pay, and they got up to leave. When they got near the door, Jack accidentally knocked a diner's coat off the back of their chair. He bent over and picked it up before apologizing to the diner. When he picked up the coat, his sleeve cuff rode up his arm slightly, exposing the start of the tattoo-like scars. After standing up, Jack quickly pulled his sleeve back up to his wrist, and they both left the pub.

#####

Just after Jack and Rhandor left, the hooded man sitting at the table near the door lifted his left hand and made a gesture with his fingers. An imp perched on the roof of the building across the street saw the hand gesture made by the hooded man through the window of the pub. After looking down the street in the direction Jack and Rhandor had walked, the imp took flight and began to follow them.

#####

Eventually, Jack and Rhandor returned to the barracks. Jack showed Rhandor how to turn the handheld radio off, and they went to their separate rooms to sleep.

#####

Outside the pub, the imp returned to the hooded man, landing on his shoulder and then whispering something in his ear. When the hooded man pulled the hood back in order to hear the imp better, his left ear was missing.

CHAPTER 19

When morning came, Jack and Rhandor woke up fairly early. Jack left his room first and waited in the hallway for Rhandor. When Rhandor opened his door, Jack popped his head right in front of Rhandor's face, startling him while he was mid-yawn.

"Morning, Rhandor!" said Jack.

Rhandor smoothed his fur back down.

"Good morning, Jack," said Rhandor.

"Question for you," said Jack.

"Ask away, my friend," said Rhandor.

"Can I wear my sword in town, or is there some rule against it, since I'm not technically a member of the Vedyrian Army?" asked Jack.

Rhandor thought for a moment.

"While civilians are discouraged from carrying bladed weapons in the town limits, it's not technically considered a crime. Aside from that, given that you are considered a personal guest of Her Highness and the fact that you are technically royalty yourself, I don't think there would be any serious objections to you wearing it," said Rhandor.

"Ok. Good to know," said Jack as he gave the sword already on his hip a few taps. "So... breakfast?"

"Indeed," said Rhandor.

"To town!" said Jack.

#####

Jack and Rhandor left the barracks and made their way to the town. As they made their way through the much less crowded streets, both Jack and Rhandor started getting the feeling that something was off. They didn't change their stride so as not to give away that they realized that they were being followed, but they did start their quiet shorthand communication.

"Rhandor?" said Jack.

"Yes, I know," said Rhandor.

"Five and seven," said Jack.

"Ten and one, as well," said Rhandor.

"Away from civilians," said Jack.

"Alley?" asked Rhandor.

"Alley," said Jack.

Jack and Rhandor continued to act casual as they made the turn into the nearest alley. Once they got a few feet into the alley, they both began to run at full speed. As they ran through the twists and turns of the back alleys of Ackhard, Rhandor's ears would twitch.

"Four... No... Five pursuers."

Jack looked up and saw that they were also being tailed in the air by an imp.

"There's an ugly-looking fairy following us, too," said Jack.

"That's an imp," said Rhandor. "That confirms it. They've found us."

"Oh joy. And we didn't even get to have breakfast. That's just rude," said Jack.

Rhandor looked up at the imp. His eyes glowed for a moment as he raised his hand and then brought it down forcefully, using his wind magic to pull the imp out of the air and slam it into the ground behind them. Looking forward, they saw that they were getting close to the wall that surrounded the town.

"When we reach the wall, you break right, and I'll break left. Then we can face these breakfast-ruining bastards head-on," said Jack.

"Understood," said Rhandor.

The moment the alley reached the wall, Rhandor cut to the right side of the alley, and Jack cut to the left side. They both stopped and turned around. Jack drew his sword. As the first pursuer came around the corner, Jack extended his left arm, clotheslining the pursuer, causing him to fall violently backward onto his head. Jack raised the sword to point it at the second pursuer. When he did so, he was momentarily surprised that there weren't any other pursuers. He looked over at Rhandor for a moment and saw one coming up behind him in the distance.

"Rhandor! Your six!" said Jack.

Rhandor turned around and unleashed some wind magic on the pursuer, sending him flying into the wall before collapsing to the ground. Turning back to the one facing the business end of Jack's sword, Jack noticed the pursuer taking out some sort of small black crystal. Rhandor saw it as well.

"No!" said Rhandor as he once again used his wind magic, this time taking the crystal from the pursuer's hand and sending it skyward. The pursuer then turned around and ran to try and catch the crystal.

"Stop him!" yelled Rhandor.

Jack switched the sword to his left hand and pulled out the Colt 1911 from its holster behind his right hip. He quickly took aim at the pursuer and fired a single shot, hitting the pursuer in the center of his back, causing him to collapse to the ground. Rhandor then used his magic to once again raise the crystal way up into the air, stopping it from hitting the ground.

"Do that again! Aim for the crystal!" yelled Rhandor.

Jack locked his eyes onto the crystal and took aim. When the crystal was at just the right angle, Jack pulled the trigger, sending a .45 caliber round directly into the crystal, causing it to shatter. When it hit the crystal, a dark cloud that spread at least five feet in each direction formed for a moment before vanishing.

"What the hell was that?!" asked Jack.

"It's a teleportation crystal! Dark magic! Very

dangerous!" said Rhandor.

With the immediate threats taken care of, with at least one pursuer dead and two others incapacitated, Rhandor crouched down to look at the pursuer that Jack had clotheslined. When he pulled the hood down, he saw elf ears.

"Wait. Elves are after us?" said Jack.

Rhandor then ran his thumb over the face of the unconscious elf, revealing the reddish-gray skin concealed beneath makeup.

"Dark elves," said Rhandor. "Agents of the Dark Army."

"You said five, right?" said Jack. "So where the hell are the other two?"

Rhandor closed his eyes and listened for the sound of footfalls.

"Left. And he's running away," said Rhandor.

"Well, let's turn the pursuers into the pursued, then," said Jack.

"Indeed," said Rhandor.

They began to run toward the direction of the fleeing dark elf. Soon, the elf was in sight, and they increased their pursuit speed. Rhandor took the lead. Just as Rhandor was within reach of the dark elf's hood, a blast of dark magic energy came from the side, hitting Rhandor and knocking him into the wall. Jack was not far behind Rhandor, so he wasn't able to dodge the second blast of dark energy in time, knocking him to the ground near Rhandor. Dazed by the impact, Jack struggled to see the face of the hidden attacker. Jack reached with his left hand to see if Rhandor was still alive. As he blindly reached, he heard Rhandor moan in pain. While Jack was thanking god that Rhandor was still alive, he was also starting to regain enough focus to make out the face of their attacker. The makeup was quite smudged from the sweat at that point, so Jack was able to see the reddish-gray skin beneath. The other notable features of the attacker were soon apparent when he lowered his hood. The left side of his face was badly burned, and his ear was gone.

"You! You did this to me!" said Corvan.

"Pal, I don't even know you," said Jack.

Corvan reached into his cloak and pulled out a black crystal. Jack saw it and quickly looked over at Rhandor, but Rhandor was still unconscious. After realizing that he had no other choice, Jack focused all that he could on using wind magic. His eyes began to glow bright yellow as he pushed his left hand forward. Jack had intended to push the crystal out of Corvan's hand, but instead, he sent Corvan flying up into the air and backward, completely clearing the street that intersected the alley before smashing through a shop window.

Jack stumbled as he tried to get to his feet, repeatedly calling out Rhandor's name to see if he was conscious. Rhandor slowly began to move and lifted his head.

"Jack... I'm ok. Ow. Are you ok?" said Rhandor.

"Sort of," said Jack.

"Where is he?" asked Rhandor.

"I used magic. I had to. No choice. I sent him flying into that window over there," said Jack.

Rhandor stumbled to his feet, assisted by the equally unstable Jack. Jack picked up the sword with his left hand and the handgun with his right hand. He looked at the handgun and saw that the magazine had been damaged, rendering it unable to function. Not wanting to mess with it at the time, Jack simply put the handgun back in the holster and used his free hand to help Rhandor. When they got to the end of the alley where it intersected with a street, they were both a bit more stable, so they carefully approached the broken window to look for Corvan. Jack held the sword out and touched the crystal on the crossguard with his thumb, causing the blade to ignite.

"Ok, Ugly, put the crystal on the ground and come out of there slowly and maybe I won't make both sides of your face match," said Jack.

Soldiers who had heard the commotion began to approach from both directions of the street. Inside the empty shop, Corvan slowly stood up. Hearing the soldiers approaching and realizing that today wasn't the day, he held up the black crystal.

"I will see you again. I guarantee it," said Corvan right before shattering the crystal in his hand.

Corvan was immediately engulfed in the black cloud, and then the cloud and he both vanished. By that time, the soldiers had reached Jack and Rhandor. While some of the soldiers were giving aid to Rhandor, he pointed toward the alley.

"There are several down back there. There may still be at least one on the loose," said Rhandor.

Jack suddenly felt very dizzy. He dropped the sword and looked down at his hands. His scars were starting to glow. Recalling the last time he felt like that, he yelled to those around him.

"Everyone! Get back! Get away from me!" he yelled.

Rhandor looked over at Jack and noticed that his arms and eyes were beginning to glow the dark purple glow.

"Everyone step away! Jack! Focus! Try to aim it upward!" yelled Rhandor.

The soldiers all began to back away from Jack. Jack fell to his knees and used every ounce of strength he had to try and lean back and look up to the sky. Just as he looked up, a burst of dark magic energy shot from his hands up into the sky. The glass in the surrounding buildings shattered from the sudden energy discharge. Given that the amount of dark magic energy he was hit with in the alley was much smaller than the massive amount of energy he had absorbed from the crimson crystal cannons when he first arrived, the amount that was discharged was significantly smaller, albeit equally as painful. The energy fired off into the sky and then quickly dissipated, leaving Jack barely conscious. After a minute or two, Jack began to gain full consciousness and struggled to stand. One of the soldiers caught him just before he fell into the broken window. Jack was still visibly shaking when he spoke to

Rhandor.

"Did I hit anyone? Did I hurt anybody?" asked Jack desperately.

"No, Jack. You didn't hit anybody. You're ok," said Rhandor.

By that point, Rhandor had regained most of his bearings. He walked over to Jack.

"Let's get you back to the barracks," said Rhandor.

"No. There's no time. They know where we are. We need to go. I don't want a battle here. Too many people could get hurt," said Jack.

"Jack, you can barely stand," said Rhandor.

"Get our things and get me to Nava. Then I won't need to stand," said Jack.

"Damn it, Jack," said Rhandor before telling the soldiers to go retrieve their belongings and meet them both at the stables.

Rhandor then put Jack's arm around his shoulder, and with the help of another soldier, they headed for the stables.

#####

By the time they reached the stables, Jack was able to walk a little easier. He climbed onto Nava's back and secured himself into the harness. The soldiers soon returned with their belongings, which were quickly secured to the harnesses. Rhandor climbed up onto Aris's back and secured himself into the harness.

"Looks like we'll be taking off from here, boys. Make way," said Rhandor to the soldiers.

The soldiers stepped back, giving the dragons some room to move.

"Stay sharp! They may come back! Send word to Her Highness about what happened here! And tell her we're making our way forward!" yelled Rhandor as the dragons began to hover.

After making sure that Jack was secure in the harness, Rhandor gave the command for both dragons to take flight. They climbed high into the sky over the town of Ackhard before heading in the direction of Firespring Mountain.

CHAPTER 20

Corvan appeared in a cloud of black smoke in the courtyard of the Emperor's palace and collapsed to his knees. A number of Demonborne guards who were patrolling the courtyard began to rush over to him.

"Don't touch me!" Corvan said as he stood back up.

Corvan began to pick the splinters of wood and small shards of broken glass out of his skin as he walked toward one of the corridors, shoving one of the guards out of the way. He let out a scream of frustration as he walked down the hallway toward the infirmary. When he walked into the infirmary, he grabbed one of the healers by the arm and pulled her away from the patient she was attending to, dragged her over to one of the empty beds and sat down.

"Do your job," he said, as he showed his wounds on his back, arms, and head and the various remaining shards of glass and splinters of wood.

The healer began to carefully pick the pieces off of him.

"Ow! Carefully, you damned fool! I'm not a pin cushion!" he said to the healer.

Soon afterward, Karvan came into the infirmary.

"I see you've returned, Brother," said Karvan. "Where is the human?"

Corvan took a deep breath and grimaced.

"He escaped," said Corvan.

"He escaped? You brought four men with you. How did one measly human escape?" asked Karvan, not hiding his anger and disappointment.

"He had a mage with him!" said Corvan.

"So what? Have you forgotten that you can use magic

as well, little brother?" asked Karvan.

"I have not forgotten, Brother! I used my magic, but have you forgotten that the human has magic as well? Have you forgotten what he did to me?!" said Corvan, pointing to the burns on his face.

"He may be strong, little brother, but he is hardly invincible. Did you not consider taking him while he slept?" asked Karvan.

"He and that mage slept in the officer barracks of the Vedyrian Army outpost! Did you expect me to just go waltzing into their base undetected? That would have been suicide!" yelled Corvan.

"There are ways, little brother," said Karvan.

"We followed them! We had a plan! We were going to grab them both in the town!" said Corvan.

"Then why have you returned empty-handed with your tail between your legs?" asked Karvan.

"The human used his magic and threw me through a damn building! The soldiers were approaching! I was the only one to return!" yelled Corvan.

"You may regret that choice, little brother. His Excellency will surely be displeased with your failure," said Karvan.

"Send me back out, brother! Give me another chance! I won't fail you!" said Corvan.

"That is to be determined, little brother. For now, follow me," said Karvan.

Corvan turned to the healer.

"Are we done?" he said.

The healer nodded.

"Then leave my sight," said Corvan as he stood and shoved the healer aside.

#####

Karvan and Corvan walked through the corridors and

left the castle. Eventually they walked into the training area. It was filled with row upon row of Demonborne, as far as the eye could see.

"Building our army, brother?" asked Corvan as they walked.

"His Excellency has been busy. We have never had more soldiers than we have now," said Karvan with a hint of pride.

"Is this what you wanted to show me?" asked Corvan.

"No. What I wish to show you is this way," said Karvan.

#####

They continued for some time before coming up at what looked like a mining operation. Goblins were moving in and out of multiple tunnels carved into the ground. Some were pushing massive carts of rocks out of tunnels while others were carrying crates of explosives into them.

"Are we looking for something, brother?" asked Corvan.

"Far too often, we have been defeated thanks to the infernal network of glorified insect spies for the Vedyrian Army. So, we've decided to take a new approach. We shall tunnel beneath the forests and valleys, far out of sight of those fairies. When these tunnels are complete, we shall hit them before they even see us coming. We will emerge from the ground and rain hell down upon them, and once we burn the Vedyrian Army camp to ash, we shall march straight into the capital city of Vedyria and bathe in the blood of the royal family as we celebrate our victory," said Karvan.

"An ambitious plan, brother. But how long will it take?" asked Corvan.

"If we continue to throw as many lives of these wretched goblins as necessary into the building of these tunnels, we shall be ready to strike within the month," said Karvan.

"And in the meantime?" asked Corvan.

"In the meantime, we shall continue to hit them wherever we can. And above all else, ensure that they do not discover our plans. There shall be no documentation, and those few commanders who are aware of this shall be forced to secrecy through a blood oath. Should they even attempt to break it, they will die most painfully as their blood boils and they self-destruct," said Karvan.

"But what of the human?" asked Carvan.

"If he is continuing north, he is most likely heading to see that damned mountain witch. Even His Excellency knows that it is best not to trifle with her. Don't worry, Brother. We will seize the human in due time," said Karvan.

CHAPTER 21

By the time mid-morning came around, Jack was nearly back to normal. He was thankful that the dark magic discharge didn't result in another three weeks of unconsciousness like the last one did. He reached into a pocket on the harness and pulled out his canteen. He drank a bit of water and then let a bit splash onto his face. Rhandor looked over at Jack and waved. Jack waved back and gave Rhandor a thumbs-up. Rhandor nodded and then pointed at the mountain in the distance. They were closing in on it quickly. Rhandor then pulled out the handheld radio that Jack had given to him and showed it to Jack, indicating that he wanted Jack to turn his radio on. Jack reached into his pocket and pulled out the radio. He turned it on.

"Are you better, my friend?" said Rhandor over the radio.

"Yeah. Much better," said Jack.

"Glad to hear it. We are only about an hour or so from our destination," said Rhandor.

"Great. Then all that's left is to see this lady that everyone seems to freak out at the mention of her name, for some reason, and ask her for help. No problem," said Jack with every ounce of sarcasm he could muster.

#####

The air was thick with the humidity of the hot springs near where they landed. A number of people were around, visiting the spa resort that had been built there. They both hopped off of their dragons, and Jack grabbed his gear before turning to Rhandor.

"I'm sure this is going to be a welcome break for you, huh? You know, given that this last part of the journey is mine and mine alone and all," Jack said with a smirk.

"Indeed, there are certainly worse places to wait, my friend," said Rhandor.

"What do you guys even do at a spa like this? Do you get your teeth cleaned and claws sharpened or something? Or do you go take a dip in the hot springs and come out all soft and floofy? If you do, please tell me you do. I really want to see you all soft and floofy. That alone would make this whole trip worth it," said Jack.

"I shall remain here and recuperate while remaining vigilant in the event of another Dark Army attack, my friend. I shall warn the protectors of the potential threat," said Rhandor, doing his best to ignore the floofy comment.

"Protectors? What protectors? I thought this was just a spa," said Jack.

"While this may look like a simple resort, it is only here because of a deal that the protectors made with Zavyra. While they operate this resort, they also serve as a means of preventing unwanted visitors from going to see Zavyra. She allows them to remain as long as they keep up their part of the deal," said Rhandor.

"Oh. That's, uh, that's kinda cool, I guess," said Jack. "So, what now?"

"Now we get you to Zavyra. Follow me," said Rhandor.

They walked through much of the resort area, passing by numerous hot spring pools with a variety of different races in various states of undress enjoying their time. They eventually reached what looked like a concierge desk. Rhandor reached into his pocket and pulled out a small folded note. He handed it to the man behind the desk.

"He has come to see Zavyra," said Rhandor to the man.

The man unfolded the note and read it. Once he realized that it was an order from Princess Lia, he immediately folded the note up again and turned to Jack.

"Please, sir. Come with me," he said.

"Well, I guess this is it," said Jack. "Try not to have too much fun while I'm gone."

"Be safe, my friend," said Rhandor.

#####

Jack then followed the man through a number of hallways before reaching a large metal gate. The man pulled out a key from a string around his neck and unlocked the gate. As it swung open, Jack could see stone stairs leading upward. The man directed Jack to go through the gate. Right after Jack crossed the threshold, the man closed the gate behind him and locked it.

"I wish you the best of luck, sir," said the man before turning and walking away.

"Gee, thanks," said Jack to himself.

He turned and looked up the stairway.

"Well, here goes nothing," he said as he began his upward climb.

#####

After climbing what seemed like a countless number of stairs, he reached a pathway that wound along the edge of the mountain. Jack let out a bit of a sigh and began his walk down the path. Much of the path was wide enough to walk comfortably, but a few places along the way had crumbled, leaving a very narrow path in sections. When he reached the end of the path, he found himself staring at what seemed to be a dead end. He looked around for a moment before realizing that the next part of the trek up to Zavyra required a bit of a climb.

"Are you freakin' kidding me?" Jack said to the mountain.

It did not reply.

Jack began to climb up the face of the mountain. It wasn't a vertical climb, which Jack was grateful for. It was only so steep that there wasn't so much a worry of falling off as there was of rolling down the side of it. After climbing about a hundred yards up, Jack came to a ledge. He sat on the ledge and looked down. He leaned over the edge and spit, just to watch it fall and hit the path below. Satisfied with that momentary break, Jack stood up and turned around to face the mountain once again. To his surprise, carved deep into the mountain on the ledge he was standing on, there was a metal door. Jack walked up to the door and knocked a few times. He waited several minutes afterward with no response, so he knocked a second time. He soon heard a rather loud and booming female voice so close that it sounded like the person it belonged to was standing right next to him.

"You may enter," said the voice.

Jack pulled the handle of the door, and it slowly began to open.

"Pardon the intrusion." Jack said quietly as he closed the door behind him.

"Proceed," said the voice.

Jack walked down the dimly lit corridor before coming to a flight of stairs leading downward.

"Yay. More stairs," said Jack.

He walked down the stairs and found himself faced with another door. This time, the door was wood. He was just about to knock when he heard the voice again.

"Open the door," it said.

So he opened the door.

He took a few steps in and looked around at what appeared to be an enormously cavernous room. There was some light near the entrance, but much of the room was still dark in its depths.

"Um, hello?" said Jack. "I'm here to see Zavyra."

"For what reason have you come to see her, human?" said the voice.

"I was told she could help me to learn how to control my magic," said Jack.

"Oh, I see. And who told you this?" she asked.

"Lia, Crown Princess of Vedyria," said Jack.

"Very well," said the voice.

Suddenly, stones around the room began to softly glow, gently illuminating the entirety of the massive cavern. As the light grew brighter, Jack found himself fixated on what the light was illuminating. In the middle of the cavernous room sat a dragon. This dragon was nothing like Nava. This dragon stood at least fifty feet tall. The scales were a pale green with copper-colored accents around the edges. The giant dragon had two slightly curved horns and eyes that seemed to glow a deep blood-red color. The dragon slowly lowered its head to take a look at Jack.

"I'm sorry. I think I may have the wrong room," said Jack as he tried to back out of the room, running into the closed door.

"You are where you are supposed to be," said the dragon.

"Wait... what?" said Jack, not sure if he heard and saw what he thought he just heard and saw.

"I said you are where you are supposed to be. Did you not say that you were here to seek Zavyra?" said the dragon.

"Um... yeah," said Jack.

"Then you have found her," said the dragon.

"Hold up. Are you telling me that you are Zavyra?" asked Jack, still in a bit of shock at the fact that he's talking to a giant dragon.

"I am," said Zavyra.

Jack just stood there, dumbfounded for a moment. He then looked up at Zavyra.

"You're a lot... taller than I expected," said Jack.

"Fascinating. What an interesting choice of wording for you to use. You felt the need to indicate the difference in our sizes but chose to use a word that could not be easily misinterpreted and potentially taken as an insult, such as 'big' or 'large.' How very diplomatic of you," said Zavyra.

"Forgive me. It's just that... of all the people I spoke to about coming to see you, not a single one of them happened to mention the part about you being a dragon," said Jack.

"People say what I allow them to say," said Zavyra.

"I see," said Jack.

"I must say, you seem surprisingly calm for someone speaking to a Grand Elder Dragon," said Zavyra.

"Part of that is probably shock. The other part is probably because I've met a few dragons, and I quite like them. You're the first dragon to speak back to me, though," said Jack.

"You speak of the lesser dragons. They are but distant cousins to my kind. We Grand Elder Dragons are far more complex," said Zavyra.

"I can see that," said Jack.

"What is your name, human?" asked Zavyra.

"Oh, yeah. It was rude of me not to introduce myself. Um, hi. I'm Jack. Jack Stobrimore."

"Stobrimore? Now that is a name I have not heard for quite some time," said Zavyra. "Do you come from the fallen kingdom?"

"Not exactly," said Jack. "Apparently my ancestors did. I came to this world through something called the Worldgate."

"You are an Otherworlder?" asked Zavyra.

"Yeah," said Jack.

"Fascinating. For an Otherworlder, you certainly appear to be handling this situation surprisingly well," said Zavyra.

"You know, that's not the first time I've heard that," said Jack.

Jack looked back at the door behind him.

"Are you expecting another visitor, Jack?" asked Zavyra.

"No. I'm just wondering how you get in here through such a tiny door," said Jack.

Zavyra chuckled, surprised by Jack's statement.

"You certainly are a peculiar human, Jack. My entrance is elsewhere," she said.

"Oh, yeah. That makes more sense. So, um, what do we do now?" asked Jack.

"All in due time. First, place your belongings down. Then we shall sleep together," said Zavyra.

"We shall what, now?" asked Jack.

"Sleep. Are you not tired from your journey?" she asked.

"Oh! Yeah. Sleep. Yes. I could definitely use some sleep right about now," said Jack.

Zavyra looked slightly confused.

"What about my statement gave you such confusion?" she asked.

"You see, where I come from, the phrase 'sleep together' can have a different meaning. It's sort of a euphemism for, um, well, uh, sex," said Jack, embarrassed by the misunderstanding.

"Oh. I see. Well, fear not, young Jack. You are at least a thousand years too young and the wrong species for me for something such as that," said Zavyra.

"Thank god," said Jack. "Because thinking about the logistics alone is just mind-boggling."

Jack rapidly shook his head, trying his best to shake the thoughts out of his mind.

"So, sleep then, huh?" said Jack.

"Yes. And as we sleep, I shall enter your mind and learn your truths," said Zavyra.

"That's not going to hurt, is it?" asked Jack.

"Of course not. We will simply be joining minds. It will cause you no pain," said Zavyra.

"Good. I've had enough pain for the day," said Jack.

"Come. Follow me," said Zavyra, as she turned around and headed deeper into the cavern.

"Right behind you," said Jack.

#####

As they walked deeper into the cavern, Jack saw all sorts of objects lining the walls. Some objects could easily be called treasure, while others could best be described as knick-knacks. When they reached a corner of the cavern, Zavyra curled up and laid down.

"You humans prefer to sleep on a soft surface, do you not?" she asked.

"Generally, yeah. But I'm a soldier, so I'm not super picky," said Jack.

Zavyra's eyes glowed yellow, and Jack was amazed to see what appeared to be a mattress gently floating over and softly landing next to Zavyra's head.

"Is that satisfactory?" she asked.

"Yeah. That's great," said Jack.

Jack removed his cloak and his outer shirt, wearing just the t-shirt underneath. He then sat down on the mattress and removed his boots. He laid down on the mattress and used his cloak as a blanket. Before closing his eyes, he looked over at Zavyra, finally getting a clear idea of the difference in size, realizing that she could swallow him whole, should she wish to, with little to no trouble at all. As he closed his eyes, he spoke to himself.

"Let's just add this to the list of things
that would immediately get me committed if I
even attempted to describe it to anyone back in
Michigan," he said before drifting off to sleep.

#####

As he slept, his dreams were more like memories. True to her word, Zavyra was watching his entire life, from birth all the way up to that point in his mind. Even through the traumatic periods of his life, he felt a peculiar calm. When his dreams reached the point up to present time, he began to wake up. When he looked over to Zavyra, she was looking back at him.

"How long was I out?" asked Jack.

"About six hours. Your pants are talking," she said.

"My what?" said Jack.

"Your trousers appear to be speaking," she said.

Jack soon realized that she was talking about the radio in his pocket.

"Wow. I can't believe I'm getting reception in here," said Jack as he pulled out the radio.

Rhandor was talking to Jack on the radio.

"Jack! Can you hear me? Are you ok?" said Rhandor.

Jack looked at Zavyra.

"I'm so sorry. I forgot I left this on. Just give me one second." Jack said.

Jack pushed the button on the radio.

"Rhandor, I'm fine. I'm here. She's lovely. Everything's good. Going radio silent."

Jack released the button and shut off the radio.

"Sorry," said Jack.

"No problem," said Zavyra, now fully familiar with Otherworld technology after joining with Jack's mind.

"So, what's the diagnosis? Why can't I control my magic?" asked Jack.

"Hmm. Let's see. Let me use some of your Otherworld technology as an analogy to try to clarify things. Since you grew up with no knowledge of magic, you were unable to truly grow into it, so for you, your magic is like a light switch. It is either off or on, so your power, which, quite surprisingly, is nearly comparable to my own, is either at no power or full power. Your body is unable to handle that binary, so when you use your magic, it takes energy from you. That's why you lose consciousness. Magic power must be slowly increased in order to use it properly. That reduces the strain on your body." she said.

"Oh. That makes sense, I think," said Jack. "So what do I

do about it?"

"I shall help you learn to control it," she said.

"What about the dark magic thing? Why does that keep happening?" asked Jack.

"That is more interesting. It appears that you are actually rejecting it. You are instinctively absorbing it, and then you are immediately rejecting it like a poison, and when you reject it, you are using your own affinity for dark magic to expel it, first purifying the tainted dark magic and then, in doing so, magnifying the power exponentially before releasing it." she said.

"Isn't rejecting it a good thing? Isn't dark magic bad?" asked Jack.

"Magic of any form is neither good nor bad if used properly. Just look at fire. It can be used to warm those who are cold. It can be used to bring a light to darkness. It can be used to cook food. Those are all good things, are they not?" she said.

"Yeah, I guess so," said Jack.

"But fire can also be used to cause immeasurable destruction. It can be used to hurt or kill. The same is true of all of the affinities of magic," she said.

"But doesn't the Dark Army use dark magic and get damaged by it?" asked Jack.

"The Dark Army uses an unnatural form of dark magic. The affinity is forced upon them, and because of that, their use of it is forced as well. It is like trying to force your hand deep into a barrel of broken glass. The more you force your hand into the broken glass, the more damage you will incur," she said.

"I see," said Jack. "Then what do they want with me?"

"Were they able to corrupt you, you would become a weapon of destruction unlike any that has been seen for millennia. Long ago, when more of my kind roamed this world, there was one Grand Elder Dragon known as Az'Drek. He became known as the Dragon of Apocalypse. He was a user of a type of dark magic, but over time he became consumed by it. Back in that time, we Grand Elder Dragons were worshiped as gods. As Az'Drek's power grew, he ruled through fear, and all who opposed him were destroyed. War was spread through continents, leaving nothing but ash. He eventually saw himself as a god above all others and even declared war on the rest of us. Many of my brothers and sisters were lost in the battle to take him down, and many millions of lives of the younger races were lost. After that, those of us who remained chose to end the time of dragon gods and went into hiding. Now we are few," she said.

Jack was left speechless by her story.

"It is rumored that the being now known as the Great Demon Emperor found Az'Drek's heart and consumed it, giving him unimaginable power but corrupting him down to his very soul," she said.

"Couldn't you and the other Grand Elder Dragons destroy him?" asked Jack.

"We are too few, and our magic is not what it used to be. The time of dragon gods is over. Should he defeat even one of us, he would only grow stronger. The risk is too great to the world. His power is strong, but not yet as strong as Az'Drek. Should another Grand Elder Dragon fall, his power may become even stronger than Az'Drek's and the world would most surely end in blood and fire," Zavyra said.

"Yeah. That would really suck," said Jack.

"Indeed," said Zavyra.

"So what can I do?" asked Jack.

"Only what you are able to do. But if we are going to discover what that is, first we need to get you to a point where you have mastery over your powers," she said.

"Sounds like a plan. So where do we start?" asked Jack.

"I shall use my ability to suppress your powers, and as you continue to train, I shall slowly reduce how much of your magic I suppress until you no longer need me to control your power," said Zavyra.

"Cool. I've never been more rested in my life, thanks to

you, so let's get this ball rolling," said Jack.

"Very well. Follow me," said Zavyra.

Jack followed her through various corridors of the mountain, eventually realizing that it wasn't a mountain but a long-dormant volcano, which explained the natural hot springs below.

#####

Over the next six days, Jack and Zavyra trained almost every hour of the day, starting with water magic, then moving onto fire, then wind, then earth, then light, and finally dark magic, taking only a few hours off to sleep each day in order to recharge. Thanks to Zavyra's magic, a few hours of sleep were all that was needed. Jack would occasionally check in with Rhandor over the radio to report his progress.

#####

On the seventh day, Jack was ready. Zavyra gave him some words of advice.

"Remember, Jack. Though you have control over your power now, you should use your full power sparingly, because it will still take its toll, especially when it comes to dark magic," she said.

"So how many times can I do that teleportation thing?" he asked.

"Very sparingly, Jack. It takes immense focus and concentration, and using it too much can drain your energy very quickly. And even the smallest mistake in your focus could result in you teleporting into a rock, a wall, the sky, or even under the ground. It is very risky magic," she said.

"I will keep that in mind. Thank you for all your help. I'll never forget it. I really don't see why everyone made that scary look whenever I mentioned your name. You've been nothing but kind. In fact, I'd even consider you a friend if you'll allow it," said Jack.

"Fear and rumors do well to keep unwanted visitors away, not to mention the dragon hunters looking to make a name for themselves, should people discover what I am. But yes, Jack. I would be honored to call you a friend," said Zavyra.

"That means a lot," said Jack.

Jack gathered his things and prepared to leave.

"I hope this isn't goodbye, so I'll just say until we meet again," said Jack.

"I have a feeling that we shall meet again," said Zavyra.

"You wouldn't happen to know an easier way back down the mountain, would you?" asked Jack.

"Since you have a handle on your magic now, why not be creative with it?" Zavyra said.

Jack thought for a moment and smiled.

"Yeah. Yeah. I think I have an idea," he said.

"Well, good luck, Jack. Until next time," said Zavyra.

"I look forward to it," said Jack before bowing, blowing her a quick kiss, and then turning to walk out the same wooden door he first entered to meet her.

#####

Jack walked back up the stairs and out the metal doorway to the ledge. He took a deep breath, closed his eyes, and when he opened them, they were glowing yellow. With a smile, he stepped off the ledge. As the path below him rapidly approached, Jack used his newly controllable wind magic to slow his descent at the last few feet, allowing him to land softly on the path. As the glow in his eyes faded, he took a quick look around before casually walking down the stairs to the gate. When he reached the gate, Jack took out the handheld radio.

"Hey, Rhandor. You on comms?" asked Jack.

"Hello, my friend," said Rhandor. "Will you be returning soon?"

"Tell the concierge that I'm waiting by the gate," said

Jack.

"Really?! We'll be right there!" said Rhandor excitedly.

A few minutes later, Rhandor and the man with the key approached the gate. The man took out the key and unlocked the gate. Jack stepped through and smiled as he gave Rhandor a hug.

"How did it go, my friend?" Rhandor asked.

"I'm new and improved, Rhandor. New and improved," said Jack happily. "Watch this."

Jack's eyes glowed a bright red. Rhandor looked concerned, given that every time he had seen that in the past, it meant that Jack was about to lose control of his magic. Jack held up his index finger on his left hand, and suddenly a small-flickering-candle-light-size flame appeared above his finger.

"How's that for control?" said Jack.

"Remarkable, Jack. Absolutely remarkable. I see that this trip was definitely not wasted," said Rhandor.

"Oh, and get this. I can use dark magic, too. And it's not that knock-off stuff that the bad guys use. I can use the real thing. I can even teleport, though I'm not supposed to do it too often," said Jack, like a kid with a new toy.

"I see," said Rhandor, with a slight degree of apprehension.

"Wanna try?" asked Jack. "I can probably cut our travel time in half, at least."

"Perhaps later," said Rhandor. "First, tell me more about your time there."

"There are some things I promised to keep secret, but what I can say is that she is incredible. She not only taught me about magic; she taught me so much about history and even psychology. She is so wise and so kind. Totally different from what I was expecting. And she is tall. I mean really tall. I'm happy to say that she is a friend," said Jack.

"I'm so glad to see that you were successful, Jack," said Rhandor.

"So, where's your floof?" asked Jack.

"I do not floof," said Rhandor.

"Sure you do," said Jack. "Free the floof, Rhandor. Free the floof."

As they walked down the hallway back to the resort area at the bottom of the mountain, Jack turned around and looked up at the top of the mountain one more time and bowed his head in thanks.

CHAPTER 22

By the time evening came, Jack and Rhandor were packed and ready to go. Rhandor wanted to wait until morning to leave, but Jack was insistent about trying out his new abilities. Eventually, he was able to convince Rhandor to allow him to try and use the teleportation magic to get them back to the town of Ackhard. It wasn't as far as Jack wanted to travel, but it would at least save them half a day's travel.

Jack told Rhandor to stand between the two dragons. He closed his eyes for a moment. When he opened them, his eyes were glowing a deep purple. A circle of purple expanded on the ground beneath the feet of Rhandor and the dragons. Jack stepped into the circle. The circle began to glow brightly before rising quickly above the heads of Jack and the dragons. For a moment their view was completely filled with the purple light.

#####

When the light faded, they found themselves standing outside the walls of Ackhard, a few hundred feet from the front gate. Rhandor began to sneeze repeatedly.

"Gesundheit," said Jack. "Okie dokey. Mental note. Teleportation makes Rhandor sneeze."

"Incredible!" said Rhandor after he finally stopped sneezing.

"I know, right?" said Jack.

"How do you feel?" asked Rhandor.

"I'm all tingly, but otherwise I feel fine," said Jack. "Let's head inside. Maybe they found something out from the dark elves that they took prisoner."

"Yes. Indeed."

Standing at the gate, he saw a familiar face.

"Marath!" said Jack.

"Sir Rhandor! Jack! Welcome back!" said Marath. "How was your journey?"

"Eventful," said Rhandor.

"Yeah. I met Zavyra. We baked cookies, played board games, and talked about our crushes as we sat by the fire in our pajamas," said Jack.

"Really?" asked Marath.

"No. I trained virtually non-stop for a week with only two hours of sleep a night, but it got the job done, and now I can use magic without giving myself brain damage or anything like that," said Jack, realizing that Marath didn't seem particularly familiar with the concept of sarcasm.

"Oh, I see," said Marath. "Please, follow me."

Jack and Rhandor entered through the gate. They handed the dragons to another soldier and followed Marath through the corridors until they reached the barracks.

"Anything to report from the Dark Army prisoners?" asked Rhandor.

"Not much to report, sir. The only thing the prisoners told us was that they were here to capture Jack and bring him back to the emperor. They claimed not to know anything else," said Marath.

"I see," said Rhandor.

"Mind if I talk to them?" asked Jack.

"You can try. But one of them died earlier today, so there's only the one left," said Marath.

"Died? How?" asked Rhandor.

"He refused to eat, but this morning he took the wooden spoon we supplied for his morning porridge and broke it into a point on his bedframe and pierced his own throat," said Marath.

Jack thought for a moment.

"Does the other one know about his death?" asked Jack.

"No. Why?" asked Marath.

"I have an idea," said Jack.

Jack looked over at Rhandor. He saw a look of confusion and concern on his face. Jack walked over and whispered his plan to him.

"I see. Interesting. A very unorthodox plan, to be sure. Do you think it will work?" asked Rhandor.

"It's worth a try," said Jack.

Jack then walked up to Marath.

"I'll need a few things and a couple of your men. One more thing. How well can you scream?" he asked Marath.

Marath's eyes went wide.

"Don't worry. I'll explain on the way," said Jack.

#####

When they arrived at the prison cells, they first placed a hood over the dead dark elf's head. Two soldiers held him up and began to carry him by the arms and walk by the other dark elf's cell. They spoke loudly so the prisoner could hear.

"It seems the human has returned and wishes to have a word with you," said one soldier.

"You may not want to talk to us. But you'll definitely talk to him," said the other soldier.

Once the dead dark elf was carried out of sight of the prisoner, he was placed down on the floor. Jack then began his performance.

"So, I hear you wanted me. You're going to tell me everything you know," he said, loudly enough for the prisoner to hear.

Marath picked up a sandbag and threw it against the wall, making a grunt sound right after it hit.

"I said talk!" yelled Jack.

Marath and Rhandor threw two more sandbags against the wall. Marath grunted after each impact.

"Don't want to talk, huh? Fine. We can do this the hard way," said Jack.

Jack stood in the empty cell and began to cast fireballs into the wall, making them bright enough to cast light on the opposite wall so the prisoner could see it.

Marath screamed, acting like he was being burned.

"No! Jack! Stop! You'll kill him!" said Rhandor.

"If he won't talk, he's not much use to me alive," said Jack.

Jack then made a large sphere of water appear and sent it cascading down the hallway in front of the prisoner's cell.

Marath poured a cup of water in his mouth and gargled it as loudly as he could, following it with hard coughs after spitting the water out.

Jack motioned for Marath, Rhandor, and the two soldiers to step up onto some wooden crates against the wall. After they were all on the crates, Jack combined wind and earth magic to kick up dust and create static electricity. The bolts of electricity arced into the water, causing the water down the hall in front of the other prisoner's cell to start sparking against his cell bars. Marath once again screamed as Rhandor shook him, making it sound like he was being electrocuted. The two soldiers that had carried the body were doing their best not to laugh at that point. After another fireball was thrown against the wall, Rhandor spoke.

"Jack! That's enough! He's dead!" he said.

Jack, Rhandor, Marath, and the others went completely silent for a few minutes. Jack then grabbed the ankle of the dead dark elf and dragged the body down the hall until it was completely in view of the other prisoner. Jack closed his eyes for a moment. When he opened them, they were glowing bright red. He released the ankle of the dead dark elf and slowly turned his head toward the other prisoner.

"Your buddy here wasn't feeling particularly talkative. That was his mistake. How about you? Are you willing to tell me everything I want to know?" Jack said in as sinister a voice as he could muster.

The dark elf prisoner was terrified. All that he did was nod vigorously. Jack's eyes returned to normal. He looked back down the hallway at the others.

"Hey, guys! This one said he'll talk!" said Jack.

The two soldiers who had dragged the body in came to the cell, unlocked it, grabbed the prisoner, and took him off to another room for interrogation. Jack walked back over to Rhandor and Marath with a big smile on his face. They began to laugh.

"Where the hell did you come up with such a crazy idea, Jack?" asked Rhandor.

"I saw something similar in a movie once, I think," said Jack.

"What's a movie?" asked Marath.

"Forget it. It's a long story," said Jack.

"There is clearly no longer any doubt that you are able to control your magic now, Jack," said Rhandor.

"Yes, but how did you make that lightning indoors?" asked Marath.

"Science, my friend. Science. I used the water magic to take all of the moisture out of that section of the cell, then I brought up the sand and wind to create friction, and that friction generated static electricity," said Jack.

"Fascinating," said Marath. "I've never seen magic affinities combined in that way before."

"Well, you did say that you wanted to see a demonstration of my magic abilities the last time I was here. I figured that I'd put on a good show," said Jack.

"A most impressive performance," said Rhandor.

"I couldn't have done it without you two. You should really consider a career in acting, Marath," said Jack.

"Perhaps, someday," said Marath. "For now, let's go see what this prisoner has to say."

#####

Over the next two hours, the prisoner told them everything he could think of. He told them not just about how the Emperor had planned to turn Jack into a weapon to destroy the Vedyrian Kingdom, but about various Dark Army outposts and surveillance operations and everything down to his childhood best friend and how he once got his head stuck in the wheel of a cart as a child and had to be taken, wheel and all, to a blacksmith in order to free his head. Eventually, Marath had to tell him to stop talking.

With the newly gathered information from the prisoner, Rhandor ordered the relevant details, minus the childhood trauma, to be reported to Lia at once through the fairy communications network so that she and the rest of the Vedyrian Army at the camp would be well prepared before Jack and Rhandor's return.

After Jack and Rhandor ate a late breakfast at the pub that they had intended to go to before being attacked the first time they were there, they got on their dragons and headed to the town of Estin. Thanks to a localized tailwind created by Jack's magic, the dragons were able to make it to Estin much sooner than before. When they arrived in Estin, Jack and Rhandor gave the dragons some time to eat and rest while they did the same, so the four of them would be able to return to the main Vedyrian Army camp early the next day.

CHAPTER 23

It was around mid-morning, and Lia found herself busy with the less glamorous or action-packed aspects of being a military commander. Supply requisition forms, field deployment rotation schedules, payroll documents, troop morale reports, and more were piled high on her desk. She had asked Alivair to review the intelligence information received from Ackhard and submit a detailed report with action plans as soon as possible. The only thing keeping her from drifting off was AC/DC's 'You Shook Me All Night Long' playing at near full volume on the music player Jack had left for her, which, as it turned out, she was not-so-quietly singing along to as she worked. Just as both Lia and Brian Johnson finished the last line of the song, a soldier opened the flap of her tent.

"Your Highness!" said the soldier.

Lia quickly pulled the earbuds out of her ears.

"Yes!" she inadvertently yelled before she cleared her throat. "Yes? What is it?"

"Two dragons, incoming," said the soldier.

Lia immediately stood up and ran out of the tent, heading toward the stables as fast as she could.

When she arrived, she was met by Bilen, Alivair, Barvan, Veris, and a number of other soldiers. They were all looking to the north. When she looked, she saw Jack and Rhandor waving from their dragons as they approached. She couldn't hide her smile when the dragons came in for a landing.

When the dragons touched down and Jack and Rhandor dismounted, there were a number of friendly hugs and handshakes welcoming them both back. When Jack looked over at Lia and saw her smile, his head was suddenly filled with questions. Should they hug? Should he give her a kiss? Did she understand the intent of the ring, or did she misinterpret it? If she did misinterpret it, would it be such a bad thing? Does she feel the same way about him that he feels about her? While his mind was completely occupied by those questions, he was awakened from his daze by the feeling of her hugging him. It was something that surprised not just Jack, but a number of others around them. Of all the things that Jack wanted to say, the only thing that came out of his mouth was one word. One syllable.

"Hi," said Jack.

"Hi," said Lia.

Jack returned the hug.

"Welcome back," said Lia.

"Thanks," said Jack.

When the embrace was over, Jack looked around and saw that there were a number of people looking at the both of them. When he looked at Rhandor, Jack saw the smirk on his face. He chose to ignore it. Jack cleared his throat and turned to Lia.

"So, did that intel help out at all?" he asked.

"Alivair is still reviewing it, but I expect it to be of great use," said Lia.

Jack looked over at Alivair and nodded. Alivair nodded in return.

"There's something else I wanted to talk to you about, actually," said Lia.

Many of the questions that were running through Jack's mind before the hug came bubbling back to the surface.

"You've been summoned by the king," said Lia.

"I've been what?" asked Jack.

"The king, my father, has heard quite a bit about what

you've done since arriving in this world. He's requested for you to appear before him so he can talk with you," said Lia.

"But I just got back," said Jack. "I have to leave you again, so soon?"

"Oh. No. I'll be joining you," said Lia.

"Wait. You will?" said Jack.

"Yes. I have also been summoned in order to make the monthly progress report and to assess new recruits. A number of my duties as commander of the army require the occasional reports to the king," said Lia.

"Oh... I see," said Jack. "So, when will we be leaving?"

"The request was for you to report to the castle as soon as you returned, but I think we can put it off for a day or so, so you have a chance to recuperate from your journey," said Lia.

"That sounds like a good plan. I could use a bit of rest," said Jack.

"Let's walk, then. Tell me more about your trip on the way to your tent," said Lia.

#####

As they walked, Jack told Lia about all that he and Rhandor had gone through on the way to see Zavyra. When they got to the subject of Zavyra, Jack wasn't sure how much he was allowed to reveal.

"She... wasn't what I expected," said Jack.

"How so?" asked Lia.

"The way everyone reacted when I mentioned her name made her sound like there was a fifty-fifty chance she was some evil witch who was going to turn me into a frog and fry my legs up and eat them with a side of zucchini. She wasn't like that at all," said Jack.

"And I imagine the fact that no one told you that she's a Grand Elder Dragon gave you quite the shock when you met her, too," said Lia.

"Yeah! I know! I walked in there and..." Jack stopped

walking. "Wait. You knew?!"

"Of course. It's a secret kept by the royal families. We're the only ones who are really able to submit people to see her without her getting upset. It's a deal that has been passed down through royal families for generations," said Lia.

"And you kept that part out when you sent me there... Why?" asked Jack.

"It's part of the deal," said Lia.

"I see," said Jack, trying to ignore the grin she had on her face as she said the last part.

"Well, at least I won't have to hide anything from you. That was the part that was bothering me the most," said Jack.

Lia was a bit surprised by the bluntness of Jack's statement and wasn't sure how to respond. Jack noticed and tried to change the subject.

"So, anyway, did you find the music player?" asked Jack.

"Yes. Though, I have to ask, do you really find me to be so predictable?" she said.

"I figured it was about a fifty-fifty chance that it would be you or Crescia who found the first note under my pillow. I doubt anyone else would have a reason to go into my tent," said Jack.

Lia thought for a moment.

"Yes. I guess that kind of makes sense," she said.

"Did you find any songs that you liked?" Jack asked.

"Yes! I'm quite fond of the one about living on a prayer, and there's one song called 'Ironic' that lists a collection of unfortunate circumstances, but none of them are actually ironic. It's fascinating. Perhaps that, in and of itself, is where the true irony lies," said Lia.

"I guess that's one way to look at it," said Jack.

As they continued walking, Jack looked over and noticed that Lia was starting to shake and tears were starting to fall down her cheeks. She started to hyperventilate.

"Jack, something's wrong," she said.

Jack took her hand, and they began to walk faster.

"I know what's happening. Come with me," said Jack.

When they got to Jack's tent, Jack had Lia sit on the bed.

"What's happening?" asked Lia as she continued to shake.

"You're having what I used to call a 'hard reset.' It happened to me a number of times after a mission in the Rangers. The stress of the war is one thing, but any feelings between us aside, you had the added stress of the Dark Army looking to capture me and turn me into a weapon of mass destruction. That kept you in a hyper-vigilant state. This is just your body getting rid of all those pent-up stress hormones now that one major stressor is gone. Here. Just put this pillow to your face and scream as loud as you can into it. It will help."

Lia did as Jack advised and screamed into his pillow. When she was done, she looked at Jack.

"Why did I have to scream into the pillow?" she asked.

"You're not hyperventilating anymore. Are you?" said Jack.

Lia realized that her breathing had returned to a more normal rate.

"The tears are just expelling all of those pent-up stress hormones and adrenaline. When you're done, you're going to feel exhausted. Lie down. Take a nap for an hour. Trust me. I've been through it enough to know. You'll feel much better afterward," said Jack.

Lia stretched out and rested her head on the pillow. She closed her eyes. Jack walked over to the small bowl on the desk. He used a bit of water magic to make some cool water, placed the facecloth next to the bowl into the water, squeezed much of the water out of the cloth, folded it and placed it over Lia's closed eyes.

"That feels nice," said Lia.

"Take a nap. I'll wake you up in about an hour," said

Jack.

#####

Over the course of the next hour, Lia slept. Jack stood outside the tent. Over that time, a few people came looking for Lia for one reason or another. Jack simply told them that she was in the middle of something important and that he would pass the information on to her when she was done. Once the hour passed, Jack walked up to the bed and gave Lia's shoulders a few gentle taps. She removed the facecloth and opened her eyes.

"Feel better?" asked Jack.

"Yes. Much, thank you," said Lia.

Jack relayed the messages he had acquired while she slept. She got off the bed and stood up.

"Weren't you the one who needed some rest?" she asked.

"Yeah, but you clearly needed it more than I did. An army needs their commander in good shape a lot more than they need some weirdo from another world who can do a few tricks," said Jack.

"Didn't you say that you were a commander in your army?" asked Lia.

"Yeah, but there was a lot less magic... and pointy ears... and fur... on the soldiers that were under my command... except this one guy. His name was Dan. We used to call him Shaggy," said Jack.

Lia started straightening her uniform. Jack noticed that her hair was somewhat disheveled, so he reached out and straightened it a bit. Lia looked at him.

"You have, uh, pillow hair," said Jack.

"Oh. I see," said Lia as she looked in the mirror and straightened her hair.

Jack walked over to the opening of the tent.

"You're not a weirdo, Jack," she said.

"What?" asked Jack.

"A moment ago, you called yourself a weirdo from another world. You're not a weirdo. You're a quite capable and honorable man, and I'm truly glad that we met," said Lia.

"Me, too," said Jack.

Just as Jack walked out of his tent, he was met by Alivair.

"Ah, yes, Jack. Have you seen Her Highness?" asked Alivair.

"Yeah. She's right behind me," said Jack, opening the flap further to reveal Lia in the tent.

Alivair looked into the tent and saw Lia straightening herself up in the mirror. He looked over at the bed and noticed that the sheets were a bit disturbed. Jack noticed the change in his expression.

"Oh! Um, it's not what you think," said Jack.

"I see," said Alivair.

Jack turned to Lia.

"I'm going to go talk to Rhandor and see if he needs any help with, uh, his after-action report. Yeah," said Jack.

"Ok, Jack," said Lia, before turning to see Alivair. "Hello, Captain. What can I do for you?"

Jack headed off to see Rhandor as Alivair stepped a bit further into the tent.

"Your Highness, I have reviewed the documents from Ackhard. I'm ready to submit my report," said Alivair.

"Very well, Captain. Let us discuss it on the way to my tent," said Lia.

Lia and Alivair left Jack's tent and made their way to hers.

Jack made his way over to Rhandor's tent in the Mage Corps section of the camp. When he arrived, Rhandor was just stepping out.

"Ah! Hello, my friend!" said Rhandor.

"Hi, Rhandor. Getting settled back in?" asked Jack.

"Yes. And how about you, Jack? Did Her Highness welcome you back?" asked Rhandor, in a suggestive tone.

"Yeah, but not like that," said Jack. "I'm taking things slow. I want to make sure that this isn't a suspension bridge effect kind of thing."

"I don't understand that reference," said Rhandor.

"Oh, yeah. Of course. It's based on an experiment that some scientists did forty-something years ago where they had a number of guys cross two bridges. One bridge was sturdy. The other one was a suspension bridge. Guys cross the bridges, and they meet a woman on the other end. The sturdy bridge doesn't cause any sort of fear or stress, but the suspension bridge is very shaky, so it causes significant anxiety, or fear or stress. The study showed that the guys who crossed the shaky bridge had a greater sexual or romantic attraction to the woman at the end of the bridge than the guys who crossed the stable one. The theory is that the guys who crossed the shaky bridge misattributed their fear- or anxiety-induced arousal from crossing the bridge for sexual arousal for the woman standing at the end of it. And it's not to say that the woman wasn't attractive. Just that the fear or anxiety made her seem even more attractive at the time," said Jack.

"That's very complicated. But I think I understand. You're trying to see if it is a fire that continues to burn as opposed to one that flashes brightly and then is gone when the smoke clears," said Rhandor.

"Yeah. Basically," said Jack.

"A quite reasonable approach. I do hope that it works out in your favor," said Rhandor.

"Yeah. Me, too," said Jack.

"So I hear that you've been summoned by the king," said Rhandor.

"You know, in all the excitement, I kind of forgot to ask about the details of that," said Jack.

"Do you think it has anything to do with the ring?" asked Rhandor.

"I hadn't thought about that. Lia said something about the king hearing reports of some of the stuff I've done since I came here. I don't know if that includes inadvertently proposing to his only daughter or what method of torture he'll order for me if he doesn't approve," said Jack.

"Should be an interesting trip," said Rhandor.

"Yeah. Speaking of anxiety and fear. I guess I'll cross that bridge, suspension or otherwise, when I come to it," said Jack.

Rhandor chuckled.

"Have you ever been summoned?" asked Jack.

"Once. When I was knighted," said Rhandor.

"Anything I should expect?" Jack asked.

"Protocol. Lots and lots of protocol. I'm sure Her Highness will advise you on the way," said Rhandor.

"Good to know," said Jack.

#####

Back in Lia's tent, Alivair was finishing his briefing.

"If the information we received is correct, I believe that we should be sending out units here and here in order to intercept the Dark Army movements," said Alivair, indicating positions on the map on Lia's desk.

"Very well, Captain. I'll leave command of this operation to you, as Jack and I will soon be heading to the castle," said Lia.

"Ah, yes," said Alivair. "Do you know the reason for the summons? Does His Majesty intend to officially recruit Jack into the army? Perhaps give him his own command?"

"I don't know. The royal summons didn't specify the reason. Only the request that we both appear," said Lia.

"Do you think it has anything to do with...," Alivair gestured to the ring on the necklace, still around Lia's neck.

Lia reached down reflexively to the ring.

"I have not spoken of such things in my reports, Alivair, and I trust that you have made no mention of it, either," said Lia.

"Of course not, Your Highness. But we were not the only ones there when Jack gave it to you. Soldiers write home to their families. It would not be impossible for rumors to start and make their way to the castle," Alivair said.

"No. You're right. It wouldn't," said Lia. "But that is a worry for tomorrow. Today, we shall focus on seeing that you have every resource necessary for these upcoming battles."

"Yes, Your Highness," said Alivair.

#####

As Jack was walking back to his tent, he heard someone in the distance calling his name. He looked around to see who it was, but it wasn't until she was mid-air, flying right at him, that he realized it was Crescia. He tried his best to catch her, and they both tumbled to the ground.

"Hi," said Crescia, laying on top of Jack, hugging him.

"Hello, Crescia," said Jack, after regaining his breath.

"How was your trip?" asked Crescia, still hugging him on the ground.

"Not bad," said Jack, still lying on the ground.

"That's good," said Crescia.

"Um, Crescia?" said Jack.

"Yes, Jack?" said Crescia.

"I'd like to stand up, please," said Jack.

"Ok," said Crescia.

Crescia released Jack from her death-grip of a hug and stood up. Jack did so soon afterward.

"Missed me, huh?" Jack asked.

"What makes you say that?" asked Crescia.

"Just got that impression. And I don't mean the one I just left in the ground behind me," said Jack.

"Did you miss me?" asked Crescia.

"Of course I did," said Jack. "You were the first friendly face I saw after waking up here."

"Good," said Crescia. "I'm happy you're back."

"Yeah, but I'm leaving again tomorrow. Apparently I have to report to the castle," said Jack.

"Yep. But this time, I'm coming with you," said Crescia.

"You are?" asked Jack.

"Of course. I'm Her Highness's attendant," she said. "What's the matter? Were you hoping to get all lovey-dovey with Her Highness on the trip?"

"No! Maybe. I don't know. Stop confusing me," said Jack.

"Don't worry. Just give me a signal, and I'll hop out of the carriage and sit with coachman," she said.

"Wait. Carriage? We're not taking dragons?" asked Jack.

"Nope. When summoned by the castle, they send a royal carriage. That's how it works," said Crescia.

"That's cool. I've never been in a royal carriage before. Though, to be fair, I've never been summoned to a castle by a monarch, either," said Jack.

"In the meantime, Her Highness has summoned you to her tent this evening for dinner," said Crescia.

"I see. Well, please inform Her Highness that I will be honored to attend and shall arrive promptly at her request," said Jack, trying to sound official.

Crescia decided to play along.

"As you wish, my lord. I shall relay your message at once," she said as she curtsied.

Crescia turned and ran back to Lia's tent, and Jack strolled back to his.

#####

That evening, Jack arrived at Lia's tent just as Crescia exited to summon him.

"Oh! You're here!" said Crescia. "Please, come in."

Jack entered the tent and greeted Lia.

"Hi," said Jack.

"Hello, Jack. Please, sit," said Lia.

Jack sat at the table, and Lia poured some wine for him and herself.

"So, I read Rhandor's report," said Lia.

"Oh?" said Jack. "And?"

"You used the sword I gave you, the sword that I had placed my very own fire magic into, to light a campfire and cook some fish, huh?" Lia said with a smirk.

Jack's eyes went wide.

"He put that in his report?" asked Jack.

"He did," said Lia.

"You wouldn't object if I shaved him bald in his sleep, would you?" asked Jack.

"Of course I would. He's a loyal knight in my army. At most, maybe a slight haircut," said Lia with a smile. "And no changing the subject."

"Ok, yes. And it was quite helpful. And the fish was delicious. But I used it against bad guys, too! I swear!" said Jack.

"Well then. You're forgiven," said Lia.

"Thank you. So, is there anything else you can tell me about this royal summons thing? I'm not in trouble or anything, am I?" asked Jack.

"No. I don't think so. There weren't too many details included in the royal summons, but I doubt very much that you're in trouble. I think my father just wants to see what kind of man you are. He's always been a bit skeptical about humans, so I'm not sure what sort of welcome you'll be getting, though," said Lia.

"Is there anything special I need to know? Rules and behaviors and such?" asked Jack.

"Of course, but we'll have more than enough time to go over them on the way," said Lia.

"Yeah. About that. Crescia mentioned something about a carriage," said Jack.

"Yes. It's part of the protocol for royal summons. It takes a little longer than dragons, but that's how it's always been done," said Lia.

"At least, that way, we can talk without having to yell between dragons," said Jack.

"Yes. Though Rhandor mentioned that you have a device from your world that allows for communication across far distances," Lia said.

"You mean the radios? Yeah. I have a few more in my bag. Would you like one?" asked Jack.

"Yes, please. From what I read in Rhandor's report, they sound like quite fascinating devices. Much like this music player," said Lia as she held up the player. "How does it work? Fairy magic allows us to store brief messages onto crystals, but this device appears to store countless hours."

"No magic in that device. Just modern technology from my world. Speaking of which..." Jack said as he reached into his pocket and pulled out a cell phone. "I've been charging this with my solar power bank in my tent forever. It's finally fully charged up."

"I'm not sure I understood even half of what you just said. What does that device do?" asked Lia.

"It's kind of a multipurpose device. It's used for communication, but I don't think that feature works here. But the reason I wanted to take it out is for this." Jack said as he turned on the camera app and took a picture of Lia. He turned the phone around and showed Lia the picture.

"Incredible! It's like you've captured a moment in time inside this little device!" said Lia.

Jack thought for a moment and realized that, in a roundabout way, that's basically what a photo is.

"It can record video, too," said Jack. He aimed the cell phone at her and pressed the 'record' button. "Say hello!"

"Um, very well. Hello," said Lia.

Jack hit the 'stop' button and showed the video to Lia.

"Your world must be filled with amazing technology,

Jack. I wish I could see it," said Lia.

"Perhaps you will, one of these days," said Jack.

As the dinner went on, they continued to talk. Jack told Lia all about his time with Rhandor during the journey and his time training with Zavyra. When Crescia came in to serve the main dishes, Jack showed her the camera app as well, and took a number of pictures of and with the two of them. When the meal was over, Jack and Lia both stood up. As they both slowly walked toward the tent opening, Jack stopped and took Lia's hands.

"I missed this. I'm glad we're able to do it again," he said.

"Me, too," said Lia.

Jack placed his hand against Lia's cheek and leaned in and kissed her. When their lips parted, Jack smiled.

"If we'll be leaving in the morning, I should probably go back to my tent and get some sleep," he said.

Just as he turned to leave, Lia stopped him.

"You know, you could always just sleep here," she said.

Jack's eyes grew wide with the surprise of her statement. He turned and looked at her.

"It's a big bed," she said.

"Are you sure?" asked Jack.

"Yes, see? It's right over there," Lia said, pointing at the bed with a grin.

Jack chuckled.

"You know what I mean," he said.

"Well, I wouldn't have suggested it, otherwise," Lia said.

"Ok," Jack said with a smile.

"Make sure to secure the straps on the tent flaps," she said, pointing to the several leather straps and buckles attached to the inner flap.

"Yes, ma'am," said Jack, giving her a quick, playful salute before securing the straps.

When he was done, he walked back over to Lia and

kissed her again. Then they made their way to the bed.

CHAPTER 24

The next morning, when Jack opened his eyes, it took a few seconds for him to recognize that he wasn't in his own tent. He looked to his left and saw that he was in the bed alone. He looked to his right and saw Crescia standing a few feet away, in front of a folding screen. She looked over at Jack and smirked.

"Jack," said Crescia.

"Crescia," said Jack.

"Sleep well?" asked Crescia.

"Yes, thank you," said Jack.

Jack heard Lia's voice from behind the folding screen.

"Jack? Are you awake? Crescia, give him the clothes," said Lia.

"Yes, Your Highness," said Crescia, before walking over to Jack and placing a wrapped bundle at the end of the bed, by Jack's feet.

Jack looked over to his clothes folded over the back of the chair near Lia's desk and then to the bundle at his feet.

"What clothes are these?" asked Jack.

"You don't expect to gain audience with the king in those clothes, do you?" said Crescia, pointing to the clothes on the chair.

"No. I guess not," said Jack, though he hadn't actually given it much thought.

Jack unwrapped the bundle at his feet. The outfit consisted of black pants, a white silk shirt with a tall banded collar, a black and gray vest with silver coin-shaped buttons, a three-quarter-length jacket with buttons down the left and right sides of the chest starting near the shoulders, fastening along the right side down to the waist, silver epaulets and a banded collar with a v-shaped gap in the front, a large belt with clips to attach a sword and a near ankle-length black cloak with an ornate clasp and a crimson lining. He got dressed.

"Don't forget the boots!" said Lia from behind the screen. "You can't wear your usual boots, Jack! You have to wear the ones Crescia brought for you!"

"Ok! Ok! I'll wear the boots," said Jack.

Jack sat down on the bed and put the boots on.

"I feel like I'm about to lead a marching band into combat," he said to himself.

"Did you say something, Jack?" asked Lia.

"Nothing!" said Jack. "This outfit isn't exactly something I'm used to. That's all."

"Let me see," said Lia, as she poked her head out from behind the screen.

Jack stood up and turned completely around.

"Put the cloak on, too," said Lia.

Jack put the cloak on and fastened the clasp.

"Now, let me see," said Lia, once again.

Jack turned to her again.

"I think you look very handsome, Jack," she said.

"Yes. Very cool. Did I use that word right?" said Crescia.

"Yes, you did," said Jack. "And thank you."

"Your hair, though," said Lia as she stepped out from behind the screen.

"Wow." Jack said almost reflexively upon seeing Lia in her elaborate dress.

It looked every bit as much like a dress you would expect to see a princess wear to appear at a fantasy castle. The purple and burgundy dress included finely embroidered gold patterns in the bodice. She was also wearing a black cloak with a purple lining and gold trim. Lia walked up to Jack and began to adjust his hair.

"You have pillow hair," she said as she ran her fingers through his hair.

"You look incredible," said Jack. "Actually, incredible doesn't even begin to describe it. Just... wow."

"Thank you, Jack," said Lia.

Alivair's voice could be heard from outside the tent.

"Your Highness. The carriage should be arriving shortly," said Alivair.

Lia walked over to the flaps of the tent and opened one of them to greet Alivair.

"We're almost ready, Alivair. We'll be out shortly." she said.

Alivair looked into the tent, expecting "we" to be Lia and Crescia. What he saw was Crescia and, over by the bed, Jack. He waited a moment for Jack to make the same statement he had made when Lia came walking out of his tent the day before, but all Jack did was smile and shrug his shoulders, all but confirming that it was what he likely thought it was.

"Morning, Alivair!" said Jack, as he gave a quick little wave.

"Yes. Good morning, Jack," said Alivair.

Jack walked up to Alivair.

"So, what do you think? How do I look?" asked Jack, trying to move beyond the uncomfortable air that was starting to form in the tent.

"You look quite ready for a meeting with the king. My compliments to Crescia for the excellent tailor work," said Alivair.

"Aww, thanks, Captain Alivair. Let me know if you ever need anything," said Crescia.

"I shall sincerely consider it," said Alivair.

"No comments on me, Captain?" said Lia, as she raised her eyebrow and smirked.

"Looking radiant, as always, Your Highness," said Alivair.

"Thank you, Captain," said Lia.

"The carriage should be arriving near the Mage Corps area of the camp, Your Highness. It should be here within the hour," said Alivair.

"Very well. We will be there shortly," said Lia.

"I shall wait outside to escort the three of you to the pick-up location," said Alivair.

"Thanks, Alivair," said Jack.

"You should probably go and retrieve your bag from your tent, Jack," said Lia.

"No need. I got it," said Crescia. "It's right outside. Sword's there, too."

"Have I told you how awesome you are, Crescia?" asked Jack.

"Yes, but I'm not opposed to hearing it again," said Crescia.

"Done. You're awesome," said Jack, giving her two thumbs up.

Crescia smiled.

Lia turned to Crescia and Jack.

"Shall we?" she said.

Jack and Crescia nodded and the three of them left the tent. Jack grabbed his bag and the sword on the way out.

The three of them, escorted by Alivair, headed toward the pick-up location for the carriage. When they arrived, Rhandor and Bilen were waiting. They both bowed as Lia approached.

"Your Highness," they both said as they bowed.

When they stood back up, Rhandor looked over to Jack.

"Looking very regal, my friend," he said.

"Thanks, Rhandor. I feel a little weird in this getup," said Jack.

"Well, it suits you," said Rhandor.

They continued to engage in idle small talk for a few minutes before the carriage appeared in the distance.

"Crap," said Jack as he looked at the carriage. "Are those

what I think they are?" he asked.

"What are you talking about, Jack?" asked Lia.

"The animals pulling the carriage," said Jack.

"What do you think they are?" asked Lia.

The animals that Jack saw pulling the carriage looked very much like horses, but with one unique feature. Located near the top of the animal's heads was a singular, slightly curved horn, similar in length and shape to the horns of a Tibetan antelope.

"Are those unicorns?" asked Jack.

"Yes. Do you not have those where you come from?" asked Lia.

"No. They're considered mythical creatures where I come from. And now I owe my former executive officer's kid sister fifty dollars. She bet me that unicorns were real, and I bet against her," said Jack.

"Well, I guess that was a foolish move on your part," said Lia. "She sounds like a smart child."

"Yeah. Fifty bucks smarter," said Jack as he pulled out his cell phone and took a picture.

Before the carriage reached the group, Jack took a few more pictures, as well as a few of Rhandor and Alivair. Just before the carriage came to a stop, Jack turned to Rhandor.

"Do you still have the radio?" he asked.

"Yes. It's in my tent," said Rhandor.

"Good. Hold onto it," said Jack before reaching in his bag and pulling out the other radio.

Jack handed it to Alivair.

"Have Rhandor explain how this works. It should help the both of you out in the field. And be sure to make good use of the nocs, too," said Jack.

"Nocs?" asked Alivair.

"Sorry. That's just slang for binoculars. Use them as much as you can. See the threats coming long before they see you. Stay safe out there, Alivair. I mean it," said Jack.

"Thank you, Jack. I shall make good use of both

devices," said Alivair.

Jack turned to Rhandor.

"Remember to watch your six, and his," he said to Rhandor.

"Indeed. I shall," said Rhandor.

Alivair looked confused by what Jack said.

"Don't worry. He'll fill you in," said Jack to Alivair.

The coachman stepped off of the carriage and opened the door. Jack rushed over and offered his hand as Lia stepped up into the carriage.

"Thank you," said Lia.

Jack shook Alivair and Rhandor's hands and gave a quick nod to Bilen before getting into the carriage. He popped his head out of the window.

"If I come back about a foot shorter and in two pieces, you'll know that I messed up somewhere," said Jack. "Wish me luck."

The carriage did a quick loop to turn around, and the long ride to the castle began.

#####

Jack sat next to Lia, and Crescia sat in the seat across from them. As they rolled along, Lia began to instruct Jack on some of the protocols he'd have to learn before appearing before the king and queen.

"When you are announced, you need to take a few steps into the room and then bow. When you bow, make your right hand into a fist and place it against your heart. Wait for my father to tell you to rise. When you speak to him, you should address him as 'Your Majesty,' and my mother should be addressed as 'Your Royal Highness' unless they say otherwise. My father has an uncanny ability to tell when someone is lying, so if he asks you a question, answer as honestly as you can. There will probably also be a number of nobles in and around the castle, so don't be surprised if some of them approach you. There's a lot of ceremony and theater involved, but as long as you don't blow anything up or burn anything down, you should be fine." she said with a grin.

"No blowing up or burning down the castle. Check," said Jack.

Whenever Lia took a few moments to look out the window, Jack noticed that she was fidgeting with something beneath the collar of her dress.

"Is it uncomfortable?" asked Jack.

"What?" asked Lia, as her attention went from the view back to Jack.

"You're fidgeting with something by your collar. Is the dress uncomfortable?" asked Jack.

Lia looked down at her left hand and saw where it was. She didn't even realize that she was fidgeting. It was just something done subconsciously out of habit. She reached into her collar and pulled out the necklace with the ring on it.

"Oh. You're still wearing it, huh?" said Jack.

"Yes. It has brought me good luck. Just as you said it would," said Lia.

"I'm happy to hear that," said Jack.

Jack looked over at Crescia. She winked at him and smiled because she had a feeling about the direction of Jack's line of questioning.

"So... On the trip to see Zavyra, I was talking to Rhandor, and he told me something about... um... the... uh... significance of... the ring," said Jack, slowly forcing the sentence out as delicately as he could.

Crescia started getting a little giddy. Lia found Jack's struggling to be a bit entertaining, so she decided to play along and see where he was going.

"Oh? He did?" said Lia.

"Yeah," said Jack.

"And what did he say?" said Lia.

"He... um... he said that... uh... in this world... presenting a family ring to a woman with whom you're...

involved... is sort of an official thing," said Jack.

"What kind of official thing?" asked Lia, trying to hold back her grin.

"Like a... like a proposal," said Jack.

"What kind of proposal?" asked Lia.

Crescia started to giggle.

"You know, like a... like a... marriage proposal," said Jack.

"I see. And?" said Lia.

"Oh. Um... Well... I was just... wondering what... your thoughts were... on the subject," said Jack.

"On the ring?" asked Lia.

"Sure," said Jack.

"It's a very nice ring," said Lia.

By that point, Jack was visibly starting to sweat.

"Is it warm in here? How do you open these windows?" said Jack, so flustered at that point that he probably wouldn't have been able to figure out how a light switch worked. Lia figured she had enough fun teasing him.

"Take a deep breath, Jack. What are you trying to say?" she said.

Jack took a deep breath and slowly let it out.

"Look. I know that I'm just some human Otherworlder and there's a whole lot of stuff about you and about this world that I don't know yet. I'm probably going to make a lot of mistakes. But would it be such a bad thing?" said Jack, trying his best to collect his thoughts.

Lia was a bit surprised at the direction the conversation was headed. Crescia was practically bug-eyed at that point.

"Jack, are you asking what I think you're asking?" said Lia.

"If I were, what would you say?" said Jack.

This time, it was Lia who was getting flustered. She figured that she would tease him a bit, but she didn't expect him to come right out and ask. She thought about it for a moment. She did have strong feelings for Jack, even though she had only known him for a fairly brief time. As often as she thought about him when he was gone, it would be fair to call her feelings for him love.

"I'd say yes," she said, after what felt like an eternity of silence.

"Oh, thank god. If you'd said no, it would have made for a really awkward carriage ride," said Jack, before fully processing her answer. After a few seconds, it sunk in.

"Wait. Did you say yes?" said Jack.

"She sure did," said Crescia.

Both Jack and Lia looked at Crescia.

"You both forgot I was here for a second, didn't you?" said Crescia.

After a moment of awkward silence, Lia began to laugh. Then Jack started, and Crescia followed. After laughing for a good few minutes, they all caught their breath and wiped away some tears before realizing that the tension was now gone.

"So we're engaged now, huh?" asked Jack.

"It seems we are," said Lia.

"Rhandor's gonna freak out when he finds out. I kind of want to see it when it happens," said Jack.

"I think it would be quite entertaining," said Lia.

#####

Over the next few hours, they all chatted, laughed, and shared stories. Jack reached into his bag and pulled out the solar-powered power bank.

"Did you bring the music player with you?" he asked Lia.

"Yes. It's right here," said Lia, taking it out of her bag.

"Give it to me and I'll recharge it," he said.

She handed him the music player, and he connected it to the power bank.

"That's a curious device. How does it work?" asked Lia.

Jack unfolded the solar panels connected to the power

bank.

"These panels take the light from the sun and convert it into energy. It stores that energy in this device, which can then be used to transfer energy to other devices that need energy to function," said Jack.

"It used sunlight to power your otherworld devices? That seems very much like magic to me," said Lia.

"It kind of does, doesn't it?" said Jack. "There's this quote by a very well-known author where I come from that says, 'Any sufficiently advanced technology is indistinguishable from magic,' or something to that effect. I guess, in a way, that's true. There may be a scientific explanation for the magic we're able to use here, but I couldn't even begin to guess what it is, so magic is the most fitting way to describe it."

The carriage suddenly came to a stop.

"Are we already there?" asked Jack.

"No. We're still a good ways away," said Lia.

Crescia opened the slider in the wall behind her to talk to the coachman.

"What's going on?" she asked.

"Bandits," said the coachman.

Jack turned to Lia.

"Bandits? Really? In a kingdom with such powerful magic users, you still have bandits?" he said.

"Of course. Where there are large groups of people, there will always be some degree of crime," she said.

"What should we do?" asked Jack. "Do you want me to do something about them?"

"Can I?" said Crescia to Lia.

"Any ideas?" Lia asked.

Jack thought for a moment and then smiled.

"Oh! I have a great idea. Crescia, come here," said Jack, gesturing for Crescia to lean in close.

Jack began to whisper in Crescia's ear. She nodded a few times as he whispered and occasionally let out a brief chuckle.

Jack and Crescia both looked at Lia.

"With your permission?" said Jack.

"You seem to have some sort of plan, so be my guest," said Lia, smiling after watching the two of them plotting something.

Crescia opened the window on the opposite side of the carriage from the door and quickly jumped out. Just then, from the door side of the carriage, a voice could be heard from one of the bandits outside.

"Come out of there with your valuables, and maybe we'll let you walk away with your lives," he said.

"Stay here. This should be fun," said Jack as he stood up and opened the door, stepped outside, and closed the door behind him. Lia slid the shade on the window to the side just enough to see outside.

When Jack looked around, he saw sixteen bandits consisting of a number of elves and various races of beastfolk. They were carrying a number of different weapons, including clubs, axes, and knives. Their leader stood in front of the group.

"Hi," said Jack.

"Did you hear what I said? Hand over your valuables, now," said the bandit leader.

"Yeah, I don't think I want to do that, though," said Jack.

"You have no choice in the matter," said the bandit leader.

"Well, we all have choices. For example, you chose to leave your house this morning with that stuff on your face," said Jack.

The bandit leader began to rub his face.

"What stuff? There's no stuff on my face. What are you talking about?" said the bandit leader.

"Oh, sorry. My bad. That's just your face. You should really get that looked at," said Jack.

"Who the hell do you think you are, human?" said the bandit leader.

"Oh, excuse me. Where are my manners? Hi. I'm Jack,"

he said.

"Well, Jack. If you don't want to spend the last moments of your life trying to gather your insides and put them back in your belly, you'll do what we tell you," said the bandit leader.

"Nope," said Jack.

"What?" said the bandit leader.

"I said no. I don't wanna," said Jack.

"Do you want to die?" asked the bandit leader.

"Nope," said Jack.

"Then what makes you think you can do anything to stop us?" asked the bandit leader.

"Nothing," said Jack. "Because I'm the... uh... what's the word?"

Jack turned toward the carriage.

"Hey, Lia! What am I again?" he asked.

"Cocky?" said Lia from inside the carriage.

"No. That's not it," said Jack.

"Are you protecting your woman inside the carriage?" said the bandit leader.

"No, of course not. She could easily kick all of your asses. It would just be a real shame to dirty the lovely dress she has on. Now, do you mind? We're talking," said Jack before turning back to Lia.

"Sexy?" said Lia.

"Hold on. I'll check," said Jack before turning toward the bandit leader again. "Do you think I'm sexy?"

The bandit leader looked like he was starting to get angry. Jack turned back to the carriage.

"No, I don't think that's it, either," said Jack. "Hold on. Let me ask him."

Jack turned to the bandit leader again.

"What's that word that means a person or thing that takes one's attention away from something that they're supposed to be paying attention to?" asked Jack.

"The word you're looking for is 'distraction,'" said the

bandit leader.

"Yep! That's the word. I'm the distraction!" said Jack with a big smile.

"Very funny. Kill him," said the bandit leader.

The other bandits didn't react.

"I said kill him!" said the bandit leader.

The bandit leader turned around to see why his men weren't doing what he told them to do. What he saw when he turned around was all of his men on the ground. He looked down just in time to see Crescia, crouched down, ready to jump. In a fraction of a second, Crescia shot straight up, kneeing the bandit leader in the chin on her way up with all the force she could hit him with. He crumbled to the ground like a house of cards in the middle of an earthquake. She landed on her feet and held her arms out.

"Ta-da!" she said.

Jack gave her two thumbs up.

"Nice!" he said.

"You wouldn't happen to have any rope in that bag of yours, would you?" Crescia asked.

"As a matter of fact, I do!" said Jack.

Crescia and the coachman tied the surviving bandits to a nearby tree, and then they and Jack returned to the coach.

"That was quite impressive," said Lia.

"Yeah. She's a furry little bad-ass, huh?" said Jack, giving Crescia a fist bump.

"What gave you the idea?" asked Lia.

"Well, in all the time I've known Crescia, I've never actually heard her coming. She walks silently. And the other day, when she tackled me like a linebacker to welcome me back, I figured that she could also move fast and with great force. And it's not like she carries those daggers for show, either. I figured that if she was your attendant, it would make sense that she could hold her own in a fight, and I was right," said Jack.

Crescia had a big grin on her face.

"That was fun," she said.

"Yeah. It was. And I didn't even get my outfit dirty," said Jack. "Shall we continue onward?"

"Yes," said Lia with a smile.

Crescia gave a few knocks on the sliding hatch on the wall behind her.

"Onward! To the castle!" she said to the coachman.

"Right away!" said the coachman as he started the carriage moving again.

"We'll inform the guards at the next town about the location of the bandits," said Lia.

Jack turned a bit in his seat to better face Lia.

"So, you think I'm sexy?" he said with a grin.

"You have your moments," said Lia.

They continued the long carriage ride toward the castle.

CHAPTER 25

As the capital city came into sight, Jack's nervousness started to become apparent. He began tapping his index finger rapidly against his knee. Not only was he about to meet the monarchs of a vast kingdom, bu he was also about to meet the parents of the woman sitting next to him that he happened to almost spontaneously propose to on the way. That's enough to make any guy nervous. A part of him felt the same way he did in school when he was called to the principal's office or when he was called to report in front of a colonel or general during his time as an Army Ranger. The capital city was immense. Races of every sort were busily going about their day, with some of them stopping and waving as the carriage made its way through the smooth, stone-paved streets. Jack thought for a moment and turned to Lia.

"About the engagement, is that something we should hold off on bringing up for now? I wouldn't want to wind up in the dungeon or something because your father didn't approve," he said.

"I wouldn't worry, Jack," said Lia.

"Ok," said Jack, before turning and looking back out the window.

The nervous tapping continued for a few more minutes before Lia finally placed her hand on top of his. She closed her fingers in between his and squeezed gently.

"It's ok, Jack. You don't have to be so tense," she said.

"Yeah, I know. I've just never been very good with formal stuff like this. Give me a weapon and point me in the direction of the enemy, and I'm fine. But put me in a fancy outfit and ask me to attend some sort of formal event, and it takes all I have not to turn and run away," said Jack.

"I've never been one for all of this, either. As a girl, I used to literally run and hide when formal events came around. My father once sent half the palace guard to find me," said Lia.

"That must have gone over well," said Jack.

"Yes. The captain of the guard found me hiding in the kitchen. He carried me back to my father on his shoulder," said Lia.

Jack chuckled at the thought of her as a child being carried around the castle.

"Oh, that reminds me. Don't be too surprised when you see the current captain of the guard. As an orc, Nadi can be pretty intimidating on first meeting her, but once you get to know her, she's really quite friendly," Lia said.

"I'll keep that in mind," said Jack, thinking back to the orcs that he saw back at the camp. The shortest one he saw there was still at least seven feet tall, if not a little taller. Given their size and strength, it came as no surprise to Jack that one would be a captain of the castle guards.

#####

Jack was in awe as the castle came into full view. As they approached the front gate, Jack could hear the rattling of the chains that operated the pulleys that opened the colossal wooden gate doors. Guards in mirror-shined steel and brass armor posted at each side of the gate stood at attention as the carriage passed by. The ornate halberds they carried, as decorated as they were deadly, were tucked firmly against their shoulders, standing perfectly vertical. Once the carriage completely cleared the threshold, Jack could hear the deep bass sound of the doors closing behind them. The carriage made its way up the winding path through the courtyard. Jack poked his head out of the window for a moment.

"That's one long driveway," said Jack. "Must take

forever to shovel in the winter."

Crescia gave him a weird look and then stuck her tongue out at him. Jack returned the gesture. As they pulled up to the front entrance of the castle, there were a number of people lined up by the stairway, including the captain of the castle guard, Nadi, and two guards on each side of her. The others appeared to be members of the castle staff. When the carriage came to a complete stop, one of the members of the staff approached, placed a small step on the ground in front of the bottom rung of the carriage steps, and opened the door. Jack turned to Lia.

"Ladies first," he said, offering his hand.

Lia took his left hand with hers and stepped out of the carriage. Jack offered the same courtesy to Crescia. Jack quickly reached into his bag and pulled out a small box, out of view of Lia and Crescia. After placing the box in his pocket, Jack stepped out of the carriage and found himself standing directly in front of Nadi. He strained his neck looking up at her face. She stood easily eight feet tall. There were multiple raised ritual scars on her face and arms. Her smoky, light bluish-gray skin was starkly contrasted by the gold trim and accents on her steel armor. Her hands were big enough that a single fist looked like it was roughly the size of Jack's head. She looked down at him.

"Are you the human called Jack?" said Nadi.

"That's what everyone keeps calling me," said Jack.

"Before you enter, I ask that you put this on," said Nadi, taking a magic suppression collar similar to the one Jack had on the first time he woke up after arriving in this parallel world.

"Nadi! That is not necessary! He is a guest!" said Lia, visibly upset at the idea of Jack being treated like a threat.

"It is by order of His Majesty, Your Highness," said Nadi. "This human is not of this kingdom, and if what I heard about him is true, he could level this entire city in a mere moment. It is a necessary precaution."

"He is my guest!" said Lia, continuing to protest.

"It's ok, Lia," said Jack.

"You dare address Her Highness so casually?" said Nadi, looking like she was getting ready to pick him up and throw him in the nearest trash can.

"He addresses me the way I asked him to address me, Captain," said Lia, very forcefully.

Jack turned to Nadi.

"If that's what it takes for things to go smoothly, then by all means, collar me," said Jack.

"But Jack!" said Lia.

"It's a security precaution. I'm not going to hold it against anyone," said Jack.

Nadi secured the collar around Jack's neck.

"I just have one question," said Jack.

"And what is your question, human Jack?" asked Nadi.

"Does it clash with my outfit?" asked Jack, trying to lower the level of tension.

Nadi smiled and gave Jack a pat on the shoulder, nearly knocking him clear off his feet.

"You are funny, Jack. I think I will like you," said Nadi.

"Always good to be on the good side of the captain of the castle guards," said Jack.

Nadi gestured for Lia to begin to make her way up the steps first. Crescia followed directly behind her. The two soldiers on each side of Nadi moved so they were surrounding Jack, with Nadi standing a few steps directly in front of him and the four soldiers forming a square around Jack.

"Ooh! Escorts," said Jack, trying his best to just go with the flow.

Jack could see that Lia was visibly upset, so he did his best not to escalate anything. As they made their way up the steps, Jack found himself reflexively matching the step of the guards surrounding him, the same way he did during marches when he was in the army. It took all he had not to start calling out some highly inappropriate cadence, so all he did was quietly whisper the basic marching cadence as he walked.

"Your left, your left, your left, right, left," he whispered.

The soldier to his back left heard this and snickered.

When they reached the top of the steps, the grand doors opened, and the group entered the castle as the staff remained to gather everyone's baggage from the carriage.

#####

Lia, Crescia, and Jack, along with Nadi and the four escorts, entered a large room with a number of couches and chairs. The guards remained at the entrance to the room.

"Please wait here until the court herald arrives," said Nadi.

Two guards waited inside the room by the door, and the other two waited outside the room with Nadi as she closed the door behind her. Lia walked up to Jack.

"I'm sorry, Jack. I didn't know that they would do this. I'm definitely going to have a word with my father about this. That's for damn sure," said Lia.

"Lia, really, it's ok. Come here. I'll tell you a secret," said Jack.

Lia leaned in close.

"Look into my eyes." Jack whispered.

As she looked into his eyes, Jack made them glow bright blue. A small sphere of water began to form in front of Jack's lips. He quickly sucked the sphere into his mouth and swallowed the water before returning his eyes to normal.

"But... the collar," said Lia.

"Zavyra told me. These collars aren't anywhere near strong enough to suppress my abilities to any significant extent," whispered Jack. "So, it's really ok. If it makes them feel more comfortable, I'm fine with wearing it."

"Still, I don't like it," said Lia.

"I know. On a happier note, while we're waiting for the herald guy to show up, I have something for you," said Jack as he reached his hand into his pocket and took out the box.

He handed the box to Lia.

"What's this?" she asked.

"Just something I picked up for you in Estin. I was waiting for the right time to give it to you."

Lia carefully unwrapped the box and opened it, revealing the brooch.

"Oh my, Jack. It's beautiful," she said.

"When I saw it in the window, I thought you might like it, so I found a way to get some money and bought it for you on our way to see Zavyra," said Jack.

"Jack, I love it," said Lia.

Lia took it out of the box and carefully pinned the brooch onto her dress.

"How does it look?" she asked.

"Perfect," said Jack.

Crescia came over to take a look.

"Oooh! Pretty!" said Crescia.

Crescia turned to Jack and lifted her fist for a fist bump.

"Nice," she said to Jack as he returned the fist bump.

Just then, the door opened and the court herald appeared.

"Greetings. I am Gilmar."

Gilmar bowed to everyone and then walked up to Jack.

"How would you like me to announce you, sir?" asked Gilmar.

"Just Jack is fine with me," said Jack.

"You wish me to announce you as Just Jack?" asked Gilmar.

Jack shrugged, and Lia immediately intervened.

"You will announce him by his official title. He is His Highness, Crown Prince Jack of the Kingdom of Stobrimore," said Lia.

"As you wish, Your Highness," said Gilmar. "This way, please."

"I'm never going to get used to that title," said Jack.

#####

Crescia remained behind as Jack and Lia followed Gilmar through the corridors until they reached the entrance of the throne room. Gilmar gestured where Jack and Lia should stand, just out of view of the entrance, before opening the doors and entering the throne room. Lia turned to Jack.

"Just wait for Gilmar to say our names and then just do what I do," she said.

"Gotcha," said Jack, giving her a thumbs up.

Jack could hear Gilmar's voice echoing in the throne room.

"Your Majesty. Presenting Her Highness, Crown Princess Lia of Vedyria, and His Highness, Crown Prince Jack of the Kingdom of Stobrimore," said Gilmar.

Jack began to move along with Lia, trying his best to not look as nervous as he felt. They walked into the throne room, and when they stopped, Lia made a fist with her right hand, placed it on her heart, and bowed. Jack did the same. Along with the king and queen, Nadi stood in the throne room.

Gilmar turned to Lia and Jack.

"It is my privilege to present His Royal Majesty, King Daven, and Her Royal Highness, Queen Liandra."

"Rise," said King Daven.

As they stood, Jack got his first good look at the king and queen. Daven stood just under six feet tall, with bright silver hair and a short beard. His eyes were a bright emerald green. An ornate crown rested on his head, and he had numerous rings on his fingers. He wore a burgundy silk full-length tunic with gold trim. Starting at the black leather belt around his waist and rising up a center line of the tunic, leading all the way up to the high standing collar, was elaborate gold and silver embroidery. Resting around his shoulders was a royal blue satin cloak trimmed in fine white fur with thin black and gray stripes.

Standing next to King Daven was the queen. She was equal in height to the king. Her hair was the same golden color as Lia's, with equally vibrant lavender eyes. Her long hair was braided into a single braid that draped over her right shoulder. An ornate crown rested on her head as well. Her dress was crimson with fuchsia sleeves and gold trim. A gold metal belt hung loosely around her waist.

Queen Liandra looked over at Jack.

"What is that around his neck?" she asked.

"It is a suppression collar, my queen," said Nadi.

"And why is it on our most welcome guest?" asked Queen Liandra.

"By order of His Majesty, my queen," said Nadi.

Queen Liandra turned to King Daven.

"Dear?" she said in a tone that clearly indicated the entirety of her intended question.

"He is not of this kingdom. Precautions must be taken," said King Daven.

"He is a guest of our daughter, has done much to protect this kingdom and its people, and above all else, is here at your own request, husband," said Queen Liandra before turning toward Jack and Lia. "Remove the collar at once."

Jack immediately reached up and grabbed the collar. His eyes glowed white for a moment, and he removed the now unlocked collar from around his neck. Queen Liandra and Nadi were both equally shocked at the fact that Jack just used magic to remove a collar that was intended to prevent him from using magic. Jack realized what he had just done, and his eyes widened.

"Oh! You meant her. I'm so sorry. I'm nervous. Sorry," said Jack as he regretfully handed the collar over to Nadi. "Here. Sorry."

"Impressive," said Queen Liandra.

Nadi took the collar from Jack while looking at him skeptically. Queen Liandra leaned in toward King Daven.

"See, dear? Had he hostile intent, the collar would have

done little good anyway." she said.

Jack's eyes were still wide and his head was lowered as he went through everything that could possibly happen as a result of his slip-up. Queen Liandra saw the panic on his face and let out a little chuckle.

"Raise your head, Prince Jack. You are in no trouble here," she said with a smile.

"So, you say you are the crown prince of the fallen kingdom of Stobrimore?" asked King Daven.

"Yes, Your Majesty. That's what I've been told," said Jack, though he would have preferred it if the king hadn't put so much emphasis on the word "fallen."

"I was under the impression that you were an Otherworlder. Was I mistaken?" asked King Daven.

"No, Your Majesty. I am an Otherworlder. But after arriving here, I learned that my family originated here," said Jack.

"I knew the last king of Stobrimore when I was a young man. He was a good man," said King Daven.

"I don't understand," said Jack.

"What do you not understand?" asked King Daven.

"From what I understand, Stobrimore fell around two hundred years ago. The last king of Stobrimore was my great-grandfather," said Jack.

"If I may ask, Prince Jack, how old are you?" asked King Daven.

"I'm thirty-five, Your Majesty," said Jack.

"Thirty-five?! You are still but a child!" said King Daven, shocked by Jack's answer.

"If I'm not out of line, Your Majesty, how old are you?" asked Jack.

"My boy, I am three hundred and fifty-six years old," said King Daven.

"Really?" asked Jack, shocked by his answer. "I never would have guessed."

"How long do you Otherworlders live?" asked King

Daven.

"Average lifespan runs somewhere around eighty five years old, Your Majesty," said Jack.

"Even with magic?" asked Queen Liandra.

"As far as I'm aware, we don't have magic in my world, Your Royal Highness," said Jack.

"Liandra is fine," said Queen Liandra.

"My queen? That is far too informal for an Otherworlder!" said Nadi.

"Would you feel more comfortable calling me Queen Liandra, Jack?" she asked.

Jack nodded.

"Very well," said Queen Liandra.

"Well, Queen Liandra, as I said, I don't think we have magic in my world, though I can't say definitively," said Jack.

"I don't know if you are aware of this, Jack, but humans capable of magic here have much longer lifespans," said Queen Liandra.

"How much longer?" asked Jack, thinking about his grandfather's running joke about being nearly 200 years old.

"If what we have been told about your magical capabilities is correct, I wouldn't be surprised if you have at least two hundred more years, if not more," said Queen Liandra.

Jack's knees began to buckle at that point.

"I think I need to sit down," said Jack.

Lia turned to Jack.

"What's wrong?"

Jack bent over and placed his hands on his knees.

"Parallel worlds? Ok. Weird, but ok. Magic is real? Took some time to accept, but sure. All that on top of being told that I'm going to outlive practically everyone I've ever known and their children, I'm going to need a minute or two to process that," he said.

Lia placed her hand on his shoulder and leaned forward.

"Just breathe, Jack. Deep breaths," said Lia.

Jack took a few deep breaths.

"You're only thirty-five?" asked Lia.

"Yeah," said Jack in between deep breaths. "Why?"

"I would have guessed you are closer to my age is all," said Lia.

"How far off am I?" asked Jack.

"About ninety years," said Lia.

Jack stood up and looked at Lia.

"You're a hundred and twenty five years old?" asked Jack.

"Yes," said Lia.

"Wow. You look fantastic," said Jack, as his breath began to return to normal.

"Thank you," she said with a smile.

Once Jack regained his composure, he turned back to the king and queen.

"My apologies," said Jack.

"No, forgive me, Jack. It was not my intent to cause you such distress," said Queen Liandra.

"It hit me a bit harder than I expected," said Jack.

King Daven cleared his throat.

"So, my boy, if what I have read is correct, it seems that you have some extraordinarily powerful magic abilities. I would love to see a demonstration. What affinities do you possess?" asked King Daven.

"All of them, sir," said Jack.

"It's true," said Lia. "I was there when he was initially tested, and he has since demonstrated each affinity."

"I would very much like to see that," said King Daven. "We shall organize a demonstration if you would be willing."

"I will do my best to put on a good show, Your Majesty," said Jack.

"Splendid, my boy. We would like you both to join us this evening for dinner. Perhaps it would be better to have any further discussion in a more casual setting," said King Daven.

"A fantastic idea, dear," said Queen Liandra. "Perhaps, in the meantime, Lia can show Jack around the castle."

"An excellent idea. Would that be acceptable, Daughter?" asked King Daven.

"Of course, Father," said Lia, before looking at Jack and smiling.

"Well then, until dinner. For now, I must attend to other duties," said King Daven as he gave a quick nod before walking out of the throne room.

After King Daven left, Queen Liandra walked over to Lia and gave her a hug.

"Welcome back home, sweetheart," she said.

"Thank you, Mother," said Lia. "It's good to be back."

Queen Liandra turned to Jack.

"Again, I'm so sorry for causing you such distress. Forgive my rudeness. May I call you Jack?" She asked.

"Oh, yes! Of course! Please, by all means," said Jack, before realizing how much he was repeating himself.

"Thank you," said Queen Liandra.

Queen Liandra looked back and forth between Jack and Lia.

"How long have you two been involved?" she asked.

Jack's and Lia's eyes both went wide.

"Mother!" said Lia.

"Wow. She's good," said Jack.

Jack then looked at Lia and made a quick gesture to his chest along with a few expressions intended to non-verbally ask Lia if she thinks her mother knows about the ring. Lia responded with a subtle shake of her head.

"I see," said Queen Liandra.

"See what?" asked Jack in a moment of panic.

"You've been together long enough to think you can have private conversations with each other without speaking. Her father and I were practically betrothed before we were able to do that," she said.

Jack and Lia looked at each other again, trying not to

panic any further.

"Really? No. Really? For how long?" said Queen Liandra.

"It would have been nice if you had told me that your mother had the ability to read minds." Jack said to Lia.

"She doesn't," said Lia, realizing that there was no point in trying to hide anything any further.

"I can't read minds, Jack. But I am quite good at reading faces," said Queen Liandra with a smile.

Lia reached under her collar and pulled out the ring attached to the necklace.

"That's wonderful. For how long?" she asked.

Jack looked at his watch.

"About seven hours, actually," said Jack.

"On the trip here?" asked Queen Liandra.

"Yes," said Lia.

"My, how romantic," said Queen Liandra.

"For the moment, can you keep this from Father?" Lia asked.

"Why?" asked Queen Liandra.

"He wanted me to wear a suppression collar just to be in this room. What's he going to do to me when he finds out I asked his only daughter to marry me? I'm hoping he gets to know me first before ordering my execution," said Jack.

Queen Liandra laughed.

"I don't think he would go that far, Jack. Now, the dungeon..." Queen Liandra said with a grin.

"Mother, don't tease him too much. I'm not sure if his heart can take it," said Lia.

"Ok. No more teasing. Do you mind if I join the two of you on the tour?" asked Queen Liandra.

"The more the merrier, I say," said Jack.

"What a remarkably quaint saying," said Queen Liandra. "May I use that?"

"Of course," said Jack.

As the three of them walked out of the throne room, Queen Liandra leaned close to Lia and whispered to her.

"I think I like him," she said.

"Me too," said Lia.

#####

As they walked through the castle, Lia and Queen Liandra pointed out the various interesting elements of the castle as they continued to talk. Jack described a number of Otherworld technologies and their uses, as well as showing the queen his cell phone and its camera feature, taking a few pictures of the three of them. When they concluded the tour, they walked to Lia's room.

"This is my bedroom," said Lia, standing at the door.

"And you shall be staying in a guest room down the hall." Queen Liandra said to Jack.

"Mother?" said Lia, wondering why they couldn't both just stay in her room.

"No, it's ok. It makes sense." Jack said to Lia. "Queen Liandra is the only one here who knows about us. If we want to keep it that way for now, it's best that we stay in separate rooms."

"I guess that is true," said Lia.

"That is quite a lovely brooch you have there, Lia," said Liandra.

"Thank you. It was a gift from Jack," said Lia.

Queen Liandra turned to Jack. He nodded and gave a little smile.

"You have excellent taste in accessories, Jack," she said.

"Well, when I looked at it, I thought the jeweled sword represented strength and the vine of gold and jeweled leaves that wrap around it represented beauty, and that embodies Lia perfectly," said Jack.

"Well stated, Jack," said Queen Liandra. "The two of you should rest until dinnertime. You've both had a long trip."

"That's not a bad idea," said Jack.

"I shall see you two at dinner, then," said Queen Liandra

before leaning in close. "And congratulations to the both of you on your betrothal."

"Thank you," said Jack and Lia.

Jack stood at attention, placed his right fist over his heart, and gave Queen Liandra a bow as she walked away. He then turned to Lia.

"So that went well. Though your father didn't really give you much of an opportunity to say much in the throne room. I kind of ended up monopolizing the conversation there. Sorry about that," he said.

"Don't worry, Jack. You seem to be a bit of a novelty for my father, and my mother clearly seems to like you, which makes me very happy. Most conversations with my father in the throne room are brief anyway. We'll talk more at dinner," said Lia.

"I just hope they don't ask me to do anything too excessive in the demonstration. I don't want to have to blow up a mountain or anything," said Jack.

Lia chuckled.

"I doubt you'll have to blow up a mountain, Jack. Maybe a hill," she said.

"Oh. That's reasonable, then," said Jack with a grin.

"Would you like to come in?" asked Lia as she opened her bedroom door.

"I'd be happy to," said Jack.

When he walked into her bedroom, Jack was surprised at the size of it.

"It's bigger than my first apartment," said Jack.

Jack and Lia sat in her room and talked until it was time for dinner.

#####

When dinnertime came, they walked to the dining hall together. When they arrived, Jack was amazed at the size of the hall and the table that occupied most of the length of it. At the head of the table sat both the king and queen. Seats were arranged so Jack was to sit at the side of the table closest to the queen, and Lia was to sit at the side closest to the king. When they were all seated, the royal servants came in with the first course. It was a vegetable soup consisting of all of the local vegetables of the kingdom. As they began eating, the king spoke.

"So, daughter. How goes the war effort?" he said.

Lia placed her spoon down.

"Thanks to the information acquired by Jack and Sir Rhandor during their trip to see Zavyra, we were able to get reliable information regarding Dark Army troop movements. As we speak, Captain Alivair is working on a comprehensive battle plan in order to intercept and eliminate the enemy units," she said.

"Excellent. Captain Alivair is a very capable officer. Perhaps, after the war is over, he might make for a good husband," said King Daven.

At that moment, Jack inhaled the soup on his spoon and broke into a coughing fit. Queen Liandra tried her best to suppress a laugh.

"Oh my! Do try to be careful, Jack. Are you all right?" asked King Daven.

In between coughs, Jack tried his best to answer.

"I'm fine, Your Majesty. A little bit of soup just went down the wrong pipe," said Jack, in a hoarse voice.

Lia was feeling a mixture of concern for Jack and frustration with her father.

"Try taking a few deep breaths… and drink some wine, Jack. It should help," she said before turning to King Daven. "And Father, I will choose whom I will marry. Is that clear?"

Jack took a sip of wine.

"This is really good wine. Not too dry. I taste a hint of cherry, maybe?" he said, trying clumsily to change the subject.

"It's zavinberries. They're one of the main crops of the western region of the kingdom. They don't just make good wine. They're also very good in desserts," said Queen Liandra, trying to give Jack a helping hand.

"Really? I'd love to try some desserts with them," said Jack, both because he was glad that she was helping him and also because he was suddenly genuinely very interested in dessert.

"Well, you're in luck. We will be having a variety of options with zavinberries come dessert time," said Queen Liandra.

"Looking forward to it," said Jack.

"So, Jack. I understand that you were a soldier in your world. Is that true?" asked King Daven.

"Yes, sir. For over ten years," said Jack.

"And what did you do in that time?" asked King Daven.

"I was in a specialized unit known as the Army Rangers. We were a highly skilled force that handled large-scale special operations," said Jack.

"What sort of special operations?" asked King Daven.

"Raids, assault missions, and special reconnaissance operations, mostly. Often behind enemy lines," said Jack.

"Fascinating. And you did this without the use of magic?" asked King Daven.

"Yes, sir. Though we were very well equipped," said Jack.

"I see," said King Daven.

"So, Jack. Being an Otherworlder, I was wondering. What do you think of our world?" asked Queen Liandra.

"It's amazing. When I first got here, I thought I was dreaming, because everything seemed so much like the stories my grandfather told me when I was young. Though, knowing what I know now about my family lineage, I guess it makes sense, since the stories I thought were just fantasy actually turned out to be stories about this world," said Jack.

"Well, I'm glad you like it here," said Queen Liandra.

They continued with general small talk throughout the meal. When dessert came, just as Queen Liandra said, there were a number of zavinberry dishes, and Jack was more than happy to sample each one. As they were finishing up, King Daven spoke to Jack again.

"I've arranged for the castle guard training grounds to be available tomorrow for a demonstration of your abilities, Jack. I very much look forward to seeing what you are capable of," he said.

"I'll try my very best to impress, Your Majesty," said Jack.

"I'm sure you will do just fine," said Queen Liandra.

"So, Jack. What do you think of my daughter?" asked King Daven.

Jack froze for a moment. He thought for a moment and decided to respond with a safe answer in order to avoid any misunderstanding.

"I have nothing but respect for her, sir. I probably wouldn't be here without Lia. She saved my life when I first arrived here. She's a remarkable leader. She's very important to me... and all of the soldiers under her command," said Jack, hoping that last slip was covered well enough.

Queen Liandra gave him a little nod, as if to say, "Good save."

"I see. I'm glad that an accomplished soldier such as yourself holds my daughter in such high regard. If I'm being perfectly honest, I had my doubts when she asked to be involved in the military when she was younger. But if an Otherworld military leader, and a special operations one at that, has that much faith and respect for my daughter's leadership abilities, then I'm fully willing to admit that I was wrong to have my doubts," said King Daven.

Lia was surprised by what her father had just said. She looked over at Jack and smiled. He was able to see the thanks contained within the smile, and he gave a slight nod in response. Queen Liandra felt that they had both been through enough, so she decided to take the opportunity to give them an out.

"Well, I think we've done enough interrogation for the night. These two had a very long trip. It's probably best that we let them get some sleep. We don't want poor Jack falling over from exhaustion during his demonstration, now do we? Let's let the young ones get their rest, dear," she said.

"Ah, yes. Of course. Forgive me for keeping you two up for so long. I'm sure you'd both like to get to your rooms for the night. We can talk more tomorrow. Good night to the both of you," said King Daven.

After that, they all stood up.

"Thank you very much for dinner," said Jack, bowing to the king and queen.

"Of course. Good night, you two," said Queen Liandra.

"Good night, Mother. Good night, Father," said Lia.

#####

After that, Jack and Lia made their way toward the hall where their bedrooms were located.

"Well... that went well," said Jack.

"...Yes," said Lia.

Jack and Lia started to chuckle. Jack walked her to the entrance of her bedroom. When she opened her door, he reached out and took her hand. After a quick look around to make sure that no one was around, Jack leaned in and kissed Lia. When their lips parted, Jack smiled.

"Good night. Sweet dreams," he said.

"May your dreams be sweet as well," said Lia.

Lia then made her way into her bedroom, and Jack made his way to his.

CHAPTER 26

Alivair was standing at the first position with his unit, scanning the horizon with the binoculars, waiting for the Dark Army squadron to appear. He reached into the bag on his hip and pulled out the handheld radio.

"Rhandor. Can you hear me?" asked Alivair.

"I hear you both loudly and clearly," said Rhandor.

"Are you in position?" asked Alivair.

"Nearly. We are almost set up," said Rhandor.

"Please explain to me again why you needed to bring those barrels of flour for a battle," said Alivair.

Rhandor, who was standing in a position with his unit a few hundred yards away from Alivair, pulled the lid off of one of the barrels of flour.

"It is something that Jack told me about. The flour will be necessary when the time comes. Please inform me when the enemy is in sight," said Rhandor.

"Understood. I shall," said Alivair.

Alivair turned to one of his soldiers.

"If the information we have is correct, the enemy should be approaching from that direction within the hour. Get into final positions and await my orders," he said.

"Yes, sir," said the soldier, before directing his squad to follow him to the designated position.

Alivair turned to another soldier.

"Spread your archers along the ridge line. Don't fire until I give the command," he said.

"Understood," said the soldier, directing the other archers to move out.

Alivair got back on the radio.

"My men are getting in position. Prepare your men as well. I will let you know when the enemy is sighted," he said.

"Understood, sir," said Rhandor over the radio.

Over at Rhandor's position, he ordered his men to get into position while he and another soldier opened up the other two barrels of flour. They positioned the barrels about six feet apart to form a triangle with Rhandor standing in the middle.

Back at the other position, Alivair was still scanning the horizon. In the distance, he started to see a fine cloud of dust being kicked up by the marching Dark Army soldiers. Alivair took out the radio.

"Rhandor. Dark Army approaching. Get ready. I'll stand by for your signal," he said.

"Understood," said Rhandor over the radio.

Alivair turned to the soldiers in his unit.

"The enemy is approaching! Archers! Wait for my order to fire! Mages! Be ready to deploy shields and lay down any cover fire! Everyone else! Draw your swords and prepare for battle on my order!" he said.

Rhandor waited until the Dark Army squadron was just in sight before closing his eyes. When he opened them, his pupils were glowing bright yellow. He raised his hands. Vortexes of wind formed above each barrel of flour, pulling it out of the barrels and keeping it contained within the vortex. As the barrels emptied, the tops of the vortexes merged, forming a growing cloud of white powder. After the barrels were completely emptied, Rhandor raised the cloud a hundred feet into the air above him, slowly spreading it out wide before sending it in the direction of the Dark Army squadron. The Dark Army soldiers stopped and looked up into the sky at the oncoming white cloud. The cloud stopped right above them. It spread out enough to encompass the entire squadron and then suddenly slammed down on top of them, creating a massive cloud of flour that completely obscured their sight of anything around them.

Rhandor grabbed the radio from his waistband and

pressed the button.

"Now! Fireball!" he said into the radio.

Alivair used his fire magic to launch a fireball into the cloud of flour. The moment the fireball reached the outer edges of the flour cloud, the entire cloud burst into flames. The explosion spread rapidly, encompassing the Dark Army squadron in fire. When the flames began to die down, a number of the Dark Army soldiers were on the ground, but many were still standing.

"Remarkable," Alivair said to himself before turning to his soldiers. "Archers! Fire at will! Everyone else, with me!"

Alivair's unit, along with Rhandor's team, charged into battle. As the magic arrows of the Vedyrian archers flew overhead, they commenced their attack. Those Demonborne who were still able to fight sent volley after volley of dark magic energy spheres and arrows at the oncoming Vedyrian soldiers. Two of the four Dark Army necromancers were still standing, and they sent large spears of dark magic flying at the Vedyrian Army soldiers. Rhandor did his best to deflect as many as possible with wind blades. One of the necromancers raised his hand toward the sky and then pointed it at Alivair's archers.

"Draphnir!" yelled Alivair as he saw a pack of at least thirty of the feral beasts heading into the battlefield.

The Vedyrian mages were doing everything they could to create wide-area shields to try and limit the damage the army was taking from the dark magic being thrown at them by the Demonborne and necromancers. The Vedyrian archers took aim at the draphnir.

Alivair built up all the strength that he had to send a series of fireballs at the draphnir in rapid succession. A Demonborne launched a final attack before dying that ran right along Alivair's arm and impacted against his side, just below his armpit. Alivair fell to the ground in pain. Rhandor saw Alivair fall and signaled for one of the mages with earth magic to form a wall along his path as he ran over to Alivair.

As he ran, Rhandor launched wind blade after wind blade at the Dark Army soldiers and draphnir that got in his way. When he reached Alivair, he was still conscious but clearly in a significant amount of pain. Rhandor picked Alivair up, threw him over his shoulder, and ran as fast as he could to the area where the healer mages were doing their work. On the way, Rhandor saw a necromancer preparing to fire a dark magic spear. Using what strength he could, Rhandor used his wind magic to lift up a boulder and send it flying at the necromancer. The boulder hit the necromancer with enough force to send him flying backward, eventually crushing him between the boulder and the rock face behind him.

The Vedyrian archers laid down heavy cover fire until Rhandor reached the healers. After placing Alivair down on one of the stretchers, Rhandor charged back into the battle. When he returned to the front lines, the majority of the Dark Army soldiers had fallen. Only a relative few remained, including the last necromancer. Rhandor ordered all Vedyrian soldiers to focus on finishing off the rest of the Dark Army while he took a run at the necromancer. As he leaped from place to place to close in on the necromancer, Rhandor pulled what magic strength he had left for a final attack. He raised both hands up at his sides, and when he got within a dozen feet of the necromancer, he sent two immense wind blades at him. The first wind blade was mostly deflected by the necromancer's staff, but the second blade cut through the staff and the necromancer, splitting them both in two.

After both pieces of the necromancer hit the ground, Rhandor looked around to see if there were any more Dark Army survivors. The few that remained were quickly picked off by the archers or run through by the swords of the soldiers. When the last one fell and Rhandor finally caught his breath, he took a deep breath in and let out an ear-piercing howl of victory. After ordering a few soldiers to scan the perimeter for any stragglers or survivors, Rhandor ran back to the area where the healers were working on Alivair. He placed a hand on the healer's shoulder.

"What's his status?" asked Rhandor.

"He sustained some significant damage, but with time and continued healing magic, I believe that he shall survive," said the healer.

"Please, see that he does. Her Highness would never forgive me otherwise," said Rhandor.

"Yes, sir," said the healer.

With Alivair temporarily out of commission, Rhandor took charge of the remaining soldiers.

"Search the bodies for any intel, attend to our wounded, and collect the dead! Burn the bodies of the Dark Army soldiers so the Emperor doesn't have a chance to use them again! Tonight we shall celebrate our victory!" he yelled.

There were cheers from many of the soldiers as they went about their designated tasks. After the bodies of the Dark Army had been searched, the wounded were collected and escorted to the healers, and the fallen Vedyrian soldiers were collected and accounted for, those who could walk began the long march back to the base camp. Those unable to walk were loaded into covered carts and carried back to the base camp.

#####

Once they returned to camp, the wounded were taken to the medical tent for treatment. By the time Alivair was taken to the tent, he was stabilized, but his wounds were still severe. His arm was badly damaged, his side was severely burned, and several of his ribs were broken. After checking the status of the other wounded soldiers, Rhandor made his way to Bilen's tent. With Alivair out of commission due to injury and Lia at the castle, command fell to Bilen, as the next highest in the chain of command.

Rhandor gave Bilen the after-action report on the operation and the casualty reports and provided all gathered intelligence collected from the fallen Dark Army soldiers. After the report, Rhandor returned to the common area of the camp to assist in the preparation of a celebration of a successful victory in battle with the other soldiers. After the celebration, Rhandor made his way back to the medical tent to check on the status of Alivair. When he got there, Alivair was conscious.

"How are you feeling, sir?" asked Rhandor.

"If I'm going to be perfectly honest, not great," said Alivair.

"Well, just rest, sir. Everything's being handled. I've briefed Bilen, and he's keeping everything in working order," said Rhandor.

"What of the troops?" asked Alivair.

"The casualty report is handled, and I've just come back from a celebration to keep troop morale up. It was a well-earned victory, and much of it is owed to your efforts," said Rhandor.

"Speaking of the battle, who would have thought that a baking ingredient could be such an effective mass weapon? However did you get that idea?" asked Alivair.

"Believe it or not, it was something that Jack told me on our trip. He said that it was something called a dust explosion and that it is a concern in his world in a number of industries that produce large amounts of dust. In his world they are generally accidental, though. It was his idea to use wind magic to try and cause a controlled one on a battlefield. I must say, it certainly proved to be quite effective," said Rhandor.

"Indeed. A most unconventional approach, but remarkably useful on the battlefield. I must give him my compliments for suggesting it when he returns. And, of course, I give you my compliments for implementing it. It was masterfully executed, Rhandor," said Alivair.

"Thank you, sir. It was an effort on both our parts that led to its success," Rhandor said.

"Here's hoping our next battle is equally as successful," said Alivair.

'Indeed, sir," said Rhandor.

CHAPTER 27

Corvan walked through the halls of the Great Demon Emperor's castle, making his way to the throne room. When he arrived, the Emperor was sitting on his throne. Corvan approached and kneeled.

"Your Excellency, I have a report in regard to our last deployment," said Corvan.

"Speak," said the Emperor.

"Unfortunately, Your Excellency, the squadron was wiped out by the Vedyrians. They appeared to use some sort of peculiar magic that turned a great white cloud into an explosion that encompassed the entire battlefield," said Corvan.

"The human?" asked the Emperor.

"He was not on the battlefield. However, I suspect his influence may have had something to do with that peculiar magic," said Corvan.

General Karvan entered the throne room.

The Emperor briefly looked at Karvan and then back at Corvan.

"You wish for victory?" asked the Emperor.

"Yes, Your Excellency. But I need to be stronger if I want to beat them. To beat him," said Corvan.

"You wish for power?" asked the Emperor.

"Yes, Your Excellency," said Corvan.

"Great power comes at a cost," said the Emperor.

Karvan approached.

"Your Excellency, might I have a moment to speak with my brother?" Karvan asked.

"As you wish," said the Emperor.

Karvan took Corvan aside.

"Brother, do you understand what you are asking?" asked Karvan.

"Yes. I do. I wish for power," said Corvan.

"You are asking for death. If His Excellency grants you more power, it will feed on your life like a vampire until you are nothing but a dried husk. Is that truly what you want?" asked Karvan.

"I want victory," said Corvan.

"Victory is never celebrated by the dead, Brother," said Karvan.

"Then you shall celebrate enough for the both of us after I win this war, Brother," said Corvan.

Corvan walked back to the Emperor.

"I am ready, Your Excellency," said Corvan.

"Very well," said the Emperor, as he held out his hand.

A deep red and purple glow began to surround the Emperor like a flame. He placed his palm on Corvan's head, and the dark magic, flame-like energy began to flow from the Emperor into Corvan. Corvan's eyes began to glow purple and black. The more energy that flowed into him, the brighter the glow became. Corvan began to scream in pain as the energy spread throughout his body. Fine glowing red cracks began to form from Corvan's eyes and traced down his cheeks like glowing trails of bloody tears. When the transfer was complete, Corvan collapsed to the floor. Karvan ran up to him.

"Corvan! Corvan!" he called out.

Corvan began to move.

"I'm all right, Brother. I was simply overwhelmed by the power," said Corvan.

When Corvan stood up, the glow in his eyes and down the lines on his cheeks began to fade.

"Are you sure that you're ok, Brother?" asked Karvan.

"I am," said Corvan before turning to the Emperor. "My deepest thanks, Your Excellency. I shall not let you down."

"See that you do not," said the Emperor.

Both Corvan and Karvan bowed to the Emperor before walking out of the throne room. As they left the castle and walked down the stairs, Corvan turned to Karvan.

"So, how goes the tunnel project, Brother?" asked Corvan.

"It is progressing, Brother. Follow me," said Karvan.

#####

They walked for a time until they came upon the entrances to all of the tunnels they had been digging.

"Digging has slowed due to metal deposits in the rocks, but we do have a single tunnel that is near completion. It is not so big as to allow our army to move through it, but a small team or, in your case, even a single powerful soldier such as yourself can make it through with little effort," said Karvan.

"Soon, brother. First, I shall test these new powers and see what I am now capable of achieving," said Corvan.

Corvan turned toward a distant hill. He concentrated and closed his eyes. When he opened them, they were glowing a red and purple swirled glow. He aimed his hand at the hill and generated a sphere of dark magic that started off the size of a golf ball and then grew to the size of an exercise ball before being compressed back down to the size of a baseball. He released the dark magic energy ball at high velocity at the distant hill. When it hit, there was a giant explosion. Shards of rock flew in every direction. Some shards flew far enough to reach both Karvan and Corvan. When the dust cleared, a crater was all that remained of the hill.

"Splendid," said Corvan.

"Yes," said Karvan.

CHAPTER 28

The next morning, Jack woke up fairly early. When he left his room, he looked toward Lia's room and noticed that the door was still closed. He figured that he would let her sleep and made his way down to the kitchen. When he arrived at the kitchen, he saw a number of the kitchen staff preparing meals for the day. He got the attention of one of the staff members.

"Excuse me. Good morning. You wouldn't happen to have any more of those zavinberry tarts that you served last night anywhere, would you?" Jack asked.

The staff member smiled.

"Yes, Your Highness. I will get some for you," said the kitchen staff member.

"Sweet! You're awesome," said Jack.

The kitchen staff member retrieved a number of the tarts on a large plate and escorted Jack to the dining room. They placed a small plate in front of Jack's seat and placed the utensils down. Jack just stood there and watched as they prepared what was intended to be just a morning snack like it was a meal for some sort of formal event. When the staff member was finished, they gestured for Jack to sit. When he sat down, they unfolded a napkin and placed it on his lap. After that, the staff member returned to the kitchen. Jack looked around the room to make sure that no one else was there. Once he confirmed he was alone, he set the utensils aside and just picked up the first tart and started eating it like a doughnut.

"Totally worth it," said Jack to himself.

After he finished the first tart and started reaching for a second one, he heard a voice coming from behind him.

"That's not a particularly healthy breakfast you're

eating, Jack," said Lia.

"You're just jealous. Want one?" said Jack.

"Yes, I do," said Lia.

Lia pushed the chair next to Jack closer to him and sat down. Jack slid his plate over so they could share it.

"You know, berries are fruit, and fruit is part of a healthy breakfast, so technically this works," he said with a grin.

"Nice try at a loophole. I'll give you half points for it," Lia said.

"Would I have gotten more points if I had also asked for whipped cream?" Jack asked with a grin.

"Maybe," said Lia.

"Where's Crescia?" asked Jack. "I haven't really seen much of her since we got here."

"She's been using this opportunity to handle some family issues, but she should be done by the time we have to head to the training grounds," said Lia.

"That's good. I've been missing the furry little bad-ass since we got here," said Jack.

Lia laughed.

"I'm sure the feeling is mutual. So, speaking of the training grounds, have you figured out what you're going to do for the demonstration?" Lia asked.

"I have a few ideas. I'm thinking about trying some flashy combinations of different types of magic," said Jack.

"I'm looking forward to it," said Lia.

"Me, too," said Jack.

Jack grabbed the last tart and carefully wrapped it in his napkin.

"I'll save one for Crescia," he said.

"I'm sure she'll appreciate it," said Lia.

#####

After they finished their tarts, Jack and Lia decided to

go for a walk in the courtyard. As they walked, Jack noticed that even though Lia was dressed in an outfit more suited to the training grounds, she still had the brooch pinned to her shirt. He smiled as they continued to stroll around the courtyard. Eventually, they came across Queen Liandra, who appeared to have the same idea to visit the courtyard.

"Good morning, Mother," said Lia.

"Good morning, Queen Liandra," said Jack.

"A good morning to the both of you, as well," said Queen Liandra. "Have you eaten yet?"

"Yes. We had zavinberry tarts for breakfast," said Jack with a big smile.

Queen Liandra was a bit surprised at Jack's enthusiasm.

"Well, I suppose that, since they have fruit, and fruit is common in a breakfast, it's not that far off from a normal breakfast food," said Queen Liandra.

"See! That's what I said! Great minds think alike. I knew I liked you." Jack said.

"Why, thank you, Jack. So, have you thought about what you plan to do for the demonstration?" said Queen Liandra.

"I have some ideas. I'm thinking of trying some combos of different types of magic," Jack said.

"Fascinating. I'm very much looking forward to it. There will be a number of nobles in attendance as well, so be sure to put on a good show," said Queen Liandra.

"Absolutely. I'm sure you won't be disappointed," said Jack.

"As someone who has witnessed Jack's magic firsthand, I'm sure you and Father will be anything but disappointed," said Lia.

Jack thought back for a moment about all the times Lia had seen Jack use magic, and given that they were almost all before he learned to control his magic, other than the time he healed the people in the medical tent, they had all either ended in explosions or property damage.

"I'm not sure how to take that," said Jack.

Lia thought for a moment and soon realized the same thing Jack had realized, though she had also taken into account the instances mentioned by Rhandor in his reports.

"Oh! As a compliment, Jack. As a compliment." she said.

"Ok, good," said Jack with a look of relief.

"Well, I'll let you two get back to your lovers' stroll, then," said Queen Liandra with a wink.

"We'll see you this afternoon, Mother," said Lia.

"I promise not to disappoint!" said Jack as they walked away.

#####

After finishing their walk around the courtyard, Jack and Lia decided to walk to the training grounds instead of taking a carriage. That way, Jack would have some time to check out the grounds to better set up his magic presentation.

When they arrived, Jack took a good look around. Fortunately there were no mountains or large hills in the area, so Jack was relieved that he wouldn't have to blow anything that big up. There was an area for hand-to-hand combat training, a target range for archery and magic, and an obstacle course that reminded Jack of the ones he went through in both Basic Training and Ranger School in the Army. There was even a 30-foot tall wooden tower similar to the Victory Tower there. Jack turned to Lia.

"You know that I can use dark magic, right?" he asked.

"Yes," she replied.

"And that the dark magic I can use is the pure kind and not the corrupted kind the Dark Army uses, right?" he asked.

"Yes," she replied.

"I've been wondering something for a while. Given that it seems to be associated with the Dark Army, would me using it be considered a taboo?" Jack asked.

"While it's rare for anyone in this kingdom to have an

affinity for dark magic, I wouldn't say that it's taboo. But given that it is primarily a destructive type of magic, those who have the affinity don't tend to use it very often," said Lia.

"Ok. There's just something I wanted to show you all that Zavyra taught me. It's not destructive, but it is dark magic. I just wanted to make sure I didn't offend anyone," said Jack.

"What do you plan on doing?" Lia asked.

"It's a surprise," said Jack. "I'm going to go check out the top of that tower."

Jack ran over to the ladder side of the tower and climbed up to the top. From the top of the tower, he was able to see for miles around. In the distance, he saw a carriage approaching. It wasn't as ornate as the royal one that the castle had sent for him and Lia, so Jack assumed that it probably wasn't the king and queen inside. He called down to Lia.

"Hey, Lia! There's a carriage approaching!" he yelled.

Lia walked over to the entrance to the training ground to greet the arriving carriage. From the tower, Jack was able to see several people, all elves in fancy clothes, step out of the carriage. Jack remembered that the queen had mentioned that some nobles would be attending. Jack climbed down off the tower as Lia greeted all of the nobles. While Lia escorted most of the nobles to their seats, one of them broke off from the group and began walking toward Jack. As Jack was wiping the dust off his hands at the bottom of the ladder, the noble spoke to him.

"So, I understand that you're Her Highness's new pet human and you'll be performing some tricks for us today." he said in a snarky tone.

"Excuse me?" said Jack.

"You heard what I said, human," said the noble.

"Oh. You're one of those, huh?" said Jack.

"One of what, human?" said the noble.

"One of those self-righteous elves who think that every other race is, or at the very least, that humans are inferior to them. I met one like you back at the base camp, but I won him over, and we eventually became friends," said Jack.

"What is the name of this fool?" asked the noble.

At that point, Lia had already directed the other nobles to their seats and noticed that one was over talking to Jack. By the expression she saw on Jack's face, she was able to figure out that it was not looking like a particularly friendly discussion. She excused herself from the other nobles and started walking over to where Jack and the noble were talking.

"His name is Alivair, and he's the second in command of the Vedyrian Army. I'm sure he wouldn't much appreciate you calling him a fool," said Jack.

The noble cleared his throat after hearing Alivair's name.

By that time, Lia was close enough to start hearing their voices.

"So, pet human, what sort of little tricks are you going to do to entertain us today?" asked the noble.

"Oh, you know, a little of this and a little of that." Jack said.

"I asked you a question, human. Give me specifics," said the noble.

Jack was getting really tired of his attitude.

"If you keep this up, one trick I'm going to love showing you is how I can make my entire boot disappear up your ass," said Jack.

Hearing this, Lia nearly snorted, trying to suppress a laugh.

"Who do you think you are, human? I am a Count of this kingdom. You will show me respect!" said the noble, raising his hand like he was about to backhand Jack.

Lia figured that it was time to step in.

"You really should learn to be respectful to those of higher status than you," she said.

"Even Her Highness agrees with me, human. Know your place," said the noble.

"I was talking to you, Count Avomir," said Lia.

"Me?!" said Count Avomir. "What status does this human have that places him above mine?"

"First, he is very dear to me. Second, he is a personal guest of the royal family, and third, his official title is Crown Prince Jack of the Kingdom of Stobrimore," said Lia.

Count Avomir's eyes widened, and he went pale. He turned back to look at Jack. Jack had a big grin on his face.

"Crown Prince?!" Count Avomir said.

Jack raised his eyebrows for a moment, keeping the grin on his face. Avomir cleared his throat and bowed.

"My deepest apologies, Your Highness. I did not mean to offend," he said.

"Yes, you did," said Jack.

"I beg your forgiveness for my rudeness," said Avomir, still bowing.

"I'll think about it," said Jack, still grinning.

"It's best that you go find your seat, now, Count Avomir," said Lia.

"Yes, Your Highness. Right away," said Count Avomir, continuing to bow as he walked backward before turning and making his way over to the spectator area of the training field.

Lia walked up to Jack and began to laugh.

"Make your entire boot disappear up his ass? The entire boot?" she said.

"Yep," said Jack. "Until he tasted leather."

Lia laughed even harder.

"A very colorful use of language, Jack," she said.

"It's a gift," said Jack.

"Well, don't worry. The other nobles in attendance are not as self-righteous as Avomir, so I don't think they'll give you any trouble. And I'm betting that he's over there making quite sure that they are all aware of your status," said Lia.

They both looked over at the spectator area, where Avomir was hurriedly talking to the other nobles. After a moment they all stood up and looked over at Jack before bowing. Jack gave a wave and a nod in response.

"Lia, you can make a shield with your light magic, right?" Jack asked.

"Yes, of course. Why?" asked Lia.

"Things might get a bit wild. I just want to make sure that I don't get everyone all dusty, dirty, or wet," said Jack.

"That shouldn't be a problem," said Lia.

Jack looked over toward the entrance to see the royal carriage approaching the entrance.

"Looks like the guests of honor are here," said Jack.

"Let's go greet them," said Lia.

Jack and Lia walked over to the entrance to greet the king and queen. When they exited the carriage, Jack and Lia bowed.

"It's quite a nice day for a magic demonstration," said King Daven.

"Indeed. It certainly is, dear," said Queen Liandra.

"I shall do my best not to disappoint," said Jack.

"I wish you luck, Jack," said Queen Liandra.

Crescia jumped out of the carriage soon afterwards.

"Hi!" she said.

"Hi, Crescia," said Jack. "I've missed you. Been busy?"

"Yep! Did some stuff with my mom and got some more training in. It's been fun," Crescia said.

"Glad to hear it. Looking forward to the presentation?" asked Jack.

"Absolutely! I can't wait to see what kind of stuff you can do," said Crescia.

"I'm sure you'll be impressed," said Jack.

Jack reached into his pocket and took out the tart wrapped in a napkin and snuck it to Crescia. She unwrapped it.

"Ooh! Yum!" she said.

Lia gestured toward the observation area.

"Shall we?" she said.

Before Lia started to walk away, Jack reached into his other pocket.

"Before you go, take this." Jack said.

He handed her one of the smaller handheld radios he had brought with him.

"This is one of the devices you mentioned that allow communication between distances, right?" asked Lia.

"Exactly. Just push the button to talk and let the button go when you're done," said Jack.

Lia then walked along with the king and queen to the observation area. Jack walked over to the center of the practice field. He held the radio to his mouth.

"Are we ready?" he asked.

Everyone in the observation seating area was surprised to hear Jack's voice over the radio.

"The magic hasn't started yet. This is just Otherworld technology. Now, for my first trick...," said Jack.

Jack closed his eyes and focused. When he opened them, they were glowing, shifting colors between blue and yellow. Jack combined wind and water magic to form a small tube of water running from his position to the observation area. Once the tube was complete, Jack spoke softly, not using the radio.

"Can you hear me?" he said softly.

Everyone was once again surprised.

"How is he able to project his voice this far without his technology?" asked one of the nobles.

"It's science," said Jack. "Sound travels in waves that spread out like ripples on a pond when you throw in a stone. The farther away those ripples travel, the weaker they get. The same is true of sound. In creating this tube, I'm making a column of cooler air surrounded by the warmer air. That cool column of air changes how the sound waves travel, focusing them and allowing them to travel further distances."

"Remarkable," said King Daven.

"For the duration of this demonstration, though, I will be using the radio for any further communication," said Jack before releasing the tube into a fine mist.

The spectators applauded. Jack took a bow.

"For my next demonstration, observe the tower behind me." Jack said as he stood at the base of the tower.

Jack looked up at the top of the tower and then lowered his head and closed his eyes. When he opened them, they glowed bright purple. A small circle formed on the ground beneath Jack's feet. The circle rose up from the ground, and Jack disappeared. Moments later, a new circle formed at the top of the tower, and Jack reappeared standing there. The spectators were all shocked. Lia tried to hide her surprise.

"Dark magic?! He can use dark magic?!" said Count Avomir.

"Of course," said Lia. "He possesses all six magic affinities."

"All six?! No one has possessed all six affinities for centuries!" said one of the other nobles.

"Yep! It's true! I was there when he was tested. He even broke the affinity gauge. It was impressive. He's really strong," said Crescia.

"How wonderful!" said Queen Liandra. "I can't wait to see what else he can do!"

Queen Liandra squeezed Lia's hand as she smiled.

Jack then walked to the edge of the tower and stepped off. Everyone was surprised that he would do something so seemingly reckless, but they were soon shown that there was no recklessness involved as Jack used the same technique to soften his landing as he did the day he left Zavyra's cave. With the wind magic, his feet touched ground as softly as they would have had he simply stepped off the bottom rung of a ladder. Lia got on the radio.

"Jack, could you warn me next time you do something like that? My heart nearly jumped out of my chest," she said softly into the radio.

"As you wish, Your Highness. Sorry about that." Jack said in reply.

"I forgive you, Jack," said Lia.

Crescia chuckled.

"Thank you. For this next one, it's going to get a little windy and dusty, so if you would, could you place a shield around everyone?" Jack asked.

"Of course," said Lia before putting the radio down and creating a dome-shaped shield around everyone with light magic.

Jack then walked over to one of the racks of blunt training swords and grabbed five of them. He stuck them blade first into five locations in the ground, forming a pentagon. As he walked, he dragged his feet to loosen up as much dirt as he could. He then placed his hand on the ground and caused the dirt inside the pentagon shape to vibrate, sending up clouds of dust into the air. After enough dust accumulated, Jack stood up and then used wind magic to spin the dust into a column. He spun it faster and faster, creating a whirlwind inside the pentagon shape. He then used one hand to grab the radio.

"You might want to cover your ears for this," he said.

Everyone inside the shield covered their ears.

Jack began spinning the dust even faster until he created static electricity. The bolts of electricity began to strike the swords. The more he spun the dust, the more frequent the strikes occurred, and each one let out a booming rumble. He raised the column higher in order to get longer and more impressive-looking bolts of electricity to shoot into the swords. He then compressed the column until it was roughly as wide as bottle, in order to build up as much static electricity as possible. In his final move, he compressed the column down to get it to discharge all remaining electricity in one giant bolt that arced to all five swords. When it was over, Jack turned toward the spectators and bowed. They applauded.

"Fantastic! He was able to create lightning from dust? Simply amazing!" said King Daven, before leaning toward Lia. "You've certainly found yourself a fascinating human, dear daughter. Fascinating indeed."

Jack got on the radio again.

"For my next demonstration, I'll be using the sand

behind me," he said as he turned toward the sand pile being used for one of the backstops.

Once again, Jack used wind magic to create a thin column, sucking the sand up into the center of it. He curved the column until it formed an arch around him. Once he had the arch shaped the way he wanted, he used fire magic on the arch. Knowing that the key to using magic involves visualization, Jack began to visualize the blue flame of natural gas fires. As he concentrated, the orange flame turned a bright blue, and the entire arch was encompassed in the blue flame. The spectators saw a dark orange glow beginning to form inside the blue flaming arch. Once the arch was fully glowing a dark orange, Jack began to introduce some water magic. Once he cooled the arch, a large volume of steam formed, completely engulfing the area where he was standing. When the steam finally cleared, the spectators saw Jack standing beneath a newly formed solid glass arch made from the sand. He once again took a bow as they applauded.

"Ooh! Pretty!" said Crescia.

He picked up the radio again.

"Are there any requests?" he asked.

One of the nobles spoke up.

"I am curious about his destructive capabilities. While very impressive, the demonstrations he has shown us so far are not necessarily tailored for combat. I'd like to see what he could do in a combat setting," said the noble.

A number of the other nobles nodded in agreement. Lia sighed and leaned in toward the nobles.

"I have personally witnessed his destructive capabilities. I'm not exaggerating when I say that he is fully capable of leveling the entire capital city in mere moments if he wished to do so," she said.

A few of the nobles looked scared at what she said. Count Avomir looked terrified, thinking back to his earlier actions, now knowing what Jack is capable of doing. Jack noticed the chatter going on and picked up his radio.

"Is there a problem?" he asked.

Lia picked up her radio.

"They would like to know what your destructive capabilities are," she said.

"They want me to blow something up?" he asked.

"They want you to blow something up," said Lia.

Jack looked around. If they really wanted to see the extent of what he could do, he needed to find something to use as a target that wouldn't result in catastrophic damage to the surrounding area. Not being able to find anything that he was willing to destroy, he got back on the radio.

"Would they settle for a big explosion?" he asked.

"What do you mean?" asked Lia.

"In the sky. Big fiery boom," said Jack.

Lia leaned toward the other spectators and asked them about Jack's suggestion.

"They would like to see a big fiery boom in the sky," she said.

"Consider it done. And they might want to cover their ears for this one, too," said Jack.

Jack walked over to one of the empty wooden barrels being used as a fighting position marker for the archery section of the training grounds. He rolled it into the middle of the field and then use wind magic to slowly lift it off the ground. He spun the barrel as fast as he could and then sent it flying high into the sky. He waited a few seconds for the barrel to reach a high altitude. He then switched to fire magic and began forming a fireball above his right hand. The fireball grew and shrank repeatedly. When he got it to the strength he wanted, he fired it up into the sky at the barrel. The fireball climbed so high that it vanished from sight. A few moments later, the fireball hit the barrel, resulting in an immense explosion that encompassed much of the sky above them. The explosion was so high up in the sky that they saw the flash of the explosion but didn't hear it. The clouds over the capital city blew away in a giant ring in the sky. Jack got on the radio.

"Prepare for the shockwave and the boom," he said on the radio.

Lia raised the shield once again and told everyone to cover their ears. A few seconds later, an earth-shattering boom shook everything around them, and the shockwave kicked up a cloud of dust everywhere. The king and queen were extremely impressed, and a number of the nobles were visibly shaken. Crescia's fur was practically standing on end. Still enveloped in a cloud of dust, Jack got on the radio.

"Too much?" he said.

"A little," said Lia.

"Sorry," said Jack.

Queen Liandra took the radio from Lia.

"How do you work this device? Press this button, right?" she said to Lia.

Lia nodded. Queen Liandra pushed the talk button on the radio.

"Jack? Can you hear me? This is Liandra." she said.

"Coming through loud and clear, Your Royal Highness," said Jack.

"That was most impressive, Jack. Most impressive. Well done. Come rest now." she said.

"Thank you. I'll be on my way once the dust clears," said Jack.

Jack once again used wind magic, and with a quick burst, he parted the dust down the middle of the training grounds, sending it far away to his left and right. Finally, he held his hands up and formed a large orb of water above his head. He released it and let it splash down on top of him.

"Ooh, that's refreshing," he said.

He shook the water off of his head and made his way toward the spectators. When he got within about ten feet from them, he spoke.

"So, how did I do?" he asked, while breathing heavily.

Queen Liandra and King Daven both stood and clapped a few times.

"You did splendidly, my boy. Absolutely splendid. A most impressive display. Yes, indeed. Most impressive," said King Daven.

"Yes, Jack. You were wonderful," said Queen Liandra.

Jack bowed.

"You honor me with your praise," he said.

When Jack stood back up, he stumbled a bit. Lia rushed to him.

"Jack! Are you all right?" she asked worriedly.

"Yeah. It just took a lot out of me. That's all," he replied.

"Please, come. Sit," said Queen Liandra.

"Yes, my boy. Sit. You've certainly earned some rest," said King Daven.

Once Jack sat down, a number of the nobles began to gather around him and bombard him with questions about his magic, about being an Otherworlder, and, much to Lia's annoyance, about whether he might be interested in marrying any of their daughters. Jack did his best to answer as many questions as he could, trying his best to ignore the ones about marriage proposals until Queen Liandra stepped in.

"Now, now. That's enough. Let the poor man rest. Can't you see that he is tired?" she said as she shooed the nobles away.

Jack mouthed the words 'thank you' to Queen Liandra, and she gave him a nod and a quick wink. King Daven noticed how exhausted Jack appeared to be and decided to help.

"Perhaps now is a good time to return to the castle. Let the young ones rest for a moment," he said, not so subtly hinting to the nobles that it was time to go.

As they left, each noble reached their hand out to shake Jack's hand as they passed by. Jack obliged and shook each of their hands. Count Avomir did his best to keep his distance from Jack, choosing to bow repeatedly as he backed toward the carriage instead of shaking his hand. Jack chuckled at Count Avomir's reactions. When the carriages left, Lia sat down next to Jack. Jack slumped over and laid his head in her lap.

"I'm spent," said Jack.

"You're all wet," said Lia.

"Sorry," said Jack.

Lia concentrated for a moment and used her water magic to try and draw some of the water away from Jack.

"That's handy," said Jack.

"How long do you plan on lying on my lap?" Lia asked as she ran her fingers through Jack's hair.

"I don't know. Perhaps two, maybe three days," said Jack.

"How about two or three more seconds?" said Lia.

"How about two or three more minutes?" asked Jack.

"Deal," said Lia.

Crescia leaned in from behind them.

"You guys are so cute together," she said.

Lia took some of the water she had pulled away from Jack and splashed it at Crescia.

"Hush, you," said Lia, smiling.

Crescia shivered at the cold water that dripped off her ears.

"Jack's right. This is refreshing," she said with a smile before shaking her head, spraying the water everywhere.

#####

After they returned to the castle, Jack took the opportunity to get some rest before dinner. Lia spent some time catching up with Crescia. When dinnertime came, Jack and Lia once again joined the king and queen. Crescia attended as well. As they ate, they discussed the events of the day, as well as going into more detail about all of the events that had led Jack to that point, including his arrival and his journey to Zavyra and the training she provided to him. Crescia, being the only one in the room who didn't know about Zavyra's true appearance, was, needless to say, quite shocked at the revelation. Afterward, Crescia was sworn to secrecy about

Zavyra's identity. Once dinner was over, everyone retired to their rooms for the night.

#####

Later that night, Jack was getting some well-earned sleep when he heard his door open. When he opened his eyes, he saw a giant silhouette standing in the doorway. He carefully pulled his left hand out from under the covers. As the silhouette approached, Jack raised his hand and began to form a fireball. The light from the fireball illuminated the room, revealing that the silhouette belonged to Nadi, the orc captain of the castle guard. Jack reached over and turned on the light.

"What are you doing here?" Jack asked.

"I have come to retrieve you. We shall mate," said Nadi.

"We shall what, now?!" said Jack, shocked by her statement.

"I observed you during your demonstration. You are strong in magic. I am strong in muscle. Our offspring shall be strong in both," said Nadi.

"No, they won't! We're not doing anything!" said Jack.

"Why do you decline?" asked Nadi.

"First, I'm seeing someone. Second, you would most definitely break me," said Jack.

"I do not wish to form a relationship with you. I simply wish to use you to create strong offspring," said Nadi, calmly.

"Well, I respectfully decline!" said Jack, backing further away in the bed.

"Come, now. I will take you to my chambers," said Nadi.

"No, you won't! No means no!" said Jack.

As Jack backed up to the edge of the bed, he knocked over the nightstand, making a large crash. Nadi took him by the leg and picked him up like he was a doll.

"Worry not, human Jack. I shall be gentle," she said.

"I don't want you to be gentle! I don't want you to be rough! I just want to get some sleep!" said Jack, struggling futilely, grasping onto the bed frame.

The commotion was loud enough to wake Lia down the hall. She and Crescia came down the hallway and stopped in front of the open door to Jack's bedroom. When they looked inside, they saw Nadi holding Jack by the ankle as he hung upside down still clinging onto the now loose board that was part of his bed frame. Jack looked over at Lia.

"Help!" said Jack.

"Nadi, would you kindly release my future husband and explain yourself?" Lia said calmly.

Nadi turned to see Lia in the doorway and immediately dropped Jack, who landed on his head on the floor.

"Ow," said Jack.

"Your Highness!" said Nadi.

"Care to tell me why I was woken up to find you preparing to carry the man I'm going to marry out of his room by the ankle?" Asked Lia.

"The man you're going to marry?!" said Nadi, surprised by what Lia had just said. "I was not informed of this!"

"It was my choice not to inform you. It was not of your concern," said Lia. "Now, return to your room and speak of this to no one, and I will do the same."

"Yes, Your Highness," said Nadi.

Nadi bowed and left the room. Crescia walked over to Jack, who was still lying face down on the floor where Nadi dropped him.

"Hey, Jack. You dead?" Crescia asked.

"Is she gone?" asked Jack.

"Yep. All gone, now," said Crescia.

Jack sat up.

"Well... That happened," said Jack.

"Are you all right, Jack?" asked Lia.

"I'm fine. Definitely not getting any more sleep for the night, but otherwise, fine," said Jack.

"Do you have your strength back yet?" asked Lia.

"For the most part, yeah. I'd say I'm pretty much

recovered from the demonstration," said Jack.

"Then how about some late-night tea and a snack back in my room?" said Lia.

"Now that's an offer I can say yes to with no hesitation. And you don't even have to drag me by the ankle to get me there," said Jack. "Just let me put some clothes on, and I'll be right there."

Jack, Lia, and Crescia spent the rest of the night chatting and eating snacks.

#####

The next morning, Jack was once again called to the throne room to appear before the king and queen. When he entered the throne room, he was a bit surprised to see Nadi standing there by the king. Given the events of the night before, Jack was worried that she had revealed Jack and Lia's engagement to the king, even after Lia ordered her not to do so. Lia arrived shortly after Jack.

"Step forward, Jack," said King Daven.

Jack reluctantly approached the king and queen as requested. When he got within eight feet of the throne, King Daven spoke again.

"That's far enough. Take a knee." King Daven said before drawing the sword that was leaned against his throne.

"*This is it,*" thought Jack. "*He knows about Lia and I, and he doesn't approve, so it's off with my head. Oh well. It was fun while it lasted.*"

As he knelt there with his head down, waiting for the end to come, he felt the blade of the sword touch his left shoulder. It didn't hurt anywhere near as much as he expected. In fact, it didn't hurt at all. He then felt the sword blade touch his right shoulder. He then heard the voice of the king again.

"Raise your head, Jack," he said.

Jack looked up at the king and queen.

"Prince Jack of the Kingdom of Stobrimore, due to

your service to the Vedyrian Kingdom, by order of the king, I now grant you the rank and authority of Vice-commander of the Vedyrian Army. Henceforth, you shall have command authority over all but the Commander, Crown Princess Lia," said King Daven.

Both Jack and Lia were shocked by what the king had just said. On one level, Jack was relieved that his head was still connected to his shoulders, but on another level, he was completely surprised to be given command of a vast army in a parallel world. It was all a lot to take in.

"Rise," said King Daven.

Jack stood.

"Well, do you have anything to say?" asked Queen Liandra.

"A lot of things I probably shouldn't say in mixed company, so I suppose that it would be best in this situation to just say thank you." Jack said before smiling and bowing.

"Congratulations, Jack," said Queen Liandra, with a chuckle.

After a few awkward moments, Jack looked at Lia and then back at the king and queen.

"Is that it?" Jack asked.

"That's it," said Queen Liandra.

"I can go now?" Jack asked.

"Yes. You can go now." Queen Liandra said with a laugh.

"Thank you," said Jack, bowing a few more times before turning and walking to Lia.

As they both walked out of the throne room, Jack turned to Lia.

"That was certainly... unexpected," said Jack.

"Indeed," said Lia.

"Does this mean that I outrank Alivair now?" asked Jack.

"I think it does," said Lia.

"And just when we were starting to become friends," said Jack.

#####

As they walked down the corridor, a soldier approached them.

"Your Highness. I have a report from the battlefront," said the soldier.

"Proceed," said Lia.

"The last battle was a victory. There were a total of twenty-eight casualties. Seventeen dead and eleven injured. Captain Alivair was among the injured," said the soldier.

"How bad?" asked Jack.

"Seven broken ribs. Severe burns to the right side of his torso and major damage to his right arm," said the soldier.

Lia turned to Jack.

"We should probably get back," she said.

"I have an idea. Tell Crescia to get our things together. I'll get us back to the camp within the hour," said Jack.

"Are you sure that's safe?" Lia asked.

"I should be able to transport us that far. I did it once with Rhandor and the dragons. Took about eight hours off our trip. It made him sneeze and made me feel a bit tingly, but I was fine. I should be able to do double that, I think," said Jack.

"Ok. I'll get things ready. Can you go tell my parents?" Lia asked.

"Sure. I'm on it," said Jack.

Lia made her way to get Crescia, and Jack made his way back to the throne room. When he got there, the king and queen were still there.

"Did you forget something, Jack?" Queen Liandra asked.

"We just got a report from the camp. There was a battle, and Captain Alivair has been badly injured. We need to get back," said Jack.

"We'll arrange for a carriage at once," said King Daven.

"Thank you, Your Majesty, but that's not necessary. I'm

going to try transporting us there. We can't waste any time," said Jack.

"Are you sure that's safe, Jack?" asked Queen Liandra.

"Yes, Your Royal Highness. I've done it before with Sir Rhandor and two lesser dragons. I don't see any reason why I couldn't do it again," said Jack.

"Very well. Let us know if there is anything we can do to assist you," said King Daven.

"Yes, Your Majesty," said Jack.

#####

Lia found Crescia in her room.

"We're returning to the camp. Gather our things and meet me in the throne room. I'll get Jack's things," said Lia.

"Yes, Your Highness," said Crescia.

After gathering their belongings, Lia and Crescia met Jack in the throne room.

"Ok. Both of you get in close," said Jack.

Lia and Crescia gathered close with the belongings in the middle of the throne room. Jack closed his eyes for a moment, and then, when he opened them, they were glowing purple. A glowing purple circle formed around Lia and Crescia. Jack walked into the circle. He turned to face the king and queen.

"Thank you for your hospitality. I'm looking forward to the next time we meet. Oh, and Your Majesty, one other thing. I'm in love with your daughter. I asked her to marry me. She said yes. Queen Liandra, could you fill him in?" Jack said.

Queen Liandra smiled and nodded. Lia looked at Jack with a shocked expression.

"Thank you," said Jack.

The circle rose from their feet, and they vanished. King Daven looked over at Queen Liandra.

"He proposed to my daughter, and she said yes?" said King Daven.

"It's really a lovely story," said Queen Liandra, smiling.

CHAPTER 29

Bilen was working on a battle plan for the next Dark Army intercept when Rhandor walked into his tent. A fairy was sitting on Rhandor's shoulder.

"Sir, we've just received reports from the fairies that there seems to be some strange rumbling coming from beneath the forest about a mile away from camp. They're not sure of the cause yet," said Rhandor.

"Very well. Send some men out to investigate," said Bilen.

"Yes, sir," said Rhandor.

Rhandor walked out of the tent to go select some soldiers to investigate.

#####

About fifteen minutes after Rhandor left, a purple circle formed on the ground in the Mage Corps section of the tent. The circle rose, and Jack, Lia, and Crescia appeared. The moment the teleportation circle vanished, Jack dropped to one knee. Blood began to drip from his nose.

"Jack! Are you all right?" asked Lia.

Jack stood up and wobbled as he tried to get his balance.

"I'm good. I'm fine. I guess I know the limit to my teleportation range now. There's a reason Zavyra told me to use it sparingly," said Jack as he wiped the blood from his nose.

"Are you sure?" asked Lia.

"Yeah. I'm all right. Just go. You have a lot to do. I'll make my way to the medical tent and check on Alivair," said Jack.

"Ok. Crescia, can you take care of our things?" asked Lia.

"Right away," said Crescia.

Lia walked over to Bilen's tent. Crescia walked up to Jack.

"Are you sure you're ok?" she asked.

"Yeah. I'm good," said Jack.

"I'll take your word for it, but don't push yourself, Jack," said Crescia.

"I won't," said Jack. "I'm going to go check in on Alivair."

"Ok," said Crescia.

Crescia began to gather up their belongings as Jack made his way to the medical tent.

#####

When he entered, Alivair was still lying on a stretcher, recuperating. Jack walked over and greeted him.

"So, I hear you got yourself a bit injured. How are you doing?" asked Jack.

"Jack? When did you return?" asked Alivair.

"Just now. A few minutes ago, actually. Heard you got into a bit of a scuffle and could use some backup. But first, let's take care of that injury of yours," said Jack.

Jack's eyes glowed white as he used his light magic to heal Alivair's injuries. When his injuries were fully healed, Alivair sat up in the bed and did a number of stretches and motions to check for any residual pain. He didn't feel any.

"The pain is gone. As are the wounds. You have my thanks, Jack," said Alivair.

"That's what friends are for," said Jack.

Alivair stood up and put his shirt on.

"So, how was your visit to the castle? Eventful, I'm guessing?" he said.

"You don't know the half of it. Get this. A few hours ago, to the shock of both me and Lia, the king granted me the rank of Vice-commander of the Vedyrian Army. How's that for eventful?" said Jack.

Alivair just stood there wide-eyed with his mouth hanging open after hearing Jack's news.

"Yeah, that's pretty much the same face I made when I heard it, too!" said Jack.

Jack thought for a moment about what he had said and tried to clarify.

"Oh! Wait! I'm not saying that I'm replacing you or anything! Not at all! It's a rank and authority thing. Not a position thing. You're still second in command. I'm just there in case the need arises. In case you or Lia are ever otherwise occupied or out of commission or anything, I can step in and take over in an official capacity. That's all." he said.

Alivair's expression changed slightly.

"I see. Well, then. It seems congratulations are in order," said Alivair.

"Thanks, but that's not important right now. Lia's back, too, and I'm sure she would like to know that her second in command was back in action," said Jack.

"Indeed," said Alivair.

Alivair left the medical tent. Just as he left, Jack's nose began to bleed again. He grabbed some gauze, rolled it up, and stuffed it up his nose.

"I must've burst a blood vessel." Jack said to himself in a now nasally voice.

With the gauze still in his nose, Jack made his way out of the medical tent and headed to the stables to say hello to Barvan and give Nava a few pets.

#####

When he got there, he saw Lia speaking with Alivair and Rhandor. They seemed to be concerned about something.

"What's going on?" Jack asked.

Rhandor turned to Jack.

"Hello, my friend. Welcome back," said Rhandor.

"Thanks. Good to be back. Is something happening?" asked Jack.

"I sent an investigation team out to go check out some strange rumbling in the forest about a mile from here. They took dragons, so they should have been there by now, but they haven't checked in yet. I loaned them one of your radios so we could stay in communication, but they don't seem to be responding," said Rhandor.

"Are you sure that their radio is on? Did you do a radio check before they left?" asked Jack.

"Of course. I did exactly as you instructed," said Rhandor. "Everything appeared to be functioning perfectly."

Jack turned to Alivair.

"Do you still have the binoculars?" Jack asked.

"Yes. I have them here," said Alivair as he handed them to Jack.

Jack then turned back to Rhandor.

"Give me the radio," he said.

Rhandor gave him the radio, and Jack ran over to Nava. After giving her a few quick pets to say hello, Jack brought Nava out of her pen and climbed onto the harness.

"We're going to get a bird's-eye view. Or, I guess, a dragon's-eye view," said Jack.

"Let's go, Nava." Jack said.

#####

Nava flew straight up, high into the sky, and after Jack gave her a few quick taps on the neck, she hovered in place. Jack took out the binoculars and scanned the horizon. Far in the distance, he saw the investigation team. They were engaged in battle against some necromancers. Jack took out the radio.

"Recon team. Does anyone hear me?" he said.

He got no response. Jack gave Nava another few taps, and she dove straight back down to the camp, hovering above Lia, Alivair, and Rhandor.

"They're fighting some necromancers at the forest's edge. We should give them some backup." Jack said.

"Good idea. Let's go," said Lia.

The three of them ran to their dragons, and they all flew toward the location of the investigation team at high speed.

#####

When the team was in sight, Alivair and Lia began launching fireballs at the necromancers. Several more necromancers emerged from the forest and began to return fire, launching bolts of dark magic energy at the dragons. Jack turned Nava around and then removed his legs from the harness cuffs and jumped.

"Is he insane?!" said Alivair as he watched Jack plummeting toward the ground.

"Just watch," said Lia.

When Jack got close to the ground, he used wind magic to slow his descent and tucked and rolled when he reached the ground. He put his hands on the ground, and his eyes glowed bright green. Walls of earth and stone rose up from the ground, creating a barrier between the investigation team and the necromancers. Rhandor landed behind one of the barriers and joined his men. Lia and Alivair continued to bombard the necromancers from the sky. Rhandor grabbed one of the injured soldiers and pulled them behind the barrier. He turned to the other soldiers.

"Is anyone else injured?" asked Rhandor.

"No, sir! But we've been pinned down!" said one of the soldiers.

"Why didn't you use the radio and call for backup?" asked Rhandor.

"The team leader dropped it during the attack as we were falling back, sir!" said the soldier.

Jack approached the soldier.

"Where?" he asked.

"Sir?" said the soldier.

"Where did he drop the radio?" Jack asked.

"Over there. About a hundred yards from the edge of the forest," said the soldier.

"Thanks," said Jack.

Jack began to walk toward the edge of the barrier.

"Where the hell do you think you're going?" asked Rhandor.

"I like that radio," said Jack. "I'm going to go get it back."

Jack raised a shield around him using light magic and started walking toward the necromancers. The soldier turned to Rhandor.

"Is he all right in the head? Is he suicidal or something?" asked the soldier.

"No. He's just really strong... and a bit weird," said Rhandor.

Jack began launching a barrage of fireballs at the necromancers as he continued to walk forward. He used wind magic to throw one necromancer into another. Lia and Alivair landed their dragons behind one of the barriers and continued to fire at the necromancers. When he located the radio on the ground, he walked over to it and bent over to pick it up. Just as he grabbed it, another necromancer appeared from the forest and pointed his staff at Jack. Lia and Alivair launched a pair of fireballs at the necromancer, launching him backward into a tree. Jack stood up with the radio in his hand.

"Got it!" he said.

As Jack began to make his way back, a voice screamed from the forest.

"Human!" the voice yelled.

Jack turned around just in time to see a massive sphere of dark magic heading right toward him at high speed. He had just enough time to put up a light magic shield, but the force of the impact still sent him flying through the air, slamming him into one of the barriers he had created earlier. Part of the barrier collapsed on top of him.

"Jack!" yelled Lia.

Lia ran over to the barrier and used her earth magic to rebuild the barrier around Jack, clearing most of the debris from him.

"Jack! Talk to me! Are you all right?" Lia said as she pushed the remaining debris off of Jack.

"Ow. That really hurt," said Jack. "What the hell hit me?"

"That was some high-level dark magic. It came from the woods," said Lia.

Another massive sphere of dark magic shattered half of the barrier where Jack and Lia were concealed.

Alivair and Rhandor called out to them.

"Your Highness! Jack!" yelled Alivair.

"Are you two all right?" yelled Rhandor.

Alivair turned to the other soldiers.

"Fall back!" he yelled.

The other soldiers began to fall back as Rhandor began launching wind blades into the woods, cutting down trees with each strike. Alivair began launching fireballs as he made his way over to Jack and Lia. The voice once again yelled out.

"I'm coming for you, human!" he said.

Lia stood up and pushed the debris off of herself and Jack. Alivair reached both of them. Jack was bleeding from his forehead, and Lia had some cuts and scratches, but they were otherwise all right.

"I'm starting to get the distinct impression that he has something against me." Jack said.

"Yes. That's the impression I'm getting as well," said Alivair.

"I'll try and draw his fire. You two hit him with everything you've got," said Jack.

"You're injured!" said Lia.

"Yeah, and if we stay here, we're all going to be injured, or worse. Let's draw him out." Jack said.

Jack stood up and started running. As he ran, he yelled at the unknown attacker in the woods.

"Here I am, Skippy! Come get me!" he yelled.

As Jack ran, a stream of deep red flame shot out from the woods and headed right for him. Jack used water magic to try and douse the flames. When it proved ineffective, he made the decision to try using the teleportation magic while running. With his eyes glowing purple, he vanished mere seconds from impact by the flame and reappeared a few dozen feet from Lia and Alivair. Being the first time he tried teleporting while moving, it didn't end well, because he wasn't able to take his forward momentum into account, resulting in him appearing at the same velocity he was moving when he teleported, sending him tumbling across the ground. After Jack stood back up, he taunted the unknown attacker again.

"Hey Skippy! How about you stop hiding in the trees like a poop-flinging monkey and show yourself!" he yelled.

The unknown attacker fell for the taunt, hook, line, and sinker, and made his way out of the woods, revealing himself to be Corvan.

"Oh... wait. I know that guy," said Jack.

"You know that dark elf?" asked Alivair.

Rhandor chimed in.

"That's the leader of the dark elves who tried to take Jack back in Ackhard," said Rhandor.

Corvan pointed both of his hands at Jack and began charging up a giant dark magic sphere to launch at Jack. The sphere grew to about the size of an exercise ball before he launched it at Jack.

"Uh oh. He looks pissed," said Jack. "Time to get serious."

Jack held out both of his hands, and his eyes began to transition back and forth between red and yellow glows. He formed an immense tornado of fire in front of him and sent it in Corvan's direction. The fire tornado dispersed part of the sphere, but the remainder continued heading toward Jack.

"Shit," said Jack. "This is really going to suck."

Jack tried to absorb the dark magic. When it hit him, he was once again sent flying backward. He used wind magic to slow himself down before hitting the ground, but he still came down hard. The scars along his arms began to glow. Jack stood up, in a significant amount of pain, and raised his hand, aiming it at Corvan. A glowing sphere of purified dark energy began to form in front of Jack's palm. After a moment, the sphere became a focused beam of dark magic energy roughly the same diameter as a tree trunk. Corvan raised his right hand to try to deflect the oncoming beam but failed, and the beam sent him flying back into a tree, completely disintegrating his right arm up to the elbow. Corvan let out a scream of agony as he looked at the smoldering stump where his right arm used to be. He stumbled to his feet and ran into the forest. Jack dropped to his knees and vomited out a black, tar-like fluid before the scars stopped glowing. After he stopped vomiting, Jack fell over on his side. Lia ran to him.

"Jack! Jack!" she yelled as she ran.

Jack held up his hand and pointed at one of the remaining necromancers that was trying to resurrect the fallen ones.

"Necromancer... is... necromancing," said Jack.

Lia turned to look where he was pointing and called to Alivair and Rhandor.

"Alivair! Rhandor! Stop him!" she said.

Alivair and Rhandor both saw the necromancer and charged toward him. Rhandor sent wind blades at him and cut off his outstretched hands. Alivair sent some fireballs at him and the fallen necromancers, setting the bodies ablaze. Lia dropped to her knees next to Jack.

"Jack! Are you all right?" she asked worriedly.

"I was right. That sucked. That sucked so bad," said Jack, still in pain.

Lia helped Jack to sit up. He wiped his mouth with his sleeve.

"What happened? I've never seen you respond like that before," said Lia.

"Zavyra told me that I apparently reject and purify the corrupted dark magic that the Dark Army uses, but this stuff was corrupted on a whole other level. It was nothing like the last time I was hit with his magic. It was way more powerful and way more tainted. Something must have happened," said Jack.

"Can you stand?" asked Lia.

"Yeah. Just let me catch my breath for a second, and I'll be good," said Jack.

After taking a few deep breaths, Jack stood up and spat out the remnants of the black ooze. Lia placed her hand on his forehead and used light magic to heal the wound.

"Thanks. That's much better," said Jack.

The soldiers who were part of the original investigation team approached as Jack, Lia, Rhandor, and Alivair gathered together.

"Who was that guy?" asked Lia.

"Based on the intel that we've gathered from our previous battles, I believe that he is called Corvan. He's the brother of Karvan, the dark elf general of the Dark Army," said Alivair.

"Well, he certainly doesn't like me very much," said Jack.

"Clearly an understatement," said Rhandor.

"We should go after him," said Jack.

"You're in no shape to continue fighting," said Lia.

"I'll be fine. We can't let him get away. He's way too volatile to let him run loose in the forest so close to base," said Jack.

"I'd have to agree, Your Highness," said Alivair.

"As do I," said Rhandor.

"Very well," said Lia, before turning to the other soldiers. "You take the wounded back to camp. You help him. The rest of you, follow us."

The group made their way into the forest. Lia and Alivair took the lead. Rhandor and Jack followed behind them, and the remaining soldiers took the rear.

#####

As they walked, Jack stumbled from time to time, and Rhandor caught him.

"Are you sure you should be accompanying us?" Rhandor asked.

"Yeah. I'm fine. Let's talk about something. I need to get my mind off of the taste of that black ooze," said Jack.

"Very well. How was your trip to the castle?" asked Rhandor.

"Pretty good. Oh, and get this. The king granted me the rank of Vice-commander of the Vedyrian Army. How's that for cool?" Jack said.

"Congratulations, my friend," said Rhandor.

"Thanks. And one more thing. I'm going to need your services as best man," said Jack.

"What are you saying, Jack?" asked Rhandor.

"I proposed to Lia. She said yes," said Jack.

"What happened to taking things slow? The shaky bridge thing and all that?" asked Rhandor.

Jack thought for a moment.

"Uh... that was superseded by the road trip effect," said Jack.

"Oh? And what is that?" asked Rhandor, with a hint of skepticism in his voice.

"It's, um, it's a thing where, if you can spend sixteen hours in a vehicle with someone and not feel like killing each other by the time the trip is done, it's a sign that it's meant to be," said Jack.

"That explanation sounds far less scientific than the last one," said Rhandor.

"It's real. Trust me. It was a study done by two very

renowned doctors in their fields. Doctor Who and... um... Doctor Pepper, I believe. Yeah," said Jack.

"Mmm hmm. Sure, Jack. Either way, congratulations on your engagement. It will be my honor to serve as your best man," said Rhandor.

"Thanks, Rhandor. I knew I could count on you," said Jack.

Alivair held up his hand to signal the group to stop. Jack and Rhandor approached Lia and Alivair.

"What is it?" asked Jack.

"Over there," said Alivair, pointing in the distance. "It appears to be a recently dug tunnel or cave. We should check it out."

"Agreed," said Lia. "But approach it with extreme caution. It could be a trap."

The group spread out and carefully approached the opening. Jack got down on the ground and low-crawled up to the entrance. He checked around the perimeter of the entrance for any signs of booby traps. He didn't find anything.

"The entrance looks clear," he said.

"Very well. I'll go in first. Jack, you follow behind me. Then Alivair, and then Rhandor. The rest follow behind him," said Lia.

"Are you sure that's a good idea?" asked Jack.

"A good commander leads their soldiers into battle from the front," said Lia.

"Ok. Just be careful," said Jack.

Lia climbed down into the tunnel, and Jack followed right behind her. When everyone was inside the tunnel, Lia held up her hand and lit the area with light magic. The tunnel seemed to be carved out of the surrounding rock, suggesting that it was not a naturally formed tunnel. It went straight for as far as they could see.

"Now I'm wishing I brought my sword with me," said Jack.

Lia stopped and looked at him.

"To fight with! I didn't mean that I wanted to use it as a torch or anything." Jack said defensively.

"I see," said Lia, turning back to face down the tunnel.

Jack looked back at Rhandor and Alivair with a slight grin and gave a quick nod, confirming that he was intending to use the sword as a torch. Alivair grinned, and Rhandor let out a little chuckle. As they slowly continued down the tunnel, Alivair began to get a closer look at the walls.

"These walls look freshly formed. I'm starting to believe that the Dark Army dug them in order to ambush us," he said.

"Quite possible," said Lia. "All the more reason we should find out where it goes."

As Lia took a few more steps forward, Jack noticed a peculiar glint from the wall. Just as Lia was about to walk by it, Jack grabbed the back of her collar and pulled her back to him. He put his right hand out to stop Alivair and Rhandor from going any further forward.

"What is it?" asked Lia.

"I saw something," said Jack.

Jack turned around to face Alivair, Rhandor, and the rest of the soldiers.

"Anyone have a piece of paper or a scrap of cloth or anything?" Jack asked.

One of the soldiers spoke up.

"I have this rag that I've been using to clean my boots," said the soldier.

"Pass it forward," said Jack.

The soldier passed the rag to Rhandor, who passed it to Alivair, who passed it to Jack. Still holding onto Lia, Jack moved the rag carefully forward around the same location as the glint he had seen. The moment he moved the rag beyond the point, the bottom half of the rag fell to the ground.

"What happened?" asked one of the soldiers.

"It looks like a tripwire or something. Let me get a closer look," said Jack.

He moved closer to the area where he saw the glint and used a small amount of fire magic to light the area. As he moved his hand, he saw what it was. There was a super-fine razor-sharp strand of some sort of crystalline material going entirely across the width of the tunnel. It had been placed there by Corvan as he escaped, with the intent to cause severe wounds to anyone who took the risk of pursuing him. Jack increased the size of the fire magic in his hand. When he held it directly under the strand, it burned away like a cannon fuse.

"That was close," said Lia.

"Too close," said Jack. "I didn't even feel any resistance passing the rag over it. Had you walked into that, who knows how bad the injuries could have been?"

"How should we proceed?" asked Alivair.

"I have an idea," said Jack.

He positioned Lia behind him and closed his eyes. When he opened them, they were glowing red and yellow. Jack used the wind and fire magic to form a disc of flame in front of him, kept flat by being held between two wind magic layers. He grew the flaming disc to be large enough to encompass the majority of the size of the tunnel path. He then used wind magic to propel the flame disc forward down the tunnel. As the disc traveled further down the tunnel, the group was able to see multiple strands of the crystalline razor wire burning away in numerous locations and at different heights along the tunnel path. One by one, they glowed and then burned away like threads of steel wool that were exposed to an open flame. The flame disc traveled a significant distance down the tunnel before they no longer saw any more crystalline razor wire burning away.

"Clearly, someone doesn't want us following him," said Jack.

"Indeed," said Rhandor.

As they continued down the tunnel, Alivair noticed something peculiar about the walls of the tunnel.

"Is it me, or do the walls appear to be getting damp?" he

asked.

"Everyone stop for a moment," said Lia.

Lia closed her eyes and focused on the sounds around her.

"Alivair, do you hear that?" asked Lia.

Alivair listened closely.

"It sounds almost like flowing water," said Alivair.

Rhandor placed his ear against the wall of the tunnel.

"Indeed. And it sounds like the water is flowing above us," said Rhandor.

"Please don't tell me that this guy dug a tunnel under a body of water," said Jack.

"It would appear so," said Lia.

"Great. That makes me feel all warm and fuzzy," said Jack.

"I'm not sure I understand that phrase," said Rhandor.

"That's because you're literally all warm and fuzzy. I was speaking metaphorically... and sarcastically," said Jack.

"I see," said Rhandor.

"We best continue with the utmost caution," said Lia.

#####

Deeper in the tunnel, Corvan reached the intersect, where the offshoot tunnel branched into the main tunnel system. He grasped the stump where his right arm once was, trying not to pass out from the pain. He closed his eyes and concentrated. When he opened them, they glowed a deep red. Black smoke-like energy emanated from the edges of his eyes. The stump began to glow. As the glow increased, bone began to grow from the stump, and black muscle followed the bone. His arm crackled like a burning log as it slowly regenerated. Corvan undid the buckle on his belt and took it off. He folded it and placed it in his mouth and did his best to muffle his screams as his arm continued to regenerate. As his hand began to form, the bony fingers stretched out into razor-sharp claws.

When the regeneration was complete, Corvan spat out the belt and looked at his new arm. It looked nothing like his old one. The flesh was pitch black and rough-textured like crocodile skin. His forearm was thin, with the bone barely covered by the black flesh, but it was by no means weakened, despite its appearance. His elongated fingers were tipped with eight-inch-long claws. As the pain subsided, Corvan could hear the distant voices of his pursuers. He placed his newly formed hand against the wall of the tunnel and sent a burst of dark energy into the wall. The energy spread down the walls of the offshoot tunnel.

#####

Further back in the tunnel, Lia, Jack, Rhandor, Alivair, and the soldiers saw a red glow approaching them rapidly. Lia and Jack both used light magic to put up a multi-layered shield to take the impact of the dark energy. The energy hit the shields and dissipated.

"What the hell was that?" asked Alivair.

"He really doesn't want us to follow him," said Jack.

"Well, he's about to be disappointed," said Lia.

Drops of water began to form in the upper left wall of the tunnel. Soon small streams began to spray from the wall.

"This tunnel isn't going to last much longer," said Lia.

"Then let's just freeze the water," said one of the soldiers as he placed his hand against the wall.

"No!" yelled Alivair, but it was too late.

The soldier used his water magic skills to freeze the spraying water. A moment later, the rock surrounding the spraying water cracked, turning the small streams into a gushing torrent. Jack and Lia immediately activated their water magic to try and stop the flow of water. The force pushed Jack backward, slamming his back against the wall behind him. They struggled, but Jack and Lia were both able to stop the water from continuing to flow, if only temporarily.

"You fool!" said Alivair to the soldier. "Ice expands! Do you want to kill us all?"

Jack's nose began to bleed again.

"Jack! Are you all right?" asked Rhandor.

"I'm holding up a damn lake! Of course I'm not all right!" said Jack.

From the other side of the suspended water, Lia yelled to the rest of the group.

"Fall back! We can't hold this forever!" she yelled.

"What about you, Your Highness?" Alivair responded.

"I'm staying with Jack! Go! Now!" said Lia.

"Can you just teleport us out of here, Jack?" asked Rhandor.

"It's too dangerous," said Jack, as he struggled with the water pressure. "I don't know where we are. I could end up teleporting us into solid rock."

"We're not leaving you two here!" yelled Alivair.

"If I let this go, we will all drown," said Jack. "Now go!"

"No!" yelled Alivair.

"Jack. Do it," said Lia.

"Rhandor! Shield!" said Jack.

Rhandor, understanding what Jack meant, pulled Alivair to him and, using his shield brace, created a spherical shield around him, Alivair, and the soldiers.

"Ready! Good luck, my friend!" said Rhandor.

Jack pointed his left hand at the group, continuing to keep his right hand up to control the flow of water. The glow of his eyes started to transition between blue and yellow.

"Brace yourselves!" yelled Rhandor.

Jack then used wind magic to propel the group back down the tunnel like a bullet down the barrel of a gun. When they were out of sight, Jack looked over at Lia.

"I don't know how we're going to get out of this one," he said, as blood continued to pour out of his nose.

Lia grabbed onto Jack's right hand and used light magic to form a shield around them.

"Earth magic, Jack. Try to seal the hole," she said.

"Ok. I'll try," said Jack, grasping her hand tightly. "I love you, Lia."

"I love you, too, Jack," said Lia.

Jack closed his eyes for a moment. When he opened them, the glow began transitioning between blue and green. The tunnel began to shake as the walls started to move, closing in on the gushing water.

"I think it's working!" said Lia.

The water flow started to lessen for a moment, but then the walls cracked further under the pressure.

"I can't hold it! Don't let go!" Jack said, realizing what was about to happen.

The wall began to crumble. The water slammed down into them, tossing them around like rag dolls. Unable to hold on, Lia's hand separated from Jack's.

"No!" yelled Jack from inside the bubble created by the shield.

Lia was carried down the tunnel by the rushing water. Jack was tumbled around and pushed up into the now gaping hole in the tunnel where the water was flowing into the tunnel. The bubble of air created by Jack's shield sent him flying up through the water like a cork as Lia disappeared into the further depths of the tunnel.

#####

At the intersect, Lia came shooting out, slamming into the wall of the connected tunnel from the main system where Corvan was standing, knocking her unconscious. Corvan dug his clawed hand into the wall to stop himself from being swept away by the water. He used magic to collapse the offshoot tunnel to stop the flow of water. As the water subsided, Corvan released the wall and walked over to the now unconscious Lia on the floor of the tunnel.

"Well, well, well. How fortuitous," said Corvan as he

reached down to grab Lia by her collar.

CHAPTER 30

At the entrance to the tunnel, Rhandor, Alivair, and the soldiers shot out like a cannonball, landing on the ground nearby. Moments later, water came gushing out of the tunnel entrance. Alivair stood up first and ran as fast as he could back toward the tunnel entrance. Rhandor caught up to him and grabbed him by the arm.

"Your Highness!" yelled Alivair.

Rhandor pulled Alivair back.

"They're gone, Captain!" said Rhandor, struggling not to break down himself.

"No! They could still be alive!" said Alivair.

"It's... unlikely," said Rhandor.

Alivair's despair turned to anger as he approached the soldier who had used the water magic. He picked the soldier up off his knees and then punched him in the face, knocking him to the ground.

"You bastard! You killed them!" he yelled.

Alivair then walked over and grabbed the soldier by the shirt with his left hand and formed a fireball with his right hand.

"Alivair!" yelled Rhandor.

"Give me one good reason! One reason why he shouldn't die right here and now!" Alivair yelled to Rhandor.

"We've lost enough today!" said Rhandor. "We need to return to camp and regroup!"

Alivair dropped the soldier back to the ground and walked away. He launched the fireball into a boulder, shattering it. He looked up to the sky and screamed. Rhandor walked over to the soldier on the ground and picked him up.

"We'll deal with the consequences of your actions later," said Rhandor.

Rhandor walked over to the other soldiers and helped them to their feet.

"Everyone form up and move out!" he said.

Rhandor then walked up to Alivair and placed his hand on his shoulder.

"Your soldiers need you. Now more than ever. We'll have time to mourn later," he said.

With tears in his eyes, Alivair nodded.

The group formed up and started their journey back to the camp.

#####

In the area above where the water had rushed into the tunnel, Jack was launched out of the water with great force, flying through the air until he impacted on a shallow area of the lake. The force of the landing knocked him unconscious, leaving him floating face up in the shallow water. The blood that continued to pour out of his nose spread out in the water around him, slowly clouding the area around his head in red. In the distance, a fairy hiding up in a tree peeked out to get a better look at the sight of the stranger who just came erupting from the lake, which was now slowly draining away.

#####

Back at the camp, Alivair, Rhandor, and the soldiers arrived on the dragons. When they came in for a landing, Barvan noticed that Jack and Lia were both missing. Alivair immediately made his way to the command tent after getting off of his dragon. Barvan walked up to Rhandor.

"Where are Jack and Her Highness? Why didn't they come back with you?" he asked.

"They're... missing," said Rhandor before taking a deep breath. "and presumed dead."

Barvan was in shock at Rhandor's words.

"What do you mean? Presumed dead? Are you sure?" asked Barvan.

"There was an incident. The tunnel we were in was flooded. We'd be dead, too, if Jack hadn't used his magic to propel us out of the tunnel. But Lia and Jack remained behind to give us a chance."

"So they may still be alive?" asked Barvan.

"It's possible, but unlikely," said Rhandor.

"Well, I'm going to hold out hope," said Barvan.

Rhandor recalled the good news that Jack had shared with him on their way to the tunnel. He thought about how Jack and Lia were engaged to be married. He thought about all of the incredible things he had seen Jack accomplish since he met them. He didn't want to believe that they were dead.

"As am I, Barvan. As am I," said Rhandor. "For now, please keep this information to yourself. The last thing we need right now is to send the thousands of soldiers here into a panic."

"Understood," said Barvan.

Rhandor gave Barvan a nod as he placed his hand on his shoulder before walking to speak to Alivair again.

#####

When he arrived at the command tent, Alivair was still furious. Papers were scattered around the tent, and a dagger was embedded into the table.

"Captain?" said Rhandor.

"Rhandor, we need to get back out there. They're alive. I know they're alive," said Alivair.

"They may be alive, but what do you propose we do? You saw the force of that water coming out of the tunnel. It was still coming out at full force even when we left. That tells me that either the other end of that tunnel has been blocked off or it is being fed by a significant body of water. It will likely be some time before we will get a chance to explore that tunnel again," said Rhandor.

"There has to be something we can do. I refuse to accept that they are dead," said Alivair.

"Why not employ the fairy network? The forests are their domain, after all." asked Rhandor.

Alivair began to calm down a bit and realized that Rhandor's suggestion made a degree of sense.

"Yes. That's a good idea. I'll summon Fyn and see what information he can find," said Alivair.

"One more thing," said Rhandor.

"What is that?" asked Alivair.

"We need to inform Crescia. She's Her Highness's personal attendant. She has a right to know," said Rhandor.

"Very well," said Alivair. "I shall take that task."

"No. I'll do it," said Rhandor.

Rhandor left the tent and made his way to Lia's tent in search of Crescia.

#####

When he got there, he found her still sorting Lia's personal items from the trip.

"Crescia, we need to talk," said Rhandor.

What is it?" asked Crescia.

"There was... an incident in the operation we just returned from," said Rhandor, trying to find the best words to use.

"What do you mean?" asked Crescia.

"It's about Her Highness and Jack," said Rhandor.

Crescia started to visibly shake due to Rhandor's tone of voice.

"What about them? Where are they?" she asked with tears starting to well up in her eyes.

"They're gone. A tunnel we were in collapsed, and water came flooding in. Jack and Her Highness used their magic to try and slow the flooding to give us a chance to escape. We made it out of the tunnel. They didn't," said Rhandor.

Crescia's knees began to buckle.

"What are you saying?" she asked.

"I'm saying that they're missing and presumed... dead. We don't know for sure, but it's not likely that they made it out of the tunnel alive," said Rhandor.

Crescia dropped to the floor of the tent.

"But... they could have, right? They could have made it out, right? They could still be alive, right, Rhandor?" she said as the tears began to stream down her cheeks.

Rhandor walked up to her and knelt down. He placed his hand on her shoulder to try and console her. She reached out and held him, burying her head in his chest as the tears poured out. Rhandor was trying his hardest not to tear up.

"I don't know. I just don't know," said Rhandor.

He continued to hold her as she cried for quite some time.

#####

Back by the lake, the fairy watched Jack for what felt like ages to see if he would get up on his own. After at least an hour of watching and waiting, she cautiously approached Jack as he still lay unconscious, floating in the shallow bank of the lake. She flew over and landed next to Jack's head. She saw the lump on the back of his head where it had struck the rocks when he came down. She then flew up and softly landed on his chest. The fairy knelt down and placed her ear against Jack's chest to listen for his heartbeat. She heard the steady beat of his heart. She flew down to his waist and began to check to see if he had any belongings on him that could be used to identify him. She reached into the pouch secured to his belt and, with some degree of effort, given her small size, she pulled out the radio that Jack had picked up earlier. Having never seen anything like it, she didn't know what to make of it. She dragged it up and set it down on Jack's chest. She then walked around it to try to figure out what it was. She started to press the various buttons to see what they did. She then turned the knobs on the top of the radio. One of the knobs made a click sound when she turned it, and then the radio beeped two times. That caught her by surprise, and she quickly flew back to the shore and hid behind a rock. She waited there for several minutes to see if anything else would happen. After making sure that the strange device wasn't dangerous, she flew back and landed next to it again. She started pressing buttons again, hearing various sounds with each button press. When she pressed the emergency alarm button, a loud tone played for five seconds. Once again, she was caught by surprise by the loud sound and flew back behind the rock.

#####

Back at the camp, having done all that he could to console Crescia, Rhandor was walking to the Mage Corps area in order to discipline the soldier who used the water magic in the tunnel. Just before reaching the soldier's tent, he heard a tone coming from the radio he still had attached to his belt. He immediately reached for the radio.

"Jack?! Jack! Is that you? Jack! Do you hear me?" he said.

Rhandor got no reply. He immediately turned around and ran back to the command tent. He burst into the tent and ran up to Alivair.

"Captain! I just got a tone on the radio!" said Rhandor.

"What does that mean?" asked Alivair.

"It could be Jack!" said Rhandor.

"Then he's alive?" asked Alivair excitedly.

"It's possible. Either that, or someone else found the radio," said Rhandor.

"Can we use the radio to find him?" asked Alivair.

"I'm not sure. I'm going to head out with Aris and try,

though. Here. Take my radio. Once I leave, press this button every few minutes. I'll see if Aris and I will be able to hear the alarm from the air," said Rhandor.

"Very well. Good luck, Rhandor," said Alivair.

#####

Rhandor left the command tent and made his way back to the stables. When he got there, Rhandor ran up to Barvan.

"Keep up that hope, Barvan. Ready Aris for a flight," Rhandor said.

Barvan's expression changed for the better when he saw Rhandor's enthusiasm, taking it as a good sign.

"Right away," said Barvan, as he made his way to Aris's pen.

Once Aris was prepped, Rhandor quickly hopped onto the harness, and they took flight and flew in the direction of the tunnel.

#####

Once they reached the forest, Rhandor directed Aris to fly at a low altitude over the trees. As he scanned the forest, he listened for the alarm tone on the radio. He reached into his pocket and pulled out a small whistle and blew into it, making a high-pitched tone. Shortly thereafter, a fairy approached Rhandor and landed on his shoulder.

"There's an ally down somewhere in the forest. They may be in possession of a device that makes an alarm sound. Spread the word throughout the network," said Rhandor.

The fairy nodded and flew down into the trees. Rhandor directed Aris to climb and hover so he could get a better view of the area. Not long after issuing the be-on-the-lookout request to the fairy, Rhandor saw a small flare-like burst of magic in the air in the distance. He pointed Aris toward the area where the magic flare had appeared, and they flew at top speed. As they got close, Rhandor was able to see a lake that seemed to be at a clearly lower level than normal. He brought Aris to a hover again as he scanned along the shoreline. The fairy that had been investigating Jack flew up to Rhandor and gestured for him to follow her. Soon afterward, Rhandor saw Jack floating face up in the water. Once Aris was close enough to the ground, Rhandor leaped off and ran to Jack. He picked up the radio that was on his chest and spoke into it as he checked for life signs on Jack.

"Alivair! Can you hear me?" he said into the radio.

A moment later, Alivair replied.

"Rhandor?" said Alivair.

"Yes! I found Jack!" said Rhandor.

"Is he alive?" asked Alivair.

"Yes, but he's unconscious," said Rhandor.

"And Her Highness?" Alivair asked.

Rhandor looked around the area.

"I don't see her. She's not here," he said.

"What's Jack's status?" asked Alivair.

"He appears to have sustained a number of injuries. I'm going to bring him back and get him treatment. Perhaps when he wakes up he can tell us something about Her Highness," said Rhandor.

"Very well. I shall meet you at the stables," said Alivair.

Rhandor examined Jack more thoroughly to see if he had any injuries that would prevent him from moving him safely. After determining that it was safe, Rhandor carefully lifted Jack up and secured him to the harness on Aris's back. He then turned to the fairy, who was still hovering around them.

"Thank you, friend. I am in your debt," said Rhandor.

The fairy nodded and then waved before flying away.

Rhandor then climbed onto the harness, and Aris took flight to head back to the camp. In the distance, concealed just under the tree canopy, a lone imp watched as Rhandor flew away.

#####

When Rhandor returned to the camp, Alivair was there to greet him. They carried Jack to the medical tent and called a healer over to treat him. Even after his wounds were healed, Jack didn't wake up.

"Why is he still unconscious?" asked Alivair.

"His body has been healed, but the amount of magic he used must have been immense. He will still need time to recover," said the healer.

"Damn. Time is the one thing we don't have," said Alivair.

"It's a good sign, Captain. If Jack lives, there's a chance that Her Highness lives as well," said Rhandor.

"We will have to wait until Jack wakes up to know," said Alivair.

"I will remain with him. The moment he wakes up, I'll retrieve you," said Rhandor.

"Very well," said Alivair. "Shall we inform Crescia?"

"Give her some time. She didn't take the news well, and she cried herself to the point of exhaustion. I will retrieve her later," said Rhandor.

Alivair nodded.

After Alivair left, Rhandor sat down on the stool next to Jack's cot. He placed his hand on Jack's shoulder. His hand was trembling. All of the mental walls that he had put up in order to try and stay objective were starting to come down, and he was just happy to see his friend again. And by seeing Jack alive, even after everything he had seen at the time told him that it would be impossible for either Jack or Lia to survive, the little flickering flame of hope he had that Lia was still alive was able to grow stronger and brighter.

#####

A few hours later, Rhandor made his way to Lia's tent. Crescia was still sleeping in Lia's bed, where Rhandor had placed her after she fell asleep from the exhaustion of crying.

He sat down on the bed and put his hand on her arm and gave it a little shake. She slowly opened her eyes and looked at him.

"What is it?" she said.

"We found Jack," said Rhandor.

Crescia darted up in the bed.

"Is he alive?!" she asked.

"Yes. But unconscious. He's in the medical tent," said Rhandor.

Barely a half a second after finishing his sentence, Crescia was already darting out of Lia's tent and heading toward the medical tent. She burst into the medical tent and immediately ran to Jack's side.

"Jack! Jack! Wake up! It's Crescia! Wake up!" she yelled.

Rhandor came into the tent.

"As I said, he's unconscious. He's sustained a number of injuries," he said.

"What about Her Highness? Did you find her, too?" she asked.

"No. We're hoping that Jack can fill us in when he wakes up," said Rhandor.

"But this means she could be alive, too. Doesn't it?" Crescia asked.

"I hope so. I really do," said Rhandor.

CHAPTER 31

Corvan emerged from the tunnel complex and was greeted by General Karvan.

"Welcome back, my brother," said Karvan, before noticing Corvan's change. "What the hell happened to your hand?"

"The human took my arm. His Excellency's power granted me a new and better one," said Corvan.

"I see," said Karvan, somewhat disgusted by his brother's new grotesque arm. "So, did you find the human?"

"He got away, but I have something else that may prove useful." Corvan said as he pulled on a rope.

From behind him, a flatbed mine cart rolled out of the tunnel and into view. Lying on the mine cart was Lia, still unconscious, with her hands tied behind her back and her legs bound.

"Is that who I think it is?" asked Karvan.

"Indeed it is," said Corvan.

Karvan summoned a number of Demonborne over.

"Take her. Have her cuffed and collared and placed in the dungeon. When she wakes, we shall bring her before His Excellency," said Karvan.

The Demonborne soldiers picked her up and carried her away. Karvan once again looked at Corvan's arm.

"Are you sure that you're all right, Corvan?" he asked.

"I'm fine, Brother. In fact, I'm better than I've ever been," said Corvan. "How goes your plan?"

"We are close. The tunnels are completed. The soldiers are ready. The attack is imminent. All that remains is His Excellency's order," said Karvan.

"Then why does he not simply give the order?" asked Corvan.

"He has a plan, Brother. It is not our place to question it. Only to implement it when the time comes," said Karvan.

"Very well. Let us go make sure we're ready when the princess awakens," said Corvan.

#####

A few hours later, Lia felt a screaming headache as she slowly opened her eyes. She found herself lying on a stone floor. As she lifted her head and looked around, she soon realized that she was in a cell. She tried to bring her hand to her face, but the cuffs that kept her hands secured behind her back prevented her from doing so. As she maneuvered her legs to allow her to sit up, she felt the pinch of the magic suppression collar around her neck. She winced in pain as she sat up. The throbbing pain of her injuries became more apparent as the fog of her recent unconsciousness lifted. She took a deep breath and felt the sharp stab of a cracked rib on her left side. A voice suddenly caught her attention.

"How do you like your accommodations, princess?" Karvan asked.

Lia cleared her throat and then winced in pain again as she felt the bite of the cracked rib.

"It's a lot less wet than the last place I was, so I'd consider it an improvement. Can't say much about the company, though," said Lia.

"So sorry to disappoint, Your Highness," said Karvan. "Fear not, though. Soon you'll find yourself in the company of His Excellency."

"Where's Jack? Is he here?" Lia asked.

"The human? He's dead," said Karvan.

"You're lying," said Lia.

"If what my little brother told me is correct, he dropped an entire lake on your human. Given that you were the only one to wash up at his feet, it's a pretty safe assumption that young Jack is no longer among the living," said Karvan.

"That thing is your little brother? You have my sympathies," said Lia.

"He always has been a bit... impulsive. He did take a great deal of joy in knowing that he killed your human after what young Jack did to him upon his arrival, though," said Karvan.

"You have no idea of how strong he really is. He's alive. I know it," said Lia.

"Perhaps. Unlikely, but possible. Either way, it's not like you'll be seeing him ever again, anyway," said Karvan.

"Why? Are you planning to kill me?" asked Lia.

"My dear, if we simply wished to kill you, we would have done so where we found you instead of bringing you here. No. We're not going to kill you. You will be presented to His Excellency. He will determine what is to be done with you," said Karvan.

"Passing me off to the boss? Of course you are," said Lia.

"What's that supposed to mean?" asked Karvan.

"Looking at the cleanliness of your uniform and boots, you don't seem like the type to get your own hands dirty. You send others into battle while you stay safe and secure here. Wherever here is," said Lia.

"You're in the dungeons of the Emperor's palace. As far as the cleanliness of my hands, I am the general of the Dark Army. Unlike your foolish kind, I know that one can best command an entire army from a central location instead of making myself a target on the battlefield for some lucky arrow or fireball to pick off. Had you done the same, you wouldn't be here," said Karvan.

"I must say, you seem a lot less bloodthirsty than I expected for the Great Demon Emperor's right-hand man," said Lia.

"I just wish for this foolish war to be over," said Karvan.

"I never did understand why you dark elves sided with

the Demon in the first place," said Lia.

"My people were the first to fall to the might of His Excellency. We asked for help from your kind, and it never came. Even before the Emperor came, your kind never much liked us dark elves. Rather than face extinction at his hands, we had no other choice but to join him. And once we defeat you, we will finally have peace," said Karvan.

"Peace will never occur as long as that demon exists," said Lia.

Karvan held up the brooch that Lia had previously had pinned on her shirt.

"A fascinating ornament. A gift from the human, I assume?" he said.

"I will be getting that back," said Lia.

"Not likely. This will be part of a message signaling the end of your army," said Karvan.

"My people will come for me, and this castle will fall," said Lia.

"I highly doubt that, princess. This palace and the surrounding land are entirely shrouded by His Excellency's dark magic. Your army could walk right by it and never even know it. We are a mere two and a half days march from your camp, and you haven't found us yet."

Lia was surprised by the revelation.

"Two and a half days? That's not possible," she said.

"Not only is it possible, princess. It is true," said Karvan.

"That would mean that..." said Lia, before being interrupted by Karvan.

"On a clear day, from the top of the highest palace tower, you can actually see the scars of Jack's handiwork in Arnin Canyon. You were so very close, and yet so far away."

Karvan then turned around and began to walk away.

"Leaving so soon?" said Lia.

"I must inform His Excellency that you are awake. Fear not, though. You won't be alone for long," said Karvan.

"Looking forward to it," said Lia sarcastically.

A few minutes later, Karvan returned with six Demonborne soldiers. He unlocked the cell door and sent the Demonborne soldiers in to pick Lia up. They brought her out into the passageway.

"Remove the cuffs," said Karvan.

One of the soldiers removed Lia's cuffs.

"Sure that's a good idea?" asked Lia.

"You're clearly seriously injured, princess. If you don't want to become further injured, you had best comply and come quietly. The other option is that we carry you, fully bound and gagged, and I don't think you want that. I will also tell you that should you try to escape, you will find that you have nowhere to run," said Karvan.

"Very well," said Lia.

"Follow me," said Karvan.

#####

Lia was escorted through the passageways of the palace until they came to the throne room doors. Before opening the door, Karvan turned to Lia.

"I wouldn't resist or try anything foolish if I were you. The Emperor will not hesitate to make it extremely painful for you should you try," he said.

Karvan put his hand on Lia's shoulder and walked her into the throne room, leaving the Demonborne soldiers to wait in the hall. He brought her to the middle of the throne room and placed her in front of a chair. He then turned to the throne, which seemed to be empty.

"Your Excellency. I have brought the princess," said Karvan.

From behind the throne, Lia heard the deep growling voice of the Emperor.

"Sit," said the Emperor.

"I'd prefer to stand, if it's all the same," said Lia.

Strands of dark magic began to crawl out from behind

the throne, like snakes, slithering across the ground until they split up and moved around Lia's feet, climbing up the back of the chair and then reaching out to Lia, wrapping around her and forcefully placing her in the chair.

"You will sit," said the Emperor.

He then emerged from behind the throne. Though the throne room was dark, Lia was still able to make out the outline of the Great Demon Emperor. The multiple layers of long black robes showed little of his nearly seven-and-a-half-foot tall frame. A heavy hood covered his head. The cloud of dark energy obscured his face, with nothing but the subtle blood-red glow of his eyes. It was Lia's first time actually seeing the Emperor. The threads of dark magic that were holding Lia to her chair began to crawl up her chest and, like the heads of small snakes, struck into her temples. Her eyes clouded over with a gray haze. Flashes of her memories began to appear, one after another, starting from the point when Jack arrived. Though Lia could no longer see the Emperor, she could still hear his voice. His words were slow and drawn out.

"Yes. I see. Such power. And what is this? You love him?" he said.

"Enough!" said Lia, as a tear fell from her eye as she watched the last moments again before she and Jack were separated. "Why are you doing this? If you're going to kill me, just kill me!"

"Child, what I have in mind for you is not death, but pain worse than death. You shall watch by my side as your world ends," said the Emperor.

The emperor formed an illusion around Lia, showing her soldiers dead at her feet. The sky was blood red. Next she was shown the capital city on fire, then the bodies of her mother and father, lying in the destroyed throne room. The final illusion she was shown was the castle exploding in a massive fireball, with Jack standing in the rubble. His eyes were black, and his skin was a dull gray. The Emperor's corrupted dark magic surrounded him like a fog. He raised his hands and brought down a rain of fire that destroyed everything in sight. When the illusion faded, Lia had tears in her eyes.

"Yes. That is only a taste of the despair you shall suffer," said the Emperor.

The strands of dark magic that were securing Lia to the chair reached up and wrapped around the collar around her neck, forming a chain.

"Come," said the Emperor.

He pulled her out of her seat and toward him. Karvan followed beside her.

#####

The Emperor walked through a doorway that led to a long spiral staircase. He, Lia, and Karvan ascended the spiral stairs until they reached a balcony at the top of the palace. From there, Karvan handed Lia's brooch to the Emperor. The Emperor secured the brooch with a strip of material taken from Lia's clothing while she was unconscious, along with a note, to a large metal spear. He then used dark magic to raise the spear up high into the air before launching it over the horizon.

"First, we shall give them hope. Then we shall rip it away," said the Emperor.

"Your Excellency. The soldiers are in place for the above-ground first wave," said Karvan.

"Very well, General. Begin the first wave," said the Emperor.

"Above-ground first wave?" asked Lia.

"Well, I suppose it couldn't hurt to tell you, given that you have no chance of escape. We're going to send a number of battalions on the ground to attack your camp. Once we lure your soldiers into the battlefield of our choosing, we will unleash the legions of soldiers we have ready underground to wipe your entire army off the map. That tunnel you were found in was merely a small offshoot of the vast tunnel complex we have constructed. Your soldiers will find themselves facing an army of more than seventy thousand Dark Army troops coming at them from every angle. You have no chance at success, princess," said Karvan.

CHAPTER 32

Alivair was preparing the next battle plan when he heard a voice yell out from outside the tent.

"Incoming!" yelled the soldier.

Alivair ran out of his tent to see what the soldier was yelling about. Just as he reached the common area of the camp, he watched as a giant steel spear plummeted out of the sky and pierced a table, missing a soldier by inches, before stabbing deep into the ground. Alivair ran up to the spear and then looked to the sky to see if any more followed. After a brief time with no signs of further attack, Alivair examined the spear. He found the strip of fabric torn from Lia's clothing tied near the tip of the spear, and when he untied it, he saw the brooch and a small note.

"Fetch Rhandor immediately!" Alivair yelled to one of the soldiers.

"Right away, sir!" said the soldier before running in the direction of the medical tent.

Alivair unrolled the note. There was a circular magic symbol on it, surrounded in runes. Rhandor ran up to Alivair and saw the spear.

"What is it? Are we under attack?" asked Rhandor.

"Here," said Alivair, as he handed the scrap of cloth and the brooch to Rhandor.

Rhandor looked at the brooch and scrap of cloth and recognized them immediately.

"This belongs to Her Highness! This is the pin that Jack gave her!" said Rhandor.

Alivair held up the note.

"This was attached. Do you recognize it?" asked Alivair.

Rhandor took the note and examined it.

"This is old magic. Ancient fairy magic, I believe. Fyn might be able to decipher it," said Rhandor.

Alivair pulled a small whistle out from his pocket. He put it to his lips and played a five-note tone. Within minutes, Fyn flew into sight and landed on Alivair's shoulder. Rhandor handed the note back to Alivair, and Alivair showed it to Fyn. Fyn looked closely at the note before whispering into Alivair's ear. After a few moments, Alivair nodded and turned to Rhandor.

"He said it is an ancient flame message. We must burn it to be able to see what it says," said Alivair.

"Then let us do so in the command tent," said Rhandor.

#####

Rhandor, Alivair, and Fyn made their way to the command tent. Once inside, Alivair formed a small fireball and touched the corner of the note to it. The note flew up into the air in front of both of them and flashed in a bright green burst of light before a smoke formed around them. In the smoke, a vision of Lia, lying unconscious in a cell, appeared before them. Along with the vision of Lia, an echoing voice was heard. It was the voice of Karvan.

"We have your princess. She lives, for now. If you want her back, come and get her," said Karvan.

In a second burst of bright green light, the smoke dissipated.

"She's alive!" said Alivair.

"Yes. But in the hands of the Dark Army," said Rhandor.

Alivair turned to Fyn.

"Send word through the network to every outpost, camp, and base of the Vedyrian Army. All soldiers are to assemble here as soon as possible. We are taking the war directly to the Emperor," he said.

Fyn nodded and flew off at high speed. Alivair then

turned to Rhandor.

"What of Jack? Is he still unconscious?" asked Alivair.

"Yes. The healers are still unable to wake him," said Rhandor.

"I pray that he wakes soon. We shall need him more than ever in the battle to come," said Alivair.

"I shall return to him," said Rhandor.

"Very well," said Alivair. "And Rhandor, inform Crescia that Her Highness is alive."

"Of course," said Rhandor.

#####

Rhandor entered the medical tent and sat down on the stool next to Jack's cot. Crescia walked in with a bowl with some cool water in it and a cloth to place on Jack's head. When she saw the expression on Rhandor's face, she immediately knew something was different.

"What happened? I heard a commotion," she said.

"I have good news and bad news," said Rhandor.

"What is it?" asked Crescia.

"The good news is that Her Highness appears to be alive," said Rhandor.

"That's amazing! Where is she?" asked Crescia.

"That's the bad news. She's currently being held by the Emperor," he said.

"What are we going to do?" asked Crescia.

"Alivair is forming a plan as we speak," he said.

But she's alive," said Crescia, just trying to confirm what Rhandor had said.

"Yes. It appears that she is alive," he said.

Rhandor then reached into his pocket and took out the brooch.

"This was attached to the spear that came down in the common area, along with a scrap of material from her clothing and a note that let us know that she's alive," he said.

Crescia took the brooch and held it tightly in her hands. "She's alive," she said.

#####

A few hours later, Rhandor was struggling to stay awake. His head would slowly lower along with his eyelids, and then he would catch himself dozing and raise his head and eyelids again. That routine was repeated eight more times before he heard a voice.

"Keep that up and you'll give yourself whiplash," said Jack in a rough voice.

Rhandor opened his eyes wide and looked at Jack.

"Jack! You're awake!" said Rhandor.

"More so than you, it seems," said Jack.

"How do you feel?" asked Rhandor.

"Well... like someone hit me with a lake to be honest," said Jack.

"I guess that would make sense," said Rhandor.

"How did I get back here?" asked Jack.

"A fairy found you in the shallows of the lake. She led me to you," said Rhandor.

"And Lia? Did you find her, too?" asked Jack.

"About that...," said Rhandor.

Jack raised his head from the pillow.

"Rhandor. Tell me you found her. Tell me she is alive," said Jack.

"She's alive," said Rhandor. "As far as we know."

"What the hell does that mean?" asked Jack.

Rhandor took a deep breath before explaining.

"She is a prisoner of the Emperor, Jack," said Rhandor.

Jack dropped his head back down on the pillow.

"Damn it. It's all my fault," said Jack in a disheartened tone.

"What's that supposed to mean?" asked Rhandor.

"If I had held on a little harder, we wouldn't have

become separated. The water just hit so hard that it ripped us apart. I should have held onto her hand," said Jack.

"The fact that either one of you, let alone the both of you, is still among the living is a miracle enough, Jack. As strong as you are, you're not all-powerful," said Rhandor.

"Clearly I'm not strong enough yet. So what are we going to do about it? What's the plan to get her back?" asked Jack as he sat up and tried to get out of the cot.

Rhandor stopped Jack from standing.

"Right now, the plan for you is to stay here and continue recovering. We're going to need you at full strength soon enough," said Rhandor.

"I can't just lay here while she's in danger, Rhandor," said Jack. "I've got to do something."

"What are you going to do, Jack? We don't even know where the Emperor's palace is," said Rhandor.

"I'll beat it out of every single Dark Army soldier I can get my hands on," said Jack.

"I share your sentiment, Jack. I really do. But before you go taking on the Dark Army all by yourself, you need to get your strength back. Otherwise, you won't be of any help to Her Highness," said Rhandor.

Jack finally realized the logic in Rhandor's argument and laid back down in the cot.

"Yeah. You're right. I hate to admit it, but you're right," he said.

"Welcome back, Jack," said Rhandor.

Jack and Rhandor were both startled by the sudden loud sound of a metal tray with several plates on it hitting the ground. They looked over to the source of the sound and saw Crescia standing there with her eyes wide and her hands covering her mouth. Jack sat up and turned to her.

"Hi," said Jack.

Crescia ran full speed at Jack and leaped at him to hug him. They both landed back down on the cot. Jack winced but held onto Crescia.

"You're back! You're alive! You scared the hell out of me!" she said as she squeezed him tight.

"Sorry. I didn't mean to," said Jack, still wincing in pain but still not letting her go.

"Crescia, he's still injured, you know," said Rhandor.

"Oh! Jack, I'm so sorry!" said Crescia as she stood back up.

"Don't worry about it. I'm always up for one of your hugs, regardless of my condition," said Jack.

Rhandor stood up.

"I'll go inform Alivair that Jack is awake," he said.

Rhandor left the tent. A few minutes later, he returned with Alivair.

"Glad to see that you're awake, Jack," said Alivair.

"That's Vice-commander, Captain," said Jack with a grin. "Just kidding. So what is the plan for getting Lia back?"

"We're assembling as much of the Vedyrian Army here as possible and prepping for a full-scale assault on the Dark Army," said Alivair.

"Do we even know where the enemy castle is?" asked Jack.

"Not exactly, but it would be safe to assume that the tunnel likely leads in the direction of it. We have two waypoints. The first is the entrance, and the second is the lake. I recall the tunnel being basically a straight shot, so even if it doesn't turn out to be an arrow pointing right at the castle, it at least gives us a heading to its general location," said Alivair.

"A reasonable assumption. How long until reinforcements arrive?" asked Jack.

"Some of them are already starting to arrive. More are to be expected over the next day and a half," said Alivair.

"Let's hope they don't arrive too late," said Jack.

Crescia turned to Alivair.

"Captain, let me fight," she said.

"The battlefield is no place for an attendant," said Alivair.

"She's a capable fighter," said Jack.

"Princess Lia is my family. And now that she and Jack are to be married, Jack is my family. I will fight for my family," said Crescia.

"As I said, the battlefield... wait. Did you say they are to be married?" asked Alivair as he looked over at Jack.

"Surprise!" said Jack. "I was planning on telling you before I got hit with a lake."

Alivair took a moment to process the unexpected news.

"We're definitely going to have a talk about that later, Jack. As far as Crescia goes, I guess it's your decision," said Alivair.

"What do you mean?" asked Jack.

"Well, given that you have the rank and authority of Vice-commander, you are technically the highest-ranking officer at this camp. Should you decide to let Crescia join the battle, it will be taken as an official order," said Alivair.

"Passing the buck, then?" said Jack with a grin.

"Please, Jack. Let me fight," said Crescia.

"You heard the lady. Get her some armor and weapons," said Jack.

Crescia hugged Jack again.

"Thank you," she said.

"Just be safe out there and don't do anything too risky. Ok? Lia and I would both be very upset if something happened to you," said Jack.

"I'll be fine. Those Dark Army monsters that took my... I mean our princess? Not so much," said Crescia.

"Give 'em hell," said Jack. "They'll regret the day they pissed you off."

"Damn right, they will," said Crescia.

Alivair turned to Rhandor.

"We should continue preparations and coordinate with the incoming soldiers. Let's give Jack some more time to recover," he said.

"Yes, sir," said Rhandor.

Rhandor left the tent with Alivair. Jack laid back down in the cot. Crescia laid down next to him.

"We're getting her back," said Jack.

"Yes, we are," said Crescia.

Soon afterward, they both drifted off to sleep.

CHAPTER 33

Having no means of escape, Lia reluctantly stayed in the vast throne room of the Great Demon Emperor. Her treatment was surprisingly hospitable considering where she was. They brought her food when she was hungry and water when she was thirsty. If not for the magic suppression collar and the fact that she couldn't leave, she could easily be mistaken for a simple guest of the court. The Emperor was walking on the second level of the throne room, casually observing Lia on the first level. As she was eating the meal she had been provided, a group of eight Demonborne soldiers approached her.

"So, this is the so-called commander of the great Vedyrian Army? She doesn't look so tough," said one of the soldiers.

"No, she doesn't. Such a delicate little flower belongs in the bedroom, not the battlefield," said another soldier.

"I'm sure His Excellency wouldn't mind if we had a little taste," said the first soldier.

Lia's fist began to clench. The Emperor's voice echoed through the throne room.

"Do as you wish. I will not interfere," he said.

"See? He's given us permission to play with his new toy, boys," said the soldier.

They began to close in on Lia.

"I wasn't speaking to you," said the Emperor.

Lia stood up and embedded her fork in the temple of the first soldier. He immediately collapsed to the floor. The other seven soldiers started to close in on her. The second soldier grabbed her left arm. Lia wrapped her arm around his, locking it in an arm bar just long enough to punch him full force in the throat, following it up with an elbow to the face. The next soldier raised his hand to create a sphere of dark magic. Lia grabbed his wrist and aimed it at another soldier's head. The sphere was released and killed the soldier. Lia then turned her back to the soldier whose arm she was holding and flipped him over her, breaking his arm after he landed. The next soldier moved in to attack her, and she kicked him in the stomach, causing him to double over, and then kneed him in the head. The remaining two soldiers raised their hands and backed away. The Emperor's voice once again echoed through the throne room.

"Remove that detritus from my floor immediately," he said.

The two remaining soldiers grabbed an arm or leg of their fallen comrades and dragged them out of the throne room. Lia looked up at the Emperor.

"A splendid display of skill, Your Highness," said the Emperor.

"Do you truly care so little about your own men that you could so arbitrarily cast them aside and refer to them as trash?" asked Lia.

"There is no room in my army for weakness. Either of mind or body. Those men were foolish enough to underestimate you based on your appearance. They deserved the defeat they received," said the Emperor.

"The fact that you see your men as so disposable is why you will lose," said Lia.

Lia walked back to the table and sat down to finish her meal. Karvan walked into the throne room and looked up to the Emperor.

"Your Excellency. I have just received news from an imp spy," said Karvan.

"Speak," said the Emperor.

"It appears that the human still lives," said Karvan.

Lia looked over at Karvan. She found it difficult to hide

her relief at hearing that Jack was still alive.

"Do we have him?" asked the Emperor.

"No, Your Excellency," said Karvan. "He was discovered by a fairy and retrieved by a beastfolk mage of the Vedyrian Army."

"Pity. Though it makes little difference. If he lives, he will be mine to control. It's only a matter of time," said the Emperor.

"You underestimate Jack if you think you'll ever be able to control him. You shouldn't be pleased that he's alive. You should be afraid," Lia said.

"I fear nothing, child," said the Emperor. "He will become my weapon."

"And how exactly do you plan to do that?" asked Lia.

The Emperor suddenly teleported from the second level to right in front of Lia. He raised his hand and lifted her off the ground with his dark magic.

"I need only drive him to the point where he loses control of his power. Once that happens, his uncontrolled magic shall corrupt him down to his very soul. Then he shall be mine. And you, my dear princess, will play a part in that corruption," said the Emperor.

"Never," said Lia.

"You will play your part, and then you will watch helplessly from my side as he becomes my deadliest weapon, wiping out all things in his path. That will be your future," said the Emperor.

He released the dark magic grip he had on Lia, dropping her back down to the floor.

"I will never cooperate with you," said Lia.

"Therein lies your first mistake, Your Highness. You're under the impression that your cooperation is necessary," said Karvan.

"How is stage one progressing, General?" asked the Emperor.

"The first wave shall arrive at the predetermined place

of battle in a little over a day's time, Your Excellency," said Karvan.

"Very well," said the Emperor.

The Emperor once again turned to Lia. He reached out the dark magic threads around her collar and pulled her closer to him.

"Come," he said.

#####

Along with Karvan, they made their way up to the same balcony where the Emperor had launched the spear. The Emperor released Lia, and Karvan took her by the arm and brought her away from where the Emperor was standing. The Emperor turned to Lia.

"Witness the beginning of your world's end," the Emperor said.

The Emperor held his hands up to the sky. Dark magic energy began to flow from the ground, surrounding him as his hands started to glow. The deep red and purple energy swirled around his body, concentrating at a single point above his hands. The more the energy built, the brighter it glowed. In a blinding flash, a beam of energy shot up into the sky. Soon, deep blood-red clouds formed from the beam, slowly spreading outward in all directions. As the clouds spread, everything around them took on a red hue. The clouds made their way across the sky, blocking out the sun.

"What's happening?" Lia asked Karvan.

"His Excellency's dark magic is spreading across the land, granting strength to our army. A blood rain shall soon fall, and as our troops grow stronger, yours shall grow weaker. You cannot win, Your Highness. It is over for you and your people," said Karvan.

"Is this the end of the war you were hoping for, General? If what you say is true, your trophy for victory will be a land of corpses and poisoned earth where nothing will grow and no one to stop him," said Lia.

"Even if I wanted to oppose him, I could not. His Excellency is far too powerful," said Karvan. "With this, this war is as good as over."

"I wouldn't count my people out just yet," said Lia.

A second bright flash signaled the end of the Emperor's spell. The blood-red clouds continued to spread. The Emperor walked over to Lia.

"Your hope for victory will only leave you that much farther to fall when that hope is crushed, Your Highness," said the Emperor.

"I could say the same to you," said Lia.

Corvan marched in front of a legion of twenty-five thousand Dark Army troops. The rattle of their armor and the thunderous sound of their steady footsteps echoed as they marched. Behind the legion of Demonborne soldiers marched a group of twenty necromancers. Between them, more than a thousand draphnir marched along, under the control of the magic of the necromancers. Corvan looked back on his soldiers as he marched and saw the blood-red clouds forming in the distance. He smiled, knowing what was coming. He yelled to the soldiers.

"Step it up! Our victory is soon at hand!" he said.

The roar of the troops was so loud that it drowned out all other sound in the area.

CHAPTER 34

The next morning, Jack woke up feeling like he was back to his usual self. Crescia was already gone, as she needed to get fitted for her armor and get some weapons in preparation for the upcoming battle. After a few stretches, he left the medical tent. The camp was far busier than he had ever seen it, due to the major influx of new soldiers. As he made his way to the command tent to speak with Alivair, he noticed what appeared to be storm clouds forming near the horizon. Something about the clouds made him feel uneasy. When he entered the command tent, Alivair was coordinating with the unit commanders of the other Vedyrian Army regiments that had made their way to the camp. Alivair looked over at Jack.

"Ah, Jack. How are you feeling?" asked Alivair.

"Better, thanks. Am I interrupting something?" asked Jack.

"Not at all. We were just coordinating," said Alivair.

"Oh. I see," said Jack.

Alivair looked at the other commanders.

"Allow me to introduce Prince Jack of Stobrimore. Be advised that His Majesty has granted Jack the rank and authority of Vice-commander of the Vedyrian Army, so should he give any of you an order on the battlefield, you are to follow it as you would follow my own. Is that understood?" Alivair said.

All but one of the unit commanders responded with a "Yes sir!" to Alivair's command. The one unit commander who remained silent was an elf. He simply looked perplexed. He leaned toward Alivair.

"Forgive me, Captain, but are you telling me that this...

human outranks even you?" said the elf unit commander.

"This human can hear you, you know," said Jack.

"You had best watch your tone, Unit Commander Beragan. I need not repeat myself," said Alivair.

"Understood, Captain Alivair," said Beragan, reluctantly.

Alivair looked over at Jack and gave him a subtle nod, as if to non-verbally suggest that Jack hit the point home with Beragan. Jack returned Alivair's subtle nod with his own before walking up to Beragan.

"Are we going to have a problem, Unit Commander... Beragan, was it?" asked Jack, in his most serious command voice.

It was the tone of voice Jack often took during his time in the Rangers whenever it was time to discipline soldiers under his command. Beragan, who stood several inches shorter than Jack, looked up at him.

"No, sir. No problems, sir," said Beragan, regretting his statement.

For about ten seconds, Jack continued to peer into the eyes of Beragan, remaining completely stone-faced and expressionless. After finishing the count to ten in his head, Jack responded in a much more cheerful tone of voice.

"Cool! Looking forward to fighting alongside you when we go to battle," said Jack, before giving Beragan a pat on the back.

Another unit commander spoke up. He was a wolf beastfolk with dark brown and light gray fur.

"Excuse me, Your Highness. Are you the human who... um... straightened out Arnin Canyon?" he asked.

"Uh... yeah," said Jack. "I'm sorry. You are?"

"Oh, forgive my rudeness, Your Highness. I am Unit Commander Saromir," he said.

"Nice to meet you, Saromir. Breaking the canyon was kind of the first thing I did after coming here," said Jack.

"I was part of the team charged with surveying the

aftermath. I must say, sir, I'm very grateful that you are on our side. The walls your magic carved are as smooth as glass," said Saromir.

"You surveyed the canyon?" asked Jack.

"Yes, sir," said Saromir.

"Did you happen to see anything that looked like an old temple?" asked Jack.

Saromir thought about it for a moment.

"Are you speaking of the ruins of the old Worldgate temple, sir?" he asked.

"Yes," said Jack.

"It was in fairly rough shape. We didn't go so far as to examine the gate itself, but, quite frankly, there isn't much left to the temple," said Saromir.

"Do you think it could be rebuilt?" asked Jack.

"Sir?" asked Saromir, a bit confused by the question.

"I realize that it's a question more appropriate for a later date, Saromir. I'm just wondering if, in your professional opinion, the temple could be resurrected," said Jack.

"I see. Without further examination, I can't say for sure, but I believe it is within the capabilities of our engineering division, sir," said Saromir.

"Good. Thank you," said Jack.

"Of course, sir," said Saromir.

"Was there something of specific interest that you wanted to talk about, Jack?" asked Alivair.

"A few things, actually. First, where is Rhandor?" asked Jack.

"He's with Bilen, coordinating operations plans for the Mage Corps in this battle to come," said Alivair.

"I see. The other thing about those strange clouds forming on the horizon," said Jack.

"Strange clouds?" asked Alivair.

"Yeah. Something about them is making me feel very uneasy. Come outside and take a look at them," said Jack.

Alivair and the unit commanders followed Jack out of

the tent, and they all looked toward the clouds that were slowly approaching. Alivair took out the binoculars.

"Yes. They certainly do look peculiar. They're certainly no normal storm clouds," said Alivair.

"I'm not even sure how to explain it, but I can practically feel the dark magic coming off of them, even from this far away," said Jack.

Beragan turned to Jack.

"What do you know of dark magic?" he asked.

"I suppose I should have mentioned this, but Jack is an omni magic user," said Alivair.

"Impossible. No one has possessed all six magic affinities in centuries," said Beragan.

Jack looked at him and focused just enough to get his eyes to glow for each of the affinities. He raised both eyebrows a few times and grinned. Alivair turned to the unit commanders.

"Make sure that your soldiers all get shield cuffs. I get the feeling that they're going to be needed more than ever in this battle," said Alivair.

The commanders all nodded in response.

"That's all for now. Go report to your respective units. Dismissed," said Alivair.

The commanders all split off to join their units. Alivair walked over to Jack.

"I fear that this oncoming storm will be unlike any we have seen before," he said.

"I plan on bringing along a storm of my own," said Jack.

"What do you mean by that?" asked Alivair.

"I have been going over the science of it in my mind since I woke up. It could be risky, though, so I may have to separate myself from the other soldiers before I try it," said Jack.

"Well, I'll be sure to keep that in mind. Let me know when you plan to attempt it, and I'll be sure to pull the troops back," said Alivair.

"Will do," said Jack. "So how many soldiers do we have here at this point?"

"Counting the ones that arrived just this morning, I believe that it brings our numbers up to nearly forty thousand," said Alivair.

A thought popped into Jack's mind.

"About those shield gauntlets. How does one infuse magic into them? Is it difficult?" he asked.

"Not too difficult with assistance from the fairies. Why?" asked Alivair.

"I'm thinking that it couldn't hurt if I gave them a bit of a supercharge. With those suspicious-looking clouds heading this way, I'd rather be safe than sorry," said Jack.

"An interesting idea. I will summon Fyn. Head over to the main supply tent. I'll send him your way after explaining the situation," said Alivair.

Jack nodded and made his way to the main supply tent.

Inside the tent was the quartermaster. He walked up to her and introduced himself.

"Hi. I don't think we've met yet. I'm Jack," he said.

"Greetings, Jack. I'm Zanovya. How may I be of assistance?" she asked.

"I'm looking to charge up the shield gauntlets with my magic. I'm going to be meeting Fyn here soon," said Jack.

"I see. I will retrieve the keystone," said Zanovya.

Zanovya disappeared into the back of the supply tent for a few moments and returned with a large quartz-like crystal. The crystal was about the same diameter as a coffee mug and came to a sharp point on the top. She placed the crystal on the table and then walked over to one of the shelves and took down a peculiar-looking device. The device consisted of a large, opaque crystal disk vertically mounted to a metal frame. The base had several small crystals of various colors in two locations. On the top of the metal frame was a fixture where the keystone was to be inserted. She set the device on the table and placed the keystone in the fixture.

"There we are. Now, all we need to do is wait for the fairies," said Zanovya.

A few minutes later, Fyn flew into the supply tent along with another fairy. Fyn waved to Jack and Zanovya and then landed on Jack's shoulder. The second fairy landed in front of one of the locations of the colored crystals at the base of the device. Fyn leaned over to Jack's ear.

"Hello, Jack," said Fyn.

"Hello, Fyn. Thanks for this," said Jack.

"I shall instruct you how to infuse magic into the gauntlets," said Fyn.

"Ok. What do I do first?" asked Jack.

"Nyl is at position one. I shall be at position two. We will use our magic to activate the infusion device. When activated, the disk will turn black, and then dots will appear. Those are the gauntlets. I shall give you a signal. When I do so, place your hand on the keystone and focus your light magic on it. The crystals on the gauntlets will glow. I will give you a second signal when to stop," said Fyn.

"Sounds easy enough," said Jack.

Fyn then hopped off of Jack's shoulder and flew to the other position on the infusion device. He and Nyl placed their hands on the crystals in front of them. Soon, the grayish opaque disk turned black. The crystal in the fixture on top of the device began to glow. Tiny white dots began to appear on the disk. Fyn looked at Jack and nodded. Jack placed his hand on the keystone crystal and closed his eyes. When he opened them, they glowed a bright white. After a few moments, the dots on the screen began to get brighter. At the same time, the crystals on the shield gauntlets in the supply room began to glow. Jack concentrated, imagining the magic flowing down his arm and into the crystal keystone. Fyn and Nyl spoke to each other in fairy language as the infusion continued. A few more moments passed before Fyn gave Jack another nod. Jack removed his hand from the keystone crystal, and his eyes returned to normal. The crystals on the gauntlets in the supply tent stopped glowing. Fyn flew up and landed back on Jack's shoulder and leaned toward his ear.

"Very well done, Jack. Your magic has infused more than three times the normal capacity of light magic into the gauntlets. I am quite impressed. I would very much like to speak with you further about your magic in the future," he said.

"Sure. Whenever you want to do it, let me know. I'm happy to be of assistance," said Jack.

Fyn flew back down onto the table and spoke to Nyl again. They both turned to Jack and bowed.

"Thank you, Fyn, Nyl. I appreciate the assistance," said Jack.

Fyn and Nyl both gave Jack and Zanovya a wave before flying out of the tent. Zanovya walked over to Jack.

"A most intriguing display of magic, Jack. I had heard things about your magic from other soldiers, but this is my first time actually witnessing it," she said.

"I just hope it helps," said Jack. "By the way, you haven't happened to see Crescia, have you?"

"Her Highness's attendant? Yes. She was here earlier this morning to get fitted for some armor and a pair of short swords," said Zanovya.

Jack thought for a moment.

"Come to think of it, I should probably get some armor for myself as well. I have all the weapons that I need, but it probably wouldn't hurt to have something beyond what I'm wearing for the battlefield," he said.

"Are you even technically part of the Vedyrian Army, Jack?" asked Zanovya.

"Well, technically speaking, as of a few days ago, I'm kind of second in command of it," said Jack.

Zanovya stopped what she was doing and froze.

"Second in command? That would make you... "
Zanovya stopped mid-sentence.

"Vice-commander of the Vedyrian Army. Yeah," said
Jack.

Zanovya snapped to attention, taking Jack a bit by
surprise.

"Sir!" said Zanovya.

"Hold up, a sec. Let's not do all of that. I'm just Jack, ok?"
he said.

Zanovya felt a bit awkward for a moment and then
relaxed.

"Ok. Sorry," she said.

"Now, about that armor?" Jack said.

"Oh, yes! I'll get right on it," Zanovya said.

She stepped out from behind the table and walked
around Jack, looking at him from every angle.

"What are you doing?" Jack asked.

"I need to get a general idea of your measurements for
the armor," Zanovya said.

"Oh, yeah. Sure. That makes sense," said Jack.

"Ok. I think I have all I need. I'll go through the armor
here and bring something worthy of your rank and authority
to your tent as soon as possible," said Zanovya.

"Thanks," said Jack.

#####

After Jack left the supply tent, the words 'worthy of
your rank and authority' started to form all sorts of mental
images of intricate and ornate armor, like something out of
a fantasy computer game. Visions of completely impractical
features like shoulder spikes, horned helmets, and long
flowing capes filled his mind. After remembering the armor of
both Lia and Alivair and how it was both ornate and practical,
he realized that he was likely overthinking things, and it
caused him to laugh. Though the course of events that led up

to him laughing made perfect sense to him, Jack realized that, to the soldiers around him who had no idea what had just played out in his mind, they probably saw only a guy who came walking out of the supply tent and suddenly started breaking into laughter like a crazy person. Jack cleared his throat after seeing the odd looks he was getting from the soldiers in the area and then made his way back to the command tent. On the way, he met Crescia.

"I was just looking for you," said Jack.

Crescia was in her armor, and she had a short sword on each hip. The swords each had single-edged blades and had a slight curve to them. The armor was form-fitting, allowing for optimum flexibility while still offering protection.

"Hi, Jack! So, what do you think?" she asked.

"You look good. You look ready for combat. Are you sure you want to do this?" said Jack.

"Of course. I can't just sit by and wait while Her Highness is being held by the enemy. You know that I can fight. You've seen me do it. You're not having doubts about me, are you?" asked Crescia apprehensively.

"Of course not. I know full well how skilled you are. I'm just a little worried. That's all. You're important to me, and I don't want you to get hurt," said Jack.

"Oh. Well, I'll be fine. I'll just stick close to you on the battlefield and watch your back. They won't know what hit them," said Crescia.

Jack grinned.

"Sounds like a plan," he said.

Crescia pointed to the shield gauntlets she had on both arms.

"These things were glowing super bright earlier. Was that you?" she asked.

"Yeah. I figured it couldn't hurt to give them a little boost," said Jack.

"So where are you headed now?" asked Crescia.

"I figured I'd coordinate with Rhandor and Bilen.

There's something about those strange clouds in the distance over there that is bothering me. I'd like to see if they might have any ideas about them," said Jack.

"Yeah. I thought those clouds were a little strange, too. For some reason, they make the fur on the back of my neck stand up on end. Mind if I join you?" she asked.

"By all means," said Jack.

#####

Jack and Crescia made their way to the Mage Corps section of the camp. When they got there, it was far more crowded than usual due to the influx of new mages. They reached Bilen's tent, and Jack popped his head in. Inside, he saw Bilen and Rhandor working on battle plans.

"Mind if we interrupt?" asked Jack.

Jack opened the flap to reveal Crescia standing behind him.

"Come on in," said Bilen.

Rhandor looked at Crescia in her armor.

"You look ready for battle, Crescia," he said.

"Absolutely," said Crescia.

"What can we help you with, Jack?" asked Bilen.

"Have either of you noticed those strange clouds on the horizon? They look like they're slowly heading this way, and there's something about them that feels off," said Jack.

"We were just talking about it, actually," said Rhandor.

"What do you make of it?" asked Jack.

"It's certainly not natural. As far as its purpose, we don't know yet," said Bilen.

"I'm getting dark magic vibes from it," said Jack.

"Even from this far away?" asked Rhandor.

"Yeah. As much as I don't want to get any closer to it, I think I should take Nava and check it out," said Jack.

"I'll join you," said Rhandor.

"Let's make our way to the command tent and inform

Alivair before you two head out," said Bilen.

"Sure. I just need to stop off at my tent on the way and grab the radios. They should all be fully charged by now, and we're probably going to need them," said Jack.

After stopping off at Jack's tent to get the radios, Jack, Crescia, Rhandor and Bilen made their way to the command tent. Once they arrived at the command tent, they filled Alivair in on the plan. Jack handed the radios out to Alivair, Bilen and Rhandor, keeping the fourth one for himself.

"These are all tuned to the same channel. They'll help us to communicate on the battlefield. First, we need to figure out what that cloud is all about, though," said Jack.

"Be careful, and keep me updated," said Alivair.

Jack and Rhandor left the command tent and headed to the stables. They filled Barvan in on their intent, and he got Nava and Aris ready for flight. Once the dragons were prepped, Jack and Rhandor climbed on their backs and took flight. They flew in the direction of the spreading clouds, taking them over the forest where Jack had been found. The closer they got to the cloud, the more they noticed something was off.

"Do you smell that?" asked Jack.

"Yes. It's a peculiar smell," said Rhandor.

"I can almost taste it. It tastes metallic," said Jack.

They both directed their dragons to hover for a moment while they checked out the surroundings. Shortly afterward, a fairy flew up to Rhandor and landed on his shoulder. As the fairy spoke to Rhandor, Jack saw another fairy approaching. The fairy appeared to be struggling to fly. It got within forty feet of Jack before it began to fall out of the sky. Jack steered Nava into a dive, and they raced down to catch the fairy. They got underneath it, and Jack reached up and grabbed the fairy. As he held it, the fairy was slipping in and out of consciousness and breathing heavily. It looked up at Jack and then pointed to a spot on the ground. Jack got on the radio to speak to Rhandor.

"Rhandor, this fairy is directing me to something. I'm going to head down and see what's going on," he said.

"This fairy with me just informed me that the oncoming clouds appear to be poisoning the fairies in this forest," said Rhandor.

Alivair entered the conversation from his radio.

"Do you require assistance?" Alivair asked.

"An evacuation of the fairies may be necessary. Stand by for incoming casualties," said Jack.

After Nava landed, Jack placed the fairy on his shoulder and went where he was directed. When he reached his destination, he found more than twenty fairies in various states of consciousness along the forest floor. He concentrated and tried using healing magic on the fairies. Some of the fairies regained consciousness but were still struggling.

"There are too many here for me to carry. I need a basket or something," said Jack.

The fairy on his shoulder flew down to the ground and began to speak with a number of other fairies who were still standing. After a brief conversation, the fairies placed their hands on the ground. Vines started to snake along the ground, interweaving beneath the fairies that were still unconscious. The vines wrapped around the waists of the fairies, securing them to the woven mat. Finally, a large handle rose up from the edges, completing the woven basket. The fairies who helped build the basket collapsed. Jack loaded them into the basket and picked it up. As he brought the basket back to Nava, a few more fairies came down out of the trees, and Jack placed them in the basket. He placed it down in front of Nava.

"Nava, carry this," said Jack.

He got on Nava's back, and she hovered for a moment before grabbing the handle of the basket with her front claws.

She slowly rose above the treetops. Jack once again got on the radio.

"Rhandor, I have a few dozen fairies. I'm going to bring them back to the camp," he said.

"We shall send out a few more soldiers to assist in the evacuations," said Alivair over the radio.

"I will remain here and coordinate the evacuation," said Rhandor.

#####

Jack steered Nava toward the camp, and they flew there as fast as they safely could while carrying the fairies. On the way back, Jack saw ten soldiers on dragons heading toward the forest to help with the evacuation. When he got to the camp, he flew right over the stable area and took Nava directly over the medical tent. He had Nava carefully lower the basket until the healers were able to safely take it and rush the fairies into the tent. After a few moments, one of the healers returned with the empty basket. He handed it up to Nava. Once she grabbed it, they made their way back to the forest.

#####

Eight trips later, nearly three hundred and fifty fairies had been brought to the medical tent. Jack made one final return to the forest. When he got there, Rhandor was finishing up with the evacuation. Jack flew Nava up to his location and hovered so they could speak.

"Is that all of them?" asked Jack.

"I believe so," said Rhandor.

"I think we've established that that's no ordinary storm cloud," said Jack.

"I think you're right," said Rhandor.

"Let's get to a higher elevation and take one more look," said Jack.

Jack and Rhandor climbed up to about fifteen hundred

feet to get a better scan of the horizon.

Something caught Jack's eye in the distance.

"What is that?" Jack asked.

Rhandor looked over in the direction where Jack was looking. Far off in the distance, he saw some movement beyond the edges of the forest. Jack reached into a pouch on his belt and pulled out the scope he had taken off his rifle and looked through it. He adjusted the zoom to get a better picture of the movement in the distance. When he brought the object into focus, he finally saw them clearly.

"That's a Dark Army unit. They're headed this way," said Jack.

"How many?" asked Rhandor.

Jack tossed the scope over to Rhandor.

"Thousands. They're not messing around this time. We're in for a major battle," said Jack.

Rhandor pulled out his radio.

"Captain Alivair, Jack and I just spotted a massive unit of Dark Army soldiers heading in this direction," he said.

"How far out?" asked Alivair.

"Looks like they're between thirty and thirty-five miles out. At their current pace, they could reach the camp in about nine hours," said Rhandor.

Jack got on the radio.

"We're looking at what appears to be at least a legion, if not more, of them heading this way. We need to mobilize everyone we can. This powder keg is about to blow," he said.

"Return to camp immediately. We will begin the mobilization," said Alivair.

"Understood. On our way," said Rhandor.

Jack and Rhandor flew back to the camp as fast as possible.

#####

When they landed, Rhandor turned to Jack.

"I'll head to the command tent. Now is probably the time for you to get your armor on, Jack," said Rhandor.

"Yeah. I'll go get it and meet you at the command tent," said Jack.

#####

Jack made his way to his tent to check out the armor Zanovya had chosen for him. When he entered his tent and saw it, the first thought in his mind was that he was glad that it didn't have spikes or a big, cumbersome cape. The armor was black and silver with gold accents. It was not all that different in design from Alivair's armor, which Jack didn't find that surprising, given that it was primarily assembled from existing armor materials in the supply tent in only a few hours, as opposed to being a custom-made suit that would likely take days to complete. As he put the armor on, the first thing he noticed was how light it was. From the looks of it, he was expecting it to be much heavier. The second thing that he noticed was how well it fit.

"Zanovya sure knows her stuff. This fits like it was custom tailored." Jack said to himself as he looked in the mirror.

Jack did a few twists and stretches to test the flexibility of the armor and was once again surprised. After he was sufficiently satisfied with testing out the armor, Jack attached the sword that Lia had given him to the mounts on the left hip. After taking one last quick look in the mirror, he made his way to the command tent.

#####

When he arrived at the command tent, all of the necessary officers and commanders were present, and the briefing had started. Jack made his way around the group until he was standing next to Rhandor.

"What did I miss?" whispered Jack.

"We're just going over the battle plan," said Rhandor.

"Oh. I'll be quiet, then," said Jack.

Alivair continued the briefing.

"Units seven and eight will position here and here," he said, indicating two areas on the large map. "We'll keep five thousand in reserve by the forest line. Without intel from the fairies, we don't know the exact numbers, so we don't want to pool all of our resources in one location. We will split the Mage Corps among each unit for wide-area attacks and magic defense. Bilen will be in charge of coordinating distribution of the mages. We will remain in communication using these radio devices supplied by Jack."

Alivair pointed to Jack as he mentioned the radios. A number of the commanders looked over at Jack, and he gave them all a quick wave. Alivair then called on Jack.

"Do you have anything you wish to add, Jack?" he asked.

Jack made his way toward the map and looked at the deployment markers.

"That cloud seems to have had a significant impact on the fairies, so we know that it's not a natural cloud. That concerns me. We should have healers ready in full force in the event that the cloud has a similar effect on the soldiers. I'd like to take Nava out and see if I can reduce the numbers of the Dark Army soldiers before they reach the main units," said Jack.

"What can one human do to reduce an army of thousands on his own?" asked one of the unit commanders.

"You heard about what happened at Arnin Canyon, right?" asked Rhandor.

"Yes, sir," said the unit commander.

"That was Jack," said Rhandor.

"Are you saying that this human wiped out more than twenty thousand soldiers on his own?" asked the unit commander.

"Yes, I am," said Rhandor.

"I don't believe it," said the unit commander.

"Believe it. I was there," said Alivair.

The unit commander looked back at Jack.

"I guess you could say that I'm kind of a walking weapon of mass destruction," said Jack.

"Once we get everyone into position, we'll send you out first, Jack," said Alivair.

"Understood," said Jack.

"Does everyone understand the plan?" asked Alivair.

All of the commanders nodded.

"Very well. Let's move out. We have no time to waste," said Alivair.

As the commanders made their way out of the tent, Crescia approached Jack.

"Well, you certainly look the part of Vice-commander of the Vedyrian Army now." she said, giving Jack a once-over.

"Indeed," said Rhandor. "The look suits you."

"Thanks," said Jack.

Alivair walked over to Jack.

"Once you've made your initial attack, I'd like you to fall back to the reserve units. I have a feeling we may need you there. I already briefed the commanders of the reserve units about your rank and authority, so there shouldn't be any issues should you need to give any commands," he said.

"Sure," said Jack.

"What about me?" asked Crescia.

"I'd like you to stick close to me," said Jack.

"Ok," said Crescia.

Jack turned to Alivair and Rhandor.

"Let's get this party started," said Jack.

They all left the command tent and made their way to the stables, where all of the troops were assembling.

#####

Once the troops were fully assembled, Alivair walked up to Jack.

"We'll contact you on the radio when we're in position. Good luck, Jack," he said.

"Good luck to us all," said Jack.

Alivair made his way to the front of the assembled soldiers.

"This war against the Dark Army has gone on for far too long. We have all lost friends and loved ones. They have spread through this land like a plague. Today, we shall ensure that they spread no further. Today is the day we all say, No more!" said Alivair.

"No more!" shouted all of the soldiers in unison.

"No more!" shouted Alivair.

"No more!" shouted all of the soldiers.

"Today is the day that we rain down hell on the Dark Army and we show the Great Demon Emperor that his reign of terror is over! We are the Vedyrian Army! We shall not fall! We shall not fail! Today we march to victory!" Alivair yelled.

The soldiers let out a deafening cheer.

"To victory!" yelled Alivair!

"To victory!" shouted all of the soldiers.

"Move out!" yelled Alivair.

The soldiers raised their weapons in the air and began the march to battle.

Jack turned to Crescia.

"I gotta admit. It was a good speech," he said.

"It certainly was," said Crescia.

"Have you ever flown a dragon before?" Jack asked.

"A few times. Why?" asked Crescia.

"I'm going to need you to fly Nava. I'll need to focus on the magic, and I'll need you to be able to take Nava back to the reserve area," said Jack.

"Without you?" Crescia asked.

"It'll be fine. I'll just use the teleportation magic to join you once I'm done," said Jack.

#####

As the soldiers marched to their first designated location, many of them saw the red clouds slowly getting closer. By the time they reached their first waypoint, the clouds were covering two-thirds of the forest. Alivair got on the radio.

"Jack, we're in position," he said.

"Understood. We're on our way," said Jack.

#####

Jack and Crescia got on Nava's back, and they took to the skies.

"Climb high, Nava," said Jack.

Nava climbed high into the sky. It wasn't long before the Vedyrian Army troops were in sight. Crescia waved to Alivair as they flew over, though they were so high that it was unlikely that Alivair actually saw it. Soon, the Dark Army legion came into view.

"Right here, Nava!" said Jack.

Nava stopped flying forward and began to hover in place.

"Are you ready, Crescia?" asked Jack.

"Ready," said Crescia.

Jack closed his eyes for a moment and held his hand to the sky. When he opened them, a dark storm cloud began to form high in the sky over the Dark Army soldiers. They stopped marching and looked up at the cloud. As high as they were, Jack and Crescia were difficult to see from the ground, which worked to their advantage. The cloud grew darker and darker as it spread out, hanging over the Dark Army formation. Soon, the cloud began to flash. The flashes were slow at first, but it wasn't long before the cloud began to flash like a strobe light. Jack directed his hand from the cloud to the ground. The moment he did that, lightning started striking from the cloud. Giant bolts of lightning struck right into the middle of the formation, and dozens of the Dark Army soldiers fell. The lightning that struck the soldiers arced between those around them, using their armor as an ideal conductor.

"Get ready to head back to the reserve waypoint, Crescia," said Jack.

"Wait. What are you going to do?" Crescia asked.

"I'm going to drop in and say hello," said Jack.

Crescia looked back at Jack just in time to see him dive off of Nava's back.

#####

Far off in the distance, the Vedyrian Army soldiers watched as the storm cloud sent down bolt after bolt of lightning. One of the unit commanders approached Alivair.

"Are you telling me that that is the act of one human?" the unit commander asked.

"Indeed, I am," said Alivair.

"I'm certainly glad he is on our side of this battle," said the unit commander.

"As am I," said Alivair.

#####

Jack used his arms to steer as he dove headfirst toward the ground. When he was a few hundred feet off the ground, he rolled forward so that his feet were pointed at the ground and used wind magic to slow his descent. Once he was about six feet off the ground and a few hundred feet in front of the Dark Army formation, he released the wind magic. Right as his feet hit the ground, the storm cloud unloaded all remaining lightning into the Dark Army formations before dissipating. Hundreds of Dark Army soldiers were killed when the dozens of lightning bolts struck them, causing them to drop in place. When Jack turned around to face the legion, he saw who was leading them. Standing at the front of the formation was Corvan. Jack shouted out to him.

"Hey, Lefty! I see you got a new arm! See if you can catch this!" he said, as he generated a fireball in each hand.

Jack's eyes glowed bright red as he put as much energy into the fireballs as he could. When he released them, they flew at high speed toward the Dark Army formation, passing just to the left and right of Corvan. They impacted at the middle of the massive formation, creating immense mushroom clouds of fire that rose from the ground, sending soldiers flying in all directions. Corvan was furious.

"Kill him! Now!" he yelled to the remaining soldiers. Soon, arrows of both the magic and the steel-tipped kind were making their way toward Jack. He raised his hands and used light magic to create a shield. The arrows bounced off before reaching their target.

"Uh oh. I think I made them angry," said Jack.

Jack sent another fireball at the Dark Army soldiers and then called out to Corvan.

"Hey, Lefty! If you want me, come and get me!" he yelled.

Corvan didn't even wait to respond. He ordered a charge, and the remainder of the Dark Army soldiers under his command started sprinting toward Jack. Jack turned around and ran at full speed. As he was running, he activated his dark magic, creating a purple circle that followed him on the ground as he ran. The circle rose up from the ground, teleporting him with a bright flash of light.

#####

He arrived back at the reserve position, still running at full speed, resulting in him running full force into a low tree branch, sending him tumbling to the ground.

"Note to self. Be careful teleporting while running in the future," he said as he winced in pain while trying to sit up.

After catching his breath, he picked up the radio.

"Alivair, I'm back at the reserve checkpoint," said Jack.

"How many did you see?" asked Alivair.

"There were a lot of them. At least twenty to twenty-five thousand, I'm guessing. Maybe more," said Jack.

"How many did you get with your light show?" asked Alivair.

"If I had to guess, I'd say probably around eight or ten," said Jack.

The unit commander overheard the radio communication between them and spoke up.

"That entire attack only resulted in eight or ten enemy losses?" said the unit commander.

"Thousand, Unit Commander. Eight or ten thousand," said Alivair to the unit commander. "Either way, that leaves us with at least fifteen thousand headed this way."

"Something felt off, though," said Jack. "My attacks should have packed a lot more punch than they did. It's like something weakened them. It might be a result of those red clouds," said Jack.

"Are you suggesting that those clouds might weaken our magic?" asked Alivair.

"It's possible. Watch yourselves," said Jack.

"Are you all right?" asked Alivair.

"I'm a bit spent, and I ran into a tree, but I should be good in a few. Call me if you need reinforcements," said Jack.

The unit commander once again spoke to Alivair.

"Did he say he ran into a tree?" he asked.

"I believe he did," said Alivair.

"That aside, he eliminated ten thousand Dark Army soldiers with weakened magic? Is that even possible?" asked the unit commander.

"As I said before, Jack has immense power. Her Highness has stated that, should he unleash it all at once, he has the potential to level an entire country, though it would likely kill him in the process," said Alivair.

"I don't know whether to find that comforting or terrifying, sir," said the unit commander.

"Perhaps a bit of both," said Alivair. "Now, get ready. The enemy should be in sight soon. The true battle is just about to begin."

As Jack stood up, he found it difficult to catch his breath. Crescia came into view with Nava. She hopped off of Nava's back and ran over to Jack.

"Jack, are you all right?" she asked.

"Yeah. I think so. That attack just took a bit more out of me than I expected. I made a dent in their numbers, but Alivair, Bilen, and Rhandor and the soldiers under their command are still in for one hell of a fight," said Jack.

Alivair looked through the binoculars and scanned the horizon. It wasn't long before the Dark Army came into view.

"Archers! Prepare to fire! Mages! Prepare for wide-range attacks! We have draphnir incoming!" he yelled.

The thunderous rumble of a thousand draphnir running full speed at the Vedyrian Army drowned out all other sounds on the battlefield. Arrows flew through the sky, leaving white streaks in their path. The mages unleashed volley after volley of fireballs behind the arrows. The earth erupted with explosions as the fireballs struck the oncoming draphnir. Though their numbers were being depleted, the remaining draphnir continued forward. Alivair launched fireballs at the oncoming horde, but hundreds continued their charge.

"Draw swords!" yelled Alivair.

The sound of thousands of swords being unsheathed rang out on the battlefield like a bell signaling the true start of the battle.

"Charge!" yelled Alivair.

The roar of the Vedyrian Army as they charged, weapons drawn, straight at the oncoming draphnir showed their determination to win. Soon, blades pierced flesh. Razor-sharp teeth pierced armor. The true battle had begun. The dark red clouds now covered the battlefield, giving everything a crimson hue. Blood-red rain began to fall. The screams of Vedyrian soldiers being torn apart by the bloodthirsty draphnir echoed throughout the battlefield. The white glow of the shields was dimmed by the blood-red rain. As the arrows continued to fly, Alivair saw the glint of the armor from the Demonborne soldiers charging behind the remaining draphnir. Alivair grabbed the radio with one hand as he drove his sword deep into the skull of the draphnir, looking to make him the next casualty.

"Rhandor! Prepare to advance!" he yelled into the radio.

"Yes, sir!" Rhandor responded.

#####

Rhandor and the troops under his command began to charge toward the Demonborne soldiers. As he ran, he launched wind blade after wind blade toward the enemy, slicing a number of Demonborne in half. The mages under his command launched volleys of fireballs into the oncoming soldiers. Once they were within reach, Rhandor began slashing at the Demonborne soldiers with his claws. He threw the eviscerated bodies into the subsequent ranks. He grabbed one soldier by the throat and lifted him up like a ragdoll before sinking his teeth deep into the soldier's neck. He tossed the corpse aside and spat out the chunk of flesh he had torn away. He reached down and drew his sword. Each swing of his blade was followed by the sprays of blackened blood of the Demonborne soldiers. Between the ferocity of his teeth, claws, and sword, his continued use of wind blades to split his enemies in two showed that he was truly a force to be reckoned with on the battlefield. Swords of the Demonborne soldiers shattered under the power of each swing of Rhandor's sword. The soldiers under Rhandor's command continued their charge, cutting down as many Dark Army soldiers as they could. Those who were successful continued to fight. Those who failed were met with the business end of a blade. When possible, the injured were escorted or carried to the healers at the rear of the formation.

#####

With the number of draphnir rapidly dwindling, Alivair redirected some of his troops to assist in the assault against the Dark Army soldiers. The more fireballs that he launched at the enemy, the more Alivair noticed their destructive power diminishing.

"Damn this poison rain!" said Alivair.

Just as the Vedyrian soldiers started to look like they were getting a handle on the Dark Army onslaught, the necromancers that had been steering and controlling the draphnir commenced their attack. Spheres of dark magic energy soared through the skies, and with every impact, Vedyrian soldiers were scattered around the blast radius. Bilen ordered the mages at the rear of the formation to put all of their strength into creating shields above the ranks of soldiers involved in battle. The dark magic spheres bombarded the shields, weakening the casters of the magic in the process. With each impact, the shields grew thinner. By that point, every soldier on the field with even a hint of magic affinity was feeling their power being drained by the blood rain. The wind blades that Rhandor continued to launch went from severing the demonborne soldiers in half to leaving shallow slices in the chests, arms, necks, and faces of them, clearly confirming Jack's theory about the clouds becoming a weakness for the magic of the Vedyrian Army. Still, they pushed forward, taking as many Dark Army soldiers down as they could. By that point, the now muddy battlefield was littered with the corpses of draphnir, Dark Army soldiers, and Vedyrians. The clashes of swords striking swords and the crunches of armor being crushed beneath the feet of those who came after were deafening. The bloodcurdling howls that came from the mouths of the draphnir, now significantly reduced in number, sent chills down the spines of the Vedyrian soldiers, but the battle continued.

#####

Far off in the distance, well outside the range of any magic from the Vedyrian Army, Corvan watched the battle. In his left hand, he held a short staff with a large circular crystal on the top. A small ring of dark magic floated above the crystal.

#####

At the Emperor's palace, the Emperor, Karvan, and Lia watched the battle on a massive crystal screen on the wall of the throne room. The battle was being displayed from the perspective of the crystal on the staff held by Corvan. A small ring of dark magic floated near the head of the Emperor. He spoke into the circle.

"Begin stage two," said the Emperor.

"Yes, Your Excellency," said Corvan.

#####

Back at the battlefield, Corvan removed a horn from his belt and raised it to his lips with his right hand. He took a deep breath and blew into the horn. The sound of the horn echoed through the battlefield. Upon hearing the horn, the Dark Army soldiers turned and ran back in Corvan's direction.

"They're retreating!" yelled one of the unit commanders.

A number of Vedyrian soldiers cheered, thinking victory was at hand. Rhandor noticed something odd about the apparent retreat. The Dark Army soldiers soon turned and headed in the direction of the forests. Rhandor took out his radio.

"Captain Alivair, can you hear me?" asked Rhandor.

Alivair took out his radio.

"Yes. What is it?" he asked.

"I don't think they're retreating. They're regrouping," said Rhandor.

"I think you're right. Something's off," said Alivair.

Alivair thought for a moment before coming to a realization.

"This wasn't their main force. This was a distraction! Jack! Jack! Can you hear me?" Alivair yelled into the radio.

"Yeah. I hear you. What's going on?" said Jack.

"Be ready! I think you're about to get hit with a much larger force!" said Alivair.

#####

Inside the tunnel complex, the Dark Army soldiers were ready. There were seven crimson crystal cannons aimed at the tunnel wall. A small circle of dark magic floated near one of the dark elf commanders. The Emperor's voice could be heard from the circle.

"Commence the second wave," said the Emperor.

"Understood, Your Excellency," said the dark elf, before yelling to his men. "Charge the cannons and prepare to fire!"

#####

Back at the reserve site, Jack was running along the lines of the reserve soldiers. He drew his sword and placed his thumb on the crystal to ignite the blade and raised the sword up above his head.

"Everyone on your feet! Weapons ready! Prepare for an attack!" he yelled.

Jack brought the radio up again.

"Where are they coming from? I don't see anything. I don't—"

Jack was caught by surprise by an immense explosion just inside the treeline that sent debris flying in all directions. Within seconds, wave after wave of Dark Army soldiers poured out of the forest. Jack stood up and picked up the radio.

"We're under attack! They're coming out of the forest!" he yelled.

Chaos ensued as the Vedyrian reserve soldiers rushed into battle with the waves of Dark Army soldiers charging at them. Crescia ran to Jack, slicing at the Dark Army soldiers that got in her way with the two short swords.

"What's the plan?" she asked.

"Stick close to me. Kill the bad guys, try your best to make sure they don't kill you, and hope we can hold out until Alivair and Rhandor's soldiers make it back here," said Jack.

Jack raised his hand and launched a series of fireballs at the treeline, turning the first few rows of trees into splinters. Through the wall of flames, more waves of Dark Army soldiers continued to advance.

"Time to get serious," said Jack.

He placed his hands on the ground, and the earth began to shake. Cracks began to form along the ground, running up to the treeline. Jack let out a guttural yell as the ground along the treeline cracked. Giant fissures opened up in the earth, swallowing trees and Dark Army soldiers, running along the length of the treeline. The fissure created a gap in the ground wide enough to slow the advance of the Dark Army. A bright glow inside the treeline preceded the firing of the seven crystal cannons at the opening of the tunnels. Giant spheres of dark energy sailed over the battlefield, heading in the direction of the Vedyrian Army base camp. Just as the energy spheres soared overhead, the blood-red rain began to fall from the dark magic clouds. Jack got on the radio.

"I've opened a crack in the ground to slow their advance, but they're launching triple-Cs toward the camp. I need to get over there and take out those cannons," he said.

"Jack, we're almost there. Don't be reckless," said Alivair.

With the fissure separating the Dark Army from the Vedyrian forces, arrows and magic became the weapons of choice for both sides. Those members of the Dark Army that made it through before Jack opened up the massive fissure in the ground fought relentlessly. Crescia moved with impressive speed from soldier to soldier, slicing and cutting as she moved. Jack continued to send volleys of fireballs across the fissure.

#####

Back at the camp, Veris and the other members of the Mage Corps that stayed behind to protect the camp saw the crystal cannon fire heading in their direction.

"Incoming!" yelled Veris.

The mages raised their hands to create shields to protect the camp, but they were only able to stop four of the seven spheres. The ones that got through hit the camp and exploded, sending debris everywhere. A number of soldiers ran to the edges of the camp carrying large spears with crystal spheres on the back ends and stabbed them into the ground. Once the spears were in place, mages made their way to the base of each spear and grabbed the shafts. As they each activated their light magic, the spheres on the top of the spears glowed. Once they were all lit up, a shield started to form along the border of the camp. The shield continued to grow, creating a protective barrier dome that covered the camp. As the second volley of crystal cannon fire started to fall out of the sky, the occupants of the camp braced for impact. The second volley impacted the shield dome. That time, none of the cannon fire made it through.

#####

Back at the forest edge, trees several hundred feet in began to shake and fall, and soon afterward, giant grotesque creatures, nearly thirty-five feet tall, emerged from the cave opening.

"What the hell are those things?" asked Jack.

Crescia yelled to Jack.

"They're mountain trolls! I thought they were extinct!" she yelled.

The flesh of the mountain trolls looked rotten, and bone was visible around their faces and hands.

"They're undead!" she yelled.

The mountain trolls lifted massive boulders from the ground and hurled them at the Vedyrian Army soldiers. Jack raised his hands and used wind magic to try and redirect some of the boulders away from the soldiers, but the more the red rain fell, the weaker his magic and the magic of all of the other Vedyrian magic users on the battlefield became. Jack used his sword to slice through a Demonborne soldier and then spoke into the radio again.

"Why did no one tell me that mountain trolls were a thing?" he yelled into the radio.

"What are you talking about?" replied Rhandor.

"They're here! They're massive, and they're attacking!" Jack yelled.

Along the edges of the fissure, where the gap wasn't as wide, Demonborne soldiers started knocking down trees in order to create makeshift bridges to cross the gap. With that, the Vedyrian Army was getting hit from three sides. Jack threw everything he had into his magic attacks against the mountain trolls. One fell, but two more appeared behind it. It wasn't long before he could no longer create fireballs. Soon after, even the flame of his sword was extinguished. However, there was one magic attribute that didn't appear to be weakened by the blood rain. If anything, he felt like it was getting stronger. But he was hesitant to use dark magic, given that Zavyra had warned him about how much of a toll it can take on his body to use it. Unfortunately, the situation left him with little choice. Jack called to Crescia.

"Crescia! Fall back!" he said as his eyes began to glow purple.

Crescia quickly moved some distance behind Jack's position. Jack held up his hands and pointed them at the mountain trolls. A sphere of dark magic slowly grew in front of each palm. Once the spheres grew to roughly the size of a basketball, a bright purple and crimson beam of energy fired from each sphere. The beams cut through the forest and the Dark Army soldiers in it like a blade through the wind. For a brief moment, all fighting stopped as both the Dark Army soldiers and the Vedyrian soldiers looked at the level of destruction Jack had unleashed. Even Jack was taken by surprise at the amount of damage he had caused. Nearly a square mile of forest was reduced to ash. A small number of Dark Army soldiers in the vicinity of Jack began to run away. A drop of blood fell from Jack's nose. Another volley of crystal cannon fire launched from the underground chamber, arcing over the battlefield and heading straight for the base camp.

#####

Far off in the distance, Corvan watched as Jack unleashed his power on the forest. He still held the staff with the seeing crystal on it, so the Great Demon Emperor also witnessed the destruction Jack had just caused.

"It has begun," said the Emperor.

#####

Jack wiped the blood from his nose.

"Looks like I overdid it again. Ok. Let's try this again, but keep it more Star Trek phaser and less Bond villain orbital death ray." Jack said to himself.

With all of the trees now rendered to ash, the opening into the tunnel complex was clearly visible. It was nearly two hundred yards from where the edge of the forest used to be. From the opening, more undead mountain trolls emerged, along with thousands more Dark Army soldiers. Once again, arrows began to fly. One of the mountain trolls threw itself into the chasm, wedging itself between the walls in order to serve as a bridge for the Demonborne to cross. Once more, the battle intensified. Jack did his best to control his dark magic attacks. The more he used them, the more his nose began to bleed. Eventually, the sheer numbers of Dark Army soldiers began to force the Vedyrian soldiers back. Jack took out the radio.

"We're losing ground here! Where the hell are you!?" he yelled.

Alivair responded.

"We are carrying many wounded! I have sent Rhandor ahead with those still able to fight! He should arrive shortly!" he yelled.

Rhandor spoke over his radio.

"We are minutes away, my friend! What of your magic? Has this cursed rain affected you as it has affected us?" he said.

"The only kind I have left is dark magic, but it's taking a toll on my body. I don't know how much longer I can control it," said Jack.

"Stay strong, my friend. We shall yet prevail," said Rhandor.

Jack slashed at a Demonborne soldier with his sword and thrust the blade deep into the chest of another one while doing his best to dodge the ever-present arrows that continued to fly. Thanks to his armor, those few arrows that did hit their mark were deflected.

#####

From the Emperor's palace, the Emperor, Lia, and Karvan all watched the battle through the view of the staff that Corvan still carried. The Emperor raised his hand and the image zoomed in until Jack was visible. Lia saw the blood pouring from his face as he continued to fight.

"He shall soon be mine," said the Emperor.

"He will never fight for you!" said Lia.

A female dark elf entered the throne room and approached the Emperor, kneeling before him.

"Your time has come to serve your purpose," said the Emperor.

Karvan placed the dark elf female in shackles and placed a magic suppression collar around her neck. The Emperor raised his hand and pulled Lia to him with his magic. He gripped Lia by her head with his left hand and placed his right hand on the head of the female dark elf. His hands glowed, and a slow transformation began to occur with the female dark elf. As his hands glowed brighter, the appearance of the dark elf began to resemble Lia's appearance. He released Lia, and she dropped to the floor, dazed by what had just occurred. When her vision started to clear, she looked over at the female dark elf and was shocked to find that the dark elf now fully resembled her.

"What sort of evil magic is this?!" Lia said.

"This shall be the final step to realizing my goals," said the Emperor.

He opened up a portal to his right.

"Go now. Do as you have been commanded," he said.

The dark elf doppelganger of Lia stood up and walked through the portal. The Emperor opened up a small, dark magic circle to communicate with Corvan.

"Has she arrived?" he said to Corvan.

"Yes, Your Excellency." responded Corvan.

"Fulfill your duty," said the Emperor.

"As you command, Your Excellency." replied Corvan.

"What is the purpose of this charade?" Lia asked.

"She is going to be the final piece on the board. She is to die," said Karvan, with a hint of sadness in his tone.

"Why is she to die?" asked Lia.

"In order to break your beloved Jack," said Karvan. "Once he sees you die, he shall unleash his full potential, and in doing so, he shall destroy everything."

"Then why not simply kill me?" Lia asked. "Why kill some cheap copy?"

The Emperor spoke.

"It is quite simple, Your Highness. As I told you before, you shall live to watch your kingdom fall. You shall watch as the man you love is shattered and reborn as a never-ending source of true dark magic. Watch as he murders friend and foe alike. Watch as your beloved exterminates everyone you have ever known and loved. Watch, knowing full well that there is nothing you can do to stop it," he said.

Lia looked at the image of Jack again. Inside, her heart was breaking as she watched him continue to struggle, knowing that with each use of dark magic, he was doing more damage to himself. A single tear rolled down her cheek before she turned to the Emperor.

"And as I told you before, you underestimate Jack," she said.

"We shall see," said the Emperor.

Back on the battlefield, Jack and Crescia were both struggling under the overwhelming numbers of Dark Army soldiers continuing to pour out of the tunnels. Bodies of both Dark Army and Vedyrian Army soldiers littered the battlefield, and the continuing blood rain had turned the terrain into a thick layer of mud. Doubt began to gnaw at Jack's mind. All around him, soldiers were continuing to fall. Though Crescia was continuing to fight, Jack could see that exhaustion was starting to set in. Jack was beginning to consider using his last resort. Up until that point, he had been using what strength he could spare to resist drawing the corrupted dark magic of the Dark Army to him, the way it had when he first arrived. Though the power would be unrivaled and could potentially wipe out the Dark Army, the eruption of the purified dark magic would be entirely indiscriminate in its destruction, likely wiping out not just the Dark Army but the Vedyrian Army as well. He looked up to the sky as the next volley of crystal cannon fire soared overhead. Just before he made the choice to drop his defenses, he heard a sound in the sky that sounded almost like a jet engine. A moment later, there was a bright orange glow above the red clouds far in the distance. The glow grew brighter, and then, in a blinding flash, the entirety of the red clouds burst into flame. The deafening roar of the rapidly spreading flame drew the eye of everyone on the battlefield. As the entire sky burned, soldiers on both sides found themselves fixated. It was as if someone had pressed the pause button on the battle.

#####

Rhandor and the troops under his command reached the battlefield just in time to see the fire in the sky. Rhandor pulled out his radio.

"Jack, was that you?" he asked.

Jack pulled out his radio.

"No. It wasn't me," he said.

In less than a minute, the flames dissipated, revealing a clear blue sky. A few moments later, Rhandor, Jack, Crescia, and the rest of the magic users in the Vedyrian Army felt their ability to use magic returning. With the arrival of Rhandor and the reinforcements and the ability to use magic returning, the Vedyrian soldiers began to feel as if the tide had turned in their favor. A number of Dark Army soldiers started to fall back.

Jack wiped the blood from his nose once again before his eyes glowed red. A fireball formed in each hand. Some of the Demonborne near Jack turned and ran. Jack launched the fireballs high up into the air. The fireballs flew through the sky and came down right at the entrance to the tunnels. The explosion that followed shook the earth, and the tunnels started to collapse. Secondary explosions followed as the crystal cannons detonated. Cheers from the Vedyrian forces rang out throughout the battlefield.

#####

Back at the Emperor's palace, the Emperor was furious. The entire palace shook as he let out a primal scream.

"You have lost," said Lia.

The Emperor raised his hand, and Lia was pulled across the room, and her throat was grasped by the Emperor. He held her close to his face. Even at the close distance, Lia was still unable to see a single feature of his face other than the glowing red eyes.

"I would not be so sure if I were you, child," he said.

The Emperor turned to General Karvan as he continued to hold Lia off the ground by her throat.

"General. We shall proceed with the final stage," he said.

The Emperor then threw Lia to Karvan. He caught her as carefully as he was able to and helped her to her feet. The Emperor then opened a teleportation portal.

"Bring her," he said to Karvan.

"Yes, Your Excellency," said Karvan as he escorted Lia through the portal behind the Emperor.

#####

On the other side of the portal, Lia found herself standing on a hill at the far edge of the battlefield. Karvan held her by the back of the collar around her neck. In the distance she saw Jack.

"Jack!" she yelled.

"It's no use, Your Highness. We are inside a null field created by His Excellency. You can neither be seen nor heard by anyone outside of the field, regardless of how much or how loud you yell," said Karvan.

The Emperor raised his hands, and pitch-black cyclone formed on the battlefield. The cyclone carved deep into the earth as it moved. It slowly made its way toward Jack and the other Vedyrian soldiers.

#####

Jack raised his hands and used wind magic to try and stop the cyclone's forward progress. The more he held it back, the larger it grew. As Jack struggled to hold it in place, he looked around the battlefield and saw the Vedyrian soldiers in its path. He yelled to Crescia.

"Crescia! When you get to Rhandor, tell him to have everyone fall back!" he yelled.

"What are you planning to do?" Crescia asked.

"I hope this works." Jack said to himself.

Jack concentrated as hard as he could, and teleportation circles started to appear at the feet of all of the Vedyrian soldiers. A circle formed at Crescia's feet as well. Once the circles formed completely, they shot up into the air, teleporting Crescia and all of the soldiers over to Rhandor's position. Crescia ran up to Rhandor.

"Jack said he wants everyone to fall back!" she said.

"What the hell is he planning?" asked Rhandor.

Once everyone was out of harm's way, Jack used the wind magic to surround the cyclone, creating a larger cyclone that rotated in the opposite direction as the one the Emperor was sending his way. Once the counter-rotation of Jack's cyclone matched the speed of the Emperor's cyclone, they canceled each other out and both were dispersed in a huge cloud of dust. Jack's vision was still obscured by the cloud of dust when a thin beam of dark magic cut through the dust and passed entirely through Jack's upper chest near his right shoulder, just below his collarbone. Jack grabbed his shoulder and let out a cry of pain. It was then that he heard a familiar voice.

"Human!" said the voice.

It was Corvan who had just fired the dark magic energy through Jack's shoulder. When the dust started to clear, Jack was able to see Corvan in the distance. He held a severely beaten Lia with his right hand. Corvan was unaware of the fact that the Lia he had brutally beaten was a fake. Jack was equally unaware, so he immediately became enraged seeing the state Lia was in.

"Lia!" Jack yelled. "Let her go!"

Jack's eyes began to glow purple. Moments later, the crack-like scars began to glow as well.

"I said let her go!" he yelled.

"I see. The whore is important to you," said Corvan. "That means that this will hurt you that much more."

Corvan raised his right hand and stabbed his razor-sharp claws through the fake Lia's back. The long claws protruded from her chest. Jack dropped to his knees.

"No!" he screamed.

Corvan pulled the claws out of her back and then placed his hand on her throat. He pulled his claws along her throat, making four deep cuts. The cuts were so deep that they nearly decapitated her. Corvan let her lifeless body fall to the ground and started to laugh as Jack screamed.

#####

Far off in the distance, Rhandor and Crescia stood there in silence as they watched what Corvan had done. Tears began to stream down Crescia's face, and she started to shake violently. Rhandor approached her and held her as she cried out in anguish.

#####

A cloud of dark magic that looked like black and purple flames engulfed Jack's entire body. The Emperor turned to the real Lia, still alive in the null space on the hill.

"Watch now, as he becomes mine," he said.

Seeing the agony that Jack was in and feeling entirely helpless to do anything about it, tears began streaming down Lia's cheeks. The dark magic flames grew brighter and more intense as Jack stood up. His eyes were locked onto Corvan. Karvan turned to the Emperor.

"Your Excellency, what are you going to do? He's going to kill my brother!" he said.

"Indeed, he is," said the Emperor.

"Are you just going to let it happen?" asked Karvan.

"He is serving his purpose," said the Emperor.

Karvan's right hand was still holding Lia's magic suppression collar. As he squeezed it tighter, he used his magic to covertly disengage the latch.

#####

Corvan held his still bloodied right hand up and fired a deep red beam of dark energy at Jack. Jack held up his right hand and unleashed a much larger, deep purple beam at Corvan. There was an explosion the moment that the beams collided. Jack let out a bloodcurdling scream, and he poured all of the power he could into the beam. The flame-like energy that had engulfed him started to flow along the beam. With each pulse of the flame-like energy, Jack's beam gained ground against Corvan's. Corvan felt his feet starting to slip from the oncoming force. He poured all of the energy he had into his beam to try and stop it from getting any closer, but he soon realized the futility of his actions. Corvan's dark magic dissipated far too quickly, and the beam that Jack fired once again obliterated Corvan's entire right arm, all the way up to the shoulder. By that point, tears of blood were streaming down Jack's face. Inside the null space the Emperor had created, Lia repeatedly called out to Jack, but he was unable to hear her.

From every Dark Army soldier, dark magic began to flow out of them and get drawn directly to Jack, as if he was forcefully pulling whatever magic affinity they had out of their bodies. Jack pointed his palms to the ground, and the earth began to violently shake. Dark magic flowed from his hands and into the ground, and glowing cracks in the ground spread out in all directions. The glowing cracks ran along the ground, heading toward each member of the Dark Army still on the battlefield. Many of the soldiers attempted to run from the cracks, but no matter where they ran, the cracks followed. When the crack reached a soldier, bright purple flames erupted from the cracks, burning the soldier alive. The soldiers screamed in pain before being reduced to ash and crumbling to the ground. The crack making its way toward Corvan was bigger and brighter than the rest. By that point, Corvan was panicking. He fired bolt after bolt of dark magic at the rapidly approaching glowing crack as he ran, but it did nothing to slow it down. Corvan screamed for help from the Emperor, completely unaware that the Emperor was watching everything happen from a nearby hill. Jack's skin was slowly turning gray, and his eyes were going from a bright purple to pitch black. The bloody tears continued to stream down his cheeks. When the crack finally reached Corvan, a column of purple fire shot out of the crack with the energy of a jet engine firing afterburners and climbed high into the sky. Corvan shrieked in agony as he burned alive. By that point, bolts of dark magic energy were firing off of the flame-like cloud surrounding Jack.

#####

Lia began to tremble as she watched what was happening to Jack. A few silent tears fell down the cheeks of Karvan as he watched his younger brother burning to death. He looked over to the Emperor with hatred. Lia once again called out to Jack.

"Jack! Please stop! Jack!" she yelled, but it was no different from the last time. Her pleas went unheard by all but Karvan and the Great Demon Emperor. The Emperor raised his hands up.

"Yes! Yes!" he said joyfully.

Suddenly, Jack turned his head and looked directly at the Emperor. A new crack formed at Jack's feet. This crack was much larger than any of the previous ones, and it increased in speed toward the Emperor.

"Impossible!" said the Emperor. "This is a null space! There is no way he should be able to find us!"

"I guess you didn't see this coming, Your Excellency." Karvan said as he backed away, taking Lia with him.

Jack's eyes remained fixated and unblinking on the Emperor and every move he made.

"I shall not end like this!" said the Emperor.

The Emperor formed a teleportation portal behind him. Karvan dropped the magic suppression collar off of Lia's neck, and she immediately turned toward the Emperor and started firing fireball after fireball at him as he continued to back up. Between the fireballs and the rapidly approaching dark magic cracks, the Emperor was struggling to remain on his feet. He continued to back up.

"This is not over! He shall be mine!" the Emperor said.

Lia fired a final large fireball directly at the Emperor's head as he passed into the portal and vanished. With the Emperor gone, the null space disappeared. Karvan spoke to Lia.

"Go. It may not yet be too late to save him," he said.

Lia ran as fast as she could toward Jack, calling out his name as she ran.

#####

In the distance, Rhandor and Crescia saw Lia appear out of nowhere and start running toward Jack.

"She's alive!" yelled Rhandor. "Crescia! She's alive!"

A moment of relief swept over Crescia, but then she looked back at Jack. At that point, Jack was looking up at the sky and screaming as the flame-like energy around him grew even more intense.

#####

Lia stopped just out of range of the bolts of energy that were shooting in every direction from Jack and called out his name again.

"Jack! Look at me! Jack! I'm here!" she yelled.

Jack slowly lowered his head and looked over at Lia. In a deep, monstrous voice, he spoke.

"Lia?" he said.

"Yes! It's me!" she yelled.

"No. You're dead," said Jack.

"I'm right here!" said Lia.

"It's not possible. You're not real," said Jack.

Lia used her light magic to form a shield and started making her way into the flames. The bolts of energy repeatedly struck her arms and legs, leaving burn marks wherever they touched. She winced in pain but continued to walk forward. When she reached Jack, she released the shield and placed her hands on his cheeks. His expression changed to one of fear and confusion.

"Lia?" he said.

"Yes, Jack. I'm here. I'm real," she said.

The tears of blood continued to stream down his cheeks.

"Is that really you?" he asked.

"Jack. It's me," she said, as tears flowed.

"Help me," he said. "I can't stop."

Lia wrapped her arms around him and spoke directly into his ear.

"Reject it, Jack. Reject the dark magic," she said.

Jack dropped to his knees, and Lia followed him down, still holding him tightly. As she held him, she put all of her strength into healing light magic. Lia then pointed at a distant mountain.

"Release it, Jack." she said.

Jack turned his head and looked over at the distant mountain. He slowly raised his right hand, and a sphere began to grow in front of his palm. The sphere continued to grow until it was nearly four feet in diameter. Jack released the sphere of purified dark magic at the distant mountain. The bolts and flame-like energy followed along his arm as he fired the sphere. The moment he released the magic, he fell unconscious and slumped over onto Lia's shoulder. In the distance, the sphere of dark magic hit the mountain, and there was a massive explosion that shook the earth. A mushroom cloud larger than a nuclear bomb detonation rose from the mountain and a shockwave spread out in all directions. Lia closed her eyes to avoid looking at the flash. Rhandor, Crescia, and the rest of the Vedyrian soldiers did the same. As the shockwave continued to spread, it gathered up dust. When it reached Jack and Lia, they became completely engulfed in the dust as the pressure of the shockwave knocked them both over.

#####

A few moments later, the shockwave reached Rhandor and everyone else, along with the deafening boom from the explosion. Some of the soldiers were knocked over to the ground. Rhandor held Crescia tightly with his back facing the shockwave. A silence fell over the battlefield as it became blanketed in a thick cloud of dust.

CHAPTER 35

When the dust finally cleared, Rhandor, Crescia, and a number of other soldiers made their way to Jack and Lia's last known location. Rhandor ordered another group of soldiers to make their way to the tunnel entrance and search for any remaining Dark Army soldiers. When they reached Lia and Jack, they were both covered in a thick layer of dust. Rhandor used his wind magic to clear the dust off of them, and Crescia moved in to check their statuses. They were both alive, and even though she was unconscious, Lia was still holding Jack tightly. The soldiers who were still able to move made a number of makeshift stretchers to transport the wounded, including Jack and Lia, back to the base camp. General Karvan surrendered without any resistance and was taken prisoner. Rhandor made his way to where the fake Lia was lying. The magic the Emperor had used to give her the appearance of Lia was gone, leaving the battered body of the female dark elf. With all of the dead and wounded gathered, they made their way back to the camp.

#####

As the camp came into sight, Alivair raced over to Rhandor.

"Is it true? Is she alive?" Alivair asked.

Rhandor nodded and pointed to the stretcher carrying Lia. Alivair made his way to Lia's stretcher. Crescia was walking between Lia's stretcher and Jack's stretcher, refusing to leave either of their sides.

"Crescia. I am pleased to see that you are well," said

Alivair. "What is their condition?"

The expression on Crescia's face showed the conflicting emotions she was feeling.

"Her Highness appears to have minor injuries. She exhausted her magic. The healers say she should be fine with rest," she said.

Alivair looked over at Jack. There was still a significant amount of blood caked on his face and his skin was pale.

"What of Jack?" asked Alivair.

"I don't know. He's alive, but... I don't know," she said.

Alivair remained next to Lia as they marched into camp and continued to accompany her all the way to the medical tent.

After reaching the medical tent, the injured were transferred to beds, and the healers began their work. Lia was treated for the burns she sustained trying to reach Jack. Once her injuries were treated, she was transferred to her tent to recover from the exhaustion of her magic, accompanied by Crescia. The healer attending to Jack examined his eyes. While they were no longer black, the whites of his eyes were a deep, dark, blood-red from the rupturing of many of the blood vessels in his eyes. The damage to his right shoulder was significant. The dark magic had burned a hole completely through his upper chest. The injuries, combined with the significant loss of blood, the damage done to his system from the overuse of dark magic, and the exhaustion of his magic as a whole, left him in critical condition. Mages capable of light magic who weren't officially part of the healers were called in to assist with all the wounded.

With Lia moved to her tent to recover and Jack receiving treatment, Alivair made his way back to the command tent to prepare for the after-action report and coordinate with unit commanders for follow-up patrols and repairs to the camp from the crystal cannon damage that made it through the shields. Rhandor chose to remain with Jack, so Bilen assisted Alivair with the coordination efforts.

#####

Several hours later, a representative of the team that Rhandor had sent to investigate the tunnels returned to report on what they had found. The report outlined a vast network of tunnels that appeared to go on for miles. Alivair ordered a squad of soldiers to explore the tunnels and report back as soon as possible.

Once the reports were all in and repairs were underway, Alivair made his way to Lia's tent to check on her.

#####

When he arrived, he was met by Crescia.

"Alivair! I was just about to come get you. She's awake," said Crescia.

"May I see her?" Alivair asked.

"Yes, but keep in mind that she's still a bit weak," said Crescia.

Crescia held open the flap of the tent, and Alivair rushed in and knelt by Lia's bedside.

"Your Highness," Alivair said as he took her hand.

"Alivair. I am glad to see you are well," said Lia.

"I am well, Your Highness, but how are you?" he asked.

"Tired, but feeling better. What of Jack? How is he?" Lia asked.

Alivair's expression darkened.

"He is... alive, Your Highness. But he is in quite rough condition. The healers are doing all that they can to help him," he said.

"I want to see him," said Lia as she started to sit up.

"In due time, Your Highness. For now, you must rest," said Crescia.

"Very well," said Lia, after seeing the looks of concern on both Crescia and Alivair's faces.

"I will go check up on him now," said Crescia.

"Please," said Lia.

Lia turned back to Alivair.

"What of the war?" she asked.

"We are encountering very few remaining Dark Army soldiers, Your Highness. I hesitate to say it, but it may very well be that this long-fought war is finally over," said Alivair.

"The Emperor?" Lia said.

"No sign of him. His general surrendered without any resistance," said Alivair.

"Karvan?" asked Lia.

"Yes, Your Highness," said Alivair.

"He shall be treated humanely for the length of his detention. Is that understood?" said Lia.

Alivair was slightly confused by her statement but knew that she had her reasons.

"Yes, Your Highness. Of course," he said.

"I should be back on my feet soon, Captain. Thank you for holding things together during my absence," said Lia.

"You need not worry, Your Highness. I have things well in hand. You need only focus on your recovery for now. Jack will likely need you as well. I can handle the day-to-day operations for as long as you wish," said Alivair.

Lia thought for a moment and considered his suggestion.

"Perhaps you're right, Captain. I shall leave things in your very capable hands for now," she said.

#####

Crescia entered the medical tent to check on Jack's status. The healers were still working hard on him. He was looking a little less pale than he was when he first arrived, and his shoulder wound was looking slightly less gruesome than before. Crescia got the attention of one of the healers.

"Where is Rhandor?" she asked.

"He just left to get some food," said the healer.

Crescia looked over at Jack.

"How is he?" she asked.

"He's no longer losing any more blood," said the healer.

"How much longer until he's back with us?" she asked.

The healer was hesitant to respond. His brow furrowed as he tried to come up with the best way to respond.

"The damage to his body was extensive. The fact that he is still alive at all could be considered a miracle. I honestly can't say with any level of certainty when... or if... he will wake up. I'm sorry. I wish I had better news." the healer said.

Crescia's facial expression was amplified by the sinking of her ears and tail. It was not the news she was hoping to hear, and with Lia now awake, it was not the news she had hoped to report, either. She lowered her head.

"Ok. Thank you. Please let me know if anything changes," she said in a depressed tone.

"I will," said the healer before returning to Jack's treatment.

Crescia left the medical tent and made her way back to Lia's tent.

#####

When she walked in, Lia could clearly see by the drooping ears and tail that Crescia was not returning with good news.

"Just tell me this. Is he still alive?" Lia asked.

"Yes, Your Highness," responded Crescia.

"Then there is still hope, Crescia. He will come back to us. I know it," Lia said.

Lia's statement was as much to reassure herself as it was to reassure Crescia. Remembering the state that Jack was in when she last saw him, there was a good deal of fear that she might never see his smiling face again, and it took all she had, even in her weakened state, to avoid breaking down. Hope was the only thing she had to hold onto until she and Jack were reunited.

"Yes, Your Highness," said Crescia.

Lia took a deep breath.

"I must get some more rest. Please see to it that I am not disturbed for the time being," she said.

"Yes, Your Highness," said Crescia.

"Come here," said Lia.

Crescia perked up somewhat and approached Lia's bed. Lia pointed to the seat next to the bed. Crescia sat down in the seat, and Lia took her hand.

"Please, can we stay like this, just until I fall asleep?" Lia asked.

Crescia's ears perked up slightly, and she smiled.

"Of course, Your Highness," said Crescia, as she squeezed Lia's hand and began to purr.

With the soothing sound of Crescia's purring, Lia was soon asleep.

CHAPTER 36

The unit that Alivair and Rhandor had deployed to investigate the tunnels was busy exploring the depths. They brought along a few fairies that had recovered from the Emperor's poison clouds. One of the first things that they noticed was the total lack of resistance. Every Dark Army soldier they found was dead. The further along the tunnels that they traveled, the more Dark Army corpses they found. Occasionally, they would come across a pile of dead goblins that had been collected and cast aside during the construction of the vast tunnel network. Some of the Vedyrian soldiers were beginning to get uncomfortable. One of them voiced their concerns to the commander.

"Sir, are you seeing these Demonborne bodies? They're all showing the same burns as the ones on the battlefield," said the soldier.

"Indeed. It would appear that the human's magic was more far-reaching than we thought," said the commander.

Another soldier chimed in.

"I get that he's supposedly on our side, and he's done a lot to help us win this war, but if I'm going to be honest, quite frankly, he terrifies me," he said.

A number of the other soldiers nodded in agreement before yet another soldier spoke up.

"I was there for the last part of the battle. I was one of the ones he transported out of the way of that cyclone with his magic. I saw what he turned into when he lost control. Captain Alivair said that, if he wanted, the human was powerful enough to level an entire country. I thought he was exaggerating, but looking at all these dead Demonborne and seeing what he did on the battlefield, I'm starting to wonder if he's too dangerous to keep around," he said.

It was at that point that the commander felt that he had to respond.

"I understand your concerns. I have some of my own. But keep in mind that you're speaking about the Vice-commander of the Vedyrian Army, a rank and position assigned to him personally by His Majesty, the king. He is second only to Her Highness in his authority, and you are getting dangerously close to treasonous speech, and it will not be tolerated. Is that clear?" said the commander.

"Yes, sir!" said the soldiers.

The commander turned to the soldier who spoke of Jack being too dangerous to keep around.

"Is that clear, footman?" he asked in a stern tone.

"Yes, sir," said the soldier.

"Now, back to work," said the commander.

#####

A few hours later, one of the soldiers noticed some daylight coming from a vertical shaft up ahead. They approached the shaft carefully and looked up. The shaft appeared to be a vent shaft to the surface to allow airflow into the tunnels. The commander spoke to the fairy on his shoulder.

"Can you fly up there and tell me what you see?" the commander asked.

The fairy nodded and flew up the vent shaft. When he emerged, he found himself on the outer edge of the vast forest. He flew up above the trees to get a better view of the area, and it was then that he saw the Emperor's palace in the distance. Having previously been concealed from view by the Emperor's dark magic, it was the first time any of the fairies had seen the palace. The fairy flew back down the vent shaft and reported to the commander.

"Very well. We shall continue onward. Return to the camp and report to Captain Alivair what you've found," said the commander.

The fairy nodded again and flew back up the vent shaft before flying at full speed back to the camp.

A few hours later, the fairy arrived at camp, and made his way to the command tent. When he entered the tent, Alivair was sitting at the desk. He flew over and landed on Alivair's shoulder to report his discovery.

"Good work. I shall take it from here. Get some rest," said Alivair.

The fairy nodded and flew away.

Alivair stood up and went to find Rhandor. He found him in the medical tent, staying with Jack.

"How is he?" asked Alivair.

"His wounds are nearly healed, but they still don't know if he will wake," said Rhandor.

"He will come back to us. I know it," said Alivair.

"Is there something you needed me for, sir?" asked Rhandor.

"Yes. I just received a report from one of the fairies that we sent with the unit to explore the tunnels. It appears that we have found the Emperor's palace. I'd like you to take a number of mages with you on dragons to investigate," said Alivair.

"Understood. Shall we report this to Her Highness?" asked Rhandor.

"I will brief her if she is done resting. Select whoever you need to proceed and head out as soon as you can. I will inform you if there are any changes with Jack," said Alivair.

"Yes, sir. Thank you, sir," said Rhandor.

Rhandor placed his hand on Jack's shoulder.

"I will return, my friend," he said.

Rhandor left the tent to select a team to investigate the

Emperor's palace. After spending a few moments in silence by Jack, wishing for his recovery, Alivair left the medical tent and made his way to Lia to report the discovery.

#####

When he reached her tent, he announced himself before asking to come in. Crescia popped her head out of the tent and waved Alivair in. When he entered the tent, Lia was sitting up on her bed. She had just gotten dressed and was securing the straps on her boots.

"Your Highness, what are you doing?" asked Alivair.

"I have spent enough time in bed, Captain. Don't worry. I'm not relieving you of your duties just yet. I just need to walk around and get the blood flowing. I also want to go check in on Jack," she said.

"Are you sure you're ready for it, Your Highness?" asked Alivair, referring both to her being mobile again so soon after recovery, as well as the potential emotional stress of seeing Jack in his present state.

"Thank you for your concern, Captain. Really, I mean that. But I can't spend any more time in here not knowing what is going on," she said.

"Yes, Your Highness," said Alivair.

"Is there something you wished to tell me?" she asked.

"Yes, of course," said Alivair, remembering the reason for his visit. "The unit we deployed to investigate the tunnels has made a discovery. They have found what we believe to be the Emperor's palace. So far, they have met with no resistance. It would seem that Jack's magic extended well beyond the battlefield."

"I'm unfortunately quite familiar with his palace. Shall I accompany a team?" Lia asked.

"No, Your Highness. That's unnecessary. I've asked Rhandor to assemble a team to get a closer look," said Alivair.

"Very well, but before they leave, have Rhandor meet

with me. I will fill him in on all I know about the layout of the palace," said Lia.

"Yes, Your Highness," said Alivair.

"Is there anything else?" Lia asked.

"No, Your Highness. I just wanted to keep you apprised of the situation," said Alivair.

"Thank you, Captain," said Lia.

Alivair gave a quick bow before leaving the tent. He made sure to catch up to Rhandor to let him know to meet with Lia before heading for the castle.

#####

After Rhandor met with Lia, she made her way to the medical tent to see Jack. When she entered the tent, she approached Jack's cot and sat down on the chair beside it and took his left hand in hers.

"Listen to me, Jack. And listen carefully. You've done enough for the Vedyrian Army. Now, I need you to do something for me. I need you to get better, and I need you to wake up. Ok? I'll be here for as long as it takes, but you need to wake up. Do you hear me, Jack?" she said.

Lia's hand began to tremble slightly. For the briefest fraction of a moment, Lia thought she might have felt Jack squeeze her hand in response to her words. That brief fraction of a moment was more than enough time to give her all the hope she needed that Jack would eventually wake up.

#####

With the briefing from Lia taken care of, Rhandor assembled his team at the stables. Barvan prepped the dragons for deployment, and before long, Rhandor and the dozen members of the Mage Corps took flight, heading in the direction of the Emperor's palace.

#####

Nearly four hours later, the palace finally came into sight. It was immense. For its size, the thing that stuck out most was that the palace and the land around it appeared to be unoccupied. The bodies of numerous Dark Army soldiers were strewn about over the landscape, but there was nothing moving that Rhandor or any of the other Mage Corps members could see. They found a place to land and dismounted from their dragons. It wasn't long before the unit responsible for exploring the tunnels appeared from the direction of the tunnel entrance. Once they were all together and the commander reported their findings inside the tunnels, Rhandor and the other Mage Corps members divided the members of the tunnel group up, and once they formed four groups, each split up to investigate and explore a different section of the palace. One team found a number of prisoners from various border villages in the dungeon, being held in preparation to be converted into Demonborne soldiers. Beyond the unsurprisingly Gothic architecture and furnishings one would expect for the evil lair of someone known to all as the Great Demon Emperor, there was actually very little of note, which, in and of itself, spoke very loudly to the Vedyrian soldiers. Three conclusions were reached while they were all standing on the main floor of the throne room. The first conclusion was that the Great Demon Emperor was nowhere to be found. The second conclusion was that the Dark Army was no more. And the first and second conclusions were what led to the third and final conclusion. The war was truly over, and the Vedyrian Army had won. At first, the conclusions were met with an eerie silence, but eventually the silence was broken by one of the soldiers who was part of the tunnel unit.

"It's over. It's really over," he said.

"I never thought that I'd be standing in the throne room of the Great Demon Emperor's palace, let alone standing here victorious," said another soldier.

Rhandor looked around the room.

"I only wish that Jack were here with us to celebrate this moment of victory. If not for our chance meeting of him, I dare say we would not be standing here right now," he said.

A number of the members of the Mage Corps wholeheartedly agreed with Rhandor. The soldiers from the tunnel who had previously spoken of their fears and doubts about Jack simply chose to remain silent.

"One final thing…," said Rhandor as he reached into the pouch on his hip.

#####

Rhandor made his way to the spiral staircase that led up to the balcony where the Emperor had launched the spear carrying the notification of Lia's capture and tore down the Dark Army flag that was connected to the pole. In its place, he unwrapped the Vedyrian Kingdom flag and firmly secured it to the line before hoisting it up the flagpole, cementing the fact that the Vedyrians had won the war. One of the soldiers approached Rhandor.

"What of the dark elves, sir? And there's bound to be draphnir roaming these areas."

"A problem for another day," said Rhandor. "Remain here. I shall return to camp and inform them of our victory."

Rhandor assigned roles to the mages and soldiers with orders to explore and inventory, as well as tend to the prisoners, and made his way back to Aris to fly back to the camp. The whole way back, there was a feeling of peace he had not dared to allow himself to feel up until that point.

#####

When he arrived at the camp and made his way to the command tent, he told Alivair to follow him to the medical tent. They entered the medical tent and approached Jack's cot. Lia was still there, still holding Jack's hand. Rhandor knelt next to Jack's cot and placed his hand on Jack's shoulder.

"This is news I wanted you to hear, my friend," said Rhandor, before turning to Alivair and Lia.

Lia gave him a nod. Rhandor took a deep breath.

"The Emperor's palace is abandoned. The Dark Army has been defeated. I never thought I'd see the day that I could say this, but here we are. I believe that we can now officially declare that this cursed war is over and we are victorious."

Lia and Alivair both smiled.

"Very well. Captain, Rhandor, spread the word among the troops. The war is over," said Lia.

"With pleasure, Your Highness," said Alivair.

Alivair and Rhandor left the medical tent and spread the word. Soon, there were cheers erupting throughout the camp. The celebrations lasted for several days.

CHAPTER 37

More than a month had passed since the official declaration of the end of the war. By that point, the camp had been packed up, and many of the soldiers had returned to their homes. Lia, Rhandor, and Alivair had returned to the castle in the capital city. While joy had spread throughout the entire kingdom, there was still one person who was unable to enjoy the victory. Jack had yet to awaken from his coma. He had been moved to a lavish room in the castle where he continued to receive daily care, but no matter how many healers they summoned, none were able to wake him. Lia spent much of her time at Jack's bedside, often with Crescia by her side. Rhandor continued to make daily visits.

"Still no change?" he asked Lia.

"No," she said.

"Keep the faith, Your Highness. I know that he will return to us," said Rhandor.

"We have exhausted every healer in the kingdom. I don't know what else we can do," said Lia, sounding a bit exhausted.

"We'll figure something out, Your Highness," said Rhandor.

A voice spoke from behind Rhandor.

"Perhaps I may be of assistance," said the voice.

Rhandor turned around just as Queen Liandra walked into the room.

"Your Royal Highness," said Rhandor as he bowed.

"No need for that, Sir Rhandor," said Queen Liandra.

Queen Liandra walked up to Jack's bed and placed her hand on his cheek.

"What did you mean, Mother?" asked Lia.

"I have sent word to Zavyra, and I just received a reply. She believes she can help," said Queen Liandra.

Lia's expression changed.

"Are you sure?" asked Lia.

"Yes, my dear. She said to bring Jack to her, and she will do all that she can to help," said Queen Liandra.

Lia stood up.

"We must make preparations immediately!" said Lia.

"Worry not, my dear daughter. The preparations have been made. The five of you can begin your journey at any time," said Queen Liandra.

"The five of us?" asked Lia.

"Of course. You, Jack, Crescia, Rhandor, and..." Queen Liandra paused as another person entered the room.

"Alivair?" said Lia. "What are you doing here?"

"You tasked me with informing all of our people of our victory over the Great Demon Emperor and the Dark Army. Jack is one of us, and until he wakes, my job is not done. I intend to see it through to completion," Alivair said with a smile.

"Thank you, Alivair," said Lia.

"The carriage awaits. I will arrange for Jack to be brought down immediately," said Queen Liandra.

Lia walked over to Queen Liandra and hugged her.

"Thank you, Mother," she said.

"Of course, my dear," said Queen Liandra.

#####

Soon, Lia, Crescia, Rhandor, and Alivair found themselves standing in front of a grand carriage. Jack was loaded in with the utmost care, and both King Daven and Queen Liandra were standing by to see them off. Once they all got into the carriage, they began the long journey to Firespring Mountain.

#####

It was eight days later when they finally arrived at the base of the mountain. Lia directed the carriage to a different entrance than the one that Jack had taken the first time he came to see Zavyra. It was an entrance exclusively for members of the royal family who came to see her.

"Shall I remain here?" asked Rhandor.

"Why?" asked Lia.

"I've heard that she is not particularly fond of beastfolk," said Rhandor.

"I'm sure that she will make an exception for you," said Lia with a smile.

"Then I shall be the one to carry Jack," Rhandor said as he lifted Jack up.

The grand doors opened to reveal a staircase, and they all stepped inside. When they reached the top of the stairs, there was a short corridor. Lia turned to Crescia, Alivair, and Rhandor.

"Before we go any further, I will ask that you keep what you are about to see a secret."

The three of them nodded.

"Of course, Your Highness," said Alivair.

It wasn't long before they heard Zavyra's voice echo through the corridor.

"Welcome, Your Highness and honored guests. Please come in," said Zavyra.

They walked through an archway, and into a large cavernous room. Crystals around the room began to glow, lighting the room. It was then that Alivair, Crescia, and Rhandor got their first glimpse of the true identity of Zavyra. They stood there in shock at the sight of the Grand Elder Dragon before them. They were rendered speechless.

"Hello," said Zavyra.

"Thank you for seeing us, Great Empress Zavyra," said

Lia.

"Of course, my dear. Come. Bring Jack here," said Zavyra.

Rhandor was still frozen in place, not quite ready to fully process what he was seeing. Lia turned to him.

"Rhandor. She's talking to you," she said.

Rhandor snapped out of his stupor and slowly approached Zavyra with Jack in his arms.

"Worry not, Sir Rhandor. I shall not bite," said Zavyra with a smile.

Zavyra used her magic to move a stone altar in front of Rhandor.

"Place him here," she said.

Rhandor gently and carefully laid Jack down on the altar. Zavyra delicately placed her clawed hand on Jack, almost completely covering him.

"Hello, my sweet young friend. This is not how I had hoped we would meet again, but worry not. I shall help you," said Zavyra.

Crescia leaned over to Alivair and whispered.

"He looks like an hors d'oeuvre on a plate." she said.

"Don't worry, little one. I have no intention of eating young Jack," said Zavyra.

Crescia was surprised and a bit embarrassed that Zavyra heard her.

"Sorry," she said.

"This may take some time. His mind and soul have been severely damaged. It will not be easy to repair. You should all get some rest. You've had a long journey," said Zavyra. "Your Highness, would you be so kind as to show them to the guest quarters?"

"Of course," said Lia.

Lia escorted Rhandor, Alivair, and Crescia out of the giant room, leaving Zavyra to do her work.

#####

In the corridor, Alivair began to speak.

"She's a dragon. She's a really big dragon. She's a really, really big dragon," said Alivair.

"She's one of the few Grand Elder Dragons remaining," said Lia.

"I thought they were a myth," said Crescia.

Rhandor was completely silent as they walked.

"Are you ok, Rhandor?" asked Lia.

"I guess Jack left a few things out when he told me about his time with Zavyra," said Rhandor. "He said she was tall."

Lia chuckled at Jack's creative use of words.

"She certainly is," she said.

"Your Highness, why does a Grand Elder Dragon have guest quarters?" asked Alivair.

"She has been a friend of the royal family for generations. On the rare occasion, she has visitors. Why wouldn't she have guest quarters?" said Lia.

Once they arrived at the guest quarters, Alivair finally finished processing what he had just witnessed.

"So, what do we do now, Your Highness?" he asked.

"There's not much else we can do other than let Zavyra do what she can for Jack," said Lia.

"The last time I was here with Jack, I stayed at the hot springs resort at the base of the mountain. Perhaps we could get some food," said Rhandor.

"I could eat," said Crescia.

"Very well. Let's head down the mountain and get something to eat. Your Highness, would you like to join us?" said Alivair.

"Thank you, but I would like to speak with Zavyra a bit more. But please, go ahead," she said.

"Would you like me to bring some food back for you,

Your Highness?" asked Crescia.

"Thank you, Crescia. That would be much appreciated," said Lia.

After Crescia, Rhandor, and Alivair left to make their way down to the hot springs resort, Lia returned to the main hall to speak with Zavyra.

#####

"Hello, Your Highness. Did you wish to talk?" asked Zavyra.

"Do you think you'll be able to help him?" Lia asked.

"It may take a few days, but I believe I can help him. First, I must heal his mind," said Zavyra.

"How will you do that?" asked Lia.

"The first time we met, I was able to synchronize with his mind as we slept. Now that we share a connection, I am able to do so simply by making physical contact."

"What do you see?" Lia asked.

"He loves you quite deeply. Seeing you die, or more accurately seeing the one he believed to be you die, fractured his mind. Seeing the real you soon afterward only fractured it further, because he could no longer tell what was real. I must first guide his mind back to reality. Something like that cannot be rushed. Attempting to do so could only fracture it further," said Zavyra.

"You mentioned that his soul was damaged as well. How do you mean to repair it?" asked Lia.

"The amount of dark magic he used not only exhausted his body. It exhausted his soul. Once his mind is healed, I shall share a part of my soul with him," said Zavyra.

"Share a part of your soul?" asked Lia. "Is that possible?"

"It is something that has rarely been done outside of the Grand Elder Dragons, and not for many centuries. But it is something that we can do... once," said Zavyra.

"You're willing to go so far to help him?" said Lia.

"I am," was all Zavyra said.

"Thank you," said Lia, realizing that it was best not to question the motivations of a Grand Elder Dragon any more than she already had.

#####

Over the next several days, Zavyra spent every moment working to heal Jack. She worked without breaks or sleep. Lia, Rhandor, Alivair, and Crescia each took shifts staying by Jack as she worked. On the evening of the fourth day, Zavyra called Lia to meet with her.

"It is time," said Zavyra.

"Time for what?" asked Lia.

"To transfer a part of my soul into Jack," said Zavyra. "I will need your assistance."

"What must I do?" asked Lia.

Zavyra's eyes glowed a bright white, and soon a thin spike and a giant spear made out of pure light magic materialized on the floor in front of Lia.

"I will pull back a scale on my chest. I will need you to take that spear and plunge it into my chest," said Zavyra.

"You want me to stab you with a spear? I couldn't!" said Lia.

"Fear not, young one. It is a spear of my own magic. It will do me no harm. And if you are unable to carry out the first task, you will certainly have trouble with the second task," said Zavyra.

"Why? What is the second task?" asked Lia.

"You are to plunge the spike into Jack's chest," said Zavyra.

Seeing Lia's reaction to that, Zavyra felt the need to once again clarify.

"As I have said, it will cause neither of us harm. It is the purest of light magic. It is necessary for the transfer. I would do it myself, but this process is delicate and is often done between two of my kind. This transfer requires precision, and as you are well aware, the difference in size between Jack and myself would make attempting it myself more complicated than it needs to be. Which is why I requested your assistance," she said.

Though hesitant, Lia finally agreed.

"I shall do as you say," said Lia, picking up the light spear.

Lia walked over to where Zavyra had lifted a scale upward to expose the flesh beneath and held up the spear.

"You must plunge it deep into my chest," said Zavyra.

"Very well," said Lia.

Lia raised the spear. She looked up at Zavyra one more time. Zavyra nodded, letting Lia know that it was ok. Lia took a deep breath and plunged the spear into Zavyra's chest. Lia was surprised when Zavyra showed no reaction to having the spear plunged at least five feet into her chest.

"I am unharmed. Now, Jack," said Zavyra.

Lia walked over to Jack and picked up the spike. She positioned it over the center of Jack's chest and once again looked up to Zavyra for confirmation. Once again, Zavyra nodded. Though apprehensive, she raised the light spike up and then plunged it into Jack's chest. Just as with Zavyra, Jack showed no reaction and no sign of actual injury.

"Very good. Now, please step away from him," said Zavyra.

Lia did as she was asked.

Zavyra's eyes once again glowed a bright, almost blinding white. Soon, a cloud of energy appeared to form around the spear in Zavyra's chest. The cloud slowly moved over to the spike in Jack's chest. Within a few moments, Jack's entire body began to glow. When the glow subsided, Zavyra was breathing heavily. Lia looked up at Zavyra with concern.

"I am fine. Just a bit tired. More importantly..." Zavyra said before looking at Jack.

Lia rushed over to Jack's side. The spike had completely vanished, leaving no sign of a wound. She placed her hand against his cheek. Her pulse began to race as she saw him slowly open his eyes and look at her.

"Is that really you?" Jack asked.

Tears began to form in Lia's eyes.

"Yes, Jack. It's me. I'm really here," said Lia.

Jack smiled gently.

"Hi," he said.

Tears started to roll down Lia's cheeks as she smiled and replied.

"Hi," she said. "How do you feel?"

"Surprisingly good, actually," said Jack as he sat up.

Jack began to look around the room. He recognized it as being vaguely familiar, right up until he looked in Zavyra's direction.

"Hi, Zavyra," said Jack.

"Hello, Jack. Welcome back," said Zavyra.

Jack looked down at himself for a moment and then back up to Zavyra.

"You healed me, didn't you?" he asked.

"I did," said Zavyra.

"I must have been in pretty bad shape if they needed to bring me to you," said Jack as he stood up from the stone altar.

Lia was trembling at that point, and the moment Jack was on his feet, she rushed in and held him tightly as the tears continued to flow down her cheeks. Seeing Lia's reaction, Jack started to worry.

"Just how bad off was I?" he asked Zavyra.

"You have been in a coma, on the verge of death, for nearly two months," said Zavyra.

Lia's reaction started to make much more sense at that point. He held her tightly.

"Thank you," he said to Zavyra. "And thank you for what you did that day, too."

"I know not of what you speak." Zavyra said in a sly

tone.

"Thank you, all the same," said Jack, winking to Zavyra.

"You're welcome," said Zavyra.

Lia got a bit excited.

"We should tell the others the good news," she said.

"Others?" asked Jack.

Lia looked up at Zavyra.

"It's ok. Go," said Zavyra.

"No words yet exist to properly convey my thanks for all you have done," Lia said to Zavyra.

Zavyra nodded in response.

Lia practically ran out of the room with Jack in tow.

#####

When they got close to the entrance to the guest quarters, Lia released Jack's hand and threw the door open, startling Alivair, Rhandor, and Crescia.

"Your Highness?! What is it?!" asked Alivair.

"It's... Jack...," said Lia, trying to catch her breath.

Rhandor, Alivair, and Crescia immediately raced out of the room and headed toward the main hall, running right by Jack. Crescia was the first one to stop. She turned around to see Jack standing there waving.

"Jack!" shouted Crescia as she leaped into the air, straight at Jack.

He caught her, and they hugged happily. Alivair and Rhandor soon turned around and ran back to Jack. The moment Crescia let him go, Rhandor hugged Jack tightly.

"Welcome back, my friend," said Rhandor.

"Careful, Rhandor. I'm still a bit fragile," said Jack.

Rhandor released Jack.

"Oh! Forgive me!" said Rhandor.

"It's ok," said Jack.

Alivair approached and offered his hand.

"Welcome back to us," he said.

"Thanks, Alivair," said Jack.

A thought occurred to Jack.

"Wait. If all of you are here, who's commanding the troops?" he asked.

Alivair smiled.

"It is my duty and honor to finally be able to say this to you, Jack. The war is over. We won," he said.

Jack smiled.

"Is it really over?" he asked.

"Indeed," said Alivair.

Jack looked over at Lia.

"You know what that means, right?" he asked with a grin.

Lia was confused for a moment, then Jack placed his index finger at the base of her neck on her left shoulder and then traced along her collarbone until he hooked the chain attached to the ring, pulling it out from her collar.

"Oh. Oh!" Lia said as she realized what he meant.

#####

A few days later, after Jack had some more time to recover, they all offered their most heartfelt thanks to Zavyra for all she had done. Jack invited her to the wedding, but she politely declined, wishing them well all the same. The carriage ride back to the capital city was filled with stories and laughter. The brief stop they took in Ackhard gave Marath the opportunity to send word of their return ahead of the carriage through the fairy communication network. As they approached the capital city, Jack saw something in the road up ahead. He opened the carriage door and poked his head out to get a better look, and what he saw took him by surprise. On each side of the road, in a line reaching as far down the road as he could see, stood soldiers of the Vedyrian Army in full dress uniforms. Jack, Lia, Rhandor, Alivair, and Crescia were all awestruck by the display as they continued down the roads to the castle. It was a welcome unlike anything they had ever seen. When they arrived at the castle, the king and queen were right there to greet them as the carriage came to a stop.

#####

The next few days were filled with the energy and excitement of preparing for the wedding. When the day finally came, Jack was dressed in his elaborate formal attire, handmade by Crescia. Rhandor stood by his side as his best man, and Alivair stood by Rhandor as Jack's other groomsman. King Daven stood at the center of the altar, ready to perform the ceremony as soon as Lia arrived. A few moments later, the horns sounded as Lia came into view, wearing a beautifully ornate, flowing wedding dress. Jack was speechless as he watched her walk down the aisle. All he could do was stand there and smile like a fool. When she reached the altar, they took each other's hands, and the ceremony continued. When the ceremony was over and Jack and Lia kissed, King Daven gave the announcement to the crowd of thousands.

"Now, it is my absolute honor and privilege to declare that my daughter, Lia, Crown Princess of the Kingdom of Vedyria, and Jack, Crown Prince of the Kingdom of Stobrimore, are officially wed!" he said.

The cheers from the crowd echoed through the capital city. After the ceremony, a great banquet was held, and countless guests made their way by to congratulate the happy couple. The celebrations lasted for several more days.

CHAPTER 38

Once things finally began to settle down again, Jack summoned the Vedyrian Army engineers. To his surprise, even while he was still unconscious, they had already begun the reconstruction of the Worldgate temple on the cliffs of Arnin Canyon. In the days after the wedding, Jack had done extensive research into the Worldgates and who could and could not travel through them. During his research, he had found that one only needed a moderate level of magical affinity in order to be able to pass through the gates. Over the decades and centuries, a number of individuals had passed through the various gates to Earth and back, leading Jack to believe that it was entirely possible that many of the myths and sightings of creatures such as werewolves, vampires, elves, fairies, and the various cryptids like Bigfoot and Yetis that have been both seen and noted in some way, shape, or form over the centuries could very well have been members of this world who had passed through the gates at various points in history and returned, giving rise to the many myths and legends of Earth.

With the war now over, having seen much of Lia's world, Jack wanted to return the favor and bring Lia over to his for a visit. In his time with Lia, Jack had found a second home. He had made friends for a lifetime and found a new family. The only thing he needed to make things complete was to share his new family with his old one. Of course, it wasn't as easy as just packing up and leaving like they were going on a quick vacation. Lia was the crown princess of a nation, so of course there were political implications. He wasn't planning to take her to the next town or even the next country. He wanted to bring her to a parallel world. That meant that there were a number of discussions with the king and queen. On top of that, even though all of his research had shown that passage both ways through the gate had been done countless times over the centuries, the scientist in him and the husband in him refused to even consider risking the travel until he was satisfied that it was safe.

#####

Over the course of a week, Jack made multiple trips to the temple to conduct experiments. Accompanied by some of the brightest minds in the Vedyrian Kingdom, Jack ran multiple tests to check the safety of traveling through the gate, starting with trying inanimate objects, since he was able to bring various things with him on his initial trip there. Eventually, he attempted to pass his phone through the portal, encased in a protective housing he had constructed and attached to a rope. By setting the phone camera to record, he was able to pass it through the portal and pull it back and then view the footage. Once he was satisfied, he moved on to living creatures. He started with insects and found that, without any affinity for magic, they simply passed through the arch and continued unharmed to the wall behind it. After moving to other various small animals, Jack was ready to try passing through the portal himself. Before Jack could pass through, one of the mages involved in the experiments volunteered to be the first to pass through. Though Jack was hesitant, he ultimately agreed. He handed his phone to the mage, and everyone held their breath as he walked through the portal. The mage vanished as he passed through the archway. A minute later, he returned. When Jack reviewed the video from the cell phone camera he was finally satisfied that it was safe.

#####

After sharing his gathered evidence with the king and

queen, ensuring that it was safe to travel, he and Lia finally made preparations to leave. When the day came, Alivair, Rhandor, and Crescia came to see them off. Crescia seemed a little sad.

"It's not going to be for too long. Think of it as a honeymoon," said Jack, trying to comfort her. "And look at it this way. You're always welcome to come visit. Trips into town might be a little hard to explain, but still... we'd figure something out."

Jack turned to Rhandor and Alivair.

"The same goes for the both of you," he said.

"You both have certainly earned some time to yourselves," said Rhandor.

Lia smiled and squeezed Jack's hand.

"We certainly have," she said.

"You have the radio, and I showed you how to charge it, right?" Jack asked Rhandor.

"Yes, Jack," he said.

"All you need to do is step through the gate and use the radio. I'll be able to hear you if you need anything," said Jack.

Rhandor started to chuckle.

"You seem more nervous than we do, my friend," he said.

"Yeah. That's weird, huh?" said Jack.

"You both will be fine, and so shall we," said Rhandor. "Enjoy your journey."

After hugs were exchanged all around, Jack took Lia's hand, and they faced the gate.

"Are you ready?" Jack asked.

Lia took a deep breath and nodded.

"Here we go," he said as they walked through the gate.

#####

When they reached the other side, they found themselves in a hallway that led to the bottom of the stairwell.

After climbing the stairs, they were greeted by the glow of the stones in the wall that illuminated the room where Artemis had made the magic stones. Lia and Jack took a moment to look around.

"I can't believe that I'm really back here." Jack said. "It seems like forever ago that I last stood in this room."

"I certainly hope there's more to your world than this room," Lia said with a chuckle.

"Oh! Yes. Sorry. It's this way," said Jack.

Jack and Lia made their way to the surface and into the woods. Once on the surface, Lia noticed that Jack was starting to get a bit jittery.

"Jack, what's wrong?" she asked.

"Um... the house is this way. It's still a bit of a hike. It's just that... it's certainly no castle," said Jack.

Lia could tell that Jack was anxious about all of the differences in lifestyles between them. Though he had told her about his life on several occasions, what were stories were now becoming a reality, and she could see the worry on his face. She knew she had to alleviate the worry.

"Jack, I didn't marry you for a castle. I already have one of those. I married you because I love you. Whether you are a prince or a pauper, it doesn't matter to me. You are all I want and all I need," she said.

The tension in his shoulders started to subside. He walked up to her and took her hands. He took a deep breath and let out a sigh of relief before leaning in and kissing her.

"You really are amazing. You know that?" he said.

"Yes, I do," said Lia with a grin.

"Come on. The house is this way," said Jack.

He took her hand, and they made the hike back to the house.

#####

When the house came into view, Jack noticed a second

vehicle in the driveway.

"What are those?" Lia asked, pointing to the vehicles.

"Oh, those are my world's alternative to... uh... unicorn-drawn carriages," said Jack.

"I see," said Lia.

Jack cautiously approached the front steps of the house, and then he saw Artemis's walking stick leaning next to the front door.

"Grampa Art is back," he said. "Let's go say hi."

Jack and Lia walked up the stairs, and Jack opened the front door.

"Grampa Art? Are you here?" Jack said.

"In the living room, Jack. Come on in," said Artemis.

Jack and Lia made their way down the hallway, and Jack poked his head into the living room.

"Grampa Art! You're back from your trip," said Jack.

Artemis looked at Jack and noticed the outfit he was wearing.

"Indeed, and I have some stories, but looking at what you're wearing, it would seem you have some stories of your own," said Artemis.

"Yeah. I now know where you got all those stories that you told me as a kid," said Jack.

Artemis smiled.

"And I look forward to hearing your new ones," he said.

"First, there's someone I'd like you to meet," said Jack.

Jack took a few steps into the living room before turning to Lia and waving her to come in.

"This is Lia. She's the Crown Princess of the Kingdom of Vedyria... and my wife," said Jack.

Lia entered the living room and smiled.

Artemis noticed her pointed ears.

"My, my, my. Hello, my dear. Jack, my boy, it would seem that your stories are just beginning. Come in, my dear. Sit. Let's talk," said Artemis.

Jack and Lia walked into the living room and sat down

on the couch. Artemis smiled as he took Lia's hand.

"I'm so happy to meet you, Your Highness. My name is Artemis. Tell me your story," he said.

#####

The glowing cloud of a teleportation portal formed in an ancient cavern. The Emperor appeared from the portal and walked over to the skeleton of a long-dead Grand Elder Dragon. He placed his hand on the skull of the dragon, and the skull began to softly glow.

Preview of
"The Stobrimore Chronicles - New Lands"

Chapter 1

Nearly three months had passed since Jack and Lia had stepped through the Worldgate to visit Jack's world. In that time, Lia had started to become used to a lot of the technologies that seem commonplace to anyone on Jack's side of the gate, though she was still fascinated by things like televisions and vehicles. Any time they left the property, Lia was careful to style her hair in a way that concealed her pointed ears so as not to draw too much attention. During their time there, Jack had made a number of trips to the Worldgate in order to deliver supplies consisting of a number of technologies, such as handheld radios and solar-powered chargers and battery banks for the Vedyrians. He refrained from supplying any weapons, however, as he understood how much it could complicate things to introduce things like firearms to a world that had never seen them before.

The smell of coffee woke Jack up on a chilly morning in October. He had spent the day before finishing up cutting a path through the woods that would make it easier to take his ATV to and from the entrance to the tunnel where the Worldgate was located. Once he was dressed, he sleepily made his way downstairs to the kitchen. In the kitchen, Artemis and Lia were preparing breakfast.

"The zombie awakens," said Artemis, as he heard Jack coming down the stairs.

Lia chuckled.

When Jack reached the kitchen, Artemis greeted him first.

"Good morning, sleepyhead," said Artemis.

"Good morning, Grampa Art," said Jack.

Jack leaned in and gave Lia a kiss on the cheek.

"Good morning, Lia," said Jack.

"Good morning, Jack," said Lia.

"Good morning, Jack," said Crescia.

Jack leaned over and kissed Crescia on the top of her head.

"Good morning, Crescia," said Jack.

Jack took a few more steps toward the coffee maker before it sunk in. He paused for a few seconds before turning around. Crescia smiled and waved as she ate a strawberry turnover.

"Crescia? When did you get here?" asked Jack.

"Early this morning," she said.

"Am I the only one who was unaware of this?" asked Jack.

"Well, you did say that I could come and visit any time," said Crescia.

Jack took a deep breath and turned around.

"Need coffee. Can't think," said Jack.

Jack made his way over to the coffee machine, pulled a cup out of the cupboard above the machine, and proceeded to fill it. He chugged the entire cup down. Lia looked at him as he downed the cup.

"Isn't that hot?" she asked.

"Yes. Very," said Jack.

He poured a second cup and took a sip.

"Ok. Now I'm awake. So, Crescia, what brings you here?" he asked.

"I missed you both, and I wanted to see if I could pass through the Worldgate. As it turns out, I can, so here I am. Are you upset?" said Crescia.

"Of course not. I'd never be upset to see you. I'm just surprised. That's all," said Jack.

"Your world sure has a lot of trees," said Crescia.

"That's certainly true about this area, but there are a lot

of other environments in this world, including vast cities with millions of people living in them," said Jack.

"Wow! I'd like to see that sometime!" said Crescia.

"I'm not sure how easy that would be, given that people in this world aren't exactly used to seeing a four-foot-ten-inch-tall walking, talking, well-dressed cat. You're kind of one of a kind here," said Jack.

"To be fair, she's one of a kind wherever she is," said Lia.

"Yeah. Fair point," said Jack as they all chuckled.

"What's that?" asked Crescia, pointing into the living room.

"That's a TV," said Jack.

"What's a TV?" asked Crescia.

Lia walked into the living room and picked up the remote control to turn on the TV. Crescia hopped over the counter and sped into the living room to study the TV.

"Ooh! Pretty! How does it work?" Crescia asked.

"TV magic," said Jack.

"I thought you didn't have magic in this world," said Crescia.

"If I told you that it takes audiovisual data recorded or broadcast from various sourcesand compiles them into a number of computers that convert the data into electrical signals that are transmitted over a vast network of cables until it reaches the TV, which converts those electrical signals back into audiovisual data, would you know what I'm talking about?" said Jack.

"Nope," said Crescia, enthusiastically.

"So?" said Jack.

"TV magic?" asked Crescia.

"TV magic," said Jack.

"Nice," said Crescia, as she turned back to the TV.

"So, how are things going in Vedyria?" Jack asked.

"Since the war ended, a lot of territory that used to

belong to the Dark Army needs to be explored. Al and Randy are leading teams to explore the territories," said Crescia.

"Al and Randy?" asked Jack.

"Oops. I mean Alivair and Rhandor. Please don't tell anyone that I call them that," said Crescia.

"Your secret is safe with me," said Jack.

When Jack heard the names Al and Randy, a vision appeared in his mind of Alivair and Rhandor wearing jeans, white tank tops, dirty plaid shirts with the sleeves rolled up, and beat-up baseball caps, and he couldn't help but laugh.

"There's also all that stuff with The Remnant." Crescia said.

"The Remnant?" asked Lia.

"Oh, yeah. You guys don't know about that yet. The Dark Army may be gone, but it seems that there are a lot of necromancers that survived and have been causing trouble. No one is entirely sure where they're coming from, but they're starting to become a bit of a headache for the exploration teams. At least, that's what I hear from the castle," said Crescia.

"How are things at the castle? How are Mother and Father?" asked Lia.

"They are doing well, though they would like you to come back soon. They would like you and Jack to be the ones to initiate discussions with the dark elf villages," said Crescia.

"Knowing what we know now about them being subjugated by the Emperor, they may not be entirely opposed to forming friendly relations with the Vedyrian Kingdom," said Jack.

"True," said Lia. "But there is still a lot of bitterness between our peoples. If what General Karvan said to me is true, the dark elves requested assistance from us before their lands were claimed by the Dark Army, and their requests for help were ignored."

"Well, let's hope the fact that we defeated the Dark Army earns us some brownie points with them," said Jack.

Artemis chimed in.

"I was still very young at the time, but as I recall, our kingdom had what I'd call a complicated relationship with a number of the dark elf settlements. I wouldn't exactly call us allies, but we did have trade agreements, and we did end up sending some of our Stobrimore Army soldiers to assist them in fighting the Dark Army. But we all know how that turned out for the Kingdom of Stobrimore," he said.

"Perhaps that could give us the way in that we need," said Jack.

"It appears that it is decided. So, when shall we return?" asked Lia.

"Well, I think we should get some supplies and at least a few souvenirs for friends and family and head back tomorrow. Any objections?" said Jack.

No objections were made.

"How about you, Grampa Art? Want to join us?" asked Jack.

"Thanks, but that's ok. I'll hold down the fort. But I'm looking forward to some new stories," said Artemis.

"Deal," said Jack.

Jack turned to Crescia.

"Come with me after breakfast. We'll set up the guest room for you." Jack said.

"Is there a TV in there?" Crescia asked.

"Yes." Jack said with a grin.

After eating breakfast, Jack and Crescia were in the guest bedroom laying out new sheets for the mattress. As Crescia tried putting the pillows into pillowcases, she talked with Jack.

"So, what's it like living in a world without magic?" she asked.

"That's the strange thing. Lia and I both have some

magic, though nowhere near what we have on the other side of the Worldgate. Over there I can blow up a mountain. From here, I can probably scorch a tree stump. From outside the property, I'd be lucky to be able to light a candle. It seems the further we get from the gate, the weaker our magic becomes. So whatever it is that allows magic in the first place, it doesn't exist naturally on this side," said Jack.

"Before you woke up, Artemis was telling me about other Worldgates here in your world," said Crescia.

"Yeah. It turns out that trip around the world he went on before I first passed through the gate was to explore the suspected locations of other Worldgates around the world. From what he was able to find, there are only a relative few that are still functional. There's one on an island south of this country's mainland called Puerto Rico. Interestingly enough, that island also happens to be the location of the first alleged sighting of a creature called a chupacabra. Most people believe it's a myth, but if you look at some of the drawings and listen to some of the descriptions of what it looks like, it looks and sounds surprisingly close to an emaciated draphnir," said Jack.

"Creepy," said Crescia.

"The one that I find the most fascinating is one of the Worldgates that's no longer active. It's in a country on the other side of this world called Russia. In the year 1908, over a hundred years ago, there was an incident that occurred near a sparsely populated area along the Podkamennaya Tunguska River. It's known to the scientists of this world as the Tunguska event. It's said that on the morning of the event, there was a massive twelve-megaton explosion in the air over what Grampa Art says was the location of a Worldgate. The explosion flattened eight hundred and thirty square miles of land, but there were no confirmed deaths. Most scientists believe that it was a meteor strike, but Grampa Art thinks that it was likely caused by a group of grand-level mages who stood just outside of the Worldgate and used some serious combined magic to ensure that the gate could never be used again after they returned through it," said Jack.

"That's scary. What's a megaton?" Crescia asked.

"Oh, of course. I keep forgetting that you're not from here. It's a measurement of explosive yield. Really big booms, basically," said Jack.

"Oh. So how many megatons was the boom that you made that blew up that mountain?" asked Crescia, referring to the last moments of the final battle against the Dark Army.

"Yeah... that," said Jack, as his expression changed.

Crescia immediately regretted mentioning it. She realized that it was not a good memory for Jack.

"Sorry, Jack. I didn't mean to bring up a bad memory," she said.

"It's ok, Crescia. To be honest, I'm actually a bit afraid to find out. Do you remember that barrel I sent high up into the upper atmosphere and blew up for the demonstration?" asked Jack.

"Yeah. That was a big one," said Crescia.

"I did the calculations that night. That one came out to somewhere between three and five kilotons, and that was hardly my full strength. Quite honestly, what I did to vaporize that mountain still terrifies me. I haven't even told Lia about this, but I still have nightmares about that day." Jack said.

From the hallway, they heard a voice.

"I know, Jack," said Lia.

Jack looked over at Lia as she entered the room. He was in a bit of a panic.

"We sleep in the same bed, Jack. Did you think I wouldn't notice when you were having a nightmare? I held you close through each one of them," said Lia.

"I never knew," said Jack.

"In Vedyria, we call it 'Warrior's Burden.' It's not that uncommon in soldiers. Zavyra told me that it was a possibility before she gave you part of her soul to bring you back," said Lia.

"We have a term for it here, too. We call it... Wait. Hold up. Gave me part of her what, now?" Jack asked, distracted from the discussion by the last thing Lia said.

"Zavyra didn't tell you?" asked Lia.

"Uh, no. I'm starting to think she left a few details out," said Jack.

"What happened on the battlefield not only injured your body, it fractured your mind and, according to Zavyra, burned through much of your soul. She shared her soul with you in order to make you whole again," said Lia.

"So you're telling me that I have part of a Grand Elder Dragon's soul floating around inside me? What does that even mean?" asked Jack.

"I don't know," said Lia.

"I mean, am I going to have a Grand Elder Dragon's lifespan now? I don't want to live for millennia. I better not grow horns or a tail," said Jack.

"What's wrong with a tail?" asked Crescia as she cradled hers.

"Nothing's wrong with yours. On me, on the other hand, it would kind of make it difficult to walk around this world with a big honkin' dragon tail attached to my backside without it getting noticed. And I'd have to get all new pants. Or start wearing a lot of trench coats. It would really complicate things," said Jack.

"I think you'd look cute with a tail," said Lia.

"You're not helping... but thank you," said Jack. "That dragon and I are definitely going to have a talk the next time I see her."

"You're welcome," said Lia.

"You know, since I met you two, I've said so many weird sentences that I never thought I'd say. Now, I love you both, but I need some air," said Jack as he started walking out of the room.

"Is he ok?" asked Crescia.

"He's fine," said Lia.

From the hallway, Crescia and Lia could hear Jack.

"I'm married to an elf princess with a talking cat attendant, and I'm frustrated with a Grand Elder Dragon! So many weird sentences!" he yelled.

Lia and Crescia started laughing.